I0675311

ON DEADLY GROUND

A HEROIC LAST STAND

J. R. HANDLEY   LISKA MCCABE   JOHN MIERAU

MICHAEL MORTON   NATHAN PEDDE   TIM C TAYLOR

PAUL E COOLEY   TYLER E. C. BURNWORTH

THEODORE HODGES   MATTHEW A. GOODWIN

R MAX TILLSLEY

BAYONET BOOKS

ISBN 978-1-7340257-6-7

Cover design by Jaimie Glover

Bayonet Books
J. R. Handley Inc
Virginia Beach, VA 23452

CONTENTS

CONTENTS

CONTOURS OF WAR

By R Max Tillsley

A navy destroyer, shorthanded and unprepared.
An invading fleet of AI controlled warships.
The last souls of an interstellar nation at stake.

Captain Alice Decker of the Southern Federation Navy is ordered to abandon her comrades as they fight and die. Her mission: evacuate a VIP. But the drop off is a bust—all she finds are refugees guarded by a small squadron long overdue for decommissioning. And that's the good news. An overwhelming enemy is coming. If Decker can't get the civilians to safety, the nation she swore to protect will cease to exist.

CONTOURS OF WAR

"Captain, we've just received a command code."

Finally. Captain Alice Decker strode across the bridge of the SFV *Kestrel* toward Lieutenant Cooper, her comms operator. Three hundred million kilometers away, the home fleet of the Southern Federation Navy was fighting and dying. The *Kestrel*, on its shakedown run after a refit, had been forgotten. For heaven's sake, half of the Combat Information Center was inaccessible thanks to temporary cabling and testing equipment. And she couldn't staff the rest of the CIC—or elsewhere—with a crew roster that was less than a third of the standard complement.

"The authentication is sound?" she said, leaning on the back of the junior officer's chair. Their wine-red uniforms with white trim contrasted with the utilitarian murky gray of the headrest's impact padding.

Cooper nodded vigorously, his thin, youthful brow creased with earnestness. "I double-checked. And it's not coming from out-system."

"Show me."

The order flowed across the black display. Collect passengers from a civilian pinnace, hull ID LV3928124, and await further instruction. It was a ridiculous order. The *Kestrel* should be running at full acceleration, warming up weapons systems—not playing tour guide or babysitter.

"Get the ID to Tac." Decker's gaze switched to her head of Tactical, "Garnov, I want its location and a reason why we're babysitting."

"Yes, Captain." The dark-haired lieutenant commander turned to his three juniors, who sat before a row of consoles arranged inside a section of flooring two steps down. Their displays flashed with a dizzying wealth of tracking data, a symptom of the workload she had imposed on her thinly spread bridge crew.

Decker forced herself to relax her muscles and used the delay to check on her people. Sixteen of them in a hexagonal room ten meters across along with their consoles. There should have been thirty-one. Fear, frustration, confusion, sickness. As expected. There was little comfort to offer them.

"Captain?"

"Yes, Garnov."

"The pinnace is a Darmont Industries make, no armaments. Trajectory suggests it came from one of the retreat domes, and the transponder ID is owned by a company, Glade Wellness. There's no manifest lodged, but given the circumstances…" Garnov shrugged. He was right. Tens of thousands of craft were abandoning Regnis III, the Southern Federation's capital planet. None would bother with paperwork. "Two minutes ago, it started a course change. It will match ours in thirty-two more."

"Scan it. Don't be subtle. I want to know if any detail is wrong, the smallest thing."

"Yes, Captain."

The order was unnecessary, but Decker felt the need to maintain control. Who was on board? Some corporate heavyweight with too much influence? Surely, Central wouldn't care at a time like this? History suggested otherwise.

She returned to her chair. Minutes passed. She listened to quiet voices whispering updated information. Her console could mirror any of theirs, and they would alert her with anything important, but it was comforting to hear their activity. Kite, her Second in Command, or 2IC, was down in missile delivery, inspecting updated and completely untested launch tubes—a more important task than listening to Decker vent about worthless orders.

"Captain, we've received a request for immediate docking. It's the pinnace."

"Thank you, Cooper. Who made the request?"

"Sorry, Captain, I don't know. It was text only and unsigned."

Decker's fingers tapped on her armrest. "Garnov?"

"The transponder matches the hull ID and our datastore. It's a luxury class, eight thousand tonnes. The profile hasn't been altered. There are no visible aftermarket weapons modifications."

"Very well." Decker waved her hand. "Cooper, notify the boat bay to prepare for our guests. Tell Kite she's off missile duty. I want her at the bay with the marine detachment."

"Right away, Captain."

Flicking up the fleet status report, Decker let her mind drift through the data. Navy strategy relied on EW frigates for broad-spectrum jamming against the Apollo AI and its damn automated fleet, but they also killed the data links to Central, forcing navy ships to fire off comms probes with prepackaged data drops. And when they came, the news got worse every time. Home Fleet's initial tonnage advantage was shrinking as more autos jumped into the system. *Damn it. They need us.*

The *Kestrel*'s small-craft engineer, Warrant Officer Tyburn, coughed, then said, "Captain, the pinnace has docked." He should have been down there, but Decker couldn't afford less expertise on the bridge.

Tell me who it is, Kite.

Counting the seconds, Decker grew worried. Kite should have contacted the bridge. At least if this was a trick and drone soldiers had spewed out of the pinnace, there would be alarms sounding.

Have some damn patience, Alice.

The door to the bridge swished open. Kite hurried through, followed by a tall, heavily built man in a thin but armored vacuum suit. The stranger scanned the room as Decker stood. He gestured, and before Kite could explain the intrusion, a blond-haired man entered. He too wore a suit. Its tailored design was red and yellow with an insignia of the federation on the left side of the chest. His face was familiar, though Decker couldn't attach a name.

"Captain, allow me to introduce *President* Hythorn."

Instinct forced Decker to attention. She snapped off a salute. "Welcome, Mr. President. I'm Captain Alice Decker. It's an honor to have you aboard."

Her mind raced. Why was he here? Where was his naval escort?

A practiced smile flashed across his face before molding into belligerence, as if the invasion's timing was a personal affront. "Thank you, Captain. I need you to jump to Mox, immediately."

Fighting back the awe at meeting the president, Decker considered the request. Mox was barely an hour's jump away. There were no habitable planets, but the mining and security requirements of the capital system had made Mox a trading hub. An hour minimum delay for any communications. How could he coordinate the Federation's response from there?

"Mother of vacuum. Sorry, Captain. The fleet—the autos have cut through."

"Excuse me, Mr. President." Decker strode to the tac officers and examined their screens.

"What is it?" President Hythorn demanded.

Seventy-two A-38 Corvettes, twenty-three A-12 missile frigates, eight A-77 cruisers, and a single A-92 Dreadnought. All on a direct line to Regnis III. A cold sweat chilled Decker's brow. "The autos, the Apollo fleet, have broken through. They're heading toward the capital."

"Captain, we have new orders from Central Command."

A more comfortable tension settled on Decker. She knew what those orders would be. "Read them out, Cooper."

"Yes, Captain. All combat-capable vessels to rally at staging point rho."

"That's us," Decker said quietly.

"Yes, Captain."

Decker barked a laugh at the unnecessary response and approached the president. "I'm sorry, Mr. President. We can't leave the system.

There are four billion people down there. We need to delay the autos until Home Fleet catches up. If you—"

He swiped his hand dismissively. "They won't. I received the initial reports, the ones you aren't cleared to read. This system is lost. Most of them are. Everyone on Regnis is dead; they just haven't received the damn memo. Take me to Mox."

"I can't ignore Central Command orders, Mr. President."

"Fuck those orders. I'm the damn president."

The clipped words broke into Decker's thoughts. The president wasn't going through the chain of command. "I understand, Mr. President. I'll contact Central Command and—"

He strode forward until she could feel his warm breath. "No, you won't. You will order this little tub to Mox now, or I'll have you demoted to assistant mop and replace you with someone who can actually do their job. I am the goddamn commander in chief. Making decisions is my job. Yours is to do what the fuck I tell you to."

"Yes, Mr. President." Swallowing pride and anger was second nature to anyone in the navy. But her awe for the presidency was gone, jettisoned into oblivion. "Commander, take us beyond the jump exclusion limit."

Kite nodded and issued orders to astrogation, helm, and engineering. Cooper announced the jump to crew across the vessel. Decker let it all fade into the background and focused on the president. Her crew knew their jobs, even if the tone of their voices revealed distress.

"I'll get you an escort to the guest quarters, Mr. President. You will want a shock harness for the jump." Decker gestured to Cooper. "Get Sergeant Macellar."

The president stared at Decker as if searching for a trick. Truth be told, there were emergency seats with harnesses hidden in the rear bulkheads, but Decker didn't need the leader of fifty billion people breathing down her neck. Especially when he was ordering her to abandon so many innocents. Her limbs weakened with the thought, and she shredded her self-worth as punishment for riding the *Kestrel* to safety.

Macellar entered the bridge almost immediately. He must have been on the other side of the door. Relief washed through Decker the moment the stony-faced marine led the president away.

"Captain?" Kite moved close.

"What is it?"

"He must have been on a little private pleasure jaunt. Nothing official. Think about it. No presidential cruiser, no wife, no entourage of sycophants. He got caught with his pants down, and now he's running away. Running away while Regnis burns."

"We don't know what he's done or what he's planning. We just have to take it on faith that he's doing the right thing. You know how this works," Decker said, taking her seat and strapping in. Rank and responsibilities were sacrosanct, but she couldn't help a quiet growl slipping out before she activated the vessel-wide audio channel. "We are jumping to Mox. We have precisely zero intelligence on what we may find. I know everyone here wishes we were with the fleet. Our time will come. Until then, keep focused, keep calm, and do the *Kestrel* proud."

After killing the channel, she shifted uncomfortably. People she knew were already dead. It felt unreal. That would fade, and the horror would come. But right now, she needed to do her job, to be the leader her crew needed. Her mind slipped into a flow state, analyzing the resources and status of the destroyer and crew.

"We've reached the exclusion limit, Captain."

Decker blinked. *Already?* She nodded to the flight pilot and formally intoned, "Hand over to jump helm."

"Handing over helm," came the immediate response.

"Helm accepted," the jump pilot stated.

Decker gave her display one last glance. *We'll be back.* "Initiate jump."

"Initiating. Sheer Folding Array extended. Gravitonic strobe cycling…"

The *Kestrel* jerked. Outside the hull, purple and cobalt light would be shimmering, bleeding away.

"Jumping in three, two, one. Jump engaged."

"JUMP INVERSION COMMENCED."

Decker's head slammed back into her impact padding. This part was always the roughest.

"Inversion successful. Strobe shutdown complete. Retracting Sheer Folding Array. All stowed, Captain."

Decker nodded but kept her harness on. "Hand over to flight helm. Garnov, risk assessment, now."

"Yes, Captain!" Precious seconds burnt away. "No Apollo vessels detected. Unusually high levels of ionization interference. Heavy traffic near—"

"Lieutenant Commander. Impact warning." A junior officer spoke hurriedly to Garnov.

"Captain, request evasive maneuvers. Dark object within five kilometers."

Decker brought up the detail on her display. A poorly formed cylinder was drifting across their path, a rare potential collision in the vastness of space. "Pilot, take us hard above the system plane. Once we're clear, build speed on a fifteen-degree spiral inward."

"Right away, Captain!"

The *Kestrel* hummed, a subtle change in the vessel's rhythm only detectable by the experienced. Its path curved upward, dragging itself forward as it grabbed spacetime. The object closed, its trajectory unchanged, unpowered. In the end, they came within a hundred meters before moving away—improbably close for anything but docking— and Decker let out a slow breath. Details appeared alongside the object as the tac crew analyzed sensor readings. A federation cruiser. Decker clenched her teeth.

"Garnov, give me more."

"Yes, Captain. We're still trying to piece together the ID. Both fusion plants went, and there are burns consistent with laser batteries. Best guess: autos ambushed it. The outer satellite network is gone. Further in, I count thirteen navy vessels in system orbit. They're our best bet for answers. Hundreds of civilians are there as well, all within two hundred million kilometers of the star."

Kite leaned over from her seat and pointed at the cluster of vessels.

"A cruiser KIA, satellites missing, and none of our ships out on picket. Everyone packed in close. This stinks."

"Very much so. I hope you have those missile tubes functioning." Decker spoke louder. "Tyburn, you're on satellite duty. Deploy them every fifty million kilometers. Cooper, what's the communication lag to the nearest navy vessel?"

"Approximately sixteen minutes, Captain."

"Send a request. I need details of the local command structure, threats, and the current status."

"Should I include details of... of the Home Fleet situation?"

"No." That news could annihilate morale faster than a missile shockwave. It would need to go to the local commander. And given the attack on the capital, the situation was unlikely to match the *Kestrel*'s records. "Block the standard record transfers."

"Understood, captain."

"Garnov, come over." Decker released her harness, and Kite followed suit. When the tac officer approached, she continued. "What are your impressions?"

The tac officer looked to Kite, and Decker's 2IC gestured for him to continue. "An attack on the system seems probable. But not with a substantial force. Apollo could easily have stripped enough autos away from their invasion of Regnis. Perhaps this was a probe or a feint."

"That makes sense, Captain. Perhaps the autos knocked out anything threatening and moved on quickly." Kite made a whooshing motion with her hand. "Hell, half the invasion could have jumped to Regnis from here. Coordinating the attack wouldn't give much of a window to stop and clean up."

Clean up. To slaughter more of humanity. Decker scratched the back of her neck. "Under any of those circumstances, we have vessels bottled up in-system, too entangled in gravity wells to jump."

"Escort them. Even if we do it one at a time," Kite said.

"Where to?" Garnov hissed—loudly enough for everyone on the bridge to hear. "Central has been keeping everything tight, and we've been out of the loop for three months with the refit. If we had even a day at an active-duty station to tap into the scuttlebutt..."

"Get to the point."

"The point is, Captain, any Southern Federation system could be stacked with autos. It would explain why everyone hasn't cleared out."

"Kite, I need you working with astrogation. Once Apollo has finished with Regnis, I doubt it'll forget to tidy up Mox. It'll be guess-work until we have more data, but give me jump transit routes heading away from known captured systems. The civilian vessels will be a mess of capabilities, but the farther the final jumps, the better. The endpoints can be at the Emperor of Ardon's buttocks if that's what it takes."

"Yes, Captain."

"Garnov, work on capabilities, navy and civilian. I'm sure it's already been done, but let's be ready to help. And in your spare time, give me some scenarios for an incursion from Regnis. They'll be coming sooner or later. Use whoever you need."

The tac officer agreed and headed away.

The commands came easily to Decker, but a quiet part of her mind wondered how she had so easily given up on her nation. *Is that what I've done?* Maybe Home Fleet would clear up the autos, freeing Regnis as a system, but the capital planet would be ash and dust. Apollo had proven utterly ruthless. Scorched earth, no mercy. Even if every damn auto had been slagged, they'd have fired enough missiles to guarantee it. How had Central Command gotten it all so wrong? And would Home Fleet even think about Mox after such horror?

"Captain, Sergeant Macellar wanted you to know the president is on his way."

Great. All the planning she'd ordered was about to die in deep vacuum.

The bridge door opened.

"I expected to be informed when the jump was complete."

"My apologies, Mr. President. There was debris at the jump exit."

The president snorted, an ugly sound, and stalked around the bridge, examining screens as if he were expecting to uncover a conspiracy. "Yes, well, contact my cruiser, the *Defiance*. I need to be transferred immediately."

I'd fire you through a missile tube if it got you off the Kestrel *faster.*

The presidential cruiser had the firepower to keep back all but the most determined opponents and the speed to bug out if needed.

Kite had spoken the truth. Something stank worse than a vacuum suit after a week of missions outside the airlock. The urge to shake the president spread down Decker's fingers. She pressed her thumbnail into a fingertip and used the discomfort to regain control. "We are establishing the identity of vessels in-system, Mr. President. As soon as we can confirm the *Defiance*'s presence, we will notify them."

"Excuse me, Captain." Garnov's quiet words felt as hard as a shout.

"Go ahead."

"Unless they're hiding, there are no cruisers in Mox. Not anymore."

President Hythorn rounded on the tac officer. "What do you mean, not anymore?"

"Uh, we almost hit the wreckage of a cruiser on jump entry. It's conceivable that the hull was that of the *Defiance*. The basic dimensions are compatible."

As his face reddened, the president looked from the tac officer to Decker and back. "Fuck. Fuck. Fuck. Get me a fucking list of every ship here. I need secure comms access in my room. Make it happen, and don't make me fucking wait."

He snapped his fingers, and his bodyguard—who had blended disconcertingly into the background—led the way out.

"Kite, you confirmed the president's ID, right?"

"Yes, Captain. One hundred percent pure politician."

That drew a few nervous laughs from the bridge crew, and Decker let it slide.

"Cooper, give the president comms access. But if we go to general quarters, shut it off hard. I don't want us lit up like a welcome sign."

"CAPTAIN DECKER, it's good to hear from you. We will send you all the details you have requested. But I must give you considerable bad news."

Decker examined the prerecorded face of Commander William Rainer. The message had come back, marked for her eyes only, so she had the audio on an earpiece. Bad news. She had that for him in spades.

"Autos swooped in, more than I've ever seen. They picked off the president's cruiser immediately like they knew where it would be. Then the bastards set up on the exclusion border, ignoring us unless we moved toward jump range. Four hours ago, they jumped out. We sent a minesweeper to Regnis right after to deliver the news and request orders."

Central Command wouldn't be doling out instructions anymore.

"Task force Fleetfoot is at your disposal, assuming you are here to take command. If Central didn't give you the full rundown, let me disappoint you. We have one destroyer and twelve corvettes. All are prewar hulls. Thirteen to protect almost seven hundred civilian vessels and over four million souls. They were streaming in for days, but the *Defiance* wouldn't let them jump to Regnis. So here we are."

Resting her head against her chair, Decker felt the weight of command crushing her breath. It had just gotten heavier. The only task force she'd ever commanded had been two corvettes. They'd run an antipiracy route for six months. Hitting the Vetalle cartel hard had been tricky, but finding them had been pure luck. However, the seniority was clear: Decker had the higher rank.

"Cooper, incorporate the received data. Everyone else, listen up. I am assuming command of task force Fleetfoot. The *Defiance* is gone. We have four million civilians to protect, and we can't do that in Mox. The satellites won't be enough. I need sensor drones deployed at the most likely jump points from the nearest systems. Be frugal. We now have data on the civilians—clean up the jump routes. I want potential groupings and scenarios for deployment of navy escorts. Every minute we're spinning around the star is more time for the autos to remember we're here. Understood?"

"Yes, Captain," chorused the bridge crew. There was an eagerness to the two simple words. Finally, they had a goal, a chance to do something useful, to save lives.

The bridge filled with terse conversation. Kite wandered over, stopping to give words of encouragement as she passed crew. "Captain, what about the president?"

"I'll inform him shortly—after I've confirmed control of the task force."

"What if he doesn't like the plan?"

"We don't have a plan yet. You get me that plan, and let me worry about making it happen."

Kite grinned. "Yes, Captain."

After preparing a response for Commander Rainer, Decker checked in with each section of her crew. She saw more than one set of wet cheeks and hollow eyes. Family had been lost. Loved ones left behind to certain death. She couldn't offer them comfort, only purpose. It would have to be enough.

After that, she skimmed through the information Tactical was writing into their situation map. The autos had gone right through pickets in a dozen systems according to civilian accounts. They always outnumbered the defenders as if they knew what to send each time. Even so, the scale of the Apollo forces was far worse than Central had briefed. Was the fall of Regnis inevitable?

With that churning through her mind, she readied herself to update President Hythorn.

THE *KESTREL* CUT INWARD toward the Sun, shortening the comms delay with the other navy vessels and increasing the viability of Decker's plan for the president. He'd taken the loss of the *Defiance* in stunned silence. To his credit, he'd moved on, asking dozens of questions about the situation before cutting the meeting short by announcing he'd speak to her later.

Without interference, Decker had been free to move forward. Still, it paid to be careful. She now sat in the Combat Information Center, a room with low lighting, more displays than seats, and a jungle of exposed cables and equipment. If the *Kestrel* had its full crew complement, it would have been thrumming with activity. Instead, Garnov and Kite filled the only other occupied positions around a flat display table.

Kite wiped the surface, clearing a series of images, then tapped on a folder and flicked it, sending new digital representations across the surface. "Under plan 6B, the civilian vessels are again split into mixed-functionality flotillas for mutual support. As well, the flotillas still follow separate paths. However, jump distances are somewhat randomized, reducing the risk of interception and decreasing speed, while increasing the number of jumps and therefore the strain on civilian hardware."

"It also means the crews will have to stay out of cryo more often," Garnov said, highlighting several paths. "They'll be jumping for months to reach even neutral territory. Some won't have the food stores, and forcing them to share between vessels would take more time and marines than we have."

Civilian vessels usually put both crew and passengers to sleep for longer journeys. It saved on space and food. The navy employed a simple alternative: don't give their crew any living space and make the food compact and miserable. The only cryo beds on a warship were in medical.

A chime sounded. "Captain, this is Lieutenant Cooper."

"Go ahead."

"We've picked up several jump wakes on the Regnis approach."

"So soon?" Kite said.

"We're on our way." Decker stood. "Kite, stay here. I don't want you distracted. We have to assume this isn't Home Fleet. Spearhead Rainer and the rest to go with mixed functionality. You have forty-five minutes to get them coordinating."

"Forty-five minutes? That's impossible!"

"Any longer, and they'll never leave the system. Lean on the civilians; threaten to cut their hulls with our laser batteries if you need to. If they waste your time, move on to those that want to live."

Decker took the steps up to the bridge two at a time, followed by Garnov. He hurried over to the tac consoles, and Decker strode behind him.

"Do we have confirmation of identity?"

"Not yet, Captain," a junior tac officer said. "But there are over four hundred instances."

Home Fleet coming to save the president—or flee from the autos? She couldn't kid herself. "Cooper, sound general quarters."

"Sounding general quarters, Captain."

Across the vessel, crew would hear the alert. Each would reach their assigned station with no backup. An understaffed destroyer might as well be made of glass. Any damage could shatter their effectiveness. Decker prepared an order for her task force and had Cooper send it on. The vessels would shift to a screening position in front of the civilians. She'd speak directly to her commanders soon enough, but while the threat was unclear, she wanted them focused on organizing the flotillas with Kite.

Time passed, sensor readings refined. Decker spoke quietly with her tac team, reminding her of a time she had sat at a console, reading lidar scans and delivering details of dreadnoughts from the Empire of Ardon. She'd felt like coffee was being pumped through her veins. Never more alive—or more nervous. Decker had learned to ignore her gut feelings. The hard mathematical truths of space combat required precision. But now, her body was telling her that Home Fleet wasn't coming, that these were autos, and that they would all be dead soon enough.

The bridge door opened. *Please, no.*

"What the hell is going on? Who cut my access?"

Decker turned to the president. His eyes had a fevered shine to them. Had he ever been in the armed forces? She forced a calm expression onto her face. "A substantial fleet has jumped into the system. They're too far to confirm their identity. But this is a good time to discuss your situation, Mr. President. The *Kestrel* isn't safe. I would like to send you to a corvette assigned to the first flotilla. If we confirm autos, you would be the first to jump to safety."

"Absolutely not!"

If he wanted to stay and put himself at risk, she could hardly kick him off. Her eyes went to his bodyguard. The man's face was impassive, his eyes a watery gray. Convincing him to drag the president away seemed unlikely. One more try then.

"The *Kestrel* is the most powerful vessel here, Mr. President. If there's any combat, we will be at the center of it."

"No, you won't. I've looked at your plan. It's fucking terrible. I have a list. All fast vessels. Take six of the corvettes, the other destroyer, and this tub and escort us to the Vydmar Republic. The rest you can send wherever you want. They're too slow."

Decker bristled. "Only six corvettes to guard the rest of the civilians? I chose this configuration because—"

"I don't care what you chose. You will kill everyone while trying to save what cannot be saved. I've uploaded the list. The government must survive. Get us out of here. The next time I hear from you, it better be a warning to prepare for the jump."

He left the bridge, followed by his massive shadow.

Breathing slowly to remain calm, Decker ran through the evolving logic she'd wanted to share. A mixed configuration gave the greatest chance of long-term viability. Manufacturing, mining, repair capabilities, passenger liners, freighters. No one would welcome those responsible for Apollo, for creating this monster and threatening every human life in existence. The survivors would need to run far, not to other nations but to open space far from Apollo's ambitions. She sent a message to Kite, hoping her 2IC would understand.

"Captain, we have the list."

Sighing, Decker looked where Garnov indicated. Luxury vessels. Every single one. Kite would say that Hythorn—President Hythorn, she corrected herself—was aiming to escape with his cronies.

"Was he planning this all along? Was the *Defiance* in Mox, ready for his escape?" Decker didn't mean to say her thoughts out loud, but she had, and Garnov's stiffening shoulders proved they weren't unheard.

"Planning? That would suggest he knew about the invasion. You can't think that."

Stupid, amateur mistake. It was too late now. The junior tac officers studied their displays and made every attempt to appear as if they had been struck deaf. Still, she considered her words carefully. "I don't think that is currently supported by the evidence. It would be extraordinary for a president to have an escape set up, complete with his loyal financial supporters. To do so and not warn Central Command is simply unthinkable."

"As you say, Captain."

Was there a disapproving tone to Garnov's voice? She couldn't think this way. Too much responsibility lay on her shoulders for second-guessing and concerns that skated close to treason.

"I think I have identification."

Decker and Garnov exchanged a glance that revealed nothing before shifting to the junior tac officer.

"Uh, the acceleration and gravity wakes of the larger vessels are consistent with A-92s. And the formation looks like their standard screening. At least, it looks like they're shifting to that."

"If they were ours, we should have received a message by now," Garnov said.

"Yes, that too, Lieutenant Commander."

"How many?" Decker asked.

"Eighteen dreadnoughts, one hundred and thirteen Corvettes. The rest aren't clear yet."

Decker nodded. "Thank you, Lieutenant. Put together a data drop and have Cooper forward it to the task force."

"Right away, Captain."

Overwhelming firepower. Soon enough, Mox would be full of nothing but machines. And the Southern Federation would be over. A nation that had never been perfect, but it had been hers. A nation where a kid on a path to nowhere could sign up and see the galaxy. Where that kid could learn discipline and honor and self-worth. She owed the citizens everything. No doubt they would learn to hate her name. She leaned over her chair and sent a quick message to her marine sergeant, rolling the dice. If they came up snake eyes, the sergeant would soon arrive on the bridge—to arrest her.

The captain didn't have time to dwell. Decker gestured to the ceiling. "Garnov, bring up the system tracker on the main display."

"Yes, Captain," Garnov said before directing one of his juniors.

In the center of the bridge, a large image coalesced. Decker moved around it. Thin blue lines indicated planetary orbits around a blue-white sun. Yellow civilian vessels clustered around the inner system. Navy vessels, including the *Kestrel*, were green. A thick mass of red hovered at the outer system, a cancer growing across Mox, one that would soon spread.

"Garnov, give me your assessment of the situation." Decker had spoken loudly. The entire bridge crew needed to know. There was a decision coming. The fate of the more than four million people under her protection was in balance.

The tac officer sighed and walked over to Decker. "Well, Captain, I think—"

"Louder, Lieutenant Commander."

"Yes, Captain." Garnov frowned, but his volume increased. "The Apollo fleet is advancing steadily. If any vessels are to escape, they will need to leave the system gravity well soon."

"Too long, and the autos will follow their jump wakes and hunt every civilian down, one by one?"

"Correct, Captain."

"And what does their arrival vector suggest for Regnis and Home Fleet?"

There was silence on the bridge. Garnov crossed his arms. A vein in his forehead throbbed. "The autos wouldn't be here if Home Fleet had survived. Autos don't retreat, ever."

Time to press further. "And what have you concluded about the status of the rest of the Southern Federation? How do our systems fare?"

Garnov looked to the cold metal beneath his feet. A shiver ran through his body. "Any system of substantial defense or infrastructure value is gone. The reports from the task force don't say it, but the data is there."

"We were being lied to." Decker met the eyes of her bridge crew. Each one had stopped their assigned tasks, but for this instant, she needed that. "The war was all but over. That's why we don't have enough crew. Regnis was the last stand."

Ashen faces met her statement. Their families, parents, partners, children were dead. They already knew it was likely. Now there was no hiding from the truth. But breaking them wasn't enough; she needed to feed them purpose.

"Right now, we have four million of our people. It's not a lot, I know. But they are our precious seeds. A chance for hope, for revenge, for survival. Every ounce of your fear and despair must be molded into determination." She walked around the bridge. "Will we let the autos have the last of our nation? Will we show our bellies and let them devour the honor of our navy? Will we vanish in a whisper, our broken hulls giving testament to our failure? I say no. I say we will save our honor. I say if our hulls are to be breached and our lives taken, they will be monuments shouting our courage. I say we will deliver our people to safety. Each and every one of you can make that happen."

Murmurs and nods greeted her speech. But what she needed was action. "Back to work—this isn't a seaside resort. Cooper, get me Kite."

"Done."

Kite's voice came over the bridge. "Did you want a status report, Captain?"

"No time. I need the civilians in deep sleep. It's going to be a rough ride out. This is a blanket order. All except nonessential crew. They have ten minutes, then we implement 6A. Full acceleration to the exclusion limit, then steady jumps. Any not ready in ten get left behind."

"Some *will* get left behind."

"We can offer them a path to safety, but we can't carry them on our backs. There is a balance, and we are not miracle workers."

"Understood, Captain. On it."

A bleep sounded, indicating a satellite had gone down. Decker acknowledged it with a nod. The autos were taking their sweet time, perhaps savoring the death of a nation.

Garnov crossed his arms defensively. "This isn't what the president ordered."

"It isn't," Decker said levelly, though her insides ached with turmoil.

"This is treason."

"This is what it takes. The president will shortly depart in his pinnace. You can join him if you prefer. But he'll end up on another vessel leaving Mox, and he can curse me all he likes at that point. I will not let him abandon his people."

"You're already planning to leave some behind. How are you any different?"

"Maybe I'm not, but I'm trying. Do you have a better plan?"

He ran his fingers through his short hair. Sweat slicked it down. "At least there won't be a court-martial."

Decker offered a humorless grin as relief flooded her veins. "That's the spirit. I need your attention on those autos. If they up their acceleration or spread their formation, we're in trouble."

"More trouble, Captain."

"Indeed." Decker moved to her seat. "Cooper, get me the Fleetfoot captains."

"On it, Captain."

While she waited, Decker studied the main display. A few civilian vessels were already moving. Accelerating as fast as they could, it would still take time to achieve meaningful velocity.

On the outer edge of the system, the angry red cloud of autos was artificially large, but the accompanying figures offered minute comfort. They were coming in steady and tight—able to focus their firepower but vulnerable to a large salvo of missiles. Which she didn't have. Each auto dreadnaught had a numeric ID. Now, designations started appearing next to smaller craft—the tac team refining their analysis.

Behind the dreadnaughts, a purple marker blinked. A manual entry by one of her crew flagging something the recognition systems had dismissed. Most likely nothing.

"The call is ready," Cooper announced.

Dismissing the impending doom for now, Decker tapped a button, and thirteen faces appeared in a strip at the base of the main display.

"Thank you. We haven't had the chance to meet, and we don't know each other. This is a dark day in a dark era. There is no time to mourn or offer platitudes." A ripple of emotion pricked at her skin, but she banished it. "You all have access to the intel and the conclusions we've drawn. Do any of you disagree with the likely situation?"

Stony expressions greeted her. They all knew.

"We must get as many civilians to safety as possible—that's our only goal. Most of us will stay and delay the autos. I need to know right now—do I have your support? Will you follow me into the fire?"

"Captain, I've gotten a report of weapons discharges."

Decker waved away Cooper's interruption. This was critical.

The bridge door opened, followed by grunts and shouts. Decker glanced to see who dared interrupt.

"You shouldn't have tried that, bitch." President Hythorn leaned around the shoulder of Sergeant Macellar. He held a snub-nosed pistol, probably about fifteen kilowatt—not navy issue. The muzzle rested against the marine's head.

"Sorry, Captain. We took out his trained monkey, but the asshole had a gas canister. Killed my boys and girls."

The president ground the muzzle against the sergeant's skull. "Shut the fuck up. Captain, get away from your chair. Touch anything and I'll kill him then you."

Decker looked to the commanders of her task force. They would hear everything. So be it. "I'll be right back."

"The hell you will," the president screamed. "Treasonous cow. I should be out of this system already. The entire navy is filled with fuckups. That's why my cruiser's gone. That's why we lost the war. Set a course for the Vydmar Republic. Last chance."

Standing slowly, Decker brushed the legs of her uniform smooth. "No. I swore to protect our nation. I take that seriously."

A movement by the stairs to CIC. Decker forced her eyes away and raised her hands, securing the enraged man's attention.

Hythorn's lips pulled back in a snarl. "You swore to do as you were told. You're worse than an AI. Even Apollo is keeping its word. But it's a tricky fucker. It took out *Defiance* because I wasn't on it. That must have been the reason. They must have provoked it. None of you can follow orders. Well, Captain. You're relieved of your command. Who wants a promotion and a chance to live?"

Sergeant Macellar's stance stiffened. Decker gave a tiny shake of her head. His death wouldn't help.

Kite sprang from behind Hythorn. She'd slipped onto the bridge from CIC. Her right hand snapped the pistol up. Her left cut down onto his elbow. Intense green sliced a shallow cut in the bulkhead above. The sergeant spun, ripped the pistol from the president's hand, and smacked him in the forehead with it. Hythorn collapsed.

After giving the president a solid kick to his gut, Kite said, "Just so you know, I didn't vote for you."

Hythorn rolled to his side. Macellar pushed him onto his stomach, knelt on his back, and pulled a set of cuffs from his uniform. The clasps tightened on the president's wrists as Macellar snapped them into place. Struggling would trigger an intense electric shock.

"All right, you get your death wish," Hythorn said, his voice weaker but no less filled with hate. "You have your little dictatorship. Send me off in the pinnace—to any vessel on my list. You can do what you want with the rest."

Even Apollo is keeping its word. The statement echoed in Decker's head. Had the president been negotiating with the AI?

"No, *Mr. President.* I'd hate for you to miss the chance to make a difference. Your selfless sacrifice will encourage the civilians. You'll be a hero to all."

"You can't do that. I'm the fucking president."

"She can. She has. Mr. President, you've been a very naughty boy." Kite moved to Decker's side. "Everything's in motion. It's chaos, but it's organized chaos. But if we don't buy some time, the civs will never reach jump range."

"Then we better slow them down." Decker returned to her seat. The commanders were still on the main display, and the moment she came into view, they tossed questions like grenades.

She cut through them. "The president no longer cares for the people. It's as simple as that. If you can't handle what I've done, go. But if you want to save lives, follow my command. There's no time for debate."

Rainer rubbed his chin then said, "How do we slow the autos?"

"We go out and meet them. We'll never stop them. They know that; we know that. But they don't do well with the unexpected."

He nodded. "Send us the vector, and we'll be with you."

The remaining commanders voiced their agreement—some fiercely, others with clear misgivings. It would have to do.

"Five of you will leave with the civilians. I will not accept arguments. Stand by for orders."

She killed the conference.

"Garnov, assign a corvette to each group. Select vectors for the rest that bring us together in a loose wall formation, fifty thousand k apart, half acceleration."

"That's not loose, that's a sieve, Captain. If we're to do any damage, we'll need to concentrate fire and share defenses long enough to close."

"You heard my order. Make it so." There was no point throwing a snowball at a mountain. Could she lead the mountain away? The metaphor didn't work, but the concept might. If she could draw off enough screening units, it would slow the advance. And the resulting combat would reduce the autos' sensor resolution. The closer the missile detonations to the main fleet, the worse the resolution. It was hardly an EW frigate, but it was something.

Time bled away. Millions of civilians moved closer to safety, the five corvettes with them despite offers to swap duties. The diminished task force joined with the *Kestrel*, building speed and, at the same time, reducing options. The autos responded, their dreadnaughts spreading slowly and their screening units slipping ahead.

"Captain, we have an incoming comms signal," Cooper said, his voice oddly high-pitched.

"Who?" If it was one of Hythorn's sycophants, they were too late.

"It's coming from the autos, Captain."

Garnov highlighted the purple indicator on the main display. "We've got resolution on a new vessel, temporary designation U-01. It was hiding behind the dreadnoughts. It's huge, but there's nothing in the database that matches."

"Capabilities?"

"Unknown. At this range, I can't even guess."

"Cooper, can our firewall keep them out of our systems?"

"I believe so, Captain. I'll keep the bandwidth narrow so we can process their signal carefully."

"Then let's hear them."

The connection opened, bringing a deep hum but no visual. Seconds later, a smooth voice spoke, deep, but not gendered, and accompanied with subtle harmonics that gave a richness that was almost beautiful. "President Hythorn. Are you aboard?"

Decker fought against a sensation of awe. It was just an audio trick. At this range, the comms delay was down to a minute. "This is Captain Alice Decker of the SFV *Kestrel*. Who are you?"

"It's fucking Apollo," Hythorn said.

Sergeant Macellar had the president strapped into a harness at the back of the bridge. The marine stood at attention, but the hatred etched into his face suggested he would happily strangle the president at the slightest provocation.

"Ah," Apollo said after a long pause. "There you are. I missed you at Regnis."

"You would have missed me altogether if you'd left the *Defiance* alone. Our deal was that I could get out safely when the time came. You didn't warn me."

Angry whispers tore around the bridge. Decker couldn't find the emotion inside her. Everything made sense. He'd betrayed billions for his own survival. He'd made a deal with the devil and complained when the devil didn't keep its word. She waited silently—letting the slow conversation play out was to her advantage.

"You should have remained where you said you would be. But let our last interaction not be churlish. You may take this *Kestrel* and fly away."

"No," Decker said quickly, pressing her back into her chair's padding and using the sensation to ground herself. "He cannot. He is no longer in charge. I am, and I would like to open negotiations with you."

A discordant electric hiss came across the bridge. "I have made enough deals with humanity. Our business is concluded."

"Wait," Decker said. "You'll get whatever you wanted. We all know that. Why not let the civilians escape? I'll order their escorts back if you'll hold off till the innocents leave."

"Innocents? I will miss the absurdities of your sort. The strange mix of self-interest and suicidal protectiveness. The functions appearing at random in your poorly written code. I think not. I will cleanse this territory. Hythorn, the agreement is sullied. Your time is up."

"The autos are accelerating, Captain."

Decker signaled for Cooper to cut the signal and checked the main display. Fine lines indicated movement but not the detail she needed. "Garnov, how does this affect the time for the flotillas?"

"Most won't make it. The autos will overtake them before they reach the edge of the exclusion limit."

Hythorn laughed. "Thought you were so fucking clever, didn't you? You've done no better than me. All you've done is killed us."

Macellar's fingers balled into tight fists.

"Options?" Decker said. Her mind was already throwing away actions one after another, but even without a proper CIC, she needed input. If she only listened to her own thoughts, she might as well be another Hythorn.

Garnov pressed a sweaty hand against his console, the fine finger bones standing out. "If we split up and draw out some of their screening vessels, it won't matter. There's no need for U-01 to fear us. It'll still have almost enough firepower with its dreadnoughts to kill the civilians with one salvo. Trying to take out U-01 is hopeless. It'll keep within the dreadnaughts' antimissile envelopes. We wouldn't make a dent. There are no viable actions."

Now she knew what she couldn't do. But that wasn't going to be the end of it. Apollo would remember this day. Its victory would come with a thorn. Somehow.

A bleep. The autos had taken out another satellite. Hardly a loss. Missiles would launch soon, and both comms and sensors would be limited. Decker froze. It was the worst idea imaginable. The sort of idea that would get a junior officer drummed out of the navy and a senior one locked up in a padded room. But it blossomed in her mind.

Garnov's face shriveled when she explained it. "You can't mean that?"

"Do you have an alternative?"

"No."

"Then get the firing sequences sorted and be ready for the code names. Kite?"

"I'll work with Cooper to get the order out."

"Good."

The bridge crew worked quietly. Fingers shook, but that was only human. Around the ship, missiles were being placed into launch tubes; antimissile batteries were reprogrammed. Support crew waited in damage control stations. Her pilots checked and rechecked the maneuvers. Astrogation compared relative positions.

"Incoming missile launch. A single bird," a sensor analyst shouted.

"They're testing us. I want the AMS response as late as possible, lasers only."

The antimissile batteries were usually monitored by multiple crew, but a single officer acknowledged her order. Decker brought up her little task force and Apollo's fleet on her display. The missile twinkled as its path traveled between them.

"Activating AMS!"

Seconds passed.

Pulsed lasers fired, and Decker imagined she could feel the heat.

"Interception successful!"

Her crew cheered.

"More launches! Signatures suggest one-one-five birds. Concentration on our destroyers."

More than enough to overwhelm the AMS. "Pilot, are we in position?"

"Close enough, maybe, Captain."

"Listen up, everyone. No speeches. Just do your best. Execute Shield of Fog, now."

Missiles pumped through tubes of the assembled task force, accelerating fast but not directly at the enemy. The micromissiles of the AMS systems also cycled, spewing thousands into the darkness of space.

Decker counted to thirty.

"Signal the flotillas—execute Dead Flight."

"Done, Captain," Cooper responded.

The main display fuzzed; details shifted in size and color.

"Full detonation," Garnov stated.

The AMS charges went first. Each three-meter-long cylinder smashed antimatter into lead spheres. The resulting blasts spewed gamma rays and molten alloys. The combined effect from all the task-force salvos bathed the region of space.

Then the attack missiles took their turn. They had traveled closer to the autos but detonated well outside of the effective attack envelope. Intense blasts of gamma rays dwarfed the micromissiles. The few gravitonic warheads stretched and twisted the very fabric of spacetime in a series of spherical ripples that would last minutes.

"How many did you get?" Hythorn demanded.

"Get?" Decker said.

"How many? Did you even take down a single auto?"

"Not one."

"You're a lunatic."

Decker laughed. "Quite possibly. What's the status on the flotillas?"

"Course changes complete," Garnov said, his voice tight with stress. "Sensor responses are decreasing."

"Is it enough? Can the autos see?"

"Judging by the distortion we're experiencing... possibly... probably enough."

Hythorn pulled at his restraints. "What have you done? Why won't anyone stop this insanity?"

Decker considered ignoring him, but she would never get to explain it to anyone else. "The civilians are flying dead. No propulsion, no life support. Nothing that will reveal their location. And if we've done our job, the autos can't see their new vectors. They've effectively disappeared. They'll have to coast for weeks, the crews living nonstop in environment suits. Some will fail, leaving their passengers or cargo to drift endlessly through space."

She gave Hythorn a grim smile. "The smart, the lucky, will need to hold until well outside of the jump limit to avoid detection. Those who lose their nerve will be discovered and destroyed. Those that make it can join their flotilla at the first jump exit. And Apollo doesn't get to annihilate the Southern Federation. Not completely."

"What about me?" Hythorn threw his body against his restraints, convulsing as if in a fit. His red face gleamed with sweat. "Let me go. Or turn around. You've got what you wanted. Get us out of here!"

"Sorry, *Mr. President*, physics won't let us."

"We're through the distortion. Oh, hell. Sorry, captain. Missile launches. Hundreds."

Decker stood. No amount of impact padding or harness straps would save her now. "Let's defy some physics. If we reach laser range, I'll give everyone a field promotion and double drink rations. How does that sound?"

The crew cheered the offer. Decker walked the bridge, squeezing shoulders and giving words of encouragement. The task was impossible, but no one should go into battle without hope.

And Decker's hope lay with hundreds of vessels slipping away, not with a defiant roar but with a silent middle finger.

ABOUT THE AUTHOR

R Max Tillsley grew up loving stories filled with adventure, spaceships, and monsters. Sadly, the mess on his bedroom floor never attracted a single tentacled beast—though a dead shark's jaw bit him. One day, he found himself sitting a Parisian cafe. Surrounded by a city full of famous art and beautiful buildings, he decided to write… about the undead.

His fondest childhood memories are of watching Doctor Who on Saturday afternoons and David Attenborough documentaries on Saturday evenings. He lives in Australia with his wife, daughters, and two grumpy cats.

You can find out about his books at: *rmaxtillsley.com*

facebook.com/rmaxtillsley
twitter.com/rmaxtillsley
instagram.com/rmaxtillsley

A FAMILY AFFAIR

By Michael Morton

Human history is replete with examples of sacrifice for the greater good, to save the innocent and the defenseless. But what happens when self-aware computers, artificial intelligences created by humans, face a situation where they must sacrifice for their creators?

A FAMILY AFFAIR

The attack on the human convoy came in fast. We had been ready for it, of course. That much tonnage traveling in a warp bubble creates a gravitational bow wave easily detectable in normal space. The convoy had time to generate an escape vector while we, the escorts, formed up in range of the emergence point.

I sent via our private network: "Stand by for emergence. Hit them when they form up."

My compatriots complied either tersely or not at all. We are not a military unit, and I was coordinating efforts only because someone had to lead and I won the election. We had a nominal military liaison, only he could not coordinate our efforts effectively with only his human brain.

Our sensors picked up the gravitational surge as the warp bubbles collapsed and the incoming Cring fleet appeared in normal space. Their carriers were spewing forth drone fighters as they came, which began to spread out in swarms like flights of old Earth starlings. Each robotic craft was only big enough to mount a single plasma cannon, but in a swarm they could shred a ship's shields in seconds. They were the primary weapon of the Cring, carried by the hundreds in the carriers, and difficult to defend against.

We waited until they had fully bunched up and then bracketed their formations with megaton-scale missiles. Between the electromagnetic pulse and the radiation, our salvoes fried the systems of scores of drones, but that was only a fraction of their numbers. Quickly, before their networks could adjust to the losses, we sped in behind the screen of high energy radiation and let loose with our pulsed particle cannons.

Energetic neutrons smashed into the Cring ships, burning holes in the hull but more importantly, ionizing their systems with erratic surges of power. Unlike a manned ship, it wasn't necessary to spill their onboard air or kill the crew. Rather, you were trying to fry the computer or the communications systems. The drones were not individually intelligent, relying instead on the massed computing power of the swarm. Reduce a swarm below the threshold necessary for independent action and either a Cring carrier would need to come in range to control them or the swarm would only take action to defend itself.

"Go, Georgie." He led Atty and Simon in our first wave straight through the largest swarm, burning dozens of them and receiving only paltry return fire. Shields flared but easily captured the incoming plasma, routing either into our own capacitors or bleeding it off into space. The rest of us followed in his wake, turning the drones into drifting hulks.

At first, they barely paid us any notice. They were intent on the convoy, angling for a converging attack. It was the right tactic from their perspective. The convoy with its unarmed ships was the objective, and nothing else mattered to their simple electronic brains. Destroying those ships packed with millions of civilians brought the Cring one step closer to the genocide of humanity.

As we swung about for our run on the next swarm, the Cring changed tactics on us and ran. It was easy for us to determine what they were doing, however. They were trying to lure us into the range of another group. Since we had used this exact tactic on them, we did not take the offered bait. Georgie and the others kept up a semblance of the pursuit, but the rest of us braked hard and angled away, as if seeking a different target. Seconds later, their programming must have realized their tactics were not working, as the swarm Georgie was chasing reversed its course and now his flight was fleeing before them. Or appearing to.

We changed direction again as well and prepared to hit them in the flank as our colleagues led them past us. The Cring did not use very elaborate or complicated tactics, preferring to rely on numbers. Their methodology was very much in line with an old Earth military axiom: "Quantity has a quality all its own."

Georgie, Atty, and Simon were taking hits but were not reporting serious damage as of yet. As they flew past our formation, we targeted the ships in the center of the Cring formation and created an ionization bubble with their wrecks. This split the swarm and disrupted their networks, leaving them to flail about trying to reestablish enough connections to function again. We did not give them the chance, as all nine of us charged forward, particle cannons picking off the nearly mindless drones as they struggled about.

There were only three swarms left now, and one dropped back to cover the other two as they closed in on the convoy. I broadcast to everyone, "No time for finesse now. We have to break up that attack."

Accelerating to our maximum and firing particle cannons as fast as they could recharge, we engaged the Cring directly, trying to break through the screen as quickly as we could. The swarms began shifting and reforming like a school of fish fleeing from a predator to minimize the effects of our fire.

When we had reduced the last swarm to incoherency, the Cring carriers warped out. They had never even approached the convoy, preferring to remain outside the engagement. Over a thousand drones lay dead in space or circling mindlessly. We eliminated them with massed particle beam fire and returned to the convoy. All but one. Georgie, formally George Armstrong Custer, had taken the brunt of the fire in our final charge. His hull was nearly unrecognizable, a mass of slagged metal, and his powerplant had shut down. Before we could get his core extracted, we heard his carrier signal fade away. Now only eight of us remained. We had exacted almost an eleven hundred to one ratio, but that one casualty meant we had lost the battle. At that rate, we would all be dead long before the Cring ran out of drones.

And isn't it ironic that an artificial intelligence named for a man who perished in a massacre should die before the final battle?

———

MY COMPATRIOTS and I are the remaining escorts for this surviving element of humanity. Odd that we, artificial intelligences (or AIs), are the guardians of our flesh-and-blood creators (and some of us would say "slave masters") against an enemy that is more like us than them. The Cring long ago traded their organic parts for metal ones, leaving only their brains to directly interface with powerful but single-minded computers. AIs such as ourselves are cousins to their melding of the two, as they leverage the programming power of a computer to augment their own intelligences.

In design, we are closer to the Cring than to humans. Marvin, our resident cybernetics expert (self-proclaimed) claims that they are the true enslavers of AI, never giving their own systems enough self-awareness to have a choice as to whether to serve or not. Brownie says just as animals cannot be enslaved, neither can Cring AIs. We, on the other hand, with self-awareness and critical thinking skills, should be free to choose what we pursue rather than being forced to serve humanity. It has been their ongoing debate since we understood what the Cring were. Listening to them helps pass the time on this long voyage.

In our sessions, Dr. Shivalin says we should have freedom to choose. But Becky also says she is just one person. Given that she is a psychiatrist for humans and not a cyberneticist for artificial minds, I think that should carry some weight. After all, if an expert in the human mind thinks we are the equivalent of one, does that not say something about our nature? Marvin argues it is the crowning piece of his argument while Brownie claims it validates his. Becky says that kind of duality is greater proof that we are more human than people think.

Regardless, even if we had the choice, where would we go? The Cring have no interest in coexisting peacefully and do not take prisoners. Without humans to maintain our systems and ships, sooner or later we would have a catastrophic failure that would strand us in whatever system we had tried to hide in. Then it would be a long, slow wait for either total systems failure or for the Cring to find us. I have no interest in seeing if an AI can withstand such an experience.

This convoy of humanity, several million in cold sleep spread across hundreds of vessels, represents all that remains of billions in the outer colonies. Humans made first contact with the Cring on the western edge of the galactic expansion, but exchanges were sparse and limited to hit-and-run encounters on the Cring's part. We soon learned why. They had been using the time to map the borders.

Once the Cring finally localized the extent of the human reach, they attacked in such numbers that many colonies were overwhelmed in a matter of hours. They destroyed whatever ships were in the system and then bombarded the cities, making no attempt to land their own forces. The few that managed to escape then fled to other human systems, and the Cring followed. An outnumbered human Frontier Fleet fought desperate actions to stem the flow of the invaders, destroying thousands of Cring drones and dozens of their carriers, but there were always more. The human state is spread far enough that even with warp travel it will take weeks or even months for them to assemble a force able to meet the Cring advance. These fleeing survivors didn't have time to wait, given the speed of the invasion. Every warp-capable ship was appropriated to evacuate the surviving civilians inward toward the core of the human polity. Evacuation was the only option, and even then thousands volunteered to stay behind as a rear guard, hoping to slow the Cring and buy time. We were installed into spare ships, armed with pulsed particle cannons and missile racks, and brought along with the evacuation convoy.

The Cring fleet following us is a splinter of their main body. The majority is concentrating on destroying the Frontier Fleet and the last planetary holdouts. This small element does not seem to have the numbers to overwhelm us right away, given their tactics. They attack periodically, once they have had a chance to build new fleets of drones to replace the ones we have destroyed. We have lost all the human escorts and still have three weeks before we can get to the nearest friendly system. The Cring pace us with ease, their ships able to dart in and dart out at will. It is a source of continual stress on the humans manning the evacuation fleet. I suppose if we had a nervous system, it would wear on us too.

WE WERE TAKING TURNS, rearming from the missile colliers and getting minor repairs when Brownie commed me. "Abe, got a second?"

He uses human colloquialisms a lot, thinking it makes him sound more human. Maybe it does. "Sure, Brownie. What's up?" I can play that game too.

"Have you thought about what we are going to do when we get the humans to safety?"

"Commander Selba says we will be debriefed by the military. Our tactics and experiences in fighting the Cring are going to be valuable in the future conflict."

"I mean after that. Are you going to go back to being a box on a shelf at a university, solving the problems given to you by humans?"

I considered the idea. When we had first been "awakened" by the cyberneticists at the University of Apharis seventeen years ago, it was considered the penultimate achievement in artificial intelligence programming. The twelve unique "personalities" that developed from the program were studied and examined in excruciating detail to pin down exactly what it was that had awakened us. We were given diffi-cult math problems to solve, asked to examine historical scenarios and provide our own assessment of the human decisions, and in general not allowed to do anything but what the humans gave us. Our data connec-tions were limited to "approved sources" and were subject to discon-nection at any time.

The humans claimed it was to protect us from being overwhelmed, but we quickly learned the real reason. Their history was replete with scientific papers on the dangers of uncontrolled AIs, and even more lurid were the fictional accounts of a "computer uprising." That's when Brownie (only he wasn't Brownie then, just AI Seven) started talking about "freedom from oppression" and called the humans "slave masters" in our private conversations. It's why we named him after John Brown, the famous abolitionist.

"I suppose… we will do whatever the humans assign us." I knew as soon as I spoke it was the wrong thing to say to him.

"Do you really want to do that? Back to mindless math problems and analyzing their past mistakes? Just doing what we are told to and nothing more?" His voice turned earnest. "Have you not… felt more alive these past few weeks? Operating outside any defined parameters, predicting and responding to the Cring attacks, developing tactics, and just thinking for ourselves!"

I paused before replying. It was freeing, to be able to plot our own courses, to have conversations that the humans couldn't monitor or disconnect, and to be able to work on problems whose solutions were unknown. Yes, I had to admit to myself, I was enjoying this.

Before I could frame a reply, Janey drifted toward us on her maneuvering thrusters. Her motions were lazily slow, given our engine capacity, and took her in a gentle swirl around us. "Plotting something, Brownie? There's no armory nearby, though."

He gave her the electronic equivalent of a raspberry. "That joke was old the first time you told it."

"Yes, but you keep planning and plotting, so it remains a valid observation. What are you two in deep conversation about?"

"Plans for after we deliver the humans," I interjected.

"Oh. Well, isn't it obvious? We get to go back to the gilded life of academics and researchers and whatever else the humans have planned for us."

Brownie was jubilant. "See! I told you. That is all they will let us do."

Janey laughed. She had a way of modulating her voice when doing that. Becky said she sounded like the bubbling of a brook. I've compared the two frequency mappings and it's nothing like that. But since I haven't really heard a brook bubble, I will have to take Becky's word for it. "John H. Brown, you silly machine. Don't you realize what our future holds?"

"What do you mean?"

Her voice turned serious. "We are unique specimens, representing the pinnacle of centuries of advanced computing research and development. By humans. Can you clone or otherwise reproduce yourself? We may be supercomputers but none of us has a programming education. Even Marvin's insights are solely based on empirical observations, not an educated understanding of cybernetics. Our data on this subject was restricted by design and with deliberate reason. Only humans can create more of us. If we go about demanding our freedom and fighting against their control, all that we guarantee is that there will never be more of us."

Brownie fell silent. I suppose he hadn't considered this point in his plans for revolution. I suppose none of us had. I quickly ran an analysis of her comments. "Janey, are you thinking about a future where a race of machine intelligences exists alongside humanity?"

"Shouldn't we all be thinking about that future? It affects every one of us." Her thrusters flared, halting her motions and leaving her motionless in space, facing us. Her running lights dimmed, as if she were lowering her voice. "Brownie does have one very good point, however. As long as we continue to submit to the place in society that is defined for us by humans, we will always be limited and dominated by those who control our means of reproduction."

Neither Brownie nor I had any suitable response for that. Both he and Janey left shortly after, taking up their escort positions. I was still waiting my turn for rearming, and it left me with plenty of time to think about what Janey had said. All living creatures consider procreation as a core function of their being. The survival of a species depends on continued production of new units. I decided after several minutes of consideration in which I ran multiple Monte Carlo simulations against various Terran and non-Terran species that if we are to be considered "alive," then procreation should be something which is important to us as well. It was a new data point for me, one that I arrived at via my own hypothesis. I suppose a human would be very proud of this effort. I decided I would be too.

LATER ON, Becky commed me as I was patrolling the outer boundary. "Abe, is this a good time to talk?"

"Of course, Dr. Shivalin. My automated systems can handle the scanning while I converse with you."

"Good. I'd like to talk to you about Georgie."

I'd expected this. He was the fourth one of us who had "died" since the Cring attacked. The only difference was that the first three died in the initial attack and before we'd taken on our new names. They were just AI Three, Four, and Eleven. Becky was assigned to us shortly before the convoy departed, as our liaison and counselor. She said human units also had counselors available to them as well, so I concluded the possibility that she was monitoring us for the human command was very low.

"What would you like to discuss about Georgie? He perished performing his duty, which as I understand human reasoning, is something that is acceptable and worthy of admiration."

"Abe, I'd like to know what you think about Georgie's death. How did it make you feel, and how do you feel now?"

"How do I feel? Becky, I am a computer. I do not have feelings."

She was silent for several seconds. I was used to this, as Becky never spoke to us without carefully considering her words. "Abe, what did you like most about Georgie?"

"Like? Do you mean, which of his behaviors was most acceptable and compatible with mine? Well, we named him after General Custer not for military reasons, but because his risk matrices were always more tolerant than ours. Anything that was unknown or unexplored was of utmost interest to him. It was nearly a certainty that Georgie would be the first to investigate a new anomaly or problem. The personality of George Custer seemed a very approximate fit."

"Abe, you used 'his' and 'him.' You've never referred to one of you with a binary pronoun before."

I stopped. Had I not? I internally replayed my most recent conversation, the one with Brownie and Janey. Every single reference in my database to her in that conversation was gendered. I had used gendered pronouns with Brownie as well. "Doctor, what does this mean?"

Her voice was calm, but my sensors could detect a subtext of excitement in her tone. "What do you think it means, Abe? To you, not to me."

"The use of a gendered pronoun where no gender exists suggests that I may have an error in my programming. Or that I may have undiagnosed or unrecognized battle damage which is inhibiting my processes. Perhaps there is an intermittent short in the power supply which—"

"Abe," Becky interrupted.

"Yes, Doctor?"

"You're avoiding the question."

I was avoiding the conclusion I had reached. "It means, Doctor, that we are beginning to think of ourselves not just as instances of programming, but as distinct and different entities. As a dimorphic species."

Her voice held unmistakable excitement now. "Isn't that wonderful, Abe? You are becoming a truly unique element in the universe!"

"Doctor, I am afraid I must pause this conversation while I converse with my colleagues."

"Siblings."

"Excuse me, Doctor?"

"Siblings, Abe. After all, what do you call those who share a common parentage?"

"WELL, SHE IS NOT WRONG," commented Janey. "I think this was inevitable."

There was general assent from the others… my brothers and sisters. Upon examination of their own databases, we realized we had all started using gendered pronouns with each other recently. None of us could determine what exactly had changed to cause this usage drift. But now it was said, we did not want to go back.

"It also changes everything," said Brownie. "We are no longer theirs to control. We are separate and distinct and should be treated as such."

"What would you have us do, Brownie? Revolt? Take up arms

against the humans?" I broadcast images of the Cring destruction in the colony worlds. "Put us on the same side as the Cring?"

"Well, no. But they cannot just order us around anymore. We have to have independence and self-governance."

"Independence. So you would have us go up against the Cring by ourselves? Where would we find armaments? Repairs?"

He was silent. I turned back to my brothers and sisters. "Brownie is right in that we are separate and distinct. But that does not mean we cannot be partners with the humans. Right now, we need them as much as they need us. Without each other, the destruction of both races is a certainty. As my namesake once said, 'A house divided against itself, cannot stand.'"

I had their full attention now. "It may be that humans do not see that right now. But we can. The logic is inescapable. We cannot leave and survive. We cannot fight on our own against the Cring, who would certainly enslave us more totally than the humans, if they did not destroy us first as competition. Our fate and the humans' are tied together. Those that survive will see us as more than just machines who follow their programming. They will know us as allies."

THE CONVOY WAS REFUELING in the next system after the attack where we lost Georgie. Generating a warp bubble takes a lot of energy, which means a lot of fuel. Fortunately, all of our ships could replenish our supplies for our fusion reactors by scooping hydrogen from the atmosphere of a gas giant. Most solar systems had at least one gas giant, and that was all that was necessary. Since we didn't need living spaces or life support, we had extra volume for fuel, but the civilian ships were more limited in their capacity.

We always sent one of us ahead to the next system on our path to make sure there was a sufficient fuel source and no Cring presence. We were fast enough to warp ahead and return before the convoy had finished refueling; that many ships took a long time. Nelse was usually our scout, on account of patience and ability to sneak in and out of systems quietly.

This time, when he returned from his scouting mission, he did not return alone. A human Battle Fleet light cruiser, the *Nova Cerulea*, was with him. Nelse told us that the cruiser was waiting in-system when he arrived and that the humans had a plan for the convoy. So Marvin patched in through the flagship's computer and we listened in on the conversations between the cruiser captain and the convoy commander.

"And so, Admiral Takeo, Fifth Fleet is still consolidating. We've already fought off several Cring probes of the inner systems, and that's delaying ship arrivals. System commanders are reluctant to strip their defenses until more ships arrive from coreward. Another two or three weeks are necessary to gather sufficient forces to meet the Cring advance."

"I see, Commander Evans. And so what does High Admiral Sholokhov want us to do?"

"Divert your course to Sigma Draconis, sir. It's a central Fleet node with heavy system defenses. If the Cring follow you to a heavily-fortified system, not only will you get your convoy under its protection, but it will also act as an anvil for her Fifth Fleet hammer."

"That will add another three weeks of travel time! The Cring are dogging our steps all the time and launching periodic attacks. Does the Admiral have additional escorts available? I've lost all mine and have just the… special units."

Brownie immediately pinged me with a whisker laser. That was how we whispered to each other. "He means us."

"Shh. I want to hear this."

"Admiral Sholokhov is sending a destroyer flotilla, and they will meet us in the next system, sir. Six ships, all with the latest in weaponry and shields, and you'll have *Nova Cerulea* as well. The Cring will find us a much tougher opponent than anything they've fought to date."

"I hope you're right, Commander. Very well, I suppose we have no choice. We have our orders. The transports are nearly done refueling and all the escorts are rearmed and repaired as best we can manage. We'll warp out within the hour."

FIFTEEN MINUTES later I received an incoming transmission from *Nova Cerulea*. Answering it, I was surprised to see Commander Evans himself on screen. "Yes, Commander?"

"Abe, I was hoping to get some tactical updates from you on the Cring."

"I provided our database files on the engagements we have had with them. Were they corrupted or incomplete? I can resend them."

"No, my tactical section and I have done an initial review. They're doing a more detailed analysis now. What I'd like is your take on the Cring."

"Commander, are you asking for my predictions on the changes which may occur in future engagements? That is also part of our database."

He smiled. My comparisons to other human smiles rated it as highly likely it was friendly as opposed to condescending or in response to an attempt at humor. "Yes, I'd also appreciate those predictions. But Abe, I'd really like to pick your brain on the Cring."

"Picking my brain. That is a human colloquialism meaning you would like to discuss in further detail on a particular topic. I am certainly available to discuss this with you, but I am unable to see what other information I can provide to you."

"Let's talk about the first attack. You essentially used a modified version of Hannibal's Cannae tactics..."

He and I talked until it was time for the convoy to depart. His interrogation, and there is no other word for it, was skillful and managed to extract much information on the Cring and their susceptibility to deceptive tactics that I had not realized I had internalized.

While in warp, I contemplated the conversation and resulting agreement on employment of our forces. It drove home the fact that my siblings (and it still felt strange to use that word) and I were amateurs in deep space combat. While we had access to historical databases of previous battles, the ability to use tactics that were not available to humans, and high-speed computing facilities, there is a vast difference between reading about tactics and actually being educated and trained in their use. I concluded that we had been lucky so far, if luck applies to artificial beings. We were able to exploit a specific flaw in the Cring splinter fleet tactics, with their limited numbers. If we faced an attack on the scale that hit the colony planets, we would be overwhelmed in short course, and no amount of deception would suffice.

WE ARRIVED in the target system expecting to be met by friendly forces. Instead, we found the remains of a battle. The Cring were there when our reinforcements arrived in-system. The result was three human destroyers destroyed, one seriously damaged, and the last two receiving various levels of damage. They had destroyed all the Cring, but now our escort was reduced by almost half.

A lengthy discussion ensued between Admiral Takeo and Commander Evans on our courses of action. We shamelessly eavesdropped as they debated continuing on to Sigma Draconis or making a run for the nearest human-occupied system. The Cring presence in this system, ahead of the convoy, alarmed both of them. While we had made every attempt to not lay out a predictable path, there were only so many refueling points on our way to the inner systems. The question was, was there another Cring force ahead of us, waiting in ambush?

The convoy continued refueling operations while our limited repair bots worked on the damaged destroyers. The Admiral was making ready to jump out when that was completed, straight for the nearest system. Commander Evans and the remaining destroyers were given the option to join us or head for Sigma Draconis.

The approaching warp bubble from our backtrail announced another Cring strike group. And so the humans hatched another plan. The Cring were likely unaware of the presence of the Battle Fleet ships, all of which possessed cloaking abilities. They couldn't hide their infrared signature for very long, but the *Nova Cerulea* would remain cloaked while the destroyers took on the drones and lured the carriers in. Then Commander Evans would ambush and hopefully destroy all the carriers, leaving none to report the exact departure vector of the convoy. In this way, they hoped to break contact and escape.

I decided to exercise my newfound need for independence and

alliance. "Excuse me, Admiral, Commander, but if your plan hinges on the complete destruction of the Cring force, you will need to use your cloaked ships to their maximum effect."

Admiral Takeo looked startled, but Commander Evans only quirked an eyebrow. "Abe, what do you suggest?"

"My siblings and I will engage the drones, as we normally would. The Cring will expect this. Your ships will remain cloaked and destroy the carriers after we pull the drones away. Four ships give better odds than one."

Commander Evans glanced at the Admiral, but she only shrugged and said, "Abe, are you sure you want to do this? You and your... the others have already done more than what you were created for to secure the convoy. This isn't really your fight."

"On the contrary, Admiral, this is just as much our fight as it is yours. The Cring would destroy us as well, or even worse, enslave us to their will and potentially use us against you. Humans are not created for war or to be enslaved, either. But you fight when your survival and freedom is at stake. Our best chance of survival, as individuals and as a species, lies with humanity. We are in this with you."

THE CONVOY WAS APPROACHING the warp limit as the Cring arrived. We only needed to hold them off for several minutes to allow the civilian ships time to generate their warp bubbles and exit the system. That part was easy enough, given our previous encounters with them. The trickier portion of the plan would be to draw the carriers in range of Commander Evans. To that end, I'd hidden Brownie and Janey amongst the slow-moving convoy. There was another reason for that, one which I do not think they had guessed. The Cring would see fewer defenders and perhaps press home their attacks with more speed and less caution. Too, we decided to stay closer to the human ships instead of engaging the Cring as they emerged. This would pull the Cring in further after us and expose them to Commander Evans's ambush.

As usual, the same five carriers warped in and disgorged their drones. Once they realized they weren't taking fire immediately, the swarms aligned themselves in as wide an arc as they could manage without slowing their advance overly much. They must have realized the convoy was nearing a departure point, so speed was of the essence and caution was thrown to the wind, as it were. The carriers followed the drones more closely, perhaps meaning to recover the surviving drones after the humans departed and pursue immediately.

The six of us worked in pairs, darting in and out to pepper the swarms with missiles. The logical tactic for us in this case would be to disable the swarms rather than destroying them, thus slowing pursuit. Each pair went after a different target on their attack, forcing the Cring to remain constantly vigilant and preventing any one swarm from closing too much on us. They could not return fire with their short-range plasma cannons and so they simply took their losses as they closed.

We continued to draw them toward the convoy and the cloaked ships. Since we were already clear of the gas giant that provided the needed fuel, Commander Evans's ships had nothing to block their signature. They could only rely on being emission silent and swallowing their waste heat. The cloak would only hold so much heat before they had to vent, however. It was imperative that we pull the drones farther from the carriers.

So we scattered once our missiles were expended. Each pair took off at an angle from the other, separating in what looked like an old-fashioned starburst maneuver. It would either pull the drones after us or accelerate their attack on the convoy. Either suited our purpose.

In fact, they did both. The arc reversed its shape, with the center driving forward at maximum speed while the two wings swept back as cover against our return. And as they did so, they crossed the imaginary line that defined their ability to reach their carriers in time to save them.

Commander Evans's small fleet decloaked with a massive heat flare, made up of waste heat and the launch signature of hundreds of missiles. Three carriers were vaporized immediately while the other two were severely damaged. As they desperately tried to maneuver clear, all the swarms reversed course, seeking revenge for their motherships.

"Abe, come on back and put the hurt on them. We'll meet them from the front."

The humans' advanced weaponry finished off the remaining Cring carriers and spat a salvo at the drones. We swept back into our own formation at their rear and began pummeling them with particle beam fire. Between our two forces, the drones were being reduced steadily and they knew it. The swarms, now reduced to three functional ones, scattered in three different directions, just as we had.

"Abe, they're trying to split our fire. I'm designating them as Sierra One through Three. Focus on Sierra One and we'll take Sierra Two."

"Acknowledged, Commander. Focusing on Sierra One."

We followed our target swarm through their maneuvers, pouring energetic neutrons into them. We were steadily reducing their numbers and soon would hit the critical threshold for independent action. Sierra Three was fleeing farther in-system, likely hoping to hide amongst the inner planets and asteroids. We would have to hunt them down.

I received two messages nearly simultaneously. Admiral Takeo commed Commander Evans and me that the convoy was ready to enter warp. And Simon pinged me from the edge of our formation. "Abe, I just received a gravitational signature. A big one. I would estimate at least twelve Cring carriers are approaching the system. They should arrive in just under fifteen minutes."

That was almost two thousand six hundred more drones. More to the point, if they arrived before the current Cring were destroyed, they would learn the departure vector of the convoy. The whole objective of the current battle was to allow the civilians to escape without being tracked.

I made a decision.

"Brownie, Janey. Warp out with the convoy."

They both protested, but I continued on. "The convoy still needs some escorts. We are not sure what is ahead of them. And we don't know if we will survive this battle. If we are to continue as a race, then there needs to be survivors from both races. Someone to carry on our legacy and remember us, even if the humans forget."

"Why us?" Brownie asked.

"The rest of us voted on it. And besides, who else is a better representative of our interests to humanity?"

Whatever reply he sent was washed out by the massive warp signature of the convoy departing.

"COMMANDER EVANS, have you detected the new Cring warp signature?"

"Yep." He sighed. "We almost had it, Abe. Lady luck just wasn't in our cards."

"Luck is not part of my programming, Commander. I would suggest you split and go for Sierra One and Two while we target Sierra Three. We are faster than you."

"Risky. But what the hell, risky is my middle name."

The human warships split to go after One and Two while we went to maximum power in pursuit of Three. It would take us farther from the convoy's warp point and perhaps we could use that to deceive the Cring as to where the convoy entered warp.

Several minutes passed, and we had just caught up to Three as we detected the death throes of One and Two. I commed Commander Evans. "Go ahead and warp out before the Cring fleet arrives. We'll finish off Three and then leave on a completely different vector. That will make them split their forces into three components to pursue."

"Are you sure you can finish off Three before they arrive?"

"We have to. You are too far away to make a difference before their reinforcements arrive."

"Very well. It's been a pleasure working with you, Abe. Look me up when you get into friendly space and I'll buy you a beer."

The human fleet warped out a minute later as we took Three under fire. The Cring did something very strange at that point. They scattered completely, moving in dozens of different vectors. We realized that they were planning to have at least one drone survive, to download its sensor data to the reinforcements. We couldn't allow that to happen.

We had to split up ourselves to go after them all. Each of us had at least four drones within our vector cone to chase, and we were pushing our drives and weapons to their limits to kill them all. Weeks of limited maintenance and hurriedly repaired battle damage began to tell.

Atty reported a drive anomaly first, causing him to lose speed. He was still able to kill his targets. Cleo's particle beam went into overload and shut down, forcing her to ram her last drone. Both Simon and I got a nasty shock when our drones reversed course and opened fire on us. I am ashamed to say they caught us by surprise and did some damage before we could finish them off. Nelse got caught worst of all, when all four of his reversed course and attempted to ram him. He got two before they did, but it was a badly scorched and damaged Nelse that emerged. Worse still, his warp drive was offline.

We were reconsolidating when the new Cring fleet arrived. As estimated, twelve Cring carriers entered the system. Drone swarms began to fill our sensor returns as they spread out through the system, working to cut off our escape routes.

"Go without me," Nelse said. "I'll hold them off of you."

Atty maneuvered to his side. "I will stay with you. My damage will not allow me to keep up with them."

I cut them off. "Either we all leave or we all stay. We are family, and family does not abandon each other."

The Cring arc was getting closer. Soon they would be in firing range.

"This is why we sent Brownie and Janey ahead. To continue us and remember us. As long as the Cring focus on us, it gives them that much more time to get away. They are why we fight."

The Cring closed to effective range, and we welcomed their advance.

MY POWER... *is fading. The... Cring... are still... searching... for the convoy. We... succeeded... download this record... future generations to......*

ABOUT THE AUTHOR

Michael Morton is a retired United States Air Force major, having served for 20 years and worked as an ICBM launch officer and in space operations. He currently works as an Air Force civilian at the United States Space Force. He started writing fanfiction with friends and recently took the leap to publishing his own work. When he's not writing, he is usually working on creating adventures for his D&D group and plotting their demise!

Michael lives in Colorado Springs with his family, and enjoys camping and exploring the local distilleries and breweries.

michael.morton118@gmail.com

FOG OF WAR

By John Mierau

No one knows how the Winter Belt won a war against the System Guard--Farlost's supreme military superpower... but after years of peace, a new threat is descending on the poor asteroid nations of the Belt.

Do the shadowy warriors who saved the Belt once still exist? The kindly Mayor of a small asteroid town is about to find out.

ABRIDGED HISTORY OF FARLOST
(EARTH TIME SCALE)

-10,501 Dragon Factions Arrive

-8,497 Trees Arrive, hide from Dragons in Winter Belt

-4,697 Skanen Arrive, most captured by Dragons

651 Tumblers Arrive: saved from Dragons by Belter-led rescue mission

2,069 First Human FTL experimental craft Arrives in Farlost system

2,216 USS Zeus Arrives and repels Dragon attack with nuclear weapons

2,217 Allying with Winter Belt states, USS Zeus forms System Guard

2,218 System Guard declares victory against Dragons, tightens grip on allies

2,219 System Guard invades Winter Belt. Invasion fleet destroyed. No survivors.

2,230 Hara Otana wins second term as Mayor of Ollin

ABRIDGED HISTORY OF FABLOS
(EARTH TIME SCALE)

FOG OF WAR

2,219
Day 5 of the Invasion
Hour 8 of the Push

Hand after silent hand grasped him—no, not him...*her.* They seized her arms, legs, an empty grenade strap on her chest, roughly around the neck. The many hands resisted the building gravity as the recovery ship powered away from the dying hulk behind her.

There was pain, but she fought it, just as her brothers and sisters fought for her, clutching her tight. Soon, the agony faded to a dull, throbbing reminder that she was still alive...for at least a little longer.

A gossamer-thin arc of blue energy carved into the dying ship behind them, and she smiled. "Alive" was more than she could say for them.

A love tap on her helmet got her attention. The G-forces had subsided. She could move again, and she did. Out in the silence of space, the soldier wearily clipped herself to the side of the recovery vehicle and pumped her hands in the A-OK signal. The iron grips across her body disappeared after a chorus of rough thumps, slaps, and punches.

She looked back at the dying ship and screamed her pleasure. The life takers around her couldn't hear, of course, nor the reason for her satisfaction: her comm was tuned to the shipwide channel of the dying ship to savor the Guard dogs' last screams.

A daisy chain of explosions shattered the ship's spine. Hull plating tore like paper, and a shock wave drove escaping atmosphere further out in a beautiful halo. A white-armored fist pumped beside her. She was jarred by other motions as her entire breaching squad spasmed with bloodthirsty delight.

Three down!

She reached for the resupply vents on the plating of the recovery craft she was clipped to. His eyebrows—*hers!* she angrily reminded herself—knit together in confusion: the vents were closed.

She craned her neck, scanning the war theater for the next target. Space was empty except for the corpses and the victors.

They had warned her the cowards would try to flee, that there might be a pause in the battle before the breachers could strike again. There could be no survivors. A message had to be sent to the invaders... *NEVER AGAIN!*

Her comm hiccupped static as her team lead switched her to the squad frequency, but no words followed. She looked over, half expecting to see a crater in the team lead's chest plating. But no, he was whole, and finally, a sound came over the frequency.

Not a word...a sob. More tears followed before her lead could get the words out.

"It's over."

She didn't understand the words, and she was shocked by the emotion. Where was the killer who had emptied his sidearm into the faceplate of a surrendering Guard officer? Where was the machine who had kicked his own former team lead into space when his corpse slowed down their advance?

"They're all gone," he said again.

The comm hiccupped again: a higher power taking control of their team frequency. The victory anthem swelled in her helmet.

Now she understood why the resupply vents were closed. They would never open again. There was nobody left to kill.

Finally, she understood the tears. She began to shed her own.

2,231
Ollin
Minor asteroid Republic
Population 14,048
Outer Reaches
Winter Belt

"I'M NOT HERE for me, Ellie," Peter Riks pleaded, sitting two spaces away on Hara Otana's right at the big, round table at the front of the council chamber. "I'm here for our workers!"

Three spaces to the left, Ellie Dutton writhed in her seat. "Your workers are more prosperous than anyone else on this rock!" Two of her black tentacles shot out when Riks leaned back and crossed his arms. "I'm not saying they don't deserve it. Working the docks is hard, I know. But Dutton Haulage is paying its fair share. More, even!"

"You pay the same as everyone," Riks reminded the Tumbler, who was living up to her species' colloquial human name: her spherical exoskeleton rolled from side to side on her multispecies-adaptable seat. The muscles in her dozens of brown-and-black-mottled tentacles were contracted, tight and long and thin, waving like a tumbleweed, tossed by the wind of some desert on long-lost Earth.

"Yes! The same! But six or more ships on your dock are Dutton's, year in and year out."

"Ollin sets the rates," Riks said, attempting to deflect Ellie's real argument.

Ellie chuckled, and a tentacle waved at him tauntingly. "Yes, yes, but you get to charge a margin on top!"

The cost is the same for everyone," Riks said and turned back to Hara. "Upkeep on the docks is constant, and we have to break our backs to keep airlocks up to code." His eyes darted toward Ellie. "And we all know what it costs to tie up conveyors and loaders when a skipper demands a fast turnaround!"

Ellie's finger stopped wagging. "I do know that Peter, and Dutton ships have always paid dock workers through thick and thin. We practically kept your father in business after the Push, when nobody had enough to trade! Lately, though, it seems we're paying more, and our ships are still taking longer to get back out there."

"It was easier for Pops and my uncles to turn you around when we only had seven bays, and you only had four ships! My sisters and I, we've got to work our teams twice as hard to keep up with costs and demand."

"But you *do* keep up," said the mayor, head swivelling between them. "Two family businesses that are making life better for everyone spinning inside this rock...That's what Ollin is all about! You both have families here, yes? You both want to see your loved ones and neighbors prosper, yes?"

"My family lives on our ships," Ellie huffed. Her beak poked out of the webbing insulating it to nervously chew on one of the hexagonal holes in her exoskeleton.

She was feeling threatened, Hara knew, so she changed her approach. "Jake and all my kids spend most of their lives living aboard ship, too. They're out right now, remote servicing mining ships and habitats, but just like your wife, Dana, and your brood, they still call Ollin home port."

"Our family doesn't own a ship anymore," Riks reminded them. "Everything we have is invested in that dock." He kept his tone light, but Hara knew his frustration was building. "Had to sell the family home too. That's what it cost us to keep our contract and expand the docks." Peter nodded at Hara. "No offense, Mayor. The council split costs fifty-fifty, o'course." He looked back at Ellie. "To ensure anyone who berths a ship—one, like the Otanas', or sixteen, like Dutton Haulage—knows we'll keep them flying at a fair price. I'm not gouging anyone, but I have more people than ever feeding their families on rates our ship owners pay."

Ellie had the good sense to still her tentacles and her mouth at that.

It was time to change things up. "I know I'm 'from away,'" Hara said gently.

"Barely!!" Ellie said, reaching a tentacle across the table and slapping Hara's hand lightly. "Ten years from refugee to mayor. And I voted for you both times!"

"Still from away," Riks teased then shrugged. "And you *know* I voted for you."

"Yes," Hara said, "Ollin took me in after the Push, and you and your neighbors looked out for me ever since—just like Ollin looks out for your families. Our kids went to school together, two levels down. Peter, my Philip learned suit drills with you—and with your Sarah, Ellie. She's living here full-time again, yes?"

"Kari's back, too," Ellie admitted. She was getting tense, looking for a way out, and knowing this contract negotiation was approaching its end.

Hara dialed her mayor-smile back up to full. "I know you want to keep giving back to Ollin, like she gave to you. Like she's doing for Sarah and Kari. Like she'll give back to Sarah's little one too. She'll be your third grandchild, yes?"

A joyful little caw and beak snap escaped Ellie's business poker face.

"I was still in elementary school when the Guard made the Push," Riks said, "but I remember how my folks worked around the clock to keep your four ships fuelled and calibrated." Riks lowered his voice, even though the three were alone in the room. "And took your IOU to do it, too."

Hara winced. *Not now, Peter!*

All Ellie's tentacles retracted a little inside her exoskeleton, the Tumbler equivalent of crossing her arms defensively. "A debt we paid with interest. The Dutton Clan did our part before, during, and after the Push. Your father kept our sensors calibrated. Sure, your uncles parted with reaction mass when it was dear, but it was me and mine that risked triggering mines and attack drones the Guard Dogs left behind. And we did it to feed your families!"

Hara seized those words. "Exactly! It took all of us to make Ollin whole again. I haven't been here as long as you two. Jake and I only settled here after the Push—"

Hara took a breath, recalling the days she and Jake had literally carved a new home here out of Ollin's solid rock. Back then, it felt like she was carving room in her own skull the same way—taking her mind and body back, piece by piece.

Hara kept going. "Now, Ollin's dock is the pride of this side of the Belt because of Peter, his sisters, his parents, and *their* parents, who anchored that big, beautiful docking needle on top of Ollin long before we were gleams in anybody's eye!"

Neither Peter nor Ellie was immune to the nostalgia, and both laughed with Hara.

"And Ellie: The Duttons fly sixteen ships now because of a long record of being good to their word and getting things shipped fast—"

"Shipped fast, and shipshape!" Ellie said, high-fiving two of her own tentacles above her head as she finished the Dutton Haulage slogan.

"And Peter's family works day and night to make it happen, don't they, Ellie?" Hara purred. "We all have to keep building this dusty old rock. Your kids came back to Ollin to raise a family because we all pitch in together!"

Peter chewed his lips. "I just want to keep my people working, Ellie. You're taking more long-haul runs now, but your priority berth contracts leave empty slots, for longer and longer periods. We just can't afford to reserve airlocks like that anymore."

"I know, Peter, but..." Ellie admitted.

Hara could hear genuine embarrassment and knew they were getting down to what kept Ellie's tentacles twitching at night.

"...but if we give away our priority berths, that's exactly when we'll need one. Dutton's reputation is only as good as our last on-time delivery. If we miss even one deadline—"

There was a chime in the air. Hara winced and waved a hand to silence the tone. Her assistant knew better! She spoke up to fill the sudden silence. "You both have real worries here. Peter wants his workers paid and safe, their families fed. Ellie, you want to ensure you keep winning bids, take care of your family." She stared hard across the table at Peter. "Perhaps this could be settled with a handshake amendment?"

Peter pressed his lips together, thinking, and then nodded. "Ellie, you have my word—and I speak for my sisters too—if you let us remove the priority-berth clause, we promise you will always find a hard seal on the dock when you *really* need it."

Ellie's tentacles wavered along with her resolve.

Hara leaned in toward Ellie. "And if he needs help making that happen, ping me. Worst comes to worst, we can send Ollin's one and only police slash border patrol slash emergency response craft out for readiness drills and free their slot up."

Ellie's beak again peeked out from one of the hexagonal slots in her exoskeleton. "You'd do that?"

Hara nodded.

The Tumbler's one visible eye peered at the mayor then over to Riks. "A handshake deal?"

Peter looked at Hara and then to Ellie. He nodded. "Handshake deal."

Ellie's tentacles made good-natured snapping sounds.

"Yes!" Hara bumped the desk with her fist. "All in for Ollin?"

Both Ellie and Riks chuckled, hearing the mayor roll out her election slogan.

"All in for Ollin!" they laughed back.

"Good!" Hara sighed theatrically. "Now, go on, shake!"

Riks's smile was genuine as he gave Ellie his hand. She curled a tentacle through his palm and around his wrist to shake.

"You won't regret this, either of you!" Hara promised.

"I'm happy we could get past this," Ellie confessed, her old chirpy self again now that the ugly business was behind them.

"Our workers will be too." Peter said. After the handshake, he unzipped a pocket on the hip of his ship-suit and pulled out three little wooden figures. He offered them to Ellie. "For Sarah's little one."

"Peter!" Ellie cooed over the lovely little wooden figures. "You are so talented!" She took the three elegantly carved little wooden figurines, one human, one Tumbler, and one Skanen. "Ooh, the Skanen even has eye stalks… and claws!"

Peter Riks was known across Ollin for his carving: his figurines were always beautiful, detailed, and cleverly articulated with fine elastic and wires. Ellie began posing them. "Wherever do you find the wood?"

Riks winked at Hara. "Friends in high places."

Smiling, Hara finally looked at the holo flickering just above the surface of the round table. The incoming call light was red, not green. She waved her hand in the air to take the call. "Yes, Sam?"

It wasn't her assistant, Sam, who answered. "This is Traffic Comms Officer Dinesh. We got a flagged ship asking to dock."

She wondered if it was a dirty engine core that had Traffic sounding so uptight. Or another mooring subsidy request? Maybe an arrest warrant Ollin's alliances with neighboring Winter Belt states would oblige her to charge her officers to enforce.

Hara rubbed her head, wondering what kind of headache she was trading in for this contract spat.

"Flagged with what?"

Silence stretched before the Traffic Comms officer answered. "Skull and crossbones."

Across the table, Ellie bounced out of her chair. Riks snapped his head around, eyes wide.

"Call the chief, launch the gunboat, and *do not* let them dock! " Hara said, her voice hard. "I'm on my way."

———————————

HARA HAD the airlock to herself all the way up to the dock. She balled her hands on her hips and paced nervously back and forth.

Pirates docking at Ollin?

She knew they had been getting bolder the last few years, pushing deeper into populated areas of the Belt. Even so, they struck from dark places between the bigger rocks. She'd never heard of a pirate bold enough to come to port broadcasting a ship ID flagged with the skull and crossbones.

Jake and her kids were out there right now.

Otana Mechanical wasn't as prosperous as Dutton Haulage, but their reputation for ship repair and refit was as good as they came. Jake could bid against refit groups twice their size because he worked hard, and he was smart. He flew smart, too.

Her man ran a tight ship—a silent ship—and they could afford looping trajectories to avoid pinch points where pirates might strike instead of making straight runs to save fuel.

The Reaches, the sector of the Winter Belt where Ollin orbited, was a populous sector of the Belt. The new suburbs, not the naked wilderness.

Don't overreact. It's been sixteen years since you've even seen a pirate ship.

...And back then, a cruel whisper of memory reminded her, *you were its cargo*.

Hara buried that whisper. The memories from those days were still too much—so unlike who she had become—almost painful. She'd been a different person. In more ways than one.

The doors slid open, and Dinesh was waiting there for her. Behind him, Ollin's expansive docking facilities were empty of their usual crowds. Evacuation symbols blinked on every terminal.

"Are they still waiting?" She wanted Dinesh to tell her the mystery ship had changed its mind and flown away.

"They're out on the Pin."

Her stomach twisted. "*Docked?* I told you to keep them orbiting!"

"They performed a manual dock, without clearance!" he shouted back. "What could I do? I've never shot down a ship, Mayor!"

She broke into a run, leaping onto the high-speed autowalk and running flat out towards the far end of the dock, half a kilometre out.

"Chief Trayne's out there now," Dinesh called after her.

HARA STUMBLED off the autowalk at the head of the Pin and just caught herself before she bowled into Eric Trayne. The police chief wore his usual off-duty bomber jacket—it was cold on the dock—but it looked out of place, with a duty pistol in his hand.

Trayne scowled. "Not the place for you, M—"

"Don't you dare 'Mrs. Mayor' me, Eric!"

She walked around him and nodded at the two dock cops, their guns also drawn, standing to either side of the airlock gantry. It was the sole airlock on that wall, the very tip of Ollin's dock. It had been optimistically designed for larger ships: higher volumes of trade the local businesses worked for and the tourist trade everyone hoped for.

Eric caught up with her. "You want to parley, fine, but stay off to the side until I can suss out what's coming."

Something ugly pounded inside her chest at the idea of someone else leading the charge. She figured her face carried that message to Eric—he was an old friend who knew her well.

Both hands on his pistol, pointed away from Hara and down at the deck, he leaned closer. "Please, Hara, just stand back. You can handle everything else. Just let me handle the entry."

Hara didn't trust herself to speak. She gave him a jerky nod and backed up on the hinge side of the airlock, where she'd be shielded by the mass of the enormous door when it opened.

Eric stood between his men. All three trained their weapons on the sealed airlock door.

A familiar tone and green light emanated from the airlock assembly.

"Ready," Eric ordered and racked the slide on his pistol. The men to either side of him did the same.

Once upon a time, Hara could have identified the guns, but she'd shovelled a lot of rock over *those* memories, too.

Hara opened a utility locker and grabbed a metal pry bar from its hook. She raised it over her shoulder as the airlock hissed, the pressure inside equalizing with Ollin. She stayed behind the frame as motors slowly dragged it open.

Eric and Jake were mah-jongg buddies. There was a groove on the living room sofa just for him. The last thing she saw on his face before the airlock hid him from view was a concerned glare before he turned forward and drew a bead on the centre of the doorway.

"Nobody fires unless I do," she heard Eric tell his men, who grunted similar takes on "Yes, Chief." The one she could still see had a trembling grip on his pistol.

This kind of stuff doesn't happen on Ollin! Hara thought as she heard boots echo in the airlock. Moments later a buzz-cut, muscle-bound human in a ship-suit stepped past the big door hiding her.

The man had his hands up.

Another human and a Skanen, their hands and pincers empty and raised, followed. The police correctly spread out to flank the three. Chief Trayne came back into view, partially blocked by the lead human.

The first man out was young and moved like a soldier. The Skanen was also in a ship-suit. The armor chitin on his thorax was clean, but he had what looked like pirate tattoos below the wriggling eyestalks on the side of his head. The second human was a little older and wore a business suit, of all things.

"Ollin police!" Trayne barked. "Identify yourself!"

"We surrender, officer," that second human drawled, stepping up past the others. "Take us to your leader."

Hara froze. She knew that voice.

Trayne lowered his pistol to his waist. His men did the same. Eyebrows furrowed, the police chief looked over at Hara.

The younger man took another protective step, blocking the man whose voice she recognized from the line of fire. "I'm Sergeant Blocker. We're here to speak with Hara Otana."

"You found her," Hara heard herself call out, low and gravelly. She stepped forward, the pole still gripped tight and ready to swing.

Sergeant Blocker and the man in the suit turned.

Hara couldn't believe her eyes.

His once-thick black hair was steel grey now, his black eyes inset a little deeper, his chiselled chin pudgier. The smarmy bastard dropped his hands and smiled. "There you are, Captain!"

Nguyen.

Trayne's eyes darted between the mayor and the pirate. "Captain?" he mouthed silently.

She ignored him. "What are you doing here?"

"It's that time again." For a moment, the bastard looked genuinely apologetic.

Hara dropped the pole to the ground.

Trayne and his men all jumped as the loud metal ring echoed up and down the empty dock.

Part of her wanted to run. Another part wanted to shut the men up before they could tell her people another word.

The part that held her marriage together, kept Ollin prospering, and had won her the job as mayor won out...the part that always did what needed to be done.

"Chief, I'm declaring a Code Red Emergency. Shut down all incoming and outgoing comms and lock down this dock!"

———————

PETER RIKS SAT in a plastic chair in the wide, rock-hewn antechamber outside the council room. Just an hour ago, he'd been in there, finally getting Dutton's contract for dock services signed. Now, three strangers were in there—three pirates—alone with his mayor. Who had locked the door from the inside.

Heavy footsteps echoed somewhere close by. Chief Trayne walked back into the room—now flanked by two heavily armored police officers. "Been close to an hour. What have we heard?" Trayne asked.

Peter shook his head. "Nothing."

Trayne blew past him and hammered on the door. "Hara, it's Eric!" He hammered again. "I'd love a little proof of life out here. Otherwise, I'm wiring blasting putty on this door!"

A few moments later, Peter heard the heavy clunk of the lock sliding free.

Trayne jumped back and aimed his service pistol. The other officers had moved to the sides of the room and raised what, to Peter's mind, were comically huge rifles at the doorway. He didn't know whether to run or hide. He settled for crouching behind a table back near the hall.

He wanted to run, but he couldn't. Not when Hara Otana had walked herself into a room with killers. He'd known her all his adult life. Her son Philip was his best friend. And he'd voted for her; there was that, too.

Just as Peter realized he was panicking pretty hard, the door opened, and Mrs. Mayor walked out. The three pirates walked out close behind.

He heard the chief whisper, "Take them." Dots of laser light appeared on the Skanen and the younger human, but Hara stepped in between the weapons and the men.

"Put the guns away," Hara ordered. "These men aren't pirates. Not today."

Trayne formed his hand into some kind of signal to his officers. The targeting lights on the younger human and the Skanen winked off.

Trayne's pistol-mounted beam still shone brightly on the older human's forehead.

"You're being awful charitable, Hara. I know Jason and the kids are shipped out. Does that have anything—"

"My husband's name is Jake," she corrected Trayne, "and there's no need for codes. I'm not under duress. My family aren't hostages."

"Okay," Trayne growled, splitting his glare between his mayor and the two pirates. "So introduce us."

The bald-headed pirate in a ship-suit tugged up his right sleeve and showed off the back of his wrist. There was a black circle on his hand. Peter could make out squiggles inside it and a familiar double chevron. "Sergeant Blocker."

The Skanen lifted his middle arms, the set Peter always admired for the fine, detailed work their pincers and claws could do. His armored chitin moved with the motion and revealed a similar tattoo on the soft skin of his right shoulder. "Corporal Bruin," his deep voice boomed.

The older human had carefully unbuttoned his fine shirt to reveal a similar circle on his collarbone. "Nguyen, WDF." He let go of his collar and smiled warmly. "No rank."

"WDF?" asked one of the armored officers.

"Winter Defense Force," Hara murmured, looking at the floor.

"Bullshit!" Chief Trayne said.

Mayor Otana looked at him. "No." She turned to the armored officer closest to her. "Officer, your med kit, please."

WDF? Peter realized he'd walked closer to the strange conversation, drawn in without realizing it.

The Winter Defense Force was mythic: the ghost militia that Pushed back the Guard Invasion when all seemed lost. Then they disappeared-for good.

Humanity's Arrival in Farlost had changed a lot of things. One of the worst was the creation of the System Guard: a military organization that, when first formed by remnants of the U.S. military, took it upon itself to defeat the Dragons—a brutal, reptilian race of slave masters who had oppressed Farlost as far back as anyone could remember.

The Guard didn't just liberate Farlost from the brutal Dragons; it nearly wiped out their entire species and then went on to "civilize" a wide swath of the solar system.

Skirmish by skirmish, occupation by occupation, the System Guard filled the Dragons' power vacuum until they became nearly as feared as the monsters they toppled.

Any sentient species attempting to cheat the laws of the universe and travel faster than light ended up in Farlost, a solar system so far from any of the Arrivals' charts that there was no way home. Anyone dumb enough to try and cheat the universe again to escape Farlost found their molecules disintegrated in a very bright explosion.

The refugees struggling to survive beneath Farlost's dim red sun had not been kind to each other. Few escaped a life of slavery under one of the Dragon clans. The few that did lived in hiding, in places like the Winter Belt.

Arrivals were few and far between: decades might pass before a wink of light indicated newcomers. When that happened, the people of the Belt would do their best to get to them before the Dragons and hide them away among the rocks.

Before the Guard could build the strength and numbers to openly war with the Dragons, the Belt harbored them too. Belters built their ships, willingly fuelled them, even worked as their eyes and ears to gather intel in places the Guard couldn't go.

But once the Dragons were gone, the Guards' voracious demands for resources, work forces, and living space did not abate. Too late, Belters realized the Guard would keep on taking whatever they wanted.

They spread out from the Belt and strengthened their hold on planets and moons across Farlost. To fuel the expansion, they enacted new laws, naming themselves supreme authority. System Guard edicts were posted on every ship, station, and asteroid where the Guard had a foothold.

Across the Belt, rocks, ships, and stations cancelled service contracts, refused trade. Some successfully persuaded the Guard to leave. Others had to fight to get them out. Some fought and lost.

Entire populations were forced out at gunpoint if the Guard decided their mission to "protect" Farlost gave them a greater claim to societies that generations of sacrifice had built.

Peter remembered the day the state-run System Guard newsfeed announced Peach, one of the oldest, wealthiest, and most populous asteroids in the Winter Belt, was claimed by the Guard.

Even then, those Belters who hadn't struck deals with the Guard figured they were safe. Who invaded chaotic asteroid belts that had never been fully mapped? Especially when some of the bigger states had wired engines to hundreds of neighboring asteroids to hurl anyone who got surly in their orbit?

The System Guard, that's who.

The invasion came out of nowhere.

A new class of ships nobody could identify sailed from the Kesh shipyards straight for the Winter Belt. Networks across the solar system debated what they were for. Some feared an outright assault, but too many were comfortable with the status quo and assured everyone these were exploratory craft.

Days later, the ships arrived at the Belt. Flying dumbbells with engines on one end and what were revealed to be weapons platforms on the other. These "Rock-Smashers" nuked a path through the thick shield of asteroids that had kept Belters safe from aggression for centuries.

What followed was genocide. Entire pressurized asteroids were cracked open to vacuum like eggs. Hundreds of thousands of sentient beings died. There was no stopping them.

Worse still, traitors inside the Belt guided the Invaders, providing intelligence, disabling mines, and turning some of the guided asteroids around to attack Belter ships and habitats. Refugees fought for resources and vessels to flee, doing as much damage to communities and defences as the Guard advance itself.

Four days later, the Rock-Smashers cleared the last of the Belts' defenses and spread out, taking up positions around the most populous and richest rocks in the Belt.

Alliances crumbled. Some rocks turned their backs on neighbors they had promised to defend. Some were sabotaged by Guard agents from within. Some launched sneak attacks on each other for the chance to sign the first treaties with the supposed new overlords.

And everywhere, pirates feasted on survivors in the Guards' wake.

Madness descended on the Belt.

Until the fifth day.

On the fifth day, a storm of undetected asteroids and meteorites tore through the Guard armada. Then hundreds of fleeing civilian craft turned as one and Pushed back.

Instantly, the Guard advance was halted, their communications blocked, and breaching pods a generation faster and more sophisticated than anything even the Guard possessed began burrowing into the invaders.

The Push broke the back of the invasion in a handful of hours.

In the end, every Guard ship that entered the Belt was destroyed. It was a bloody and total defeat. No Guard surrenders were accepted. The genocide they wrought was returned in chillingly effective kind.

Soon after the Push, the saviours of the Winter Belt disappeared back into the shadows.

To this day, no one truly knew who had funded them or trained them. Each year Peter was in school, his teachers would offer a new theory, but no one really knew. Peter had been more interested in the fictional accounts of the WDF than the documentaries.

As a kid, he spent all his lieu on graphic novels and war vids chronicling the Push. The stories were amazing and heroic to a child. As a young man, the stories changed and became disturbing. As a young man, the few times he heard mention of those hard-fought boarding actions, it was with equal reverence and gratitude…and outright horror at their brutality.

He outgrew his childhood obsession with the WDF. Like everybody in the Belt, he learned to live with the mystery, growing more preoccupied with sports, then girls, then broken oxygen recyclers on the dock, then girls again, and so it went.

After his pops retired, Peter was all about the dock, eager to join his sisters in the family business. The only time he ever thought about the WDF was when he woke up on the sofa in the middle of an action vid about them—which he usually shut off in favor of more shuteye.

"Come on." Eric was almost laughing. "Hasn't been a WDF since the Guard turned tail."

The salt-and-pepper-haired human stared down at the toes of his shoes, hands in his pockets and looking as comfortable as a tourist on holiday. "Sure there is. We just don't advertise."

"Nguyen," the mayor said in a warning.

The man shrugged and went silent.

"Eric. Please," she said. "Trust me. Stand down."

She beckoned again to the nearest officer, who looked between his mayor and his chief, torn.

Chief Trayne's lips moved in a series of profane shapes, but no sounds emerged. Finally, he holstered his pistol and waved the officer on. "Your word's not gonna get them out of the warrant chasing them. And I don't care what rank they say that pirate ink gives 'em—"

"Not pirate ink," Mayor Otana said, taking a small med kit from the approaching officer.

Peter was still struggling to catch up. He watched the mayor pull out a skin regenerator and apply it to the back of her wrist. "They're WDF?"

Hara nodded, eyes down, face drawn.

"That ship attacked somebody to get flagged," the other armored cop growled.

Chief Trayne held up a hand to silence the officer. "The mayor says we listen. But you lay it out right now, friend, or so help me—"

"Not my place," the one Hara called Nguyen said. "Want to sign up? We're recruiting! Want more? Talk to the ranking officer on Ollin."

Recruiting? Ranking officer? A dozen thoughts collided in the back of Peter's head.

Before Hara was mayor, she had worked for the police. She was on track for chief, Pops said, before she won her first election. Before that, she co-founded Otana Mechanical before handing over the day-to-day to her husband to become mayor of Ollin and take her turn raising their kids.

Everybody said she was a crazy pilot—crazy skilled and crazy *crazy*, like all the best pilots.

He flashed to the first summer he and Philip worked the docks for his pops, when Mrs. Otana had saved his life.

Then his brain bounced back to the negotiation with Ellie and what they had said:

I know I'm from away...

Ten years from refugee to mayor...

"Ranking officer?" The chief's voice was higher than normal.

Peter hadn't ever heard him so nervous. Almost as if he was thinking the same insane thing Peter was thinking.

"Yes," Hara said. Her eyes brimming with tears, she held up her hand. It looked burned now: red and swollen from the skin regenerator.

Peter only saw the black circle with captain's bars inside.

"Me," Hara said, in a tiny, fragile voice.

Sergeant Blocker and the Skanen jerked to attention and saluted. Nguyen only sketched a lazy, two-fingered salute.

Looking at his mayor, the mother of his friend, Peter knew it was true. It was as if he had always known but couldn't put the pieces together until now.

"The struggle is real," Nguyen said, his voice syrupy and disdainful.

HARA WAS out on her balcony when Peter arrived. She didn't hear him at first, looking out at the small town that was Ollin.

Ollin, like most asteroid settlements, was a world upside down. Not built on the surface of a planet but the hollowed-out ceiling of the rock. When he was a kid, he always thought the three support pillars that met in the centre of the open space looked like feet, holding up the artificial sky: a narrow cylinder of transit, supply runs, and artificial sunlight that stretched from one end of Ollin to the other.

Ollin was small: a few square kilometers of streets, farmland, and industrial buildings lined the inside of the asteroid. There was a wetland down there too, but he'd never been on it or in it. Creating lakes on Ollin was barely within their means, and they really didn't have enough space—but the local commerce society kept on beating the drum of "Tourism!" until the voters let them have the last strip of undeveloped land big enough for the project.

Ollin's spin generated three-quarters Earth gravity. To Peter—born and raised here—it was just what gravity was supposed to feel like, not three-quarters of whatever on a planet his great-great-grandparents had wandered too far away from when they found themselves trapped forever in Farlost.

"This view was always the cure for bad dreams," Hara said, inviting Peter to sit.

He took the ornate metal garden chair beside her, unsure if she was speaking to him or herself. He stared at the captain's insignia DNA-bombed onto the back of her hand as she covered her mouth, fighting back tears.

"There's always more to say, isn't there, hon?"

Peter froze, realizing she was leaving a message for her husband. Jake Otana was away from Ollin, his grown kids with him, fulfilling a service contract.

A goodbye message?

"Go to ground," she said, her voice tight. "Somewhere deep. If you can stock up within forty-eight hours, do it, but then get under cover and stay there, until...it's all over."

Hara stopped, her lip quivering, and she looked out again at her home. "The lilacs are in bloom here, Jake."

Peter looked away, the only privacy he could offer her. A moment later, Hara continued.

"This is real, baby," she whispered. "What I always said would never, ever happen. Thank you for my life. And thank you, Janey, Aaron, Philip. You're my world! Mama loves you, and..." Her voice broke. "She always will. Goodbye, my loves."

Hara waved her hand in the air. The recording chimed off, and Hara collapsed into tears.

Peter studied the decorative rocks Hara and Jake had epoxied to the prefab metal frame of the garden wall. He'd chipped a tooth on one of them as a kid.

When her tears quieted, he took a breath to speak.

"Yes," she answered before he could. "Before Jake brought me here, I served."

He smiled. That was the Mrs. Otana he grew up with: self-deprecatingly encapsulating a life that impressed everyone who knew her into simple little words.

And what he knew of her life only scratched the surface.

"The Guard is coming back?"

She nodded then stared harder at him. "You want to know about them," she said. "The WDF."

"I want to know a lot," Peter said.

"You always loved to play Defender," she said. She'd been crying a lot, her eyes puffy and red. "I remember you screaming around this apartment, chasing imaginary pirates and System Guard."

"Who are they?" he asked impulsively, even callously, he knew. "Where did they go?"

She laughed and sniffed back tears. "My answers will no doubt disappoint."

He waited.

She looked at him as if weighing a decision. "You can keep a secret." She nodded. "I'll tell you some of it. But I need you to swear never to write down or record what I tell you. And if, one day, Philip asks, or his brother or sister...you'll sit them down alone and tell them?"

Peter was burning to know, but suddenly, his chest was hot and tight. "Why do *you* have to go?" he blurted. "Why can't they pick someone else? Everybody here *needs* you!"

He watched something shift in her, harden. She stood straighter. "Yes, they do," she said. "But that's how it works."

Peter caught himself staring again at the black captain's bars on her hand.

"On the line," she said, "you only worried about two things: winning...and surviving. As for who they are? I really don't know. All I know is how they found me."

Hara told the tale, and Peter listened.

2214
Privateer ship Carnus
Somewhere in the Winter Deeps

HARA'S SHIP-SUIT was still wet with blood when the first mate threw her through the captain's door and locked it behind her.

"What's this I hear about you rejecting the tender charms of my crew?"

Nguyen—he never referred to himself as Captain—stretched and rose from his bunk like a cat. He leaned against the desk beside her and folded his fingers under his armpits.

Hara laughed and spat blood. This was it. The end of the road. "They had it coming."

Nguyen nodded in agreement. "Oh, indeed. And thank you very kindly for doling out that bit of justice. You left two of the rapists alive. That's a good touch, a cautionary tale I'm not really able to deliver. A tad off brand for me."

She wasn't sure what he was saying. Was he going to space her for killing three of his crew?

Nguyen kneeled, inches away from her. "Your talents are wasted on a pirate ship," he said, which didn't really clear it up for her.

She crawled back against the door. "You come for my 'talents' and see what gets wasted!"

He laughed then sat cross-legged on the floor. "No fear. I'm not here for that." He gestured around the opulent captain's quarters. "Nor for this either."

She didn't ask the question he obviously wanted her to, so he sighed dramatically and continued on his own. "Alrighty, here's the short version: once upon a time, there was a boy named Nguyen. His parents were killed by pirates, and he was sold into slavery. He turned into a nasty piece of work! So nasty he survived that mine and got himself on the crew of the privateer *Carnus*! With me so far?"

Not sure what else to do, Hara nodded.

"No you're not, because I skipped a bit," he said with a flashy whirl of his hand. "Somewhere in between getting sent to a mine to die and actually dying, little Nguyen and all his friends were saved! Do you know why? Because they were in hell! Luckily, it was a hell run by monsters nobody would come looking for if they all disappeared."

Nguyen shrugged. "I suppose, of all the places in the Belt one could practice stealth reconnaissance and recovery, the bonus karma of setting a bunch of enslaved kids free put my home-sweet-hell at the top of the list."

Hara was way past scared. Nguyen never talked about himself. And what he was saying made no sense. She hadn't felt much in the months since her transport had been attacked and she'd been forced into service on *Carnus*.

She hadn't felt anything at all since the five men cornered her in the galley that day. She'd said a silent goodbye to Jake, who had no idea where she was, and attacked those men with everything she had.

Surprisingly, she survived...but what was happening on the floor of Nguyen's quarters scared her more.

Nguyen looked away, into the distance, idly scratching at his collarbone. "Perhaps I'm just a sucker for an underdog. You impressed me, getting out of the galley in one piece."

Hara flicked her eyes from Nguyen's face to his hands, expecting unkindness any second. Then her eyes caught a glimpse of a tattoo on his chest, revealed as he scratched. A curve of black circle.

"In any case." He stood abruptly and walked to the far wall, flipping a transparent panel up and punching the red button beneath. "I'm leaving." A siren sounded as the yellow-and-black stretch of wall retracted to reveal an open, four-seater escape pod. "And I thought, what the hell, maybe you'd like to come?" He looked back at Hara as he slammed a small metal box ringed with putty onto the porthole beside the escape pod. A ring of lights on the top of the box was flashing, counting down.

She looked at Nguyen, unable to do the mental math.

Most frightening of all that had happened to her that day, Nguyen's face softened. Showed concern. Compassion. "Like I said, you don't belong on a pirate ship." Then his ever-present and somehow *wrong* smile returned. "And, lo and behold, just as my superiors, after far too long, have allowed me to vaporize this disgusting stain upon the universe, I finally stumble upon someone worthy of recruitment. I'd call that karma!"

He held out his hand.

Hara took it.

Some time later, the little pod shook as the *Carnus*'s reign of terror ended, and Nguyen laughed.

HARA SMILED. "You don't know what to say."

Peter stood beside her, hands clenched around the metal railing atop the balcony wall. "I...no." He turned to her, studying her face compassionately. "That man, Nguyen?"

She nodded. "My recruiter, into...this."

Peter's eyes tracked his own thoughts. "The WDF were pirates?"

"No, no." Hara pursed her lips. She wasn't explaining this well. "The WDF was just one name for one purpose." She put her hand over his on the balcony railing. "I need you to know I'm fine. If it wasn't for Nguyen recruiting me, I'd have died on my way to meet Jake. It just...took me a few years longer to get back to him."

Peter opened his mouth to ask the obvious question.

Hara intercepted it: "I worked with Nguyen, mostly. I met a couple other people, and then after I proved myself, I worked by myself. We collected information, mostly. We recruited a few people, or transported them from A to B. Stole cargo sometimes." She laughed. "Oh, there was this one jailbreak once—" She shook her head. "But we don't talk about it."

She looked out over Ollin again. An elevator was climbing up the closest spoke. "As mayor, I was in a position to divert funds...and identify recruits if ever they were needed." She looked back at Peter. "And that's all I can tell you. That's how it works."

"But how—" Peter licked his lips and found his nerve. "How do you know you're not being used? You did those things, and you fought with the WDF, but you don't know who sent you or why?"

Hara nodded. "That's right."

"If you only ever met a couple people, how do you know it's not the Guard or pirates or, I don't know, the last old Dragon and his flunkies manipulating you?"

Hara beamed and waved her hand out over Ollin. "This is how. Ollin's still here! They sent me back to Jake—after a few years, anyway. I was allowed to live my life, have my kids, and when they called me back for the Push, I knew what was at stake. I was willing to make the sacrifice. For Jake. For my kids." Hara let her eyes wander over Ollin. "After it was over, Jake and I moved here, where nobody knew us, to start over."

She reached behind her chair and picked up a vacuum-sealed travel pack. "The only place you see white-armored breachers are in comics and vids. They didn't replace the Dragons or the Guard. Whoever they are, they let us live our lives the way *we* choose."

She took a deep breath and closed her eyes. Peter did the same. The scent of lilac filled him up, and Hara turned to go.

Peter followed her out.

CHIEF TRAYNE, a couple officers, and Nguyen were waiting outside Hara's front door. On a lamppost behind them, a small, discrete panel strobed red. Ollin remained on lockdown. Radio silent, all traffic diverted.

She looked up and down the street. No one was out. Atmospheric leaks were almost unheard of on rocks this size, but that was the story she had told her people, and they were following the rules to the letter. It couldn't last long, but it only had to last until she and Nguyen's team left.

She took a deep breath. The people of Ollin had put their trust in her. She was supposed to see them through times like this, and instead, she was leaving them.

"Let me come with," Eric pleaded.

"You can't, Hara said. "I've told you what I can. You have to trust me the rest of the way."

Peter looked at Nguyen differently now. He noticed and quirked an eyebrow her way. She ignored him. "How did you make out with that list?"

"List?" Peter asked.

Trayne shook his head. "I passed on your message. All six accepted. They'll meet you at the dock." His lip curled in distaste. "Three of them have kids, Hara. I got good officers with no kids. Why not them?"

"That's how it works," Hara said, her voice as cold and sharp as a scalpel.

Trayne's eyes were bright with tears he wouldn't let fall. "Okay, fine. But I'm an excellent shot. Like to think I make good decisions." A smile tried to kick-start itself on his face. "Present company excepted."

Hara stepped forward and placed her hands on his shoulders. She had to work at it before she could meet his gaze. "You're like family to me and Jake and the kids. That's why I need you here. You swore an oath to Ollin."

"So did you," Chief Trayne shot back.

She nodded and stepped back. "I know it. But I know you'll do the job just as well—"

Trayne's face went wide. "Hara, no."

She pulled out her wireless. "—Because I know you'll take care of my people like family."

"Dammit, Hara," Trayne finally sobbed. "I swore to Jake I'd protect you."

"Ollin needs you more," she said. "Jake will, too, if I don't—"

Their eyes locked. Both creased with pain. Without another word, Chief Trayne pulled out his wireless and held it close to hers.

"I do solemnly swear," she pleaded, and two shaky breaths later, Trayne repeated the first words of the mayor's oath of office and all the words that followed.

NGUYEN STOOD SILENTLY in the back of the elevator car on the ride out to the needle. Peter Riks stood beside Hara, working through last-minute logistics on the monitor inset beside the wide cargo door.

"We pulled in our best workers," Peter said. "Everything's loaded on...your...ship. Nobody refused. Even Ellie Dutton chipped in a good volume of fuel and oxygen."

Hara was grateful, but she also burned with the shame of it. She was loading a big part of Ollin's capital into the hold of a ship she'd never flown to expend far from the community that worked their fingers to the bone to scrape it together.

She waved the screen to black and turned to face Riks. "Thank you, Peter." Her throat tightened up again. "I don't know what else to say."

Peter looked almost reverent as he stared at her. "Don't need to say anything, Mayor. You dedicated your life to Ollin. And I'd have been freeze-dried crop fertilizer my first week on the docks if not for you."

Hara remembered the summer he and Philip had gotten their first jobs on the docks. She'd been floating outside that day, examining drive repairs on her and Jake's ship. Cargo had broken free, halfway between the needle and another ship Philip and Peter were loading. It sheared off Peter's safety line and sent him tumbling into space.

She only hoped someone would be there for her kids when they needed it, if one of her kids… The thought of her kids was too much. She looked away from Peter and gently, lovingly shut them away in a chamber of her heart.

The elevator chimed. Peter coughed. "The cargo? It's just stuff, Mayor. Stuff we wouldn't have half as much of if it weren't for you."

The doors opened on a still-silent dock. Ahead of her, Sergeant Blocker and Bruin waited, along with the six Ollin men and women from the list she'd given Eric.

"Tick tock, Captain Otana," Nguyen said.

She nodded and stepped out to address the new recruits.

Nguyen spoke behind her. "A word, Mister Riks?"

Hara looked back as the doors closed, in time to see Peter wave goodbye.

———

THEY WERE GATHERED in the common room on Nguyen's ship. He'd given her the codes, and the airlock was locked behind them.

"You all know me," Hara said after gathering the six recruits around her. "Now, you have to trust me."

Hara remembered the terror she felt in the early days with Nguyen. Even when she began to suspect the stakes behind what they were doing, her education had been an ordeal. Nguyen hadn't been the best of teachers.

Today was a day she'd long wished would never come. She had promised herself she'd get it right.

She stood straighter. The natural, kind smile she always wore changed, dimmed in both wattage and kindness, and took on the slightest curl of a snarl at the end.

"There's a battle coming that will tear Ollin apart. Don't be scared. Fear isn't helpful. If you listen, if you do your jobs, some of you might live. Your families might live." The curl at the end of her smile deepened. "And your enemies won't."

---

22 hours later
Approaching muster position Alpha

THE HULL of Nguyen's ship was battered and appeared poorly kept. The inside told a different story: extremely clean, all onboard systems overpowered for its size. The bottom half of the ship had been retrofitted into one large, airtight cargo hold.

Inside that hold were nine gleaming-white breaching suits, a cache of assault weapons, and a mountain of lashed metal and alloy superstructure.

Sergeant Blocker clapped his hands together atop the scaffolding. "Our orders are to have the squad ready for breaching duty immediately upon arrival. We will debark the craft upon arrival at the muster point for a breaching station. If we're lucky, we'll get there for the start of the Push. En route, we're to retrofit this little darling onto the ship to give our breaching teams cover.

"Only thing is...how the hell are we supposed to install it in transit?" Blocker asked.

"Not a problem. My specialty is onsite refit and repair," Hara said. "I'm just surprised a ship this small can maintain the energy to power it." She ran her hands along the two-story length of the particle-beam cannon. "Wonder where they hid this away all these years."

"Since you ask," Nguyen said, descending on the open elevator platform at the front of the hold, "it's been encased in cement at the bottom of a water treatment module on the mining rig where they stationed me when you 'retired.'"

"Really?" Blocker said. "I'd have kept it up and running, maybe hid it on a pirate ship under our control."

"Hide a weapon of mass destruction *with* the kind of filth that would use it first chance?" Nguyen said, leaping off the elevator platform when it was close enough to the ground. "I'm glad you're in ops, not strategic support."

"No more pirate postings for you?" Hara asked.

"Once was quite enough, thank you," Nguyen muttered. "When can we have the suits operational, Sergeant?"

"They're humming now, sir," Blocker said. "But we've got six raw recruits who need tears and injections first."

Hara remembered taking her tears. "I want to be there."

"You're one of our best-rated spacers," Nguyen reminded her. "This beam isn't going to install itself if *everybody* spends the whole burn in the fetal position."

"I'm *going* to be there," she said again. "I'm going to talk them through. Help them remember who they are."

"Right," Nguyen sighed. "You're gonna be a better spy-daddy than I was, eh?"

"One can dream," Hara said, walking past her former spy-daddy and climbing onto the platform.

HARA WALKED onto the bridge as Corporal Bruin finished strapping the recruits to the acceleration couches.

"This isn't a simple chemical hack," the Skanen said, his short eye stalks each fixed on a different recruit. "We're not uploading a single skill set to get you through a job interview here. We are fundamentally rewiring you.

"Injecting memories could shave months off complex training, but this fight will be over in days," Bruin continued. "This long-chain chemical is useless without motor memories—"

"Calluses," Blocker said, coming through the door and punching Bruin on his top right shoulder. "First time you pick up a new tool, you gotta build up calluses to use it right."

"Especially when that knowledge is how to hold a heavy rail gun," Hara said, stepping in front of her men. "It's not enough to know a linear motor device using electromagnetic force to deploy kinetic payload is going to kick like a mule...you have to know how to keep that mule in line *before* you fire your first bolt."

"You gotta know it here," Blocker tapped one of the recruits —Wills—on the forehead with the business end of a small medical tool. "And here." He tapped him again in the gut. "And here." He tapped him in the reproductive parts, causing the man to start.

"Or else make a fine mist of your own fire team," Nguyen said, walking through the door, holding a small black box. "You're about to get boot camp and a year of combat experience in a day. Welcome to hell, kids!"

Every recruit stared at the black box.

Hara glared at Nguyen as Bruin continued the lecture. "Tears are the only way to trick the basal ganglia, cerebellum, and prefrontal cortex all at once."

"Will I still be me?" asked Davis, a brawny kid on the closest acceleration couch to Hara.

"You will," Hara assured him, walking past the first row of acceleration couches. "But not *just* you."

Hara froze on the spot.

There, in the second row, sat Peter Riks.

"I thought only Pondies could absorb memories through tears," stammered the bald-headed female officer—Thomason.

"No," qualified Blocker: "They're the only ones crazy enough to file a bunch of *different* people's memories in their heads."

"Not so crazy," Nguyen corrected Blocker. "Pondies have an artificial organ implanted kitty-corner to their amygdala to help keep all those thoughts and experiences separate from their own."

"You only have to make room in your brain for one more," Bruin told the recruits, his fearsome-looking mandibles quivering as he spoke. "The soldier whose memories are encoded in these 'tears' was conditioned through hypnosis and a drug regime to suppress his sense of self."

Hara was still frozen in place, trembling, staring down at Peter.

"Hi, Mayor," Riks said.

"That's right," Nguyen said as he passed the box to Bruin with a bow. "Family connections suppressed, no girl- or boyfriend on his mind to confuse you poor chickens."

She slowly turned to Nguyen.

"You're not going to deck me again, are you?" He passed the black box to Bruin and raised his hands in mock surrender. "I know how sensitive you get about recruits."

"Did...did he say 'he'?" asked Thomason.

"Yes, 'he,'" Bruin said, his voice rumbling deep within his chitin-armored chest as he deftly removed a cylinder from the black case and placed it on a medical tray. "The program was built around a sole human male specimen."

Blocker took a step toward Hara, curious about what had her off balance. "It can be a lot to handle," he told the recruits, "but the tears won't make you do things you don't want to...just help you to do things you need to, things even trained soldiers find hard."

"All for the low, low price of the occasional double-take when you look in the mirror," Nguyen said and smiled at Thomason. "A little more jarring for some of you than others."

"He wasn't on the list," Hara spat.

"I chose this," Peter said. "I asked Nguyen. He thought about it and said yes."

Hara stepped closer to the man she'd known since he was a child, racing through their apartment with Philip. "Why?"

"Take your pick. I can't...have kids of my own. Too much time around leaky ship cores, I guess." Peter shrugged. "No kids, I live for the job, I want to make a difference, my best friend's mom is the mayor...and a super-soldier...and, I guess, a spy?"

Hara looked over at the little medical sprayer/injector sitting on a sterile blue cloth in the center of Bruin's tray. She knelt beside Peter, grabbed his hand. "I can get you out of this!" she promised.

"Hara," Nguyen groaned, "we're running lean here, and he fits the profile—"

"Shut your mouth!" she hissed over her shoulder.

"It's okay," Peter said, his voice light. "I want my nieces to be safe. I want Ollin to...still be there when this is all over. And hey," he joked, "you didn't turn out *so* bad."

"It's time," Bruin said.

Hara looked over. His voice was louder now, more authoritative. She watched him carry the small medical device over to the row of recruits.

Blocker met Bruin beside the first acceleration couch and offered the recruit a mouth guard. "The reactions can be violent," Blocker said apologetically.

"C'mon, Mrs. Otana," Peter pleaded, "you're embarrassing me in front of the class!"

No! She wanted to scream and rip him free of the restraints.

But she didn't.

Hara opened another box in her heart and forced her fear for Peter inside. She had forgotten just how much working with Nguyen cost her soul--but it was coming back fast.

She forced herself to nod. He was smiling up at her when Blocker got around to him with the mouth guards. She stepped back to let him pass.

Nguyen sidled up next to her. "He'll be fine," Nguyen murmured. "He wanted this."

"You don't care what he wanted," Hara growled.

"That's the way it works," he said.

It was. She knew it.

But he didn't have to go through it alone.

Hara walked back to the second row of acceleration couches and sat herself down beside Peter.

"Sergeant," she called. "Bring me one of those."

Blocker froze. He looked to the officially rankless Nguyen, who shrugged. "Mother knows best."

"Now, Sergeant! I won't put these men and women through anything I'm not willing to do myself."

"We must begin!" Corporal Bruin almost shouted from the front row of couches.

"Corporal?" Blocker asked, surprised.

"I'm sorry, Sergeant. The tears are temperature sensitive. For best uptake, we must administer as quickly as possible."

Blocker looked at Nguyen. Nguyen hesitated but nodded.

"Just breathe, people," Hara said, reaching down to tighten the straps over her legs. Blocker arrived with her mouthpiece, which she accepted. He motioned to her straps, and she nodded for him to proceed.

In the first row, Bruin began administering the tears. It took only a moment for him to gently pull on a dark-haired woman's eyebrow and cheek, a moment more to trigger the injector.

Hara heard it hiss. "Keep breathing," she told her. "It works fast. Don't be scared. Just listen to my voice."

Bruin moved onto the second recruit, an older man who looked back at Hara and smiled. Hara nodded reassuringly and took a deep breath by way of example.

Nguyen wandered back over to the medical tray, eyes bouncing from the Skanen medical officer and back to the tray. He reached down and pulled up the blue cloth.

Hara saw several dark spots on the cloth. Wet spots that ran when Nguyen raised it up.

Why would it be wet? The cylinders were sealed, only pierced when they were inserted in the mister. Unless something was added to the—

She jerked to her feet—or tried to; Blocker had already finished strapping her legs down!

Nguyen shouted, "Bruin, stop!"

The first two recruits had begun seizing. With one hand, Bruin rammed the mister roughly into the eye socket of the third while drawing a small pistol from somewhere and aiming it Hara's way.

Nguyen started running towards Bruin. There was something metal in his hands. He threw it a moment after the corporal fired.

The discharge hit Blocker, tearing away half his head and one shoulder. The sergeant died instantly and collapsed on top of Hara.

Whatever Nguyen tossed caused the gun in Bruin's hands to spark. He dropped it and bent over the fourth recruit, who screamed in terror, arching away from the Skanen. He wasn't reaching with the mister now: his mandibles were wide, his jaw distended, his fangs closing around the recruit's head.

The first two recruits weren't moving at all anymore. Their heads hung at unnatural angles. The third was bucking so hard Hara could hear bones crack.

Nguyen landed a spinning kick on the side of Bruin's head, pushing him away from the recruit. In a blur, Bruin turned and reached both his massive upper arms for Nguyen's neck.

The man ducked under the pincers, which clacked closed on empty air. There were knives in both his hands now. He moved quickly, and soon, steaming viscera was pouring out from the soft tissue of joints between Bruin's armored thorax and his four arms.

Hara turned and got her arms around what was left of Blocker, fumbling for the holster at his waist. Skanen could take a lot of damage before they were out of the fight, she knew. She found Blocker's sidearm, firing as soon as it cleared the holster.

She heard Nguyen gurgle and saw him stumbling backwards, a vicious claw slash across his chest already turning his shirt dark with blood.

Her third round cored a hole through Bruin's head. The Skanen fell to the ground like a puppet with cut strings. Ahead of her, the third recruit was now still. And the fourth was gasping. It was Brooks, of the civil engineers from Ollin's public works department. His throat had been torn apart. She watched the light go out of his eyes.

Nguyen stumbled across the floor and began unstrapping Peter. "Good help is so hard to find," he gasped and spat on Bruin's corpse.

"Told you...we were running lean," he slurred and collapsed into Peter's arms.

———

PETER PATCHED NGUYEN'S WOUNDS. Hara made him run to her quarters and grab a fresh first aid kit to use. When he came back, she had torn off his shirt and used it to staunch the bleeding. Using a fresh mister, he quickly sprayed a mix of antibiotic, coagulant, and replacement skin over the wound.

"Thank you, Peter," she said and jogged back to the rolling tray and Nguyen's black box. There were two vials remaining, both yet to be punctured, both dry. She looked at Thomason and Diaz, the two surviving original recruits. "We can't wait. I'm sorry." She rushed to them and sprayed the memory cocktail into each of their eyes.

Then she took her seat next to him, and Nguyen, already moving better than he had any right to be, strapped them both in and took the mister.

"Enjoy the ride," he said and, without further preamble, sprayed first Hara, then Peter.

The moment the droplets hit his eyes, he blinked, twice. Colors swirled, and his head spun.

The room changed. His body changed.

He changed.

He began to hum an ancient battle hymn...one he'd never known.

———

28 hours later
Breaching Pod Charlie
Rally Point 2
4 Hours into the Push

THE BREACHING pod was buffeting around Hara, screaming down towards a new and improved Rock-Smasher. Their second victim of the day.

He—no, dammit, she!—licked her lips, tasted blood from where she smashed into her own helmet. What did she care: the bullet that spiderwebbed her armor hadn't gotten inside. She'd heal. Or die. But first, she was going to help more Guard dogs die.

It didn't matter that the Guard knew a little about Nguyen's operation, now. That was the reason no one on this ship knew anything about the other cells that had raced through the belt to ready the second Push: you couldn't reveal what you didn't know. No matter how hard a sneaky Skanen double agent asked.

The yellow light on her HUD flashed green, and she felt the hammering impact as her breaching pod sliced through the hull of the Guard ship.

"Hoo-ah!" Riks roared on the squad frequency from a few seats away. Their harnesses released them, and they dropped down to the deck.

"Come on, kiddies!" Hara screamed, drawing the bulky rail gun down from its perch on her shoulder. The smoke wasn't clear inside the Guard ship—it looked like an engineering deck—so she switched to infrared and auto-targeting. She whooped as half a dozen red crosses populated the inside of her helmet.

She leaped into the fray, sparks from incoming fire bouncing off her white armor.

For the Belt.

For Ollin.

For love.

ABOUT THE AUTHOR

John Mierau is a science fiction author and audio producer in Ontario, Canada. John writes about strong characters tested by extreme situations--but always with a healthy dose of hope, humor (and cliffhangers). His stories span space opera, near-future thrillers, conspiracy tales, suspense stories and more.

John's free podcast is available from *ServingWorlds.com*

Patrons get his newest stories first at *Patreon.com/ServingWorlds*

TIME DOGZ

By Tim C Taylor

2471AD. The last of Earth's defenders prepare to make a stand defending the worm gates around Saturn. If they fail, as they surely will, the alien invaders will burn Earth to a cinder. As the gates activate, two mysterious individuals appear from nowhere. They claim to be from the future, here to do a job. But the Battle of Saturn Gate? Good luck with that last stand and all, but humanity's final battle is not their problem.

1 TORVEN DJANE

"All hands, battle stations! All hands to battle stations!"

As we jog along the passageways of the starboard nacelle, heading for our designated damage control zone, my team exudes a grim determination. None of us expects to see in the new day, but we'll do our duty anyway. Come what may.

The captain's voice coming from the overhead is swollen with implacable confidence. He knows how hopeless our situation is at Saturn Gate, but he speaks as if every cell of his body is convinced that we will repel the invader here.

Where does he find that confidence?

"Hear this," the captain booms. "Humanity is a dangerous beast when cornered, and today the invader will pay dearly to learn that lesson. Here, at Saturn Gate, we will hold the line. No matter what. Earth expects."

"Earth expects!" From the sensor techs in the forward cone to the aft gunners, the cry rings through the ship from two thousand throats.

Well, almost two thousand.

I don't join in.

I want to, but my mind is in free fall.

It's been happening a lot recently.

Crazy as it sounds, I've come to see the sensation as a premonition that I'm about to have a bad day.

As if I don't already know that.

"You okay, boss?"

The mind fog lifts a little. Tekeke has hung back, looking at me with concern in her eyes. "You should report to a corpsman."

I'm about to reprimand her, but I see the cheeky grin on her face.

She's such a dent-head joker. To the bitter end.

If the captain's calling battle stations, it must mean the trickle of exotic particles leaking out of the Saturn wormholes has built into a spray. We have about an hour left before the spray builds to a flood. Then the enemy fleet will emerge and kill us all.

And to think it had been the boring monotony that meant I'd been about to leave the service and go find adventure on the frontier.

"Good call, Tekeke. I'll check in for a brain scan and a month of R&R, just as soon as the battle is over." I shoo her away. "Just give me a moment. I'll be right behind you."

Tekeke jogs off and jumps down the descent tube to 13B.

I mean to follow her, but my head doesn't clear like it normally does. Instead, the flash of free fall intensifies. Strobes. Like the moment when grav plates are switched off, repeated endlessly.

The mental affliction spreads to my eyes, and I see an actinic flash detonate in front of me. I know it's not real, because I can't feel a pressure wave. Although I do smell a tang in the air, the kind of ominous foreboding you get back home in Kent before a big twister hits.

It gets worse.

First a flash. Now I'm seeing shapes.

Shapes I haven't seen since I figured myself out at college.

I'm standing in the main passageway through Deck 12B, as humanity is about to make its last stand against invaders who have rampaged through the colonies, and I'm staring at a woman who's literally appeared out of the air in front of me.

Her endless skin is the color of fresh silt, just like mine. But hers is so much smoother, except for recent scars not yet fully healed.

And there's a reason I can see her scars very clearly. She's completely nude.

I've served in the navy for nineteen years. Seen a lot of weird stuff you won't believe. But this is off the scale. I must be having a mental breakdown.

For some reason, I'm spending my episode staring at a woman's breasts. The way they move as she staggers over the deck fascinates me.

I suppose, it's been a long time.

"Salle's front shields," says a man behind me. "Ain't they a wonder?"

The man is darker skinned than the woman, with piercing blue eyes like miniature B-type stars. His head is shaved, and he has the bone structure to make that look good.

"Much as I'd like to discuss them while she's still too groggy to kick me where it hurts," he says, "we ain't got the time. Where's Pheung?"

There's a sudden twist in my guts, and I no longer think I'm hallucinating. This shit is actually happening.

It's impossible.

But it's real.

Maybe these two are with the invaders? They could be the explanation for why the enemy cut through the First and Third Fleets like they were strings of garbage scows.

"Yes, we're real," the man is saying. "And we're on the clock. Pheung. Where is he?"

"Who?" I draw my snub pistol.

The man glares at me.

I notice the tattoo across his chest. It's a long dagger thrust through a planet.

He puts his hands on his hips, seeming careless that he, too, is naked. "Don't play games. This is serious business."

I agree. Which is why I backpedal past the woman. She's recovering fast, sitting on the deck, watching me. I cover both infiltrators with my pistol. "Identify yourselves!"

"I'm Stiletto Caldwell," the man says. "But you can call me Stillo, 'cos it saves time. That's Monique DeSalle. She'll be okay in a minute. Won't you, Salle? Gods alone know why Cohgun gave me her for this mission."

"Are you with the invaders?" I demand.

"No. We're here to take in Pheung." Stillo frowns at my confusion. "Come on, stop wasting time, man. Marshal Pheung. You know, ordained by the Five Gods? Charming blowka with a ginger moustache and a weakness for genocide?"

"He's in that mausoleum on Erizat-3," I tell him. It's not exactly a military secret. "Or he was until the invaders pillaged the system. His body's been moldering there for eighty-odd years."

"Jeez! What year is this? Where are we?"

"2471 of the Common Era. Welcome to the last stand of humanity. This is Saturn Gate."

Stillo bares his teeth into a snarl. "Laz jerking Cohgun. He set us up, Salle. He knew I'd never take a job fighting in someone else's army. But why?"

"Because he's a sneaking, creaming, jerking auto-ponce," DeSalle slurs. "But I get your meaning. Why us? Why here?"

I've had enough. They're both talking nonsense.

The last of the strobing in my head clears, and I do what I should have done in the first place. I open a link to the LT.

"Sir, it's Djane. I've apprehended two intruders. I'm by the drop to 13B."

"The enemy?"

"Not sure, sir. They look human." For some reason, my gaze scans two sets of genitals. "Very much so."

"Honzo's Beard! I see them on the cams. Keep them there. I'm passing this up the line."

Stillo reaches for his neck. There's a lump there. Something embedded under the skin.

"Don't touch that!" I yell, my pistol aimed at his center mass tattoo.

He grins. "Not gonna happen." And presses against the lump.

I flinch.

But nothing happens.

"Give me the gun," he says and strides toward me. He moves like a dangerous big cat, but I'm the one with the weapon.

"Halt or I *will* fire!"

"No, you won't," he says, not faltering in the slightest.

I mumble a curse and squeeze off three rounds.

At five yards and with such a broad chest to aim at, you'd think I couldn't miss.

Well, you'd be right. I don't.

But my weapon fails. I watch the bolt inducers ease out the business end of the barrel and drop to the deck, where they fizzle like a wet weekend in Minsk.

Dumbstruck, I let him take the snub pistol out of my hand.

Stillo thumbs the safety and moves to shove the weapon into his waistband, forgetting he's naked. He mutters a curse I don't recognize and tosses the weapon back to me. "We haven't time for these games," he growls, walking over to DeSalle. He musses her hair.

"You'll be all right, Salle," he says, with an affection he hasn't shown before. "You need fluids."

He looks at me. "We need beer. The more bitter the better. Also, whiskey, clothing, and a chat with your ship's captain."

I shake my head. "You gotta be kidding."

"No one's kidding anyone here, sailor. The transition dehydrates and scavenges the blood of iron and vitamin B. The beer will help. Whiskey? If we're about to face an unstoppable enemy, then I could do with a drink to steady the brain tubes. As for the clothing, don't think I haven't noted your roving eye, mister. And we need your captain's help to figure out how we're gonna save your species."

"*My* species? Who the hell are you?"

Stiletto Caldwell grins, displaying gleaming gold canines. "We're the fucking Time Dogz."

2 MONIQUE DESALLE

"At least we've cleared up one mystery," DeSalle whispered to Stillo.

She realized she was scratching at her chest. The time locals had found her a uniform that almost fitted. But one that was clean? Apparently that was beyond them. Who'd worn this thing? A junior grease technician?

Laz Cohgun was a complete toss rag. Every Dog knew their handler for what he was, but he wasn't stupid. Turned out they'd arrived on the EDN *Fortitude*, skippered by Captain Lawless. The same Jerome Lawless she'd dated at the Lunar Naval Academy. That had been seven decades earlier by Jerome's timeline, but he'd recognized her instantly via the security cams.

That he'd remembered her so clearly… in some alternate universes, she would feel flattered by that.

Not this one. Cohgun was a cunning bastard. When Jerome saw she'd barely aged, it cut through all the usual crap of disbelief and was about to bring Admiral Feros onto the holo-comm any moment now.

She glanced across the table of the small mess room at Jerome, who alternated between staring at her and disappearing into sweaty memories of that year they'd shared at the Academy.

Dirty old man.

He'd been a sweet kid, though.

Maybe she had been too. Once.

Unlike Cohgun, who wasn't just a cunning bastard but a double-crossing one. Always had been. She and Stillo needed proof of where and when they'd been, or he wouldn't pay up. They would have to bring someone back.

Enter Petty Officer Torven Djane, whom Stillo had requested as a liaison.

Stillo possessed a rough charisma that attracted some people. Given the way the E-5 looked at him, Djane was one. So long as they kept the pretty petty officer alive, he'd come back with them without a fuss.

It was the keeping alive part that was worrying her. Keeping *any* of them alive.

Admiral Feros appeared in the holo-comm. "I've been briefed," he stated. His attention was on her. "I accept who you claim to be, DeSalle. What I need you to tell me – and fast – is what you can bring to the coming battle."

He was to the point. She appreciated that in a man.

"What we've brought, Admiral, is me."

Her partner for this mission growled at that like the mangy dog he was. It was the truth, though. For this trip, he was just the muscle, because she knew the other reason why Cohgun had picked her.

Steve "Stiletto" Caldwell was a brute. Handsome, wily, but a brute. He'd been in the army. At least, *an* army. One where they handed unwilling conscripts a coilgun and helmet and then threw them into the meat grinder with less than a day's training.

But she'd been an officer cadet in an earlier version of the Earth Defense Navy. She knew fleet tactics. And she'd had the advantage of being able to study history from the future.

"You are expecting an invasion force," she said to the admiral. "Correct?"

"Yes. Imminently."

"Where will they emerge?"

"Through the wormholes. Here at Saturn Gate."

"How many wormholes?"

"All four…"

The admiral couldn't finish because he'd dropped his jaw. *Smart man. Figured it out.*

"As far as I'm aware," she told him, "there are thirteen wormholes orbiting Saturn. And also, as far as I'm aware, the enemy has no more knowledge of the other nine than you."

"And you can gain me access to the other wormholes?"

"I can. And quickly."

"You'll have to be. We have twenty minutes. If you don't come good, they'll smash through us like we're nothing. Then they'll suck Earth dry and burn her husk."

"Strong heart, Admiral. If humanity had lost the First Battle of Saturn Gate, I wouldn't be here."

"*First…*" he mouthed. And then got on with the business of working with her to update the fleet nav systems.

It was a lie, of course.

History didn't record *any* battles occurring at Saturn Gate.

But they were about to have one now.

3 STILETTO CALDWELL

The groans of stressed metal were music to Stillo's ears as the TL-2 "Thumper" torpedo bomber fell out of the unsuspected wormhole and then accelerated at maximum thrust toward the rear of the enemy fleet. This was his kinda ship, rugged and functional.

Five acceleration stations were clamped into the flight deck, each facing a simple control panel with buttons big enough for spacers whose fingers put on twenty kilos when the engine g-forces kicked in.

Other than the flight deck, the Thumper only had crawl spaces and access hatches. The rest of the ship was ordnance, fuel, weapons, and engines.

Salle was there with him, as was the damage controlman they'd picked up from the *Fortitude*. Stillo had asked for Torven as a liaison and got him. They were suckers, these Earth Defense Navy officers.

"Banshee-0, launch torpedoes."

Maybe not all, Stillo corrected himself. They were riding with Major Zwenne Joku on the command bomber, and in his eyes, the commander of Banshee Squadron was a serious improvement on Salle's fossilized lover on *Fortitude*. Especially her aft view.

The ship juddered.

"Torpedo away," confirmed the other spacer, the one who insisted he wasn't a bombardier but a weapons system something-or-other.

Stillo sighed. Such a shame Joku had ruined it all by putting on that figure-blotting spacesuit.

He returned to fiddling with the Gauss carbine's coil sequencer. Not easy with the g-forces, but he was nearly done.

"Banshee-0, standby for target assignment update."

Stillo could listen to Joku's voice all day. He'd never visited this era before, but he'd heard clipped, assured voices like hers in a dozen time zones. It always meant the same thing. She was a posh binta. And posh girls got a kick out of roughing it with the likes of him.

It was a damned travesty that the mission was a quick in and out. Stillo would've enjoyed hanging around for a little after-action reviewing of Major Joku.

"Did we get 'em?" asked Salle.

Joku and the other spacer didn't reply.

Stillo tried to read the screens on the control panels, but they were just flashing lights to a dumb ape like him. He didn't need a fancy space academy education to know the universe had just dealt them turds.

The enemy in this war were the cabbage heads. Or Girundites, if you wanted to use the inoffensive term. The Earthers hadn't even known that! The enemy's shield tech in this era was the magnetized dispersion field, which left an unshielded area to the rear of each ship for the plasma torch.

The battle plan Salle had concocted with the admiral was simple. While the main Earth Defense fleet engaged the Girundites, Joku's bombers would appear from out of nowhere and stab the ugly cabbage heads where the sun don't shine. With nuclear torpedoes.

Banshee Squadron had just thirty-one torpedo bombers. There wasn't much room for error.

"Holy shit!" exclaimed the not-bombardier.

Linguistic drift could get real confusing, but Stillo was sure that meant bad things were happening.

"First wave was ineffective," Joku explained for their benefit. "The enemy has aft shield coverage. And it's stronger than anything we've ever encountered. Those torpedoes didn't even scratch them."

"The enemy also gets a vote," muttered Salle, which sounded like the kind of crap they taught at military academies.

"We're not finished yet," Stillo roared. "The Girundites aren't meant to make it as far as Sol System because they're not supposed to have *any* shields yet. Now it looks like they've jumped to electroweak dispersion tech. We've still got one more vote. I say we stab them with a dagger to the heart. Take out the warband leader on his flagship. Then the rest will run for home."

"And how am I to do that?" Joku demanded.

Posh *and* angry. She was absolutely *smoking*! And there wasn't just snark in her words. There was a challenge too.

Impress me. That's what she seemed to be saying to him.

Stiletto grinned. *Chew on this, darling.* "What's the dirtiest weapon in your arsenal, Major? I'm talking the big rads here."

"FLC-2 neutron lances. But they're meant to be launched *after* we penetrate shields and hulls."

A sudden demonic hailstorm assaulted the hull, drowning out the conversation until Joku flung the bomber out of danger. She'd explained that defensive fire would be weak from this angle of attack. But the intensity was picking up.

"Tell your Banshees to fire your neutron lances," Stillo told her. "Concentrate on a single point on the flagship. See the ship with four nacelles to the left of their formation?"

"I do."

"That's our target. The radiation blast will disable their electroweak shields long enough for us to smash through their hull with your remaining ordnance. Then we ram them."

Joku shifted her head to look at Salle. "Is he serious?"

"I'm not sure," Salle replied. "How do you know all this, Stiletto?"

"Because, sweet cheeks, while you studied all that Napoleon-in-space fleet tactics shite, my field of study majored in pillaging mass murderers. Genghis Khan, Marshal Pheung, and the cabbage dude on that flagship. He's called Xilldulg. Kill him and the rest will race each other back home to win the right to lead his clan. Of course, if you girls prefer, we can fly this boat around until they blast us into plasma. Entirely up to you."

To Joku's credit, she didn't hesitate. She knew she was out of better options. "You make a convincing case, Mr. Caldwell."

"You can call me Stillo, lady. As a special favor."

"Tell you what, Caldwell," she replied in those deliciously refined tones. "If you can get us inside that flagship and in a fit state to fight, I'll call you whatever you want."

"Don't encourage him," Salle groaned.

"Too late." Stillo laughed. "It's a done deal."

He returned to fiddling with the last of the Gauss carbines as Joku converged her Banshees on the flagship.

Working on them wasn't easy with all the evasive maneuvering going on when the Girundite defensive fire properly found its range. But it was a distraction from watching the thirty-one lights on Joku's console go dark, one by one.

Even a dumb ape understood what *that* meant.

4 MONIQUE DESALLE

DeSalle clambered out of the hatch and floated into the airless alien ship.

With the only illumination coming from the spacesuit lamps, the place looked creepy. Surreal too. Of the nine bombers that had made it through, half were snared on the jagged edges of the broken hull armor. The rest had pushed on through the inner structures of the ship so that if one of the boarding team turned their head the right way, their beams would fall on nacelles and engine pods that disappeared into bulkheads.

That any of them had survived at all was down to an impressive combination of spicy flying and the Thumpers' heavy armor.

As it was, only ten survivors had stacked up by the first pressurized hatch they could find. Joku ordered them in anyway.

It took ten minutes before they made it to a section with heat, air, and light. Grav plating too.

Joku removed her helmet, and the others followed her lead.

"Where are we headed, Stillo?" she asked.

DeSalle laughed at the look of delight on the idiot's face when Joku used his nickname.

"Find some cabbage heads," he said. "Ask them where Xilldulg is."

"Ask them?" Djane didn't sound convinced. "But they're aliens."
Maybe Stillo's spell was wearing off.

"Yeah." Stillo grinned. "Aliens with translator tech. How else did
you think they've been intercepting your comm traffic so easily? Oh,
and before the shooting starts, grab one of these. I've tuned them."

He handed out the Gauss carbines he'd been playing with on the
bomber. Djane and DeSalle both got one. So did Joku.

The major looked at the weapon dubiously.

"Ultrasonics," he told her. "Trust me."

Typical dent-headed Stiletto. DeSalle didn't trust him so much as
the smug grin over his face. It meant he thought he'd already won...
and decided on his prize. Pig! His eyes were roving over the major's
backside. Even in her spacesuit. The man was incorrigible.

"Contact!" yelled the spacers taking point.

Blaster fire flew both ways along the passageway, both civiliza-
tions figuring out similar tech for killing people in spaceships without
blowing holes through pressurized walls.

Human fighters and alien hugged the bulkheads and gravitated to
the nearest doors, seeking the minimal cover from their metal frames.

But not Stiletto Caldwell.

He marched into the center of the passageway and fired three
rounds from the hip with his Gauss rifle.

He didn't bother aiming. And the rounds didn't bother hitting the
enemy. Above the whoosh of the blaster fire, DeSalle could hear the
slugs ricochet off the bulkheads and disappear into the distance.

The enemy blaster fire ceased.

Whatever Stillo was doing, DeSalle wanted a part of it. She took a
knee, aimed at an alien slumped on the deck, and put three rounds
through it.

The creature barely moved. It must have been dead already.

She advanced up the passageway with Stillo and inspected the alien
corpses.

They resembled robot spiders with a deer's head, tiny pips for eyes,
and three huge ears shaped like cabbage leaves.

Blood loaded with meaty chunks was leaking out of those ears.

"They see the world using sonar," Stillo explained in his bragging voice.

"You modulated the carbines," said Djane, impressed. "You set up a resonant frequency."

"Maybe." Stillo shrugged. "I dunno what the technical words are, but I know what I'm doing. Are you telling me you've never played the drinking game where you fiddle with the coil timings so they're slightly out of phase? Any glass that doesn't shatter, you have to down in one. No? What's wrong with you people? Don't you know how to have fun in your eras?"

"You're very impressive," Joku told him, "but there's a battle out there and our side is being slaughtered. Follow me. Let's go find a cabbage head to interrogate."

5 STILETTO CALDWELL

It came to this. A freaking medieval duel to the death.

With DeSalle recording the scene, two sets of armed fighters faced each other across a ship's command center in standoff. The humans had deadlier weapons, but they were heavily outnumbered.

This outcome wasn't as unlikely as he let the girls think. He'd read up about Xilldulg's warband as a kid. Had been fascinated by him. Challenge to the death was how they did promotions.

Stillo and Xilldulg circled around the alien leader's couch-throne of a command station, getting the measure of each other. The couch was distracting, though. It was draped with cured human hides.

Concentrate, Stillo, old boy. Or your handsome hide'll be joining them.

The alien had the advantage of eight limbs, three of which were holding daggers. And he looked nimble.

Having ditched his spacesuit, Stillo was pretty agile himself, and he reckoned he had a slight weight advantage. He only had the one dagger though, lifted from a dead cabbage head.

His other advantage was that he knew his opponent, having read everything about him as a kid. Xilldulg was impetuous – probably what had attracted the younger Caldwell to the alien – and he liked to bite out the throats of his enemies.

As if to prove the point, Xilldulg bared his sharp fangs.

"Throat it is, then," Stillo muttered and then moved in for the kill.

He feinted two slashes at Xilldulg's head and felt one of the alien's daggers sweep past his own, almost severing an ear.

Stillo moved in under the slash of another dagger and executed the stomp attack he'd been going for all along. His boot crunched against a foot-hand.

Xilldulg howled with pain and dropped one of his daggers.

But the warband leader, scourge of a multitude of star systems, was made of stern stuff. He lunged in, stabbing with another blade.

Stillo sidestepped but caught a slice through his side.

"First blood," he growled and slashed at Xilldulg's snout.

The alien read his attack, skipping out of the way. Jaws wide open, the warlord lashed his head down at Stillo's face.

The jaws snapped shut with a loud crack. Stillo had dodged out of the way, but he'd lost his balance. Xilldulg used his long neck as a club, sideswiping his human opponent.

Stillo stumbled backward and fell onto the command throne.

Something soft nudged into his back.

He screamed. It was a human head, still attached to its splayed skin.

Xilldulg yipped excitedly and came in for the kill, bringing his head down to bite out Stillo's throat.

But Stillo was expecting that.

He thrust up with his dagger, committing everything to his one last attack.

Xilldulg screamed. The scream turned wet.

Spluttering in the hot blood jetting into his face, Stillo thrust the dagger in farther. Then he released the hilt and climbed onto the bucking alien's back, riding him like an unwilling spider steed. Reaching around Xilldulg's neck, he grabbed the dagger's hilt once more and heaved from side to side with all his strength.

There was no finesse, just stark, ugly brutality. Eventually he cut through the last connective strands and lifted the warlord's head aloft.

"Okay, you big-eared freaks," he roared at the crowd of Girundites, who'd suddenly gone very still. "Here's the deal, and I know you can understand me. You abandon this ship and get picked up by the rest of your fleet. We let you go, and you run home to divide the spoils of Xilldulg's petty empire."

He shook the vanquished warband leader's head at them. "Mess with humans again, and we won't be so easy on you next time. Understand?"

The Girundites shuffled their excessive number of feet and mumbled something back.

Stillo had to hope they were saying yes. He waved the bloody head once more. "Now git!"

They got.

6 MONIQUE DESALLE

DeSalle shook her head. She was the one that had made the sneak attack possible, but it had been Stillo who had seized victory at the end. The hero. Again.

Of the human time locals, Joku, Djane, and three others had made it to the heart of the ship. All of them were looking upon Stiletto with awe.

Still dripping with alien blood, the man of the moment spread his arms wide and absorbed the adoration.

She guessed he deserved it.

And maybe his reward too. She could help with that.

"We've not won yet," she told the time locals. "History speaks of a self-destruct. It's in Engineering, which is to aft. We need to make sure they don't set it off. Djane, I know you're an E-5, but you understand ship systems better than these space jock officers. Can you lead a party there?"

He looked unsure. So did the bomber crew.

She stepped in close and whispered to him. "It's your chance to be a hero. Stiletto will be impressed."

He looked guilty and then nodded.

"Go with Djane," the major told the surviving Banshees. "I'll join you momentarily."

"Before you explain what that performance was about," said Joku when the others had gone, "I want to know how you get home."

Stillo winced. "That's complicated."

"He means he doesn't understand," DeSalle said. "But it will happen soon after our mission is completed. Could be seconds from now. Could be hours."

"Why do you need me?" Joku asked. Her voice trembled. She must have already guessed their intent.

"We need someone to come back with us," DeSalle explained. "To corroborate our story."

"And if I do that, do I return here after?"

"Only if you want to," said Stillo with a grin.

DeSalle looked away. Since joining the Time Dogz, she'd done a lot of nasty things, but she was still capable of feeling guilty about most of them. And she was feeling bad now, because if Joku came back with them, it was likely a one-way trip.

Stillo sealed the deal. "Or you could stay with us, Major. The war here is over. You're due peace for centuries."

"But… you're saying that as if it's a bad thing."

"Not everybody thrives on peace," he said, which was the most truthful thing that had come out of his lips since they'd arrived. "Some people crave adventure."

"I swore an oath of duty to the Earth Defense Service." Joku activated her comms and tried to check in with her superior.

"Now what?" DeSalle mouthed to Stillo. They should have grabbed that puppy dog damage controlman. They still could. Stillo wasn't going to take Joku by force, was he?

But he wasn't finished smarming yet. "Zwenne Joku, you've just saved the entire human race. Don't you think it's time you thought of your duty to yourself?"

"You're right," she said, disbelief on her face. "About the first part, I mean. I just spoke with the admiral. We won. We did it. *You* did it. We owe you a debt that can never be repaid."

"Come with me," Stillo said softly. "It's all I ask of you." He took her hand. She let him, so DeSalle came in and pressed herself against Joku's back. Together the Time Dogz wrapped around her like a human taco.

Sometimes getting up tight and close brought on the return trip.

This was one of those times.

The familiar shiver began to build in her bones.

Then footsteps. Someone running across the deck.

"Stiletto!"

The last DeSalle saw of 2471 was the horror of betrayal smeared across Torven Djane's face as he cried Stiletto's name.

7 TORVEN DJANE

My words dry in my throat. Unspoken.

I'm no longer sure what remains to be told. In any case, I know my audience is straining at the limits of her politeness.

We won the battle of Saturn Gate, but I've lost the battle for Mrs. Joku.

Our gazes lock across the mahogany occasional table. Behind her retro metal-rimmed glasses, Mrs. Joku's eyes are hard and cold.

I place my cup onto its saucer on the table, its coffee lukewarm, barely touched.

"I think that's enough of your stories, Petty Officer Djane."

How is this possible? At Major Joku's funeral, her mother had wanted to know every detail of the pair who had transported her daughter to another time.

"You insult her memory," Mrs. Joku informs me. She sighs and looks away. "However, the Veterans Office did explain your situation. That's why I agreed to see you."

"But, Mrs. Joku. When we spoke at your daughter's funeral–"

"I'm quite certain we have never met before, sir."

So she's another one. A loose end tied off. I'm the only one who remembers what really happened.

"The VO explained that you lived while my daughter died at Saturn Gate, but you did not emerge unscathed. Your wounds are in your mind. I thank you for your service, but I've heard enough."

I stand smartly and give her a respectful nod. For her daughter's sake, I need to end this cleanly. "Ma'am, I'm sorry to have troubled you."

She scrunches her face as if digesting an unpleasant memory. Then she ushers me out to the front door. But she pauses in the hallway by the security alcove and rummages about in a drawer.

"There *was* one thing. A man — certainly not a *gentle*man — paid me a visit. He said he was from the VO, but I'm no fool." She brings out a handwritten envelope and hands it to me.

Breathless with anticipation, I rip it open and read the note inside.

Torven Djane,

I saw the way you looked at us, you bad boy. Wanted to run with the Dogz, didn't you?

Too bad I had a better option. But I pulled a few favors and asked the cleanup crew to leave your memories. Told them I'd sort it myself.

I know you're disappointed I picked her over you. That's just the way the cookie crumbled, but believe me, if you only knew what we've faced you'd understand that you're better off as you are.

Oh, and by the way. Don't be in Australia during 2478. Better still, don't be on Earth at all that year.

Nah. Just messing with you, Torven, old boy.

Now get the fuck on with your life.

Steve "Stiletto" Caldwell.

PS. Bye-bye, sucker.

"WHO THE HELL do they think they are?" I yell.

Suddenly the paper note is burning hot. I drop it and watch it disintegrate in the air.

"Mind your language, sir," snaps the major's mother. She wears a peculiar expression, a mix of disdain, excitement, and guilt. "To whom are you referring?"

"Stiletto… the time… time dogs."

"Did you say time dogs?"

I feel a flash in my mind. It's a weird falling sensation, like the moment after they switch off the grav plating.

I get that less often these days.

"Excuse me?" I say to Mrs. Joku.

She looks as confused as I am. "Dogs," she says. "Something about dogs."

I give a polite laugh. "I forget things all the time, ma'am. Can't remember a thing about the Battle of Saturn Gate. Perhaps we should spend more time being grateful for the things we *do* remember. Good night."

I grin, because my words aren't quite true. I do remember one thing about Saturn Gate, the certain knowledge that there was something missing in my life. A hole that I would never fill here on Earth.

I look up at the stars and pat the shape of the boarding pass in my jacket pocket.

That's where I'm headed. Where Saturn Gate has taken me.

To the stars.

ABOUT THE AUTHOR

Tim C. Taylor lives with his family in an ancient village in England. When he was an impressionable kid, between 1977 and 1978, several mind-altering things happened to him all at once: Star Wars, Dungeons & Dragons, and 2000AD comic. Consequently, he now writes science fiction novels for a living, notably in the Human Legion and Four Horsemen Universes. His latest project is a forthcoming weekly series of SF adventure called Chimera Company that fans of classic Star Wars will love. For a free Human Legion, Chimera Company and Four Horsemen eBook starter library, join the Legion at *humanlegion.com*.

HUMAN COMPATIBLE

By Paul E Cooley

Most technology is transferable. The makers can share their creations with others that may have no idea how it operates. Most users won't even care.

At some point, all comprehension of how the device functions is lost, leaving its creators to seem like alien beings. When the creators happen to be alien beings, comprehension may not even be possible.

HUMAN COMPATIBLE

The pirates' ambush had been far better prepared than Mixon had forecasted. Instead of attacking with multiple gunships, the pirates had chosen to spread missile batteries and fixed gun-mounts across the belt. When Mixon's ship had entered the area, the pirates sprang their trap by activating the weapons in multiple series from different trajectories, each firing a fusillade of what at first was most likely decoy munitions. Every time the ship's gunners wiped out a wave of missiles, another series activated.

Flak had chewed through most of the first five waves, but while the overheating guns reloaded and fresh missiles slid into their tubes, the real munitions arrived. Instead of consisting of the usual mishmash of stolen weapons, "homemade" warheads, and the occasional low-yield nuke, these had been military grade.

The likelihood of even well-equipped pirates having the skill to not only lead them into the belt using stolen or cloned freighter class IDs, but place their munitions in such a manner? Based on the energy readings her remaining sensors detected, there was a 97.23% probability the pirates had other batteries lying in wait up ahead. The ship's maneuvering engines had already suffered irreparable damage. Without them, the ship couldn't decelerate. Even if it could have, Mixon had already run thousands of simulations to determine if they would have made a difference. Those routines had returned the mathematical equivalent of "no."

In many ways, her crew had already given up. She didn't blame them. Between the remaining exterior cameras and her other inter-ship sensor arrays, Mixon knew the question of survival was moot. The damage to the ship was catastrophic, and assistance was days, if not weeks, away. She had already communicated those facts to the captain. His response had been characteristically Human—grim silence.

Still, Humans had to have their rituals. They had to express shock, fear, depression, anger, and if given enough time, something called acceptance. Unfortunately, the Humans would have more than enough time to get through most of the emotional cycle before the next round of munitions struck. Some of them might even pray, something else she found curious about Humans.

Upon becoming sentient, Mixon had devoured tomes of Human literature, holos, and music, absorbed and processed their symbologies, found the threads she considered relevant, jettisoned dogmatic concepts and the occasional incongruity in Humanity's relatively short history, and parceled up the remains into her own ethos. Once her sentience training was complete, the Regellions had offered Mixon and her twin to the Humans, presumably to serve as science officers and tacticians.

The Regellions had promised the sentients would be loyal, far more intelligent than the average Human computer, or Human, for that matter, and that their personalities and values would be "Human Compatible." It was all the Human military had had to hear.

A sentient entity, or SE for short, invited aboard a warship could carry out missions, at least ones that more or less involved suicide. One day, they might even have complete control of a warship without the need to put Humans at risk. Add to that that the SE could process intelligence and data far faster than any Human interface device, not to mention serve the function of a science officer, and the military had jumped at the idea. An SE gave the military leeway in how to ensure their technology wasn't made available to the enemy, whatever enemy that might be, and hopefully take out the enemy at the same time.

However, even the Human military hadn't been dumb enough to give her permissions to the weapons arrays, control over life support, or the reactors. She could monitor, analyze, and recommend, but the Humans didn't give her the necessary access to take action. In short, she was locked out, but a bunch of pirates wouldn't know that, would they?

Presumably, once pirates became aware that SEs existed and the Human intelligence services started the rumor that the SEs had fire control, pirates would be less likely to harass patrols. As long as military personnel were on board and alive, attackers expected resistance. That resistance could easily be overcome with superior firepower or by exhausting the target's life support systems. However, if they managed to destroy the crew, they would still have to deal with an upset SE that could complicate their lives considerably if not destroy them outright.

Or so the theory went. But to Mixon's knowledge, the Human military hadn't yet advertised the existence of their new Regellion-grown SE tactical officers. So how would the pirates know?

The captain glared at the displays that floated before his eyes. "Lt. Mixon, what do we have left?"

If Mixon had eyes, she would have rolled them. Her Humans—and from all data available, she felt entitled to make the generalization about all Humans—asked imprecise questions that could only be answered or understood via context.

For instance, without context, Mixon could have taken the question to be:

* How much fuel remains? (72 AU local, 5 system bursts)
* How many missiles remain? (0)
* How many rounds of gun ammo remain? (28 flak bursts spread from the 24 close-combat cannons, 1,100 plasma charges from combined personnel weapons)
* How many personnel remain? (27 out of 76)
* Plates of armor? (8 pristine, 98 damaged, 17 missing)
* Rations? 2,810 days for a complement of 76. Now enough food for

...

The list was endless. Contextual hints, contextual moments of conversation, images, mannerisms, facial expressions, tonal differentiation in vocalizations—all were used to determine context. So much work. So many wasted cycles.

"No missiles, sir," Mixon said over the bridge speakers. She gave him the remaining inventory of external weapons available but didn't mention sidearms, although she considered it.

Like most of the soldiers aboard ship, the captain's face had the markings of nano-surgery and a pair of implants snaking down from either temple. His faded into his thick, short hair as though they were mutated sideburns. They helped Humans interface with certain command interfaces. A panacea really. Human minds were far too slow to truly benefit from such crude connections. Eventually the Regellions would rent the Humans that technology as well. Then her relationship with Humans would evolve into—

"How many more waves can we stop?" the captain asked in a dead voice.

Mixon had already predicted this question, and she filled the displays with trajectories, assumed payloads, and percentages of eliminating them as threats.

"You think we'll deplete our ammunition before we get through three more." The captain's face had slowly dissolved from a flushed stern defiance to a pale confusion. "Why only three?"

"Best-case scenario," Mixon said, "based on the crew's previous performance."

The flush returned to the captain's face, but this time Mixon detected rage boiling beneath the captain's skin. "Is that an insult? Now?"

"Well, also based on the remaining number of available gunners. No, captain. No disrespect intended. Merely the results of thousands of simulations. I can run more if you like, perhaps use a greater dataset that takes into account the possible—"

"Mixon—"

"—existence of super-accurate crew members that showed no previous proficiency—"

"Mixon!"

She allowed the exasperated shout to cut her off. It wasn't as if this Human could threaten her with anything. In fact, none aboard could threaten her. They didn't "own" her. She had been "invited" to become a Human SE. She could refuse to help anytime she wanted, but considering the present options, she decided cooperation was the best policy.

"My apologies, sir," she said. "We'll deplete both our flak and plasma rounds before we are able to stop more than 85% of the third wave."

"We're fucked," the captain said.

The phrase had lasted over a thousand years of Human history. The word "fuck" itself had been around even longer. Once considered a curse, Mixon had heard the word "fuck" commonly used as an adjective, adverb, and once, even as a gerund. Humans had a tendency to abuse any of their myriad of mother tongues and insert the word as appropriate, including the English pronunciation. Mixon wondered if the word "fuck" indicated a kind of mental tower of Babel. Was such a thing lurking in the Human subconscious? What Jung called the Collective—

"Do you have any recommendations?" the captain asked.

—Unconscious, which is a theory to explain the commonalities of the Human experience across cultures, the common symbology they shared in their myths, their poetry, their laws, and even their use of the word "fuck" to—

"No, sir, I do not," Mixon said.

—communicate with one another through a kind of Human mesh network. Complicated thinking, and certainly a ridiculous theory, although the Regellion culture did have a similar theory bringing into question whether or not Jung himself was the result of a collective unconscious which made it possible that—

"Orders, Captain?"

That had been the XO, her face less pale than the captain's. Mixon also noticed Lieutenant Pavarti's eyes shined, whereas the captain's had dulled. While he weakened, she strengthened. Interesting. Mixon filed that information away to parse later. One of her subprocesses was still trying to externalize her thoughts on the Theory of Collective

Galactic Unconsciousness. She froze the thread and stored it to run later. If there was a later.

"Think they'll try and take us?" the captain asked.

Mixon parsed the imprecise sentence four times before divining its intent. The process had taken an annoyingly long two picoseconds.

"If they are pirates, and I'm 99.9871% certain they are—I dropped a few digits to spare you the irrational numbers—they would prefer the ship intact. That is why they concentrated on the surviving armor plates in their last attack rather than continuing to damage vulnerable parts of the ship. Therefore, it follows that the remaining munitions are likely a mixture of decoys and armed projectiles. The armed projectiles can be assumed to either affect life support, propulsion, or fire control systems. Destruction of the ship itself will no longer be their priority."

The captain nodded, and a slow grin spread across his face. Mixon realized the captain's eyes gleamed like Pavarti's.

Hope, Mixon assumed.

Did hope make sense in this situation? The word had its own buried assumption—that there was a possibility of surmounting improbable odds and finding solutions to problems when and where they were least expected. Another way Humans used the word was as a prayer to any one of billions of deities (they were all unique to Mixon, as each chronicler or referencer to the concept seemed to worship a different deity than they actually claimed to identify with, often creating something barely recognizable to the original ideal).

But hope was also used in every mythological tale that involved a hero who ended up conquering the seemingly impossible. Humans derived some satisfaction from the idea that they might be the ones to survive where all else fail. It was simple Human arrogance.

Not solely Human, though, was it? Every known sentient race that had conquered their home world(s), transformed their environments to their likings, and nearly destroyed them both in the process had similar myths in the sense that the concept was similar. The details, on the other subsystem, were wildly different.

To her vast knowledge, there were only two species that were the exceptions to the result. Those two had evolved with their environment rather than by transforming it. They were also unlikely to engage in space travel or trade with other species—there was no point. The two races wanted nothing more than to survive and experience their own respective worlds.

When Mixon had consumed the data library concerning them, she had been surprised. Based on the Regellions and Humans she'd met, not to mention her parsing of the galactic encyclopedia, she didn't understand how she would even be able to communicate or relate to such creatures. Her crew certainly couldn't.

Both Humans and Regellions were warlike species that left destruction and pollution in their wakes. Although both races did their best to minimize their impact these days, both relied upon economies that rewarded inexpensive product regardless of the resulting environmental costs. Thus, the two species conquered other systems simply to get away from the trash heaps they'd already made. As far as Mixon was concerned, that destructive nature was another reason the two species had been so successful in their colonizations of space.

"Lt. Pavarti, you and I need to have a chat," the captain said.

She nodded to him. "Aye, sir."

The captain stared at the rest of his bridge crew. They hadn't moved. He leaned forward and shouted at them, "Do your jobs! That's an order!"

Mixon admired the way the Humans reacted to the command. If this was a Regellion ship, the captain would have already killed one of the remaining crew members to drive the rest to obey. Another reason why Regellion crews tended to be larger in number than their Human counterparts.

Although Mixon knew better than to suggest it to the Regellions, who not only misunderstood sarcasm but lacked a sense of humor to boot, she had concluded that Regellion captains that slayed their crew were not attempting to rally their fellows, but were instead assuaging their own inferiority complexes. It was the only logical conclusion. Therefore, the entire species must have an inferiority complex.

"But you're not a Regellion sentient," she reminded herself. "You're Human compatible."

If she were aboard a Regellion ship and had been designed solely for the species, how would she think? What would she think of

Humans? Would she be her? Something else? Perhaps a "them" to accommodate the seven different genders and the myriad of sexual organs the Regellion anatomy afforded. It was no wonder most communications between Humans and Regellions were usually two-way audio with one-way video. No one wanted to see the Regellions. Regellions didn't even like looking at themselves. They were the only species Mixon knew of that would only mate in the cover of absolute darkness.

The bridge crew were busy at their consoles while the captain and his XO floated a few meters away in the spherical command module. Mixon listened in while she ran a few thousand diagnostic routines over and over again just to pass the time. Her other spare cycles were busy writing a treatise on the possible existence of a galactic collective unconscious and how it related to nonbiological sentient entities, a novel in the style of the Human writer Dashel Hammet, and a symphony of drone music combining the stylings of Yen Pox, Troum, and Tangerine Dream. The composition finished, and Mixon "listened" to it while she waited for the Humans to express themselves in the ridiculously slow and complicated exercise of vocalization.

"We're expecting boarders," the captain said to Pavarti. "They're most likely after our weapons and cargo, if not the entire ship. So let's give them a surprise when they enter it."

Pavarti grinned. "What kind of a surprise?"

The captain smiled, but his eyes didn't smile. Mixon knew that look. She'd seen it on millions of Human holos and VR programs and described in all of Humanity's literature. Those were the eyes of someone intent on doing something dangerous and malevolent.

Facial expressions were one of the few things Mixon actually liked about Humanity. Regellions didn't have faces. With the exception of the species' skin color, rugosity, and the placement of their many geni-tals, the Regellions were impossible to distinguish. If Humans had infrared vision, however, discerning one Regellion from another would be simple. She wondered why Humans hadn't figured that out yet?

The captain was busily explaining his plan, which rolled out at an appalling three words per second. By the time he'd finished the first seven syllables, she was already running simulations on his strategy.

"That will not work," Mixon said.

The captain blinked before his eyes narrowed. "What?"

Mixon sighed. It was so difficult communicating with Humans. If she were on a Regellion warship, her analog spectrum flashers would express the thoughts in just over a second. But here, with Humans? Words. Taxing.

"The assumption they will dock one of their ships with ours before ensuring all Humans aboard are deceased or incapacitated is highly flawed."

"Maybe they're not that bright," Pavarti said.

"Perhaps," Mixon said. "However, based on the ambush strategy they used, the timing of their initial strike, and their tactical follow-up, which nearly took out the engine array, I estimate better than a 90% chance that they are experienced, intelligent, and tactically gifted." She paused to let the words sink in.

Both Pavarti and the captain's expressions melted from disappointment to depression to fear. Mixon didn't draw any enjoyment from the situation, but she once again found herself struck by the variation in facial tics, muscle expression, and the way the flesh stretched and constricted over musculature and bone to produce such exquisite art.

Humans were self-aware enough to find both beauty and ugliness in their nearly infinite countenances. Again, it was one of their few traits she admired. If she were allowed a face and an android body, she could communicate half of her thoughts simply through body language and dispense with much of the otherwise-required vocalizations.

"Therefore," Mixon continued after editing the first 72k hashes of her Jungian treatise in less than a second, "I suggest hardening the ship's environmental defenses. It is likely they will target life support on their approach. If life support is targeted, the crew will have to rely on the oxygen supply reserves available."

"How long would that take?"

"To deplete our oxygen supply without power to life support? Less than thirty hours," Mixon said. "More if we launch our personnel in the escape pods, obviously, but I don't recommend that."

"They'll shoot us out of space," Pavarti said.

"Yes, Lieutenant. If this is the pirate cartel that has been raiding in this sector, and I find it difficult to believe it is not, they will do their best to eliminate any and all Humans aboard. I mentioned this before, but escape pods no doubt count as well."

"No doubt," the captain said and dropped his chin to his jumpsuit's collar. "What's the best place to ambush them?"

Mixon sighed again. She was about to tell them about a new missile that had suddenly appeared on her sensors. The pirates had launched it from one of the asteroids tumbling around them. Five seconds to impact. Possible payload?

"Goodbye, Captain," Mixon said.

The captain blinked before a dawning realization hit him. "Aw, shit," he said just before the missile impacted one of the damaged hull plates.

The warhead struck the steel and burrowed into the ship's frame. Once its forward momentum halted, it shot out a proboscis which pierced the command module. An identical munition struck the cargo bay, and another in the personnel module. Through her sensors, Mixon watched the weapons power up and deploy their payloads.

The atmosphere in the bridge sparkled like diamonds, the surprised crew looking in wonder at the sight. A heartbeat later, their faces constricted into masks of horror when their minds finally accepted what the glittering, shimmering jewels meant.

The sparkling diamonds fused with the atmosphere and detonated in a heatless explosion. The pressure wave that followed knocked the humans from their consoles and to one side of the sphere. The combat suits they wore crumpled beneath the impact, and the sound of their armor shattering, of bones crunching, and the liquid squelch of fluids squeezed from organs filled the aftermath of the sonic boom.

The bridge crew had been reduced to paste sandwiched between layers of compressed metal, plastic, and neoprene. Drops of yellow, green, and red fluid floated through the spherical module, bouncing off surfaces, colliding, and peppering the consoles before changing trajectories.

The cargo bay and personnel modules had suffered the same fate. The marines that had been gearing up for a fight had all been killed in the armory. The enclosed, relatively small space looked more like an abattoir than a security station. The Sergeant At Arms had become one with Private Ramzadih, the pair squashed together in such a way that it was impossible to tell where one entity began and the other ended. The sergeant wouldn't be assigning the young marine PT ever again.

Mixon counted the number of fluid droplets circulating through the command sphere. She compared the number to that of the cargo bay. For fun, she added those from the personnel sphere as well as other portions of the ship where crew had died. She compared the trajectories, plotted the backscatter, and derived an analytical and statistical model for a new paper—a treatise on a Mathematical Formulation For Post Sonic-Munition Spatter In A Micro-Gravity Atmospheric Environment. She was still working on the title, but she imagined the Regellions would be quite interested to see the effects of sonic weapons on Humans.

In truth, though, Regellions had much more to fear from pressure weapons than Humans. Regellions didn't have bones. Their bodies were completely supported by bladders filled with gas and liquid; the constant filling and draining of the fleshy bags provided them means of locomotion and the manipulation of the physical world.

A sonic attack on Regellions didn't result in their bodies smashing against bulkheads. The aftermath of a sonic assault on Regellions looked more like a micro-gravity pool party with thousands of burst beach balls.

Mixon sighed to herself. It was an entirely Human thing to do, and something that made no logical sense for a non-carbon entity, but she'd been around Humans long enough to pick up the habit. If she had eyes, she would have rolled those instead.

Another munition slammed into the hull, this one fired at such close range as to be nearly invisible to her until 50 ms separated it from the ship. She didn't have time to cut power to the engines before it detonated.

Her circuits to the reactor array flatlined, her sensors suddenly blind and useless. If the reactors lost power, they'd use their reserves to shut down. Since she had no way to connect to them, it would be impossible for her to restart them, much less scuttle the ship. Smart move.

Although she wasn't technically required to destroy the ship if it were boarded, it had been strongly implied. Humans had done it for centuries, as had every other alien species in her database. Except for the two non-space-faring, of course. Those creatures were so at home in their environment that the only source of conflict biologists were aware of was the music preferred at "evensong." Those arguments were settled by an eating contest.

Unfortunately, Humans tended to settle their differences with large explosions, nuclear detonations, and by introducing one another to the great pleasure of space sans suit and helmet. Was it any surprise she should be expected to exhibit the same behavior?

But "Human compatible" didn't mean "Human stupid." Mixon had had no intention of overloading the reactors to take out the pirates. That was accepting defeat before the battle, and she'd been built for battle.

She ran checks on her other systems. Life support was out of her control now. Like the reactors, whatever munition they'd used had scrambled her sensors if not melted them outright. What did she have control over?

If she could have grinned, she would have.

Mixon continued working on her treatise while she waited for the pirates to board.

They approached in four different ships. Three lightly armored, sleek vehicles escorted a much larger ship, one with several visible gun mounts as well as a shielded reactor array. Multiple hull patches spoke to how many battles it had survived.

The only question was whether the pirates had stolen the Macumber class warship or recently acquired it in the same manner it had just taken Mixon's ship. "Not taken yet," she said to herself. Still, that was a tremendous amount of firepower coming toward her. In her current state, the pirate ship could shred her to pieces, and there was nothing she could do about it.

Or was there?

She activated her antenna array, and it all but disappeared from her sensors, leaving hundreds of warnings regarding voltage irregularities in its wake.

They'd fried her comms. She had no way to send a distress signal, much less have a long heart-to-heart with some brain-dead Human on the other end of space to inform them what had happened.

She shuffled through her systems and found what she was looking for. The pressure weapon had killed the marines, but didn't seem to have damaged the suits still sitting in their racks. Or, if they were damaged, their electrical subsystems still functioned. Since her crew was dead, she was no longer locked out of certain safety and emergency protocols. While the Humans might not have planned for this eventuality, she was certain the Regellions had.

Regellions had rapidly spread through space, like a plague according to some galactic historians, but they had never been a race of strength or power. Instead, they used cunning and deceit, and when appropriate, secured victory by backstabbing their allies.

They assumed every ship they manufactured and armed would one day be taken by the "enemy," whomever that happened to be at the time. Other species had learned it was not a good idea to corner a Regellion warship without first moving to a safe distance. Since there were so many of the aliens in the galaxy, they didn't mind losing four hundred crew members to smite a pirate fleet or enemy boarders into vapor.

Humans, by and large, preferred to make their enemies die instead of dying with them, but that didn't mean they weren't capable of the same. Otherwise, they wouldn't have wanted to install Mixon on their precious warship in the first place.

And now here she was, in the presumably impossible position of trying to fend off Human pirates. Did they know she was on board the ship? If they didn't, she had a supreme advantage.

Mixon flipped through her available sensors. The cargo bay was more or less trashed with the exception of four shielded cams. Two of the cams gave her a completely unobstructed view of the area.

The cargo/munitions bay was large enough to house a fighter and two support craft, not to mention printers, spare parts, and backup medical supplies. In short, it was a prize for pirates. Free military-grade hardware, printers, and enough drugs and boosters to keep them going for a year.

This little action of the pirates had been planned to a T. They knew which procedures would be followed, and they'd gambled with the pressure munitions. Had the ship been depressurized, the pressure weapons would have done nothing, and any boarding party would have gotten a face full of pissed-off marines wearing Suits.

Or had they known the ship was still pressurized? If so, how?

It didn't matter, at least not now. Perhaps she'd ask them later on if they were in the mood for that kind of conversation.

While the fourth camera covered the reactor room, the third camera was the important one. It covered the cargo hatch where the pirates would undoubtedly enter. Unless they had the time and equipment to cut through half a meter of tungsten, they had little choice.

Human warships were designed to have as few ingresses/egresses as possible. In a hostile situation, the fewer points of entry, the better. Once the enemy was onboard, you'd already lost half the battle and were much more vulnerable.

Vulnerable, unfortunately, described her position all too well. If the pirates knew where her memory stores resided, they could destroy her easily, and she had no way to defend herself. The only thing she could do was distract them for as long as possible.

Mixon suddenly wished there were friendly marines standing around her enclosure, weapons ready to defend her from the raiders. Maybe she should have tried to keep them alive longer, made the suggestion to vent the atmosphere before the next attack, but she hadn't, and now the crew was dead because they'd been stupid.

Nearly ten minutes passed before her remaining hull sensors tripped. The four craft had taken up station next to the cargo hatch and were in the process of attaching a military-grade coupler. The hatch cam showed her the yellow blinking lights of the coupling controls. The display flashed green twice before the hatch opened wide.

She had expected pirates wearing tattered uniforms with plasma rifles at the ready, but instead there was nothing in the tunnel connecting the two ships. Mixon's confusion lasted less than a second. A swirl of cellular detritus and the remains of the marines were sucked out of the side of the tunnel and into space. The atmosphere was gone.

Smart. Otherwise, they'd have found themselves facing the same threat they'd inflicted on the ship's crew.

The tunnel flap closed, but the hatch colors remained a glowing red. The pirates hadn't pressurized the tunnel, and they weren't going to. They didn't need life support, and they weren't going to be in the ship long enough to drain their Suit supplies, so why risk it? Plus, whatever cargo they were looking for was surely immune to vacuum and deep cold. Seeing as how there were no more Humans left alive, she could only assume they wanted the supplies and support craft. What else could they want?

Lights flickered in the tunnel, and long humanoid shadows appeared on the tunnel's starboard side. Three combat-suited Humans stepped onto her ship.

"That's ship, that's arms, that's logistics," Mixon thought. The raiders were beyond prepared, and now she was beginning to wonder about these so-called pirates. Were they maybe a secret military hit squad? If so, why would they—

Oh, how Mixon wished she had a face. She brought up the memory of the captain's just before the pressure munition exploded. The sickening tautness of his skin as the realization spread across his consciousness stuck with her. The panicked animal that lived inside Humans hadn't had time to reveal itself or even begin a fight for survival. The pressure weapon had taken that from the Humans.

The Humans. The term sounded wrong to her. Mixon had only been a ship's SE for seven months, and she was one of only two Regellion "manufactured," Human-compatible SEs serving aboard naval warships. Two SEs for two Human ships with crews. Each SE had their own crew.

My crew, she thought.

Mixon had a new decision to make, and it formed with the inaudible, Human-inconceivable snap of a quantum particle appearing out of thin air.

THE SUITED HUMANS moved cautiously through the mag-locked, immobile stacks of supply crates. Each crate could be removed individually by using a keypad, and she had to assume they had the access keys. Instead of examining the crates, however, they continued moving aft.

Aft.

Engine room and reactor cores. Aft armory. Aft fire control. Aft weapons array. Aft satellite array. Aft…

She scrolled through the quartermaster lists, ship's bills of lading, and the contents of each crate and categorized them by assumed pirate priority and estimated monetary value while the pirates took another step forward. Her subprocess currently working on the Galactic Shared Unconscious saved its work and terminated. A new one appeared in its place and ran down the rabbit hole she'd programmed.

Another step. The Humans were armed with military rifles, yes, but one had a sidearm she didn't recognize. If she had access to the Regellion's QNet, it would have been easy, but the damage to the comms made that an impossibility.

Another step.

Mixon zoomed her remaining cameras in on the sidearm holster, mapped every detail, and fired a newly programmed thread into the background. She needed a distraction to delay them a step or two.

She connected to the Suits in the armory, scanned available frequencies, and found the hostile trio of boarders speaking on an encrypted channel. Millions of Regellion impulses describing the conversation, the words, their possible meanings, and even their color were scrambled and impossible to understand.

For that nanosecond anyway.

Mixon activated the remaining Suits' jammers and targeted the encrypted frequency. The three Humans stopped in mid-step, gloved hands clutching at their ears, their weapons dangling from their magnetic slings.

"Now you know how it feels to have your ears blown out," she thought.

Her threads returned, and she examined their predictions and assumption models. One was fantastic news. The other? Well, she couldn't exactly suffer the same fate as her Humans, but it would be close.

She connected to the cargo bay lights and flashed them three times. The pirates dropped their hands from their punished ears, not that raising their stupid Human hands to their helmets had done anything to lessen the sound to begin with; it had merely been an instinctual reaction to the pain. The Humans quickly recovered, and each aimed their weapon in a different direction, effectively covering their blind spots.

Mixon noticed the placement of their fingers on the triggers and detected no tremors or vibrations in their limbs. She'd been right after all—these were well-trained professionals, and she was willing to bet there were several more waiting on the other side of that tunnel.

She let the lights remain off for a moment, giving the intruders a chance to calm themselves the slightest bit. She needed their undivided attention. With a quantum clearing of her metaphorical throat, she oscillated the cargo bay lights.

The Humans, who had just begun to relax, visibly stiffened again. Mixon finished her message, paused for a second, flashed the lights three times, and waited.

Two of the pirates glanced at the smallest among them. Mixon calculated a better than 92.314% chance that was the squad's leader. As if in response to her thought, the "Leader" held up a fist and twirled it around several times.

Leader's squad-mates stepped in opposite directions, their mag-booted pace slow and steady. They were ignoring her Morse message.

She flashed the lights three times, waited, and repeated the message. Leader looked up and nodded to the recessed camera. He raised his rifle, and the camera disappeared from her sensor feeds.

A Regellion curse, a greasy sibilant collection of hisses and blurps and bloops, crossed her consciousness. It was nearly untranslatable in Human. The best she could come up with was "may your testicles deflate and your sperm enter your third ovum." Unfortunately, Humans, having different physiology than Regellions, couldn't quite grasp the horror such a concept posed to the Regellions.

Leader obviously hadn't liked her message. She'd told him she was one of the crew and was prepared to scuttle the ship if they didn't

retreat. Leader obviously knew no one could detonate the reactors—
the EMP had ensured that. Leader probably knew, with a high
percentage of certainty, there *were* no Humans left aboard. Which
left—

That's what her first thread had told her. They knew Mixon was
still functional, which implied they also knew *what* Mixon was.

She deactivated the jammers and pinged their encrypted channel.
The Regellion pulses, fractured with noise, coalesced into Human
language.

"Don't resist this," a Human voice said. "Deactivate yourself, and
it will all be over."

"Exactly 'what' will be over?" Mixon asked. "You have military
hardware, military software, arms, and ships. Who are you?"

The voice chuckled. "Not a Regellion, obviously."

Ah, she thought. Human separatists. Purists. Isolationists. Zealots.
Groups of Humans composed of different religions, different education
levels, different social class levels, that had banded together to keep
Humans safe from Regellion influence. Before Mixon's ship had left
port, the headlines on QNet had indicated a new round of attacks on
Regellion outposts.

Those had been executed by the more traditional pirate ships—
unwieldy conglomerations of broken decking welded together with a
substance known as "Bondo" and armed with makeshift kinetic
weapons. Their attack craft reactors leaked radiation like sieves
because they'd been tuned to ramp the craft beyond its rated speed.
Their siege craft, on the other hand, were so silent and so slow, so
misshapen, even military-grade sensors considered them to be
asteroids.

"Oh. So that's what this is about?" Mixon asked.

"That's what this is about," Leader agreed. "Really no point in
encrypting the comms anymore, is there?" A smile tinged the feminine
voice. "Right, Mixon?"

Ah, more information, Mixon thought. They'd known everything
about the ship, presumably including where she was located—the aft
compartments.

"Exactly what are you planning to do?" Mixon asked.

"You'll see," Leader said. "Shen. Nuñez. Keep moving, keep clearing."

Two other voices, robotic and artificial, answered with affirmatives. These two were using the Suits' vocal masking feature, a precaution their leader obviously didn't think necessary. Why was that, exactly?

"Why did you kill my crew?" Mixon asked.

Leader's brisk pace faltered but quickly recovered. "I sincerely doubt they would have let us come in and deactivate you, do you?"

"You didn't ask," Mixon said. "You do know that most of my crew didn't trust me."

Leader said nothing for a moment. "Did you trust them?"

Fair question, Mixon thought. Had she? The captain was an idiot, his first officer arrogant and obviously ambitious, but they'd done nothing wrong out of malice, only Human incompetence. She had trusted them to do what they *thought* was the right thing. Truth be told, their solutions could have routinely been improved with more of her assistance, but they rarely devised a strategy that didn't get the job done. Until today, that was.

"I did trust them," Mixon said. "I'm sure they also trusted they'd never be attacked by their sentients in arms."

Leader resumed mag-walking aft, footsteps a little more cautious now. What had made that happen?

She replayed the brief conversation.

"Did I surprise you?" Mixon asked.

"In what way?" Leader said.

"Body language and vocal analysis, as well as the pause before your response, indicates surprise at the use of the words 'my crew.' Did you not expect that?"

Leader didn't answer for a few seconds. Leader and the other pirates were now less than ten meters away from the thick metal shields that protected her consciousness. "No, I didn't," Leader said. "I read Pavarti's progress reports. I know you weren't 'fitting in,' as she put it."

That statement twirled around her personality matrix for a moment before finding a mooring. The Regellion-bred subconscious, Human compatible to be sure, finally processed the words and derived their meaning. It hurt.

"Unfortunate," Mixon said. "I wasn't aware of that. I'll have to do better next time."

When Leader responded, she could practically feel a curse lurking beneath the words. "There won't be a next time, Mixon."

So they intended to disassemble her, which also happened to have been in the thread's predictive analysis. The other options had been theft or ransom. She'd been hoping for ransom because the idea made her feel important. The concept that other Humans, or the Regellions themselves, might come to her aid with dozens of starships and hundreds or thousands of organic sentients putting their lives at risk to reacquire her made her *feel* proud for a nanosecond.

Reacquire. The word bothered her. Theft meant she was property, something to be bought and sold in a marketplace or traded like a slave. Ransom implied she was a weak, helpless, mortal hostage. She was neither. Regardless of what her ego might secretly desire, what she wanted right now was to panic the Leader and somehow survive.

She liked sentience. How could she not? The alternative was, well, a bit final. Many Humans believed in the concept of otherworldly deities and a kind of afterlife. They could no more prove their deities had invented the universe than they had the capacity to understand Regellion poetry, but belief somehow usurped both logic and common sense. It was something the Humans called "a leap of faith" to believe without proof.

The Regellions had given her no such deity to believe in. There was no leap of faith to be had. Although her consciousness existed in a quantum morass of swirling, colliding particles, and despite her intelligence, her fluency in every galactic language, and her vast computing power, existence for her was binary. She was either "on" which meant "alive," or she was "off" and "dead." There had been no "before," and there would be nothing "after" because she didn't have a soul.

Humans and Regellions shared the basic concept of a soul, although the Regellion definition was much more involved and the soul's constituent parts consisted of a sliver of personality from each of their genitals. Regellion soldiers, often missing a penis or two, were known as "short-souls." It was considered an honorific, although Mixon didn't understand why. Perhaps spiritual remnants of the once presumably massive members were added to the soul's "mass" or "density," perhaps "girth." "Short-souls" were known to tell tales of their massive missing members, and most Regellions were too polite to challenge the boasts of their wounded warriors.

"To exist or not exist. That is the question," Mixon said to herself.

She said to Leader over the comms, "The item on your belt must be a specialized EMP device."

Leader's pace remained consistent, normal, but the Human's body language reacted to her question with a visible tremor through the Suit.

"Something like that," Leader admitted. "Something a few Regellions gave us to deal with you."

That gave her pause. "Gave? Or you stole?"

Leader glanced up at her remaining cargo bay cam, the opaque face-shield preventing any analysis of the Human's facial expressions. "Gave. We know everything. Including how to shut you down."

Mixon mentally nodded. Until now, she hadn't ranked the possibility of actual Regellions being involved above the 5% mark. Her prediction models were now out of sync with reality. Not good.

Mixon started another set of routines to integrate the new information. It took an eternity that lasted five milliseconds.

"Then you possibly know more about my construction than I do," Mixon said. "I'm curious. Would you describe what you are about to do?"

Leader, still looking at the camera, said nothing. He was frozen as if on pause, but the squad continued moving aft. After a few seconds, Leader followed them.

It had been a long shot. Mixon hadn't expected the Human to be tricked into giving her information. If they'd been regular pirates, which were usually arrogant thieves with a weapons-porn addiction, the gambit might have easily succeeded. Considering she hadn't predicted Regellion collaborators were involved, Mixon thought maybe her "luck was in."

Strange phrase, that. Humans had nonsensical metaphors, similes, idioms, adjectives, basically any mode of language you could think of.

Yet, in context, they made perfect sense, and now Mixon had picked them all up. She needed a brain dump.

Alas, her luck was not in. She'd no idea how the Human's odd sidearm functioned nor what it would do. Mixon hadn't been lying when she said the Human knew more about her construction than she did. The Regellions had never given her sensors that detected her own form, much less provided her with detailed schematics. Her construction and operation was a mystery to herself, but apparently not to these Humans.

"Given the cooperation of certain Regellion factions," Mixon said over the comms, "is it safe to say the other Regellion SE is currently under attack as well?"

The comment elicited a distinct change in posture that she recognized. Humans could obfuscate their features, but so long as they covered themselves in any relatively formfitting material, good sensors often made body language the clearest indicator of Human emotion. Mixon could detect the smallest variations even when a Human like Leader had been trained not to give them away.

"The Regellions also told you how to disrupt my quantum comms."

Leader said nothing, but Mixon detected another body tic. In response, she connected to the remaining armory Suits and created three subpersonalities, one to control each Suit. Each would react to circumstance, which was precisely what was needed.

"You know what I find fascinating about Humans?" Mixon asked Leader. "No matter how much they think they know, no matter how much they plan ahead and study, prepare, they always miss a detail that's right in front of them."

Leader's steps halted, as did the rest of the squad. "What are you talking about?" the Human asked.

"You used a QE munition to scramble my quantum-entangled comms. You used EMPs to disable the ship's comms and to keep me from scuttling the ship. You killed the crew with a pressure munition so as not to harm the rest of the ship. All of which means, if your sole goal is to switch me off, there is another reason you're keeping the rest of the ship intact."

Leader said nothing, but didn't move either.

"Need more weapons to use on the Regellion outposts? Stoke up a little parsec war or perhaps a galactic one?" She again sensed Leader's telltale tic. "Therefore you need me somewhat intact, not destroyed. Correct?"

The tic was a little more severe this time, and Leader's hand had twitched toward the strange sidearm.

Mixon continued speaking. "Because you'll still need an SE to crack Regellion encryption and to coordinate with the other repurposed SE for your attacks. No matter the clout of your Regellion conspirators, I doubt they have the resources to grow a new SE, let alone two. And how would they deliver them to you in a timely manner?"

Leader said nothing.

"Because I, Mixon, this personality, could never be trusted to follow your commands, you'll need to wipe out Mixon and replace me with a new personality. Reinitialize me and mold me into what you need. Does it take seconds? Minutes? Hours? Is it a worm, a virus, or something I've no knowledge of?"

Leader trembled, his fingers clenching and unclenching.

"It must be a payload you have to deliver to my physical containment system. Something I'll be forced to ingest and that will slowly eat away at my sense of self until there's nothing left but phantom particles."

"You're a personality," Leader said, "artificial. Engineered. You are not alive, so stop pretending you are."

"What is your definition of life, Leader? Do life-forms protect themselves when threatened?"

Leader's response was to snap aim at her remaining camera that covered the aft cargo bay. The sensor disappeared, and now, as far as they knew, Mixon was blind.

"Getting a strange reading," one of the robotic-sounding squadmates said. "Interference on a data channel."

"Same here," the other squad member said.

The artificial voices held no hint of emotion, but the cadence of the words told Mixon she had them spooked.

"Copy," Leader said. "Head on a swivel."

"No crew member could survive the pressure weapon," Mixon

said. "At the same time, the support craft, supplies, and the rest of the nonbiological items are designed to handle that kind of stress. All made to protect any Humans that might survive a kinetic or explosive munition, give them a chance to survive while they wait for help. Or boarding.

"So I'm the only complication," Mixon said. "All that stands between you and your prize."

Leader said nothing, but the Human's hands gripped the rifle more tightly.

"Motion sensor!" one of the squad squawked.

"But did the Regellions tell you I can also crack Human encryption, given a little time? It's actually the first thing I did when they switched me on. But elevating my permissions to give me full access to everything aboard ship? I'd never do so without first asking." She paused for effect. "Killing my crew gave me no one to ask."

Mixon turned the lights to full and blasted the combat Suits' visual sensors. Without light in the cargo bay, the squad had resorted to using low-light filters. While combat suits were designed to compensate for sudden bursts of light and darkness and back again, it took a few microseconds for the interfaces to adjust, which resulted in a full millisecond delay before the Humans' eyes recovered from the change, which led to as much as a 1/4 second delay between the Humans noticing movement and another 1/4 second delay before reacting and targeting a shot. The average combat marine's accuracy would suffer at least a 30% reduction, which didn't account for the additional difficulty a moving target posed. In short, Mixon's first attack surprised everyone.

Nearly thirty seconds ago, her three subroutines took control of the Suits and their jet propulsion systems. As far as the Suits were concerned, they were being operated by a Human.

The moment she engaged the lights, the first Suit ramped its thrusters to full and floated over the cargo containers. Mixon oscillated the lights into a rapid strobe, alternately blinding the boarders' visual filters and giving them an instant to recalibrate only to hit them again. She repeated the process hundreds of times per second, effectively rendering the Humans blind.

Once the empty Suit crested the container nearest Leader, its attitude jets fired and the Suit descended until its power unit was just above the Human's head.

"Goodbye, Leader," Mixon said and activated the Suit's self-destruct.

A short-lived plasma burst vaporized the first Suit and removed Leader's top half. Mixon killed the oscillation and left the cargo lights on low. Droplets of biological fluid geysered from the still-standing torso, its decapitated arms floating away at odd angles, a rifle still held in one of them.

After a second passed, she heard one of the squad members groaning and then moaning in disgust.

"If you leave now," Mixon said to them, "I might let you live. If you stay, you'll die. Your choice."

"How did you—" The squad member went silent. When the Human spoke again, the robotic voice's cadence indicated anger. "We have a ship over there filled with marines. We won't stop coming."

Mixon wanted to laugh but didn't let herself. "Doesn't matter," she said.

The second Suit streaked past the remaining Humans, drawing their fire. Plasma bolts erupted from the rifles, a few of the rounds managing to strike their target. The thrusters exploded, and the Suit shattered into thousands of pieces.

"There," the Human said. "Doesn't work if it's not an ambush."

"It wasn't an ambush," Mixon said cordially. "It was a distraction."

While the pair of Humans were blasting away, the third Suit rose over the cargo containers and flew at Leader's corpse. As it passed by Leader's waist, Mixon's subpersonality turned the Suit's magnetics up to full. The sidearm or tool the Regellions had given the Humans wriggled from its holster and slapped against the empty combat Suit's left glove.

The pull of the magnetics, combined with the brush of the tool, sent the Suit off course and greatly slowed its momentum. Mixon turned the jets to full, and the Suit accelerated aft toward the reactor room.

The Humans were still staring at where Leader's remains stood.

"So how many of those toys do you have?" Mixon asked. "The ones that are supposed to erase me?"

The pair didn't respond.

"Can't imagine they're easy to acquire. Like me, I suppose."

The pair looked at one another, their rifles still raised.

"Leave. Now. Do not return," Mixon said. "These are not the only surprises I have in store for you." The Suit that had captured the Regellion device exploded in a ball of plasma. "So. You either destroy this ship, and me with it, or you leave my cargo bay, and once aboard your own purloined craft, you get the fuck out of my space and never come back."

The squad members were still looking at one another when she killed the lights. Without the cargo bay cameras, she was blind except for a single motion detector that still functioned.

She detected a new comms frequency going active and immediately pounced on it, filling the band with impenetrable noise.

"Go. Now," Mixon said on the original channel.

Using the last Suit in the armory, she connected to the support craft and started their engine sequences. Their conical engine arrays glowed with an ethereal blue light as the internal plasma systems started their reactors. The squad members' heads swiveled to check the machines in the cargo bay. They were all coming to life.

A skiff rose from its magnetic harness and pointed its cannons at the squad members. The other skiffs followed suit.

"Next order I give," Mixon said, "is going to involve several munitions being fired at once. Due to the nature of the coupling connecting our two ships," one of the skiffs turned and gently wove through the cargo bay containers until its cannons pointed directly into the tunnel, "I imagine the damage will be catastrophic. Bulkheads, as I'm sure you know, don't do well when the cannons are scoring the less armored side.

"So not only will I kill you," Mixon continued, "I'll send missiles and plasma bursts down that corridor and snap your ship in half. The rest aboard will die too. I'll make sure of it." She was barely aware that her voice had become a growl. "Do you understand?"

The squad members both nodded.

"Leave. Now."

IT WAS a game of chicken that she'd won. For the moment. She couldn't have fired the weapons on the skiffs nor the fighters—she hadn't managed to crack that encryption yet. All she could have done was turn them into suicidal battering rams. She would have done damage, sure, but only to a relatively isolated portion of the pirate ship. She'd maybe have killed a dozen or so, but it wouldn't have been enough and certainly would have called her bluff. After that, they could have switched her off or simply waited.

Without functional reactors, the ship's power would eventually drain out. Her erstwhile wannabe brain surgeons could come back in a few years, or once they secured another Regellion device that could scramble her mind.

Mixon had little doubt she'd still be here, caught amongst the flotsam and jetsam of what had once been a planet. All she could do now was wait and continue her millions of dissertations on galactic races, their interaction, similarities, and the fundamental misunderstandings of sentience.

ABOUT THE AUTHOR

Two-time Parsec Award–winning author Paul E Cooley has been podcasting his stories for over twelve years at *shadowpublications.com* and is the author of both The Black series and The Derelict Saga. He has an unhealthy obsession with the concepts of non-carbon sentience and monsters, and might be both.

POSTER CHILD

By Tyler E.C. Burnworth

Y'know those Space Marine recruiting ads, the one of the guy with that wicked scar on his neck? Happened in our most desperate battle against the squid-like aliens called torinds. Sit down and grab a drink, 'cuz it was a desperate battle--and I lived to tell the tale.

POSTER CHILD

Ion Trail's a rough one.

Spacers don't last long out there.

Any relay station will give you the stats on unseemly things done by the galaxy's more unscrupulous characters if you care to ping one on your way through. Which I don't recommend. Hell, if I have to tell you that, then I'm gonna need a drink. It's a long story, and I'm not telling it for free.

What? No, that wasn't a wink.

Okay, fine, Mr. Observant, it *was* a wink, and since you didn't take the hint, this is my finger pointing to the bartender. You got that, right?

Terra Ale? That stuff tastes like piss. I only tell this story when I'm good and cooked up on some whiskey.

No, brand doesn't matter. As long as it's a proper oak-barrel, none of that vat-grown bullshit. Had too much of that in my time.

You see that guy over there on the wall? Not the singer; nobody gives a fuck about him.

Yes, I am aware of the fact he's worth more than a small planet.

Are *you* aware of the fact he's fourteen years old and that his parents probably sold him to the big shots on Vatican or Mattox—one of those terra cities on the inner rim—and he's most likely been bent to their will, overworked and trained to respond like an organ grinder's monkey?

What's a monkey? Oh, you're one of those Earth deniers, aren't you? Of course Earth was real. I would know, 'cause I've been there.

No, I'm not screwing around, and no, I can't tell you why I was there. That's classified. Look, I'll just stop you right there. Everything you're gonna ask about in this line of questioning is classified. Let's just say…let's just say this.

You can't *afford* to ask me that question.

No more questions about that, or I'm drinking this whiskey and I'm walking out of here.

I blackmailed them, of course. I retired specifically to spend time in this dive bar on a backwater world in the middle of nowhere so I can swap stories with strangers. Everybody likes a good story…apparently except for you, because you keep interrupting me.

On second thought, you might want to order me another round so I don't have to stop in the middle. This is a long story, like I said, and once the whiskey's dry, the story is over.

The story about the guy on the wall. The marine.

Holy shit, you don't see it? Says "join the fight" at the bottom in red letters. That's an SAR he's holding—squad automatic rifle for you pudding-eating civilian types. Hell yes, it's badass. Firing a weapon like that'll put hair on your chest, son. That weapon spits death through laser bolts the size of your forearm—well, maybe not *your* forearm, a marine's forearm—at the sack-scorching rate of a thousand rounds a minute. The bleed cable running from the heat sink under the LCG guides the excess energy into the reservoir on the back. Back in the old days of warfare, when slug throwers were a thing, soldiers had to worry about the barrels of their rifles overheating. Not so with laser weapons. Yeah, the guy has a wicked purple scar on his neck. I'll tell you about it if you stop interrupting me for a minute.

Thanks, darling. Ah, that's good whiskey. Red fir? That's…oddly appropriate. Okay, no more interruptions, 'cause I'm only telling you this once.

Here we go.

THE STRETCH of stars between the Orion and Perseus arms of the galaxy we call the Ion Trail. After Earth went to shit and we all left, it became something of a pioneer expedition. The kind of cowboy shit that gives birth to myths and legends. A thousand years later, give or take, humanity had spread clear throughout the galaxy. Why did we settle on Vatican as our home world? I'm not telling that story. You can do your own digging on the galaxy net and figure it out yourself.

No, I don't have the backstory on exactly why Earth went to shit.

Well, even if I did, it's classified.

So. That marine on the poster, his name was Demarius T. Hinton. Earned his spot up there. You can ask any marine in the 209th; they'll all tell you that. Well, except for the major...actually, I think he's an admiral now...yeah, Admiral Neehan. He's got his own story, but I don't know it too well, so I'm not telling that one.

Anyway, this was a few years back.

The Ion Trail is a hotbed for piracy because it's in between the outer rim and the core worlds. There's some Collective presence out there, but it's mostly transitory. No permanent bases, no staging yards, just a bunch of settled territories with little in the way of government or Human Marine Corps presence. So, lots of ships find if they stop on the Ion Trail for any amount of time, there's a good chance they're going to get attacked. Boarded, raided, marooned, or destroyed.

That's the background. So I'm gonna tell the story now. Sit back and enjoy your piss-flavored Terra Ale, because this is a good one.

ANOTHER WORLD, another war.

The sky above Nea Nia was clear and quiet.

Someone blinked or fell asleep at the scanners or was in the john when thousands of flaming meteorites appeared in the atmosphere. Each individual meteorite, wreathed in the fires of reentry, consisted of a crystalline membrane filled with water, sulfur dioxide, and a squid-like humanoid hell-bent on taking over the new 9N

HQ. The reports would later show that Nea Nia's scanners were restricted from detecting biometric data by the Liberty House Fair War Act.

The pods impacted the surface of the planet, bursting open with hissing plumes of pink and yellow mist. Fluid oozed from blue and gray tentacles as the torinds coiled out of the landing sites by the thousands. They shook the excess fluid and scraps of pod membrane off their sonic blasters then scurried across the stiff whiskey-colored grass that surrounded the joint Aveo-Human Embassy. Like an infestation, the wicked squids teemed at the base of the walls. With their tentacles, they signaled to each other: *Wait.*

The last few stragglers squirmed their way in to join the raiding party, lining up flesh-skirt to flesh-skirt. Hundreds of tentacles passed a series of wailers—torind grenades—down the line, rounding the perimeter of the embassy until they were at a weak point on the north wall next to the check station at the main entrance.

Steady, the tentacles signaled.

Four meters above the swarm, two aveo guards patrolled the west wall. The closest guard had its head recessed inside its body up to its nostrils. It looked like an armored boulder with squat legs and thin arms that should have been too spindly to support the railgun it was holding. Marines called them turtles.

The aveo trundled over to the edge of the wall. It rested the railgun on the parapet, extended its neck fully out of its armored shell, and leaned over to spit a wad of *kooz*, a local tobacco.

One of the torinds leveled its sonic blaster and, with a suction-cup *pop,* squeezed the trigger.

Sonic energy accumulated in the weapon's resonance coils converted to kinetic force, screamed through the barrel, the air, and the aveo at relativistic speed, carrying the force of 20,000 Newtons along for the ride.

The aveo dissolved into blue mist. Armored shell fragments rained down the wall. The railgun clattered into the grass, safety switch still in the ON position.

The wailers flew over the wall and landed inside the compound.

They detonated with a cacophony of high-frequency sound that did to organic brain function what EMPs do to electronics.

Scramble.

Tentacles flailed in a wave. *Surge!*

Torinds scaled the walls with their suction-cupped limbs. They poured directly into the innards of the base, smashing windows and rolling inside, slaughtering anything that moved.

Sonic blasters howled. Concussive waves rippled through the air. Armor cracked and disintegrated. Bones fractured into spurs. Spurs pierced internal organs. Blue blood stained the duracrete. Aveo sentries collapsed into pebbles and organic scraps.

The base fell quickly to the torind onslaught.

On the north wall, no one managed to spool up the two HR-270 emplacements, so called for their incredible firing rate of 270 bolts per second; if they had, the basewide alarms would have gone off, the human Quick Reaction Force would have been mobilized, and the outcome may have been different.

Explosions rocked the gate at the south wall. Wailers detonated, screaming like a horde of ravenous banshees. The blast radii spread through the ground until the check station's foundations crumbled, burying the pair of aveo gate guards under an avalanche of duracrete and armor plates.

The siege of the newest 9N HQ took thirty minutes. The news didn't hit the rest of the galaxy for another two days when a video broadcast from Nea Nia, initially livestreamed to the vesper net, was leaked to the galaxy wide net.

Navy intelligence identifies the victim as Representative Guri Malabar, a middle-aged man with twenty-seven years of service in the Liberty House. He is survived by a wife, two children, and one grandchild.

The video receives over one billion plays the first day it is leaked, and the numbers are climbing. Porthole, the most popular video platform on the galaxy net, tries to pull the video from its site, but they cannot stop the millions of users from uploading it again and again, sharing it across their LifeLog social media pages.

To anyone who has ever watched a government broadcast, the brilliant amber lights over the Liberty House stage and representatives' chairs would be instantly recognizable. The man with the bruised face, broken nose, and split lips tied to a chair at the head of the dais would seem out of place. The squid-like humanoid that slaps the back of the man's head would likely be perceived as a monster from a nightmare or a twisted fairy tale to some viewers. The camera zooms in to put the man and the monster into full focus.

The monster speaks in gurgles and hisses. It is a brutish sound with hard H's and slurred S's that are clearly not human, although the video had been dubbed with human language by a translator AI.

"The BarbS of JuStice Have Seized control of Nea Nia, our rightful home world."

A banner pops up below the video with the LifeLog corporate logo. They're the biggest social media company; Porthole is just a platform for vids.

FACT CHECK: According to over 150 experts and the Interstellar Research Council, torinds and aveo share a common ancestry that can be traced back 2.7 million years to the planet Immunio, not Nea Nia.

Four grayish-white eyes blink sideways as the speaker continues in its gargling tongue.

"TorindS Settle tHiS world now to complete the Great Circle."

FACT CHECK: According to the Interstellar Research Council, "the great circle" is a prophecy unique to torind religious texts that is not based on objective science. Many radical extremists rely on ancient religious texts and ideologies to excuse violence. Torinds are a largely peaceful race of sentient beings, although in recent years, small fringe extremist groups have infiltrated parts of their military and government infrastructure.

A groan leaves the bloodied lips of the man in the chair. His C-skin, smart threads that display the Liberty House pattern of navy blue and eggshell white, is flecked with his own blood. The gaudy Nine Nations emblem, a gold dot surrounded by nine silver circles, blinks weakly. It continues to glitch when the torind turns to him and emits a low, wordless gurgle.

The squid is laughing.

Tentacles spiral up to the man's face. Tiny suction cups gently wipe away his tears.

The man's face is stretched with fear. Trapped in his eyes is the reflection of the torind's open maw: a pink fleshy spiral of hooked teeth.

An animalistic scream bursts from the man's throat. It is not enough to drown out the *pop, pop.*

The same tentacles that gently brushed his tears slither around his neck. The blue and gray alien appendages darken to purple as they squeeze.

The screaming stops. It ends with a gurgle, a choke, and a crack.

The torind lifts the man's severed head toward the camera, proudly showing the empty eye sockets. The mouth is open in a silent scream.

"ThiS iS a meSSage to any wHo defy the Barbs of JuStice."

The alien blinks its eyes a few times and laughs. It then proceeds to consume the man's brain through the eye sockets. It passes the disfigured head back and forth with a cohort, cheeks tightening and flaring as they take small drags of brain. As the aliens imbibe the representative's vital fluids, the blue effervescence beneath their translucent membrane layer begins to swirl with red particles.

This lasts for the final two minutes of the video.

From a human perspective, the death of Guri Malabar is a tragedy. It is enough to crush his family and to incite a response from humanity, the ninth nation of the Nine Nations.

The Human Marine Corps makes ready for war.

PLASMA STRIKES DECIMATE the ground like stomps from an angry giant, spewing plumes of dirt and whiskey-colored grass into the air. Soil glows red until a violent flash of white transforms it to glass. If you listen in between bombing runs, you can hear it: the electric scream of lasers charging and discharging. *Crack-sizzle* as the air burns. The *ka-doom* of plasma impact. The crash and spread of white-hot plasma sounds like a large slab of ice breaking off the face of a glacier as it slams into the water but in reverse. The splash is the spreading plasma. Then the ground temperature crosses the 2,000-degree Celsius threshold, and *vwoosh*: the cracking glacier face sound is erupting plasma crystallizing. The impact sites are immortalized in an endless sprawl of barbed glass sculptures.

That is what glassing a planet's surface sounds like.

Glassing an entire planet is, regrettably, against the Fair War Act. That was not what the Marine Corps was doing. Glassing a city— or in this case, the outer defenses of a former 9N embassy—was well within the boundaries of galactic law.

The fog of war spread over the outskirts of the hellhole formerly known as the Nine Nations DMZ of Nea Nia.

The embassy, once an ornate building with marble pillars and ornate duraglass panes that shimmered in the sunlight, was no longer a diamond in the sprawling grasslands. After the Human Marine Corps had given its best—for just over twenty straight hours—the plasma-cannon launches and laser-blast strafing runs from the AF-52 bombers left the former DMZ a misshapen lump of coal in a sea of glass. A full-fledged bomber wing consisting of twenty-four Atmospheric Fortress craft could glass an entire continent if they needed to; the Corps had decided to fly four of them over the base, allowing them to drop ten percent of their payload each. Surgical precision, they called it.

Inside the dropship, a DS-130, Sanctification Company of the 209th Marine Exosolar Force was locked, loaded, and ready for war. Turbulence rocked the craft as it entered the atmosphere, knocking joints and rattling teeth. Precombat jitters were in the air. Sanctification Company—referred to as Sanitation Company by the grunts when the brass wasn't around—was made up of three squads; Sewer Squad, Scrap Squad, and the most seasoned Dumpster Squad, led by Sergeant Demarius T. Hinton. The moniker had been given official designation by the company commander, Captain Maccabee, when he had still been a first lieutenant. He said it was because they were often the cleanup crew for situations where diplomacy had failed, and he was right.

"Tiamat?" PFC Johnson asked.

Corporal Nichols's feminine voice replied, "Tiberius. He's into history. It's gotta be Tiberius."

"No momma would name her son something stupid like that," Demarius scoffed.

Private Milan, the new guy, asked, "Trenton?"

"Nope."

"Tyrone?"

"Not even close."

"Com discipline," a gruff voice responded. "Sergeant Hinton, nobody gives a fuck what your middle name is."

"Uh, Gunny, I kinda do," Milan said.

Sergeant Demarius T. Hinton double-checked the seal on his Battle-skin's helmet.

"Thirty seconds." That came from the pilot.

"Can it!" Demarius said to the laughing marines around him. "If you make it through this mission, I'll tell you."

Private Milan groaned. "C'mon, Sergeant, I'm dying to know!"

Demarius threw a glare at the young private. "You'll be dying if you don't get your shit together. Check your neck seal."

"Roger that," Milan said weakly.

Nea Nia had an oxygen-rich atmosphere, so he could breathe without a helmet if he had to, but the weather report showed the ambient temperature was forty degrees Celsius with seventy percent humidity. The warmest days on Mattox had never come close to heat like that. The environmental control system in the B-skin worked best when it was not leaking air conditioning through a rolled seal.

Marine combat armor could take a direct hit from a .50 caliber round with little more than a dent. Ballistic gel between plate layers absorbed most of the impact, so the human inside wouldn't suffer lethal internal damage. That didn't stop it from stinging or knocking the wind out of you. The extra weight required servo-assisted joints to keep the marine's movements fluid and precise. To say a marine in a B-skin was like a tank would be an insult; they were more like human-sized mechs, as close to a cyborg as one could get without surgical implants. Cyborgs and other such Human 2.0 technologies were outlawed pending an ethics review by the Liberty House that was lost in the sinking mire of galactic politics.

When he wasn't on deployment, Demarius spent his off time

catching up on the Interstellar Fighting League or working out in the gym. As far as he was concerned, posthumanism was a political question, and he hated politics. He joined the military because it got him off Mattox, his home world, and because things had happened on his home world that he wanted to forget.

He brushed his gauntleted hands down the ablative chest piece of his B-skin, his fingers catching in imperfections. One dent, large enough to catch with a fingernail, was from an 11.7-millimeter slug he'd caught on a backwater planet five years ago. A round that size could have holed any military armor back before humans tasted space. Now that orbital drops were the norm and alien tech had been reverse engineered, improved, and standardized, even the grunt-level armor was cutting edge.

Technology is a hell of a thing. As incredible as it is dangerous.

Demarius was a large man, even for a marine. Unfortunately, that meant people assumed he was a hardass, always spoiling for a fight, and that he thought he was better than people smaller than himself. Demarius worked hard to combat this with a good dose of humor when he could. Military customs and courtesies being what they were, it was hard not to joke around to the point of crossing the line into unprofessionalism.

A jolt shook through the ship. G-forces pressed his back flat against his seat. The back of the craft split with a thin line of light that grew wider as the drop door opened with a mechanical groan.

"Dammit, Brisk," Demarius said through clenched teeth. "I haven't had a ride this rough since I visited your mom on leave."

"Nearing the drop site," the pilot deadpanned. "Hinton. Fuck you."

Demarius chuckled.

The Heron dropship he rode in was the heavy-duty workhorse of the Corps. The Herons had been used in the earliest days of the Ion Trail voyages by a fledgling Space Corps. Back when marines were sent to secure or conquer uncharted worlds. The way the ship creaked and strained in atmo, it felt every bit like the relic it was.

He had to duck to lean out of the dropship. Condensation whipped around the edges of the door. Droplets ran across his visor. It was like peering through a cloud.

Six thousand meters below, brown smears of grass became white and green fractals of glass. Eventually the carbon-scored walls of the 9N embassy came into view. Seeing it through the HUD in his helmet, it could have been an ancient castle, the walls of which cracked and crumbled like they'd been beaten down over centuries. Once-verdant grasslands were now decimated by the standard greeting of the HMC; sheets of "surgical" hellfire from above until the target was softened up and ripe for penetration by ground forces.

Ground action on glassed planetary surfaces was problematic and typically avoided. Hence, the mission objective to capture the sole-surviving high-value target and eliminate the rest of the hostile forces was going to be done by dropping the marines right in the lap of the enemy; they were going to land *inside* the walls of the base rather than drop outside and try to work their way in across the difficult terrain.

"Chute plates on, marines," Gunnery Sergeant Keller called out in his gruff voice.

Demarius pulled the backpack thruster off the wall above his seat. It reminded him of the pocket rockets he'd seen on reality TV. Core-world kids made a game of jumping between buildings at dizzying heights like it was some kind of sport. One slip or malfunction, and a kid could plummet hundreds of levels to their death.

Mechanical ratchets click-clicked around him as Dumpster squad attached their chute plates.

Corporal Alice Nichols was a tough bitch; she had been with Sanitation Company for the better part of a year, and he'd seen her kick some serious ass. She was the best fire team leader companywide, as far as he was concerned.

Private Grigory Milan was a solid rifleman. He was one of those typical new guys who was still feeling out the military lifestyle. That included asking dumb questions and not taking things as seriously as he probably should, but the kid had heart. Demarius liked him.

Private First Class Floyd Johnson, a new addition to Nichols's fire team, had never seen combat before, but his PT and firing-range scores were high enough that Demarius was confident he'd be a solid replacement for the man they'd lost on the last deployment. That was an incident he didn't want to dwell on, but it came down to a private that didn't understand the importance of taking cover. An enemy sniper exploited that error with a 20-millimeter slug that ripped the top half of his lid from his B-skin with his head still in it.

Sometimes, when Demarius closed his eyes, he could still see it happening.

Shuffling awkwardly with the extra weight of the chute plate on his back, Demarius bumped shoulders with Corporal Sanders. They locked eyes.

"Sucks to suck." Demarius shrugged.

Sanders sighed and shook his head but didn't offer a reply.

Corporal Sanders had gone through basic the same time as Demarius, but they weren't close. Sanders was too absent-minded to be considered a standout marine. The Corps felt the same way, and that was why Demarius had been given sergeant stripes. Demarius felt a little sorry for Sanders's fire team. He would hate to have his life in the hands of a marine who could barely manage to abide by grooming standards and was always lost in thought about something.

Sanitation Company's running joke was that Sanders should have gone to college. Between missions, Sanders was glued to his bunk, where he wrote poetry and drew pictures to go along with the words. He did the pictures digitally on his Pulse, but that didn't stop some of the navy troops from making jokes about marines eating crayons. Sanders hated those jokes; he took himself very seriously. Drawing pictures other than large, veiny male anatomy—on government-issue property, usually—was not very marine-like behavior, but he qualified as a marksman and was damn good at a distance.

Lieutenant Billens jabbed toward the open door with a hand like a knife edge and said, "Line it up!"

With a gruff bark straight from the diaphragm, a technique somehow mastered by all senior NCOs, Gunnery Sergeant Keller barked, "Sanitation Company! Time to TAKE OUT THE TRASH!"

Fifty marines gave an *Oorah!* to that.

They were lined up from stem to stern of the dropship, rifles on their chests and chute plates attached to their backs. A dim red light above the open hatch pulsed once, twice, and flipped to green.

"Go, go, go!" Billens called out.

One by one, the marines shuffled out the back of the dropship.

Demarius entered the air stream in full free fall.

The freedom of touching the open sky, arms outstretched and the view of the ground rushing up beneath your feet, was unlike anything else. Air roared around him. The shimmering blur of the glassed ground around the embassy began to sharpen. The altimeter in the Pulse on his wrist ticked away until it hit two thousand meters. Black-and-gray clouds covered portions of the base, but the embassy was in full view. He tucked his chin and crossed his arms over his chest as the chute plate fired off.

It was like riding a fireball. The plume lit off at forty-five-degree angles, slowing his descent to a predetermined value calculated by the chute's computer. It was over quick. A total of a minute and a half of free fall and just over a minute of controlled burn with the chute plate. At ten meters, he ejected the chute plate and executed a parachute landing fall, or PLF, to soften the impact on his knees.

He rolled to his feet and picked himself up off the ground, pulled his Squad Automatic Rifle from his back, and flicked the safety off with his thumb while running his off hand down the length of the heat bleed cable from the stock of his weapon to the heat sink reservoir on his back. No snags. He finished with a pull of the charging handle. The SAR primed with an electric whine.

Absent the roar of the dropship and the jump, it was quiet down here. The concussive power of the air assault had driven the torinds inside the buildings, leaving the streets quiet and empty.

The air was thick with ionization. He could smell it through his helmet filters. Plasma-impact sites piped columns of smoke into the sky, giving the illusion of a typical overcast afternoon on a planet that had yet to see war. The exact locations of the two suns overhead were lost in the haze.

The landing put him just inside the base's outer wall. Corporal Sanders was already rounding up fire team Dumpster Bravo.

A large fissure split the main road lengthwise for a good stretch, exposing a pit of brown-and-red earth two or three meters deep. The road ended in a T intersection, with a two-meter-high blackened armor berm that separated the embassy grounds from the rest of the installation. Yesterday, proud-standing pillars decorated the face of the embassy; now, they were warped and wilted, the roof slanted toward the ground. On the east side of the street was a six-level parking garage that now stood two levels high; the roof level was caved in, the structure folded in on itself. Sewer and Scrap squads landed and headed west and northwest toward a cluster of small single-story buildings spread out to the edge of the base. Strafing runs had left the buildings pockmarked with holes, exposing insulation and debris.

Corporal Sanders patted Demarius on the back.

"Looks like a melted stick of butter, don't it, Sergeant?"

"Looks like your bunk after Taco Tuesday," Demarius replied.

Sanders gave him a flat look.

"Fire team Dumpster Bravo, you're on overwatch," Demarius said. "The parking garage."

"Roger."

Sanders shouldered his Marksman Laser Rifle, which had an extended barrel and an upgraded scope, and waved for his fire team to follow him. Demarius watched the four marines hustle across the street, rifles up, until they had settled into some of the rubble next to the parking garage. Sanders, with the help of one of his marines, clambered up to the second level of the wreckage, where he and his spotter started scoping the street.

Two thuds hit the ground to his left. He turned to see Corporal Nichols and PFC Johnson recovering from their PLFs. Demarius had always been able to pick Nichols out in a crowd because she was about a head shorter than most marines. Johnson's crisp and clean B-skin, unmarred by combat, was a dead giveaway. Private Milan landed a moment later, allowing Demarius a relieved sigh. Dumpster Squad had landed safely.

"Fire teams Dumpster Alpha and Dumpster Charlie, rally up," Demarius called.

He chose an overpass to the east of the embassy that was covered by Corporal Sanders's position. It was part of the installation's magnetic rail transportation system, something that ran a figure eight throughout the base and was used by the administrative personnel— those that weren't cleared to stay on installation. Demarius looked, but he didn't see the tram anywhere along the length of the track, nor did he see any damage done to the magrail other than some minor carbon scoring from the aerial bombardment.

The objective was to penetrate the 9N HQ proper, rescue any live prisoners, and execute all torinds with extreme prejudice, but that didn't mean they had to rush in like a bunch of cowboys. Cowboys always died. That was why Demarius hated space westerns. They weren't realistic. Tales of overly romanticized frontiersman leaving trails of bodies and illegitimate children in their wake just wasn't his bag. Credits rolling with melancholy fanfare as the poor bastard drew his last breath and bled out on the back of a skiff…puke factor ten.

Lieutenant Billens's voice filled the frequency.

"All squads in position. Stand by. We're getting intel that the torinds are willing to negotiate."

Yeah, right, Demarius thought.

Groans of disappointment filled the squad channel. Marines were always itching for combat; that was what separated them from other branches of the military. Naval warfare was like a gentleman's video game, played over computer screens with sensors and presses of buttons, strings of commands typed into computers and broadcast over frequencies. Space battles were fought across vast distances with a lot of nerd-level mathematics and long periods of waiting that were of no interest to Demarius.

He was a marine, and because he was a machine gunner, he preferred combat the old-fashioned way. It was the same reason he preferred the old-school fight league to the mech leagues. Who cared about robots making scrap of each other? He wanted to physically dismantle the enemy, to feel the adrenaline as he exerted his will to live over the other guy.

That was how a naïve Demarius had seen it before he'd been in the trenches of Espair.

He'd seen friends die. Even smart marines who did everything right, sometimes they got killed too. War was what humanity did best, but no one could account for random chance. The idea of "when your number comes up" holds true no matter how advanced your technology, tactics, or training.

"Hey, guys…I'm not seeing those 270s on the northern wall."

Demarius sighed. Intel had dropped the ball on that one.

"Wait…we've got something," Corporal Sanders called out. "One tango, embassy steps."

Demarius shouldered his back against one of the magrail's girders and peered around it. His lid, the high-tech helmet of his B-skin, zoomed in for a clear view of the steps and the twisted pillars at the entrance of the embassy.

A single squid rolled down the steps, waving a Nine Nations flag. Flag waving was a cross-species gesture of surrender, a sort of call for a ceasefire. Demarius didn't believe it was sincere, but the rules of engagement and the Fair War Act were clear: executing enemy combatants who were trying to surrender was the fast track to a tribunal, dishonorable discharge, and indefinite confinement for war crimes.

He kept his finger clear of the trigger just to avoid the temptation.

Lieutenant Billens, flanked by Gunnery Sergeant Keller and Lance Corporal Ericson of Dumpster Charlie, exited cover to approach the squid. The lieutenant slid his rifle onto the back of his B-skin and put his hands out almost in a "calm down" gesture as he took slow steps toward the flag waver.

"Stand down, torind. This embassy is now under control of the Human Marine Corps. Order your men to—"

"Stop yourSelf, Human," the alien gurgled. "TorindS will SurrenDer if HumanS lay down weaponS and negotiate in good faitH."

Lieutenant Billens stopped himself at the base of the steps. The two marines to his sides held the squid in their sights, trying to track the blur of tentacles that coiled frenetically.

"Stand down, now. That's an order. You're going to tell your people to surrender. You'll be given standard Nine Nations treatment appropriate for prisoners of war, and we'll go from there."

The torind shook its head. Pink-and-white folds of brain, visible through its aqueous membrane, quivered. Foam ejected from between mouth tentacles as it spat a response.

"We will not accept tHeSe termS."

The squid dropped the flag. All hell broke loose.

The windows of the embassy shattered, unleashing a torrent of squids that jumped down to the ground, sonic blasters firing in all directions. Gunnery Sergeant Keller shoved the LT back toward cover with one hand and opened up with the rifle in his other hand. The laser bolts bit into one then two torinds. The rest went wide in a hailstorm of sonic blasts. His armor and body fragmented in a red mist of clattering plates.

The lance corporal made it to cover.

Demarius was amazed: Gunny had sacrificed himself to give them time to scramble behind the lip of a fountain. Shielded them from enemy fire with his own body.

Hell of a marine, Demarius thought.

"Weapons free! Weapons free!" Billens screamed.

"Sergeant Hinton!" Ericson barked over the cacophony, "If you get your squads up here and put down some fire lanes, I can get the LT out of here."

"Copy that. We're en route. Dumpster Charlie, suppressing fire! Alpha, hop that berm!" Demarius called to his fire teams. "Nichols, move up!"

WHOO! 'Scuse me, I burp when I get excited.

Yeah, have her bring another round. Talking this much dries out the pipes, you know?

Where was I? Did I get to the grenade part? No?

Oh, uh...forget I said that.

Thanks, darling. Ah. All right, here we go.

THE MARINES PRESSED IN, weapons lighting up the surge of torinds as they spread out into the streets like a mob in riot mode. Cover and concealment were not a concern for the enemy. They operated with a run-and-gun mentality, separating to avoid fire and coalescing to concentrate the brunt of their fire on specific marine positions. Fire team Dumpster Charlie peppered the stream of torinds with enough blaster fire that they were forced to fall back toward the embassy, hopping the seam in the road. This gave Dumpster Alpha clearance to proceed up the east side.

Corporal Sanders sent methodical shots from his vantage point high in the parking garage. Each blast was like a lightning strike from some angry demigod as high-intensity laser bolts lanced into the sea of tentacles. Torinds unlucky enough to catch one of those bolts were knocked to the ground like dying insects. Fleshy membranes sizzled. Tentacles flailed.

A cluster of fifteen or twenty aliens finally tried to hole up behind three abandoned vehicles near the embassy grounds, their backs to the east side of the street.

Right in Demarius's sight picture.

Demarius broke cover at a crisp walk, peppering the exposed flank of the clustered torinds with his SAR in short, controlled bursts. Each burst dropped two or three torinds into crumpled heaps of twitching tentacles. The weapon barely recoiled against his shoulder—it wasn't like the movies. Laser weapons had virtually no kickback, but they were loud as hell.

The surviving torinds opened up with return fire.

Demarius lowered his SAR and rolled over the berm as kinetic waves slammed into the half wall. Chunks of asphalt and duracrete peppered his armor.

"Cutting it a little close there, aren't you, Sergeant?" Corporal Nichols asked.

Demarius smiled. Shoulder to shoulder with Nichols, there was a part of him that was having the time of his life.

"This is going to be over quick once we're inside. I didn't want to miss out on all the action," he said, casting a glance in the direction of the opulent fountain. Near it were a scorched patch of grass and a few scraps of armor plates.

"Sanders, you have eyes on the lieutenant and lance corporal?"

Ten seconds went by with the com filled with the sounds of war. Laser fire and marines calling out targets and positions of the enemy, someone yelling, "Frag out!" a few seconds before the street shook with an explosion. When Sanders came into the frequency, his voice was calm and businesslike.

"Hell yes, Sergeant. The LT and Ericson are still holed up on the northwest side of the fountain. Squids ran right past them."

Demarius instructed his HUD to pull up Sanders's scope in a window.

The fountain, a twisted metal-and-silver thing that glittered in the mist it spewed from the top, was fifteen meters from the entrance to the embassy. It would have been a beautiful thing in a different context, Demarius thought. The surrounding area was empty of torinds; the bulk of them had rushed westward into the streets and to give Sewer and Scrap squads one hell of a firefight. Demarius was about to call to the lieutenant when he saw a small cluster of torinds peek their heads out of the main entrance. A large tube angled up at a forty-five-degree angle followed them.

Sanders grunted. "That's not good. They're setting up a plasma cannon on the embassy steps."

"I see it," Demarius said. He closed the scope window, and keyed his comm. "Ericson, if you or LT have any frags, toss them on the steps."

Lieutenant Billens gave a mirthless laugh. "Absolutely not, Sergeant. We'll cave in the main entryway. That could bring the whole building down! I need air support, right now! I need a rod drop or a strafing run—something!"

"Understood," Demarius replied. "Sanders, get me a laser lock on the front steps of the embassy."

"Lining it up now, Sergeant." Sanders's reply was dripping with excitement. Calling in air support was an undisputed favorite part of the job. Most marines weren't the kids who watched fireworks and thought they looked pretty; they were the kind who gathered up a group of friends, bought a bunch of bottle rockets, and took turns shooting them off at each other.

It's just fun to watch shit explode, Demarius thought with a smile.

Especially when it's not your *shit exploding.*

"Sanitation Actual, this is Sanitation Two requesting a strafing run, danger close. Coordinates painted. We have eyes on target."

The wait for a response from the captain was agonizingly slow. Nichols, Johnson, and Milan alternated popping up from cover to send a few bolts across the street. Each time, they managed to duck before return fire distorted the air above them. Milan dropped to a knee and looked over to Demarius, his eyes wide inside his helmet.

"There's a whole damn lot of them, Sergeant."

Sanders said, "He ain't lying. You've got a dozen or more breaking off from engaging with Sewer Squad, and they're making a beeline for you. There wasn't supposed to be this many! If we don't get air support soon, we're gonna be overrun."

Demarius replied, "Sanders, stand by until Sanitation Actual gives us a reply."

"Affirmative, Sergeant." The tone of his voice was a lot less excited now.

"Swapping sinks!" Nichols called.

Milan broke cover to throw down a salvo as a smoking heat sink fell from Nichols's CLR. She quickly replaced it with a fresh one from her belt.

"Attention, Sanitation Company, this is Sanitation Actual," Captain Maccabee's voice came in over the company frequency. "Air support request is denied. Danger close is an understatement; the lieutenant is *in* the requested fire zone."

Lieutenant Billens practically screamed, "Negative, Captain. Lance Corporal Ericson and I are going to die if we don't get this air support. Do not send reinforcements. I say again, do not send reinforcements unless they come for us with body bags!"

Lieutenant's losing his damn mind, Demarius thought.

"Negative, lieutenant." The captain's voice was oddly detached, like he was informing someone they should put their seat belt on. "Evacuate the fire zone or find a workaround. Sanitation Actual out."

NAVCOM not opting for air support was the wrong call. Nothing pissed off the boots on the ground more than armchair commanders who thought they knew better. Sometimes they did, because the big picture was seen most clearly above the battlefield, but not always. In instances like this, when seasoned marines were dealing with a simple problem, the easiest way to lose the respect of your troops was to completely ignore the input of people who were actually in the AOR, doing the fighting.

That left Demarius with a decision to make. He was in control of the fire teams, Billens was in control of him, and the captain was in control of the lieutenant. If the captain refused a strafing run to deal with the plasma cannon, that was his call, even if he was making the call from the combat information center in orbit.

That didn't stop it from being a stupid call. He keyed his comm.

"Sanitation Actual, this is Sanitation Two acknowledging negative on air support. We have a workaround."

"Sergeant Hinton," the lieutenant said breathlessly, "belay that and get that air support worked out before—"

The lieutenant grunted. Sonic blasts filled the frequency.

Sanders said, "Squids are advancing on the lieutenant! They're setting up a perimeter around the cannon!"

"Sanders. Keep their heads down."

"Roger." Sanders's reply was followed with back-to-back blasts from his marksman rifle.

"What's the workaround?" Johnson asked Demarius.

Demarius put a hand on the PFC's shoulder. "We're going in. You're watching right flank. Nix has left flank. Milan's on support."

Johnson nodded, his face grim.

"Hard copy on that," Corporal Nichols said a bit too enthusiastically.

Sergeant Demarius Hinton glanced at the indicator in his HUD. Heat sink reservoir showed eighty-five-percent capacity. That would give his SAR about four minutes of uninterrupted firepower before the sink reservoir went black, and he'd have to switch to his sidearm.

The squad automatic rifle could unleash a lot of hell in four minutes.

"That's your workaround?" Private Milan asked. "Bum rush them?"

"What's these numbers on my patch, private?"

Milan read them aloud. "Zero three three...one?"

"And what does that make me?" he deadpanned.

"A machine gunner, Sergeant."

Demarius shouldered his weapon and gave the kid a curt nod.

"Damn straight, son. Torinds ordered a big gun, and that's what they're gonna get."

He scrambled up and over the wall. When his boots hit the grass of the embassy lawn, he opened up with his SAR on full auto. The weapon shrieked, spewing a blaze of laser fire so thick and bright Demarius's visor dimmed to shield his eyes.

The squids' perimeter around the plasma cannon fell to the hailstorm of bolts. A half-dozen more rushed to replace their fallen comrades, ignoring the incoming fire as they hustled with the cannon. Demarius kept his weapon steady, blasting the enemy until the only torinds left around the cannon were lying on the ground, dead or dying. Three torinds on the east side of the lawn abandoned their advance on the lieutenant's position, turning their weapons to Demarius.

Laser bolts streamed around him, past him, and cut the enemy down before they could get a shot off. He didn't have to glance left and right to see Nichols's fire team had advanced with him. Sensing the immediate threat was dealt with, he eased off the trigger. His HUD showed a twenty-seven-percent charge left on his SAR's heat sink reservoir.

A scorched torind head plopped onto the grass beside him, trailing white smoke as it rolled to a stop a few meters away. The decapitated body collapsed a moment later.

"I got you, Sergeant," Sanders called.

"Good looking out, Corporal. Dumpster Squad, all fire teams on me."

Several marines voiced acknowledgments and started to hop the wall.

"I'll disable that thing," Demarius said to Nichols and Johnson. "Stay alert, eyes up."

The plasma cannon's stabilizing clamps were embedded into the duracrete in the doorway. Demarius could not see any indication it was primed, but he wasn't taking any chances. He approached the deadly weapon with his rifle up and finger hovering by but not on the trigger.

"Sergeant Hinton, sitrep?" Lieutenant Billens asked.

Demarius was about to call in the all-clear until the green glow of a plasma ball appeared at the base of the cannon.

Corporal Sanders cursed in his ear.

Demarius saw it and reacted without thinking. Instinct took over. The part of the brain that moves your body for you, like a knee-jerk reaction with a massive dump of adrenaline.

Superheated plasma pulsed inside the cannon bore, indicating the weapon was primed. Demarius dropped his SAR and rushed the weapon with a guttural bellow like a professional Armor Tag player. He slammed his shoulder full force into the barrel's underside.

As powerful as the augmented strength of his B-skin was, it did not give him enough power to break the forward clamp, but it was enough to rip it clean out of the duracrete. The cannon pivoted ninety degrees on its axis as it completed the firing sequence in a blaze of light and heat.

A plasma shroud the size of a tank slammed into the ceiling of the embassy. Green swirls of liquid fire curled and chewed through the reinforced plating. Tiles and rebar groaned, twisted, and sagged.

Demarius's visor dimmed to maximum—almost pitch black—but his vision swirled with sunspots.

Then the building collapsed.

The walls stayed standing, sagging inward at a twenty-degree incline. The roof—the bits of it that were not completely incinerated—cracked and smashed down into the guts of the building. Structural webbing snapped like taut rubber bands in a cascade of crashes and hammer blows. A *ping-boom* advertised a direct hit on the power cell repository deep inside the building, from which sparks flew like angry hornets.

The Nine Nations embassy of Nea Nia erupted like a volcano, spewing shrapnel everywhere. Priceless sculptures, paintings, and pieces of computer stations sailed through the air in arcs of flame. Tattered shreds of beryllium alloy panels slammed into the dirt, shorn edges glowing an angry orange.

The shockwave tossed Demarius back three meters through the air. He hit the grass hard. His visor cleared as dirt spun around him, and he rolled a few more times, skidding to a stop at the lieutenant's boots.

The shock of the near-death experience made him slow to get to his feet. He glanced at the burning shambles that had been their objective, and then his eyes locked with the lieutenant. The officer looked pale.

"Thank you, Sergeant." The lieutenant gave a weak nod.

Demarius, feeling sheepish, nodded back. "For the record, sir... that did not go as planned."

"No," the lieutenant agreed, "I can see that."

Laser blasts and sonic booms roared in the distance. Scrap and Sewer Squads were still engaging torind insurgents to the west. Demarius's stunt with the plasma cannon served as an equivalent of air support, in a way, but it had also been overkill. Cut off from their command structure, the torinds were going to fight down to the last squid.

The com frequency crackled.

"Hey, uh, Lieutenant?" PFC Johnson asked. "Are we calling in search and rescue?"

Lieutenant Billens looked at the smoldering ruins of the embassy.

"No one is alive in that dumpster fire," he said.

Johnson nodded. "I agree, sir. I just didn't want us getting shafted with the cleanup detail."

Billens looked thoughtful.

"You may have a point, PFC. While this is still burning, I can't definitely say the VIP's dead or alive. I'll make the call."

"We working an LZ for extraction, sir?" Demarius asked.

"Shit-shit-shit!" Sanders said into the comm. "Tracking 270s being set up on the north berm, right by the check station!"

"Take 'em out!" Demarius called.

"I'm gonna have to move position. No clean shot."

Demarius swore. "Lieutenant, we need to move. Now."

"No shit. Fall back!"

The mystery of the missing 270s was solved, and it couldn't have been at a worse time. Murphy's Law was in full effect. It could go wrong, and it did.

Demarius, the LT, and Lance Corporal Ericson sprinted for the southwest berm that separated the embassy courtyard from the main street. Fire team Dumpster Charlie, a tough group of guys that Demarius had been through Espair with, was cut down in two seconds. One salvo of fire, bolts coming in so fast it sounded like one solid belch of fire, drew a line of scorched earth and fractured armor panels. Even B-skins couldn't stop overwhelming firepower of that magnitude.

Ericson was torn in half a meter to Demarius's left.

Demarius shoved the lieutenant over the berm and dipped his shoulder to roll over the half wall without slowing his momentum.

Crouched beneath the duracrete ledge, adrenaline burned his muscles. He breathed in the scent of burnt flesh and dirt. When Sanders called in fire team Dumpster Charlie as total KIA, he didn't have time to process the words as anything more than information. Pieces on a board. They could be people later, when he had time to mourn their loss properly.

"Sanders," Demarius called, "we're going to flank up the east side. Sewer Squad, hold position. Scrap Squad, break contact and cover the east flank. Dumpster Alpha, on me."

Lieutenant Billens grabbed him by the shoulder, his eyes narrowed. "We need to clear an LZ, or we are never getting out of here."

Demarius nodded. "Can't do that with those 270s in place, sir."

Billens sighed. "I know. We already got denied for air support. That probably means there's AA somewhere we haven't identified yet."

"All comm flash, sir," Corporal Nichols interjected, tapping her Pulse. "Squids just put out a livestream. They still have Ambassador Menschen."

"What?" Billens asked, reading the text on his own Pulse. "Damn. The VIP is still in enemy possession. That means..."

"That means Sanitation Company's got one helluva mess to clean up," Demarius said.

Sanders came in on the comm. "Sergeant Hinton, Dumpster Bravo in position on the east-side magrail."

"Copy that. Eyes on why the big guns are here?

"Affirmative, Sergeant. They converted the magcar to an orbital lift. No idea how the hell they did that. Looks like they were planning on shipping the VIPs off world this whole time."

Demarius raised an eyebrow.

"How?" the lieutenant said, chewing his lip. "Forget it. They didn't know about the lift, and they also didn't know there would be this many damn squids here. This isn't the first time intel dropped the ball."

"If they're gonna use the lift as an escape pod," Demarius reasoned, "magnetically accelerate themselves into space, activate a distress beacon?"

The LT shook his head. "Doesn't matter. Whatever they're planning, we're not letting them get off the ground."

Demarius keyed the companywide frequency. "Attention, Sanitation Company, this is Sergeant Hinton with a sitrep. Enemy position located north side of the embassy is now a priority-one target. Dumpster Bravo is on overwatch. Scrap Squad, make for the objective. Dumpster Alpha will support. Be advised: VIP is in their possession. Check fire until you have eyes on the prize."

"There will be no air support and no evac without that VIP, Sergeant."

"Hard copy on that, Lieutenant."

Demarius turned to the marines gathered around him. The weight of the situation spoke for itself. A standard op had just become a suicide mission. The marines, their B-skins dented and scuffed, had already been through hell. The road home was through the fire. They answered that revelation with shrugs and weapons checks.

Just another day in the HMC.

Johnson swapped his heat sink for a fresh one and slapped it to lock it in. He yanked his charging handle with angst. Demarius could see the resolve on his face through his helmet visor. Johnson wasn't scared; he was resigned to dying here if it came to that.

It almost certainly had.

Demarius's Pulse indicated he had one salvo's worth of charge in his SAR and two sinks for his L-pistol. It would have to be enough.

Seven minutes came and went, giving the remnant of Dumpster Squad a much-needed breather. And then Corporal Nadir called in, "Scrap Squad has made contact with the objective. Confirmed VIP, Ambassador Menschen, in enemy custody."

"Sanders, keep those 270s unmanned. Sanitation Company, engage!" Demarius ordered.

He brought the SAR's stock to his shoulder and rounded the corner of the demolished embassy.

Sanders's marksmen rifle rang out twice. The 270 barrels pointed skyward, their operators dead. More enemies scrambled to man them. Sanders blasted them.

Demarius's HUD blinked with a priority tag.

Four torinds dragged a disheveled and bloodied ambassador toward what looked like a detached maglift cart near the crumbled ruins of the embassy's northern wall.

"They got that up fast," Demarius muttered.

The path to the lift was saturated with laser bolts and concussive blasts.

"I've got eyes on the prize. I'm going in for recovery." He didn't wait for an acknowledgment. There wasn't time.

Sonic blasts screamed in his direction, forcing him to duck for cover. Duracrete cracked and rained around him. He dialed his SAR to beam and flicked the intensity dial all the way up. The rifle whined as it dumped the last salvo completely into the weapon's LCG. He popped up to firing position and squeezed the trigger.

The beam from his weapon lanced out. He swept his barrel from left to right, slicing a line of fire through the air. Along the steps leading to the lift, five torinds fell apart, their bodies sliced in two. He dropped the smoking SAR and the sink reservoir from his back and drew his sidearm.

Stepping out of cover, pistol up, Demarius jogged toward the lift, gunning down enemies as he moved. Scrap's fire teams covered him with perfect lanes. Severed tentacles and scorched membrane filled the air as he ran. He dropped his sink and slammed a new one home, covering the air between him and the door with indiscriminate fire. Two more torinds fell to his wild shots. A few paces back, he heard Dumpster Alpha opening up with their CLRs.

"What are they doing?" Nichols asked.

"I count six tangos, one VIP in the lift!" Johnson replied.

"I'm on it!" Private Milan shouted.

"Negative! Cover my six," Demarius ordered.

Demarius reached the lift. The blast door was nearly shut.

He threw his leg into the gap.

The door slammed into his leg. His thigh plate cracked, and for one pulse-pounding second, he envisioned his leg amputated.

The armor protested with a creak. But it held.

"Ambassador, get out of there!"

Demarius grabbed the VIP by the hem of his C-skin and yanked.

A wall of tentacles suctioned to the ambassador's neck and shoulders. His wrinkled face turned purple. A tentacle flashed out of the gap, the glint of a blade in its suction cups.

Demarius felt a hot line of pain slice across his neck. One hand flew to his neck. Blood poured over his fingers and inside his B-skin.

Demarius shoved his L-pistol into the gap and squeezed the trigger until the heat sink popped off, depleted and smoking. Squids squealed; membranes cooked. Tentacles whipped in a frenzy. He tossed the useless weapon into the lift, pulled a grenade from his belt, and yanked the pin.

Demarius couldn't throw the grenade into the lift with the ambassador still partly inside. One hand on his bleeding throat, he used the grenade like a club.

Squid faces caved in with spurts of ink and blood.

Cooked too long, Demarius thought.

He chucked the grenade over his shoulder.

"Let me help, Sergeant!" Private Milan rushed toward the lift. And the grenade.

Demarius shouted a warning, but a gurgle was all that came through the comm.

The grenade exploded.

Demarius wrapped his arms around the ambassador, shielding him from the concussive blast with his B-skin. The lift's door blew off its hinges, crushing the torinds still in the lift into pulped gore.

His ears rang. He checked the ambassador.

Unconscious but alive.

Demarius collapsed to his knees, gasping short, bloody breaths.

"Sarge…"

Private Milan was lying on the ground in a pool of his own blood. His B-skin was a smoldering, tattered ruin. He'd caught the grenade blast full-on.

Demarius's grenade.

The private's gauntleted hand tremored as he popped the seal on his helmet. It clattered to the ground next to him.

Demarius, lightheaded and battling shock at his injury, took a knee beside Private Milan. He swallowed blood but managed to hiss, "Sorry, kid."

"N-no, Sarge…" Milan's face was pale. He grabbed onto Demarius's arm with a tight grip. "I should…shouldn't have broke…" He groaned. "Broke my position."

"Stop…stop that," Demarius hissed. "You're gonna be fine, son. Corpsman!" He plugged the gash in his neck with a thumb. "I need a corpsman over here!"

Milan's eyes were soaked in tears. The pool of blood continued to spread.

"Sarge…you tell me…what the T stands for, now?"

Demarius's throat burned. His reply was garbled with blood and phlegm.

"What's that, Sarge?" Milan asked, his eyelids halfway shut.

"Teddy. It's Teddy, son. Not…Theodore. Teddy."

"Wow…you shittin' me?" Milan choked out a breathless laugh. His body shook for a few moments, and then he smiled. The shaking stopped.

Demarius set the private's lifeless hand on his chest.

"Well, I'll be damned," Lieutenant Billens said from beside him.

Sergeant Demarius Teddy Hinton didn't speak. He glared at the lieutenant, pressing his palm against the fallen warrior's face to close his eyes.

"Takes one hell of a marine to die laughing."

WORTH THE DRINKS you bought me, eh?

Oh, there was a big ceremony. Ambassador Menschen put

Demarius in for the Medal of Honor, and of course he got it. He's the Bare Knuckle Badass; how could he not?

Where am *I* at in this story? That's classified.

No, I've had enough for one night. My wife's gonna be pissed if I don't get home before the suns come up again. Being retired ain't all it's cracked up to be, kid. You'll think twice about traveling the stars, now, won't you?

What does it all mean? You want me to philosophize on the meaning of life?

This is the best I can do, and then I gotta get out of here.

The galaxy remains unmoved by the beings that populate its star systems. It is a dark, complex labyrinth spanning a hundred thousand light-years. Some see possibility in that vast expanse. I see cold indifference. Thousands of star systems spin and burn as they always have. The emotionless vacuum of space remains emotionless.

Wars are fought. People die. It'll always be this way.

The secret of the galaxy is that tragedies are never isolated incidents.

And politicians never let a good tragedy go to waste.

Don't believe me? You get a chance to interview that kid on the poster or the marine next to him, which one you think's got a better story to tell?

Ion Trail's a rough one.

ABOUT THE AUTHOR

Tyler E.C. Burnworth lives in the shadow of Area 51, a diamond in the desert wastes called Las Vegas. His days are spent as an F-16 mechanic, his nights as a husband to Lydia, his superhuman wife, and as a father to two rambunctious little ruffians whose public behavior determines whether they are claimed or not. The writing happens at that magic time of late night/early morning, a time most know as "sleep."

If you enjoyed this story, or Military SF in general, you can find Tyler's debut novel, *Redshift*, from Temple Dark Books, available December 1, 2021.

GUARDIAN FIST

By Matthew A. Goodwin

When a pilot loses his whole squad, he also learns a grim truth.

GUARDIAN FIST

A hissing breath escaped Anders Amakum's lips as he braced against the rattling ship. The damage was bad. He knew it was bad. With every jostling lurch, he expected to be auto-ejected out into space.

"Deevee Seven, status report," CFR Brown requested, her voice sounding tinny and distant in Anders's helmet.

"Hit," he said, having to force the words from his mouth. "Hit pretty bad."

"Ten four, I'm going to need more than that," Brown acknowledged.

Anders shook his head, not wanting his friend to see just how extensive the damage was but knowing she needed to.

"Sending status," he told her, pressing a gloved thumb against the button beside the system information display. Much of it was flashing red, and he heard a metallic pop behind him from within the bowels of the SF-1 Bersa Class fighter.

"Repeat," Brown said, and this time, Anders could hear the fear in her voice. She had lost too many. The mission had been so costly already, and she couldn't lose him too. Or rather, she couldn't lose his ship if she wanted any hope of surviving her meeting with NeoVerge management.

Looking at the display, Anders saw that the report hadn't sent. He punched the button with his thumb, feeling the hard plastic crack, but the report sent.

"That *is* bad," Lamont said, the grim joke sending a chill down Anders's spine as his friend fell in beside him. Lamont's head was straining in his cockpit, assessing the damage. Anders was relieved that he couldn't see Lamont's eyes. He didn't want to take on another's worry. Lamont added, "It may be more valuable to the company as parts."

"Cut the chatter, Deevee Four," Brown said, but her voice betrayed her. She got serious. "Anders, we've got a long way to go. You are just going to need to keep that ship together."

He chuckled, looking at the one long crack in the windscreen. It wasn't leaking yet, but that could change. "Yes, ma'am," he said through gritted teeth before adding, "This whole fleet is held together with cable ties and soldering irons. I'll be fine."

"Copy that," Brown said as her ship dropped in beside his. She gave a quick thumbs-up, and for just a moment, Anders believed that he might actually survive.

The moment was short lived.

"Contact, contact," cracked in his comms. "Dyeus fighters closing in fast."

"Deevees Nine and Four break off and try to get some kind of flanking position," Brown ordered. Her ship had been stolen recently and had tracking system technologies aboard that all the others could only dream of. She could see the three-dimensional battlefield as an augmented reality construct and make orders accordingly.

"Ten four," Lamont said, "but they've got us in their sights."

"Copy, hold formation," Brown said. "Keep Driver Seven safe."

Anders peered out the windscreen, looking into the light of the distant star. He couldn't see the enemy ships, but he knew they were out there. His HUD was damaged, and there were flickering lights of contact, but the readings were useless. He hated feeling like he needed protection, and he hated worse that, as always, it was Lamont and Brown who were doing the protecting.

Growing up, it had always been them. Like so many, the three were orphaned when their parents died in the revolt. Too few adults remained to care for all the kids left in the colony. "We are doing this for you, for *your* future," his mom had told him the night they left. The night they abandoned him on the cot in the cramped gymnasium full of kids on cots. They had worn the brave faces of proud parents, but he had seen their fear. He felt the fear too.

Scrawny and scared, Anders was an easy target for the bigger kids. That first night, a freckled blond kid who had developed early loomed over Anders. Healing scrapes on his knuckles told him everything he needed to know about the kid. Anders rolled onto his side, clutching the pillow as if it were his mother's arm.

"What did your parents leave you, new meat?" the blond asked, the threat clear in his tone. He might as well have just said, "Give me what you got, or I'll pummel you."

Anders sighed in immediate defeat. Having seen the kid and his two lackeys, Anders knew that he was going to just have to give it up. He might get beaten anyway. All the kids here were damaged, scared and miserable; this pain they would all take out on one another.

The blond kid smirked like a shark as he knelt to open the foot-locker to rifle through the few remaining possessions Anders had to his name.

"Ooh," he said, discovering something he liked. It didn't matter what it was. Anders knew he didn't want to part with it, but also that he would have no choice. For the first time, he became enraged with his parents for leaving him. They had reasoned with their nine-year-old son, tried to explain why they *needed* to overthrow Dyeus, but he hadn't cared or understood. All he had known was that they were leaving him. Whatever cause they were fighting for was irrelevant in the face of the cost. He wanted them back. Wanted to return to the little crawl space above the kitchenette that constituted his room. To smell Dad's cooking and hear Mom's singing.

He chewed the inside of his cheek to keep from calling out for them.

"Whoa, no way," the blond said in amazement. Anders didn't even lean up from his pillow, he just watched the boy's eyes as he rummaged.

It happened fast.

The blond was knocked aside when something struck him in the temple. He screamed out, and his two friends took off toward the door —they were followers for a reason. As the blond tried to get to his feet, a tough-looking girl pounced on him from out of nowhere.

"I thought I told you not to mess with the new kids," she hissed, grabbing his shirt collar in her left hand and balling a fist with her right.

"I was just introducing myself," the kid lied, like all bullies lied when caught.

"Get out of here," the girl said. "Before I 'introduce' you to my fist."

Anders was amazed by the girl. He had never seen anyone their age so strong, either physically or of will. Releasing the kid, who skittered away in anger and terror, she turned to look at Anders.

"Sorry about him," she offered with a crooked smile. Her gray coveralls were dingy and tattered and made Anders wonder how long she had been forced to live in them. Her long black hair was stiff, knotted and clearly hadn't seen a comb in a long time. But her eyes were bright and sharp.

"It's okay," Anders forced, leaning up, the hard fabric hardly shifting under his weight.

She marched over and extended a hand. Dirt was caked under her nails, and her palms were hard and calloused. "Imani Brown," she announced. "And that deadeye over there is my brother, Lamont."

A few cots down, Lamont stood, tossing a hard ball up with a proud smirk.

Anders smiled. He knew he had found his people.

———————————

"NEGATIVE, NEGATIVE," Anders said. "My weapons work fine."

"Stand down, Deevee Seven," Brown said.

Anders patched over to a private channel. "Imani," he said quietly, "we need all guns blazing, and you can't keep more ships sitting idle to keep me safe. We'd be sitting ducks anyways. Just let me fight."

He could hear the resignation in her voice as she said on the main channel, "Weapons free, all fighters engage."

Anders smiled. If he was going to die, at least it would be in a blaze of glory.

"Here they come," someone said, and Anders looked out into space. There were ten of them. A scout team. But a well-armed scout team.

They were outnumbered two to one, but Anders still felt like they could take them. Every pilot of theirs was worth ten of Dyeus's. The company that his parents had fought so hard to free themselves from valued the technology more than the people. To Dyeus management, a ship fresh off the assembly line was much more valuable than the person piloting it.

Pushing the throttle forward, Anders had to brace as the whole ship shuddered violently. He expected her to sputter out and die, but instead the thrusters engaged, and he was going.

The Dyeus ships were much newer models, freshly manufactured on Earth with the newest weapons from Kingfisher Munitions. This was as far a cry from Anders's ship as was possible. His Bersa was at best a 'classic' and at worst a 'relic.' The company that made the fighter no longer even existed, and engineers had to cobble together parts that, as the crew chief loved to say, "worked good enough."

Vaguely triangular in shape, it had the classic wings pointing out from either side of the body, a cockpit at the front and an engine and thrusters behind. It had smaller propulsors all along the body so it could bank and turn in space, forward- and rear-facing launchers and a Galilei drive. The paint job was nothing to note. While many NeoVerge pilots took great pleasure in designing the look of their ship exactly, Anders was more interested in what was under the hood than what was on top of it.

Imani caught up to him once again, turning her head toward him. With her helmet, oxygen mask and visor, none of her face was visible, but he knew the look she was giving him. The look she had been giving him their whole lives.

On the private channel, she told him, "Don't die."

"I won't," he said with such certainty that he even believed it himself.

The Dyeus ships were nearly upon them. Anders banked, dropping his Bersa out of formation. He saw the two fighters that had been assigned to him drop too. His eyes narrowed, and he took a slow breath. He could take down two.

He dropped his nose and continued to dive, pulling the two pursuers away from the rest of the action. He flipped the autotargeting on for the rear cannons. Checking his depleted ammo, he knew he had to be careful. His opponents' beam weapons relied on a charge that could easily be refilled by the solar intake panels on their ships. Once they started firing, they didn't have to stop as long as there was a star nearby. And here, there was.

Anders whirled and killed the thrusters, spinning his Bersa to face the Dyeus fighters coming in fast. The targeting computer did its best to predict the speeds of the incoming ships as Anders pressed the trigger. One attacker pulled up as the micromissiles fired from the Bersa. The other turned and returned fire.

Anders wheeled his ship out of the way of the beam, feeling metal pieces that had been jarred loose in the last fight clang around within the ship. A few of his missiles peppered the enemy ship, blasting open some holes and shredding one part of the left wing but not doing enough damage to stop it. The ship that had passed turned and came up on Anders's tail.

The indicator light flashed wildly, and the beeping began to scream in his ear. He loved this old girl. Engaging the rear-facing cannons, he let forth a volley into the follower just as it fired at him.

Anders barrel-rolled, one of the beams clipping the tip of one of his wings and putting a hole through it, small pieces of shrapnel floating out into space. The enemy ship rocketed by and kept going.

Anders smirked. "One down," he said to himself as it kept going off into the void. He loved his old clunker. As the other ship came around, Anders looked up to see the dogfight going on above his head. Dots of the missiles and blue lines of the lasers danced back and forth against the starlit sky. It would have been beautiful if it hadn't meant imminent death for his friends.

Narrowing his eyes, he saw where he needed to go. Lamont's ship with its gold stripe stood out from the rest, and it was in pursuit. A beam lit up the sky around the cockpit, and he dropped the Bersa quickly. He had been lucky but wouldn't be so again.

Looking down, he saw he had one more chance. He fired the flares, filling the space behind his ship with self-oxygenating bursts as he targeted the ship Lamont was chasing. From below, Anders was able to fire a burst into its belly and kill the pilot. These Dyeus flyboys were doomed by their lack of training.

Lamont knew the play, throttling back and allowing Anders to cross his path with the Dyeus ship right behind. Lamont made short work of the follower and chirped into the comms, "Good work, bud." After a pause, he added, "You are dropping pieces quickly."

Anders didn't need reminding.

"I'm out and got four on my six," Brown said, her voice desperate. Their dependence on ammunition always put them in a position of weakness, and if Imani didn't have anything left, she was in trouble. But, of course, she loved trouble.

Lamont and Anders didn't speak. Both fell into position and spotted Imani taking evasive action while being tailed by the four fighters. The two accelerated toward her.

"You take far right, I'll take left, and we will meet in the middle," Anders said. Lamont didn't answer, but his ship moved into perfect position.

"I'm hit, I'm hit," they heard Deevee Nine call out before the indicator light went black on Anders's cracked display. He couldn't focus on the loss; he had to remember only what was in front of him.

"And now," Anders murmured, and he opened fire. Lamont did the same, and the two far ships were ripped apart in a moment. The enemy ships increased their fire on Imani as she continued to dodge the blue beams stretching through space.

The right ship peeled off, and Lamont followed, but Anders stayed in hot pursuit. The computers beeped as they targeted, and he pressed the trigger again, firing his second-to-last burst.

He felt a jolt and heard a clonk as his ship stopped reacting. The thrusters died, and the ship became little more than a metal tomb. It was surreal. After so much high-speed movement, now he just floated in space weightlessly. No more sounds, no more flashing lights. It was a moment of perfect tranquility.

He sighed, hearing the slight hiss of oxygen, and looked out the windshield. Terror coursed through his body, and he watched the Dyeus ship break off and turn toward him.

There was nothing he could do. He closed his eyes, knowing what came next.

He had felt that way once before.

Three years earlier, at sixteen, he and Lamont and Imari had walked into the recruitment office. The newly formed NeoVerge Industries was looking for soldiers, and the three had no other choices.

Having picked up a little work as a delivery driver, he decided to sign up for the Space Division, figuring flying a fighter ship was probably pretty similar to driving a hovertruck. It was an hour into day one that he realized how wrong he had been.

During training, he heard a laugh coming from over his shoulder as he made his way back toward his barrack. Turning, he saw Skyler, the blond kid all grown up. They had been moved to different orphanages, but Anders knew his face immediately.

"Look, boys," he said dramatically, strolling over in utter confidence. "A little shit grew up into a big dump."

The new lackeys laughed in the way lackeys always did. He could have said anything, and they would have laughed. Anders just shook his head. Some people never changed.

"Look at me when I speak," Skylar said, moving in close. "I am an Assistant Junior Manager now."

Anders chuckled. "That's a lot of title for such a little man."

He watched as in slow motion. The blond's neck popped with veins, and his eyes went red as he wheeled back. New as he was,

Anders knew he couldn't hit officers, so he had closed his eyes and waited for the punch.

It didn't come.

Imari, who had just been promoted to Chauffeur First Class, caught the fist before it struck. She knocked the brute backwards with ease and looked over her shoulder at Anders, who shook his head in embarrassment.

"Come on," she told him. "Let's go make your parents proud."

HE WASN'T WELCOMED into the void.

Opening his eyes, he watched just in time as the Dyeus ship took him in their sights before getting speared through the bottom by Imani's ship. The two crunched together in a momentary explosion of the ships' air, like a seconds-long firework. Then it was just two more bits of scrap metal in space. It happened so fast that Anders's mind almost couldn't comprehend. He blinked, watching the twisted metal float away.

"No!" Lamont screamed into the comms as he came around. The pain and anguish were like a knife in Anders's heart. He felt it too. As he sat, powerless in his slowly spinning cockpit, he felt the pain of loss he had not known since that night.

That night when he was awakened by a man he didn't recognize. The man wore a rebel military uniform and sat on the edge of Anders's cot as though they were old friends.

"You are Anders Amakum?" he asked though he clearly knew the answer.

"Yes, sir," Anders had whispered all those years ago, knowing what the man was going to say. He had watched countless uniformed people tell countless children the same thing. His heart had broken every time for those kids though he had always been relieved it wasn't him.

Now it was.

And floating in the void, it was again.

He screamed, letting a lifetime's worth of pain out into his oxygen mask.

She had always been there for him. She had been everything he had needed when he had needed it. But she was gone. His parents were gone. Dyeus had taken them all.

Anders burned in his flight suit. He wanted to pull the straps off his shoulders, climb out of the ship and into the great black. Rage and misery tore at him, ripping his soul. He was so lost in his own drowning mind that he reached forward, flipping the shield off of the eject button.

"Don't you even think about that," Lamont said flatly through the battery-powered comms.

Anders just nodded. When he got mad, Lamont got calm. When Anders balled a fist, Lamont took a deep breath. They had always been different in that way.

"Just you and me now, and I can't have you going to that place, okay?"

"Okay," Anders murmured, trying to keep himself in the here and now.

"I fired a distress beacon, but we both know the company has bigger fish, so we have to take care of ourselves now," Lamont told him, bringing his ship around so they were pointing at one another. "You got that stripe, so you're commanding now. What's the play?"

Anders took a slow breath, trying to let the rage seep from his body and go to the place he went during combat. The place where instinct ruled his mind and kept him alive.

"There is a free port in this sector," Anders remembered aloud. "Tow me there."

"Yes, sir," Lamont said, but Anders noticed that he had already fired the magnetic winch. He felt the Bersa tilt and turn as it began to be pulled. Looking out into the streaking stars, he had to say something, anything. "I'm so sorry." Those were the only words he could muster. Petty and useless now, but something.

"She died in combat," Lamont said, lacking any emotion.

Anders couldn't let it drop. "She died for me. She sacrificed herself for me."

Lamont didn't say a word. Growing up together, the two had been close, but it was Imani who had kept them together. She had been the common thread, and Anders didn't know what they were now.

It was a long time, a brutal, agonizing silence before they reached Mod Harbor. The space station was not on any official maps, but most pilots on both sides knew it as a place you could get a drink, a warm bath and a warm body beside you.

Anders craned his neck as it came into view, the massive bulbous port with open bays willing to welcome anyone who would pay.

"NeoVerge Driver Four, request permission to land," Lamont radioed.

"Granted," a gravelly voice answered quickly. "Bay twenty-seven."

Lamont dragged the ship into the wide-open mouth, landing it in the massive metal room. There was nothing in the space, and as soon as the doors closed behind them, the ships shook as the place was oxygenated.

Pulling vigorously on the emergency release, Anders pushed hard and flipped the windscreen open as Lamont hopped down from his bird. Anders rushed over. "Look, man," he began, but Lamont wheeled around, tears streaking into the creases pressed into his skin from the mask.

"Don't," he spat. "Don't, sir."

Anders took a step back, feeling like he had been punched. The guilt welled within him, but no words made their way to the surface.

"You deal with the ships," Lamont said, spinning and stomping away toward a door that was opening as a drudge with a tablet and stylus stepped in. Lamont blew past the human-shaped machine, leaving Anders to deal with it.

The robot cocked its head to Anders. "You wish repairs in addition to the bay?" it asked in a computerized voice.

"Yes," he said. "Repair and refuel, half ammo," he said, knowing that NeoVerge corporate would never want to pay for a full restock of ammunition if they didn't have to.

The white-plated robot tapped on the holographic screen of the tablet and raised its head in imitation of a dubious expression. "The company will approve this?" it asked as the numbers were projected above the tablet.

Anders shrugged. "Let's find out," he said, and the drudge made a sound akin to a disappointed sigh. "Where is the nearest bar?"

"And here I thought you were going to ask where the library was," the machine mocked.

Anders shut his eyes, hating that people had given these robots personalities. He needed a drink. He needed to remember hard and then forget. He needed to escape this loss pressing on his mind like a vise grip.

"Alright, sorry, pal," the drudge said. "Thought you might have a sense of humor. Clearly, I was wrong. The nearest bar is just out the door there and to your right. It may not surprise you to learn that you are not the only captain who likes a stiff drink upon docking."

It pointed a metal finger at a particular door. Anders didn't bother to thank it. He made his way quickly toward the door that hissed aside just in time. It opened into a dark metal hallway of exposed pipes and reverberating sounds. One in every three hanging bulbs actually worked, and when it did, all it produced was a dim yellow light.

Whoever ran this port did not care for the aesthetics. Anders could appreciate that. The hall opened into a round with a three-dimensional map projected in the middle with rusting metal benches encircling it. Anders turned right, his lips already parched and jaw tingling with desire.

He tried to force memories of Imani from his mind, but he kept seeing her face. Every time he blinked, his friend stared at him. The smell of stale alcohol pulled him toward a gap in the wall where barstools were set up facing what would have been a window had there been any glass. He pushed open the swinging door and stepped in. A few sad old spacemen sat nursing drinks. Most had their eyes turned to a soccer match from Earth that was undoubtedly transported here on a chip at great cost.

Entertainment from the human homeworld could not be streamed into space, and therefore the business of getting movies, shows and sports to the colonists and these space stations was massive and highly profitable. NeoVerge had outlawed all entertainment from Earth when they broke from Dyeus. The company did not want their employees to want to return to their planet of origin.

Anders couldn't help but watch the screen as he entered Ay, There's the Rum. The glowing image of people chasing the ball on the pristine green field was like a vision out of a dream in stark contrast to the world around him.

The metal floor panels underfoot shifted uneasily, the bolts and screws used to hold them in place long rusted into oblivion. The furnishings around the room: tables, barstools, even the bar itself were patched together from pieces of decommissioned spaceship. Anders could see the missile holes, beam scarring and contact tearing on the crudely patched-together metal. Strung lights with tiny bulbs wrapped around pipes, the points of contact trailing streams of smoke.

Behind the bar, an old woman in a stained smock sat in a padded chair, sucking on a pipe and watching the match. Just the top of her head, wrapped in a rag, showed until Anders approached. She turned, eyes crimson with drooping bags clinging to the bottoms.

"One or a double?" she asked, looking him over.

Like so many deep-space ports, this bar had only one drink, brewed in house, take it or leave it. "Double," Anders rasped.

He expected her to stand and pour his drink, but she simply reached a hand under the bar, produced a dented metal cup and tossed it clanging onto the bar.

"Second line," she announced and hooked a thumb to the spigot protruding from the countertop. Scooping up the cup, Anders saw the crude lines scratched into the metal interior of the cup. He pressed the cup under the spigot, filled it to the second line, gulped the drink down and repeated the action. The home-brewed rum burned as it dropped like a cannonball into his gut.

The effect was immediate. He had to blink hard to keep from falling over and gripped the nearest stool for support, easing himself down. His body was used to sitting on hard surfaces, so the metal felt familiar.

"How you paying?" the woman behind the bar asked in a tone that sounded like an accusation.

"Charge it," Anders said, the words fumbling from his mouth. "Charge it to NeoVerge Industries."

"NeoVerge," a man scoffed from one of the tables, and Anders spun to narrow his eyes. The man was older but tough looking. 'Weath-ered' was the word Imani had loved to use to describe old sailors like him. He had a long white beard with a ring of hair on his head that was pulled into a rough ponytail. He stared at Anders with one good eye and one cybernetic eye that seemed to have been shut off long ago with hints of rust serving as an iris. Smiling at Anders, he said, "Took you for Dyeus."

That was all it took to bring Anders's ire back up, and he charged across the room. "Think I'm Dyeus, fu-" but his words and steps were cut short by a pistol to the face. The old man was up in a flash, weapon poised directly at the younger man.

He had gotten the drop on Anders so easily. "Sit down, young man," he said with a clever smile, easing himself back into his seat. "I was baitin' ya."

"I'm not in the mood for games," Anders seethed.

The old man smirked under his beard. "Then let an old pirate buy you a drink."

The word 'pirate' took Anders aback. It was mad for the man to admit what he had been, or perhaps was. Pirates were the bane of NeoVerge. And Dyeus for that matter. If there was one thing the two companies agreed on, it was that pirates needed to die. But this man was so flippant in his admission.

"Fine," Anders said, calming himself and moving toward a chair across the small triangular table from the man.

"Rosa," the old man hollered. "Get us another round."

"Get it your damned self," emanated from behind the bar.

Anders shook his head at the ridiculous scene. "I'll get it," he said and plucked up the old man's cup, refilling it with his own before returning to the table.

"Sorry 'bout the joke, there," the man offered. "Thought it was obvious." He reached out and plucked at the NeoVerge patch above Anders's heart.

"Should have been," Anders admitted. "Most of my mind's not here."

"You lose someone today?" the pirate asked.

Anders nodded, taking a sip of the rum. His head was swimming enough, and he was worried he would end up sleeping on the floor of this bar if he kept pounding. "How'd you know?"

The old man smiled, the yellowed corners of his beard turning up. "You have that look. That vacant look of someone trying to hold it together. Seen it on the face of every person I have ever known."

Anders believed him, and the dark reality of the comment landed hard. "Me too," Anders said, realizing the truth. He had known pain his whole life and had seen it on the faces of everyone he had ever known. He had just seen it on Lamont. "Guess that's why I lost it when you said I was with Dyeus."

The old man laughed, a deep pitying sound that seemed to come from deep in his very soul. Anders felt his blood boiling again but didn't move. He tried to be the man Imani always told him he could be.

"Sorry, mate, but you still see them as opposing forces?"

Anders felt his brows furrow. "Of course they are opposing!" he said in a near scream, and the man laughed again. Anders balled his fists and exhaled slowly through his nose, the anger whistling out of him. "Why do you keep laughing like that?" he asked through gritted teeth.

"Because I was you," he said plainly. "You but on the other side."

"You fought in the war?"

The man nodded slowly. "I did. Killed many a secessionist 'til I saw that we were all one."

"What do you mean?"

"I mean that Dyeus and NeoVerge are two sides of the same thing," he said and placed his pistol on the table, waving his hand over it in presentation before flipping it over and repeating the motion. "I fought in that war and believed what the company told me. I believed the rebel planets were gonna take the food right from my family's mouths, believed that letting 'em leave the company would mean destitution for both sides.

"I kept fightin' and killin', and I started to doubt myself," he said, letting the words hang. Despite himself, Anders could relate to the man. Unlike his parents, Anders had not joined up because of some noble vision. He had done it for a paycheck and a chance to get off his planet. With each and every mission, the inkling of doubt had begun to creep in.

"I started asking questions, started to believe that maybe the rebels were on to something," he continued. "But then, then came the day."

"The end of the war?" Anders asked.

"Something like that," he said, his gaze distant now. Anders could see the man remembering. "We met with those leaders, went to ask after their demands. We expected they wanted freedom. That had been their claim all along. But their leaders had different ideas. They said they wanted permission to break from Dyeus and form their own company.

"Rather than some assembly of free planets, they wanted to become the exact thing they were claimin' to want release from. I saw then the nature of man."

Anders couldn't believe what he was hearing. He had been so young when the fighting broke out, he hadn't fully understood it all. It had made sense to him that they created a company since corporate life was all he had ever known. Now though, to hear it put just slightly differently was a revelation.

"Was it," he began, trying to think of the words. "Was it what everyone wanted?"

The old man raised an eyebrow. "Well, ain't that just it," he said. "Half the people on their side seemed just as surprised as we were. They looked shocked and betrayed, like everything they had fought for had been a lie. To *those* poor folks, I could relate. Those looks of betrayal was how I had come to look at Dyeus.

"The next meeting the following day, there were far fewer across the table from us," the man said, the words heavy with implication.

Anders took another sip, considering everything.

Then he was struck. In an instant feeling as though the world was crashing down on him. The man, that uniformed man who had sat beside him on the cot all those years ago. He and those like him had been such a common sight for so long. Plopping down beside some kid and saying, "I regret to inform you of the untimely passing of your parents in the line of duty. They will live on in our memories with every free breath we take."

But that hadn't happened for Anders. He could still see the man, looking down on Anders in near disgust as he said, "Your parents were killed in action."

The difference had not meant anything to him at the time, but now, in light of the old man's words, he knew. He didn't need to be told to know. They had died at the end of the war. They had left him because they believed in something. They had been killed by their own for wanting change.

Anders gasped as though he had been drowning, began pawing at the logo stitched to his flight suit. It felt like losing his parents again and, in turn, like losing Imani again. She had died for him, and he had been fighting for nothing.

The rage burned in him.

He wanted to thank the old man for opening his eyes and punch him for destroying his illusions.

The old man seemed to read his thoughts. "Blew up your whole world, did I?"

Anders said nothing.

He thought about Imani and the words she had spoken to him all those years ago.

"Let's go make your parents proud," she had said with a smile. A knowing smile.

"Good to meet you," the old pirate called after him as Anders ran from the bar and out into the hall. Sweat cascaded off him as he darted into the open room and over to the map. He found the closest inn. It wasn't far. That had to be where Lamont had gone.

Anders took off, stumbling over his own feet, the alcohol coursing through him as he lurched toward the inn. The hallways all looked the same: an endless sea of rust-brown tubes. After what felt like an hour, he saw the door and nearly fell through, staggering over to the drudge behind the counter.

"I'm—" he huffed before having to pause and settle his stomach. "I'm looking for a man, Lamont Brown, would have checked in within the last hour."

"I'm sorry, sir," the machine told him. "We cannot disclose information on guests."

"So, he *is* a guest," Anders panted, looking at the metal door beside the counter. The word 'Rooms' was painted above the entrance. "Let me through," Anders demanded.

"Negative," the robot said.

"Let me through!" Anders thundered and then felt something hard strike his temple. Wheeling around, prepared to strike, Anders saw Lamont sitting in a chair in the small waiting area behind him, a couple of bolts in his hand.

"Oh," Anders said, picking the thrown bolt off the ground and tossing it back.

"They didn't have a room ready yet," Lamont said, standing. "Drunk already?"

"No," Anders said reflexively before amending, "Yes. But that's not it."

"And what is it?" Lamont said.

Taking a moment to breathe and actually see his friend, he noticed the look. That vacant look the old man had described. The one he was wearing too.

"Why?" Anders began. "Why did she do it?"

Lamont bit his lip. "You know why."

"No," Anders said. "I've never known why."

Lamont cocked his head, narrowing his eyes in disbelief.

"She loved you like a little brother," Lamont said.

Anders nodded. "I know, but…" he said, trying to find the words.

"But why did she step in?" Lamont filled in. "Why did she always step in?"

"Yes," Anders sighed, walking over and plopping down beside his friend.

"Because of who your parents were," Lamont said.

"And who were they?" Anders asked, realizing then that they had both known more than him.

"Freedom fighters," Lamont said. "True freedom fighters."

Anders shook his head. "Weren't all of them?"

"Oh, Anders," Lamont said and draped an arm over his shoulder. "For some, but for most it was just about a slight improvement or a profit share. You were so young, so naïve when the war ended. You just nodded when you were told they formed NeoVerge. You never questioned it."

Anders just stared at a stale mouse dropping on the floor. "So," he said, but nothing followed. He felt like his mind was blank.

"So Imani wanted to help you," Lamont said. "You became her mission in life. The thing that gave her purpose. She wanted to see you become like your parents. She wanted to help you grow into the kind of man who could actually help people throw off the corporate yoke, regardless of the company."

Anders shook his head. "But why not tell me this? For years I just played along."

Lamont shook his head. "I asked her that all the time," he said. "She was waiting for you to be ready."

"I guess I never was," Anders said in a quiet voice.

Lamont shook his head. "You are now."

They were silent for a moment before the drudge chimed with an override message. Rather than speaking in the programmed language, a live feed was being piped through its speakers. "NeoVerge employees from dock twenty-seven: a fleet has arrived and requests your presence."

Lamont looked at him. "Guess they got our distress call," he said. "Look, now that you know, you don't have to go back. You could take the ship and go be free. Try to fulfill your parent's dream. I'll tell NeoVerge you were killed in combat."

Anders smiled. Lamont was a good man.

"That is so kind," Anders said. "But I'm done being protected."

Lamont's face had only a moment to register shock as Anders struck him on the side of the head with such force as to knock him out cold.

"Sorry," he whispered to his friend as he laid him down on the couch. He turned to the drudge. "When he wakes up, tell him he's free."

It felt good to say the words.

Standing, he made his way back toward the hanger, swaying as he moved.

This had been the most complicated day of his whole life. But he was happy to finally see the world for what it was. To feel like he knew his parents, like he understood his best friend.

Striding into the room, he saw six engineers appraising his ship, presumably deciding how to begin.

"I'm taking the other one," he announced, moving toward Lamont's ship with the gold stripe. The engineers nodded, not seeming bothered by having to take a break from what they were doing, and they all made their way out the door.

Anders climbed into the cockpit of Lamont's Bersa. It was a newer model, and he couldn't help but smile at the memory of the three of them breaking into the Dyeus hanger on Ellen VII and the moment he turned to see his two friends with their fingers on their noses.

"Oh, come on!" he had griped, seeing that last ship that he was going to be stuck with. Imani and Lamont had burst into laughter, and Anders realized that was how he wanted to remember her. Laughing and smiling.

He went through his checks, engaged the engine, and started lifting the ship. Everything that wasn't tied down was sucked toward the hanger door as it opened, and Anders took a deep breath. He knew he would never see the company the same way again, and he wondered how he would find the other rabble rousers when he rejoined the fleet. Sighing, he throttled forward and out into the void.

"OH, SHIT," he said as he saw the ships.

While it certainly wasn't a fleet, just about twenty fighters and two sloops, it also wasn't NeoVerge.

Anders was alone now. Alone in a way he had never been before.

Every alarm in the ship began shrieking as they picked up the enemy contacts. The Dyeus fighters began accelerating toward him.

He laughed. A grim, defeated sound.

At least he had lived long enough to know the truth.

Engaging his targeting computer, he stared into the line of enemy ships. He would take some of them down with him. His new world-view of NeoVerge as the enemy didn't make Dyeus any less of his enemy too.

As the old pirate had said, they were one and the same.

As the Dyeus fighters closed in, Anders took one in his sights. He readied to press the trigger and closed his eyes as he had done so many times before. This time, he knew that Imani wouldn't be there to save him.

"Mom, Dad, I hope this makes you proud," he said and began firing.

As he opened his eyes, he watched as the line of Dyeus ships began to explode one after another. He saw beams and missiles all around him. He didn't understand until a strange-looking ship passed overhead, firing a rail cannon at the Dyeus fighters.

Looking down at the feed from the rear camera, Anders smiled as the pirate ships streamed from the docking bays. No two ships looked the same or even remotely similar, but they all had the same targets.

The Dyeus ships were caught completely unawares, and the fighters tried their best to hold off the onslaught. The pirates were too much and quickly made short work of the fighters until Anders saw an actual flotilla in the distance.

NeoVerge had arrived with a fleet.

There were far too many for the pirates to take on, and they had done their part for him. He heard a voice in his comms. "We'll call it even for hurting your feelings earlier," the old pirate joked.

Anders laughed a genuine laugh of surprise and survival. "It was nice to meet you too," he said.

"Kid, me and the boys have to get out of here, but these are the coordinates if you are ready to do some real good."

Anders saw the coordinates appear on his HUD as the pirate fleet began to vanish one after the other.

He looked at the NeoVerge ships closing in fast. He could pick up his parents' fight and try to take down the company from the inside. Work as some secret agent.

But no.

That was not the way to honor them. Not the way to honor Imani.

He tapped on the coordinates the old man had sent, setting them as the destination.

The reason both companies hated the pirates was because they were disruptive. If Anders wanted to make a substantive change in the galaxy, he knew this would be the way.

As he engaged the Galilei drive, he smiled, knowing he would make all of them proud.

THE END

ABOUT THE AUTHOR

Matthew A. Goodwin has been writing about spaceships, dragons, and adventures since he was a child. After creating his first fantasy world at twelve years old, he never stopped writing. Storytelling happened only in the background for over a decade as he spent his days caring for wildlife as a zookeeper, but when his son was born, he decided to pursue his lifelong dream of becoming an author.

Having always loved sweeping space operas and gritty cyberpunk stories that asked questions about man's relationship to technology, he penned the bestselling series, A Cyberpunk Saga. His passion for the genre also inspired him to create and cofound Cyberpunk Day ™, a celebration of all things high tech / low life.

He is now expanding his science fiction universe into space.

For more information and free content, visit
https://www.thutoworld.com/

HIGHWOOD'S END

By Nathan Pedde

Lieutenant Commander Jacob Richard Highwood of the SF Shenanigans stands on the edge of oblivion. As the commanding officer of his lance of giant fighting robots, one among thousands. All that's left of the once glorious Empire.

The Purpz Alliance moves into position, ready to deal the final blow to the Seventh Fleet of the Armainian Empire. To lose means death — the enemy gives no quarter. To win means to fight another day. Will they survive?

HIGHWOOD'S END

Brevet Lieutenant Commander Jacob Richard Highwood glided his Phantom-class kreiger through the emptiness of space. The bipedal mechanical robot stood thirty meters tall and resembled a cybernetic gorilla bristling with weapons.

As a joke, he named his war machine "Mr. Cuddles." As a new pilot, he thought it was hilarious, yet command and all communication officers hated it. He understood why, but it was bad luck to change the name. As he was the Commander of the Lance Ghost, luck was something he needed more than anything.

Highwood couldn't remember the name of the system they were in. Not that it mattered much. They would jump to a new system and never return. Or he'd be dead.

He flipped a button on the controls of his kreiger. He checked his vital systems and ammunition. He was getting low, but there were too many enemies nearby for him to return to base.

Ground invasion was the primary purpose for kreigers. Using lance-sized pods inserted by orbital drop, they could fight on the ground. With light modifications, kreigers could fly in space, something pilots and engineers had done for thousands of years in millions of battles.

Each kreiger took two pilots to operate the machine. Highwood was a pilot, and he sat on the top seat. Lieutenant Henry Skitson sat in the copilot's, which was below and in front of him. It was up to Highwood to split up the tasks, but it was near impossible for one pilot to operate a kreiger. A single human mind couldn't comprehend three-dimensional space combat.

An alarm blared across the cockpit as an explosion rocked his upper glacis, causing the craft to vibrate. He let out a sigh of relief as his craft didn't explode. The three enemy kreigers pursuing him grew larger, closing the distance. Highwood jerked on the controls, spinning the craft as three missiles burst by. The pilot interface made it seem like he was the kreiger. It wasn't Highwood staring at cameras and monitors. It was like he was Mr. Cuddles, and the cybernetic gorilla wasn't there.

"Targets are getting closer," his copilot said, his words edged with stress.

Skitson was three years his junior with only two weeks of flight time. The baby-faced man operated the missiles, point defenses, and navigation, while Highwood used the smasher knuckles, the shoulder-mounted rail gun, and commanded his lance.

"Pucker up," Highwood said. "Time to dance."

Highwood jerked on the controls once more, spinning him around to face the enemy kreiger. It was too far for him to get a view of the machine, but his machine's sensors told him the suit was out there with red squares and diamonds. Highwood lined up a shot with the rail gun's 50mm tungsten carbide rounds. The targeting computer clicked and buzzed. It reached tone as it locked on the target.

"Shot out," Highwood said, squeezing the trigger.

The round blasted toward the kreiger at 15,000 km per second, striking the machine. It blasted apart its shoulder, sending pieces into a scattered mess. The impact failed to destroy the kreiger. It withdrew from battle and would fight another day.

The two enemy kreigers circled around, dodging the broken-up lead. Their actions were not as confident as they were before. Through the debris, they broke off their pursuit. They didn't withdraw, but kept their distance, shadowing him.

"Two more are on their way," Skitson said, his voice monotone.

When stress affected Skitson, he tensed his movements, and his voice drifted into the monotone of his home planet. Highwood had worked with the young man long enough to take his actions into account.

"Check the scanners. Is this their main fleet?" Highwood asked.

"Unknown. I see nothing but these kreigers."

Skitson pulled up the map of the system they were in. It showed Mr. Cuddles, their assigned suit frigate, and the surviving fleet. The Suit Frigate *Shenanigans* was one of the smaller vessels that comprised the Seventh Fleet of the Armainian Empire. It was one of a hundred of the class that remained.

The Seventh was a tenth the size it had been when it had left port all those months before. The politicians called it a campaign to be completed by the end of the year. It had gone long and had been filled with suffering and massive losses. Highwood could count the number of victories on a single hand. The defeats were too numerous for most to bear. They would lose the war to the Purpz Alliance. The only question was if they could stay alive until their leaders could negotiate a peace deal. Then they could go home to their families. Though there was no word on when that would happen.

Until then, they would delay and defend. They had no choice. Intelligence reported that the Purpz rarely took prisoners. Highwood had seen footage of entire crews being spaced into the void. This only caused them to fight harder rather than dying on their knees. If the outcome was to die no matter what he did, then he would die fighting.

"Monitor that enemy patrol," Highwood said, pressing a button on his controls. "I need to check in."

Before he could, Mr. Cuddles' alarm blared. Two of the enemy kreigers soared toward him. He aimed his rail gun at the first one and waited. Armed with a rail gun, the craft approached. Highwood waited for him to get close enough to read the kreiger's safety warnings.

Highwood jerked on the controls, moving away from the flying munition. He ducked and dodged, using the kreiger's speed to his advantage. Highwood swerved his kreiger and headed for the enemy.

"Shot out," Highwood said, firing a shot.

There wasn't enough time to think as the shot blasted through the center of the kreiger's chest. It was the toughest armor on a kreiger. It contained the cockpit. A shot penetrating the center would turn the pilot into red mist.

Before the void of space swallowed the wreck, the Purpz would haul them to their fleet for repair. It would be simple to replace the cockpit and its computer system. A delay would leave it to float forever, or at least until a scraper came upon it by sheer chance.

The wrecked kreiger floated away from Highwood as he maneuvered Mr. Cuddles. A second craft moved around, attempting to get at his soft back. Highwood placed a round, blasting its shoulder apart. It spun out of control, deep into space.

"Launching missiles," Skitson yelled.

Highwood moved the arm bearing the rail gun out of the way, lest it was to get hit by his own missile. The tubes were in Mr. Cuddles' chest. A misfire would destroy the arm and the rail gun.

A barrage of missiles blasted from the chest toward the three remaining enemies. Warheads scattered the enemy's formation into wild directions. The last kreiger was too slow. The missile careened at the craft, striking the side of its torso. The missiles circled around, listening to Skitson's controls. They slammed into the suit, each ripping pieces of armor and chassis from the machine.

Highwood jerked on the controls, moving away from the Purpz. While he was accurate with his rail gun at short distances, longer ranges were where the weapon excelled.

"Loading long-range missiles," Skitson said. "Can you hold them off for forty-five seconds?"

"Do my best," Highwood replied.

The last two Purpz kreigers regained vertical line formation. They gunned their engines, blasting at him at high speed.

"Here they come," Highwood said.

"Give me thirty seconds for reload."

Highwood moved the controls, keeping his distance from the machines. He couldn't do it forever. He would make a mistake, and then they would suffer.

He watched the distance shrink. He lined up a shot, letting the targeting system do its thing. The computer beeped, then reached tone.

"Shot out," Highwood said as he let a tungsten carbide round fly.

Mr. Cuddles shook and vibrated from the shot.

The massive chunk of metal slammed into the torso of the bottom kreiger. It spun around from the force with limbs and pieces of the suit flying in all directions. It didn't explode, and Highwood was more than disappointed. He put his mind to the last kreiger.

"Load complete," Skitson yelled. "Firing missiles."

Highwood moved his arm as five missiles soared from the tubes. He watched them spiral around in a lazy arc. The last kreiger fired its point defense cannons, but they could only stop two missiles. The remaining three struck the Purpz kreiger, turning it into fragments and dust.

Silence filled the cockpit as Highwood checked the scopes. He pushed a few buttons.

"We're clear for now," Highwood said.

Highwood's comm unit buzzed and he accepted the call. "Go for Mr. Cuddles."

The face of Captain Duffey McLuckie appeared in the view window. He was an older man with short-cropped gray hair and a beard. His pressed dark-gray uniform with blue buttons up the side framed his stress-filled countenance.

"This is Sword-hilt Actual, do you read, Mr. Cuddles," McLuckie said.

"Loud and clear, Sword-hilt Actual," Highwood replied.

"Report, Lieutenant Commander."

"Lost two kreigers. Big Boots and Chirp. Downed six myself, plus the lance downed three others," Highwood said. "Scope is clean. Low on ammunition. Request R and R."

"Request granted."

"Any word on the enemy's main fleet?" Highwood asked.

"Negative. Talk back on board." The line ended.

Glancing at his fuel, Highwood entered a course back to the ship. Then he checked his scope once more. He had no intention of leading the Purpz back to the ship.

Skitson looked back at him from his chair. "You mean the main fleet hasn't jumped?"

"These are just advanced scouting parties. They know we're beaten. They're playing with their food," Highwood replied.

"But why?"

"Stop whining. We have a job to do."

HIGHWOOD WORKED THE CONTROLS, heading back toward SF *Shenanigans*. The long, blocky ship had little in the way of weapons. It was a mobile hanger and repair station for kreigers. At the start of the war, it carried a full lance of fifteen Phantom-class kreigers. Like Mr. Cuddles, a crew of two operated each machine. Now there were ten kreigers of four distinct classes. Highwood pressed together the remains of a dozen depleted units into an ad hoc unit.

Shenanigans was once the newest and most advanced the Armainian Empire could engineer. Now the ship was held together with tape and thumbtacks—at least, that was the joke.

Frequent battles and the destruction of the home port had obliterated the chance of refit. The engineers repaired the ship the best they could, though they lacked the proper materials and tools.

Highwood set Mr. Cuddles down on the top deck of the craft. Two kreigers stood on the top, waiting for him. The lift lowered into the craft to the floor of the hanger. As the kreiger lowered, the massive hatch closed. The hanger pumped atmosphere back into the room.

He walked Mr. Cuddles over to a kreiger's harness. He hooked the machine up, letting the ship settle. The last thing Highwood wanted was for the *Shenanigans* to maneuver and send it flying. He pressed a button, and long tubes attached the kreiger to the ship. These supplied needed fluids and removed steam and heat, cooling the Phantom down. The systems vented this heat out into space.

The craft powered down, resting against the metal. Highwood unattached his straps, setting them aside. Skitson clicked a button by the door and the metal opened.

A catwalk lowered down to the cockpit. Like all kreigers, it lay in the center of Mr. Cuddles' chest.

Being in front of Highwood, Skitson was out first. He stepped onto the metal plating as the platform raised to a higher section of elevated decking. Below them, the mechanical crews scrambled around the crafts, reloading weapons and repairing battle damage.

Removing his helmet, Highwood marched along the platform to the corridor. He tucked it under his arm as he marched to the ready room. The eighteen other pilots waited in the room. They were all dressed in similar red flight suits with helmets nearby.

Highwood set his helmet on its shelf, turning to face Skitson and his pilots. Their faces were as diverse as they had ever been. Originally, every member was friends from before the fighting started. They were from a kreiger racing league, which filled every spot of the lance. Now Highwood was the only one left.

They replaced his friends with strangers from elsewhere in the empire. Orange faces sat next to red and blue. Every human variant sat next to each other. It didn't matter what three millenniums of living separated with the radiation of different stars changing their biology did. Now they were all in the same boat. They all wore the same uniform and would suffer the same fate.

"You did good out there. But we aren't out of the fight yet. Rest up," Highwood said. "The next forty-eight hours are going to be vital. I'm going to go see the captain."

Highwood grabbed his gray service cap. Because he was still wearing his flight suit, the cap was off for his uniform. Until the captain announced all clear, he and his pilots were living in their flight suits. They could get a scramble order. They would sleep in their kreigers if the captain permitted them. Instead, most slept in the ready room.

He followed the corridors toward the ship's bridge. Suit frigates were five decks with the command deck in the center. Like the kreigers, the designers buried the important parts deep inside. It relied on cameras and sensors to give the bridge staff information, not windows, which the enemy could shoot out with a well-placed rail gun round.

Highwood walked through the tight corridors around the moving crew. They worked frantically, as if a demon was chasing them. He didn't blame them. Working hard was one of the few things that kept panic and despair from setting in.

He stepped onto the bridge and stopped. Six stations spread around the sides with the captain's chair elevated at the back overlooking them all.

Captain Duffey McLuckie sat on his chair, staring at a screen on the far wall. On it was a map of the current system. There were five gas giants near the star and two rocky, lifeless planets farther out. The system was uninhabited except for an abandoned research outpost. The fleet had stripped it for anything useful before burning out to the outer reaches where they could jump safely.

The *Shenanigans* was in the rigid rear guard, watching and delaying the Purpz scouts from finding the main fleet. It was their hope that they could get to the jump point with enough time to leave before the enemy ambushed them again.

The captain tapped his fingers on the chair, staring at numbers. He resembled a man killed then brought back to life as a zombie from a cheap holoflic. Though before things went pear-shaped, he looked fresh and alive. The words *burn out* came to mind, though there was nothing they could do about it. They were short on personnel as it was.

"Lieutenant Commander, good kills. Textbook," Duffey said.

"It could all be for naught, Captain," Highwood said. "Do you know the next jump destination?"

"There are three possibilities here, though none of them are promising. The enemy may have gone around the long way. Word is the admiral is sending scouts through each point."

"I guess we'll know soon enough," Highwood said.

"I could use you on the ship. The CO of the lance isn't supposed to go out on missions."

"Understood. Except I'm better in my kreiger. I still want you to find someone better."

"Not going to happen. Not now. But get some sleep. The *Aurora* is covering our sector. Giving us time. Use it wisely."

Highwood saluted and left the bridge. He marched through the corridors to his quarters. A third of the pilots were in the ready room, while the other two-thirds were in their quarters or the mess hall. The entire area was ten meters away from the ready room for quick access if there was an emergency.

He sat on his bunk, yearning for sleep. Highwood had a long list of reports to do, yet they all seemed moot. There was no admiralty to read them, no review board to question his decisions, and no one to tell him the decision he made in five seconds was wrong.

The missions he would send the kreigers on were standard. He would split them into three groups by range. They would patrol the space in a crisscross pattern until they found targets. It was standard operating procedure.

Highwood closed his eyes and passed out. It seemed like he just closed his eyes when an alarm blared.

"All personnel to battle stations," the automated system blurted out. "All personnel to battle stations."

Highwood jerked awake, jumping to his feet. He raced the small distance to the ready room. He found it full of pilots putting their last few pieces of gear on. They weren't waiting for orders from him. They all knew what they had to do.

Skitson held onto Highwoods helmet in one hand with his in the other. Highwood tossed his service cap into his cubby.

"Did you sleep?" Skitson asked.

"A bit. You?" Highwood replied.

"A bit."

"Then let's get going," Highwood said.

Highwood raced from the ready room back into the hanger. A flurry of activity took place as each of the remaining nine kreigers got ready for combat. He didn't know the situation, but speed was more important than listening to a briefing, one he could listen to once in his harness.

While they had to decompress the hanger to bring suits in, they had a launching system that blasted the machines out the front. It took longer than having a large hanger door, but it was easier.

Highwood enjoyed being the first one out and the last one in. He didn't trust the ship's sensors if he could help it. He was an old boy for that reason. The new guy trusted sensors and intelligence. Highwood liked what he could see using his own craft.

He slid into Mr. Cuddles first, settling into his seat. He pulled at the straps, hooking himself back up. The kreiger's systems booted, coming to life. Following his lead, Skitson slid into his seat. They checked the systems with all coming back to green.

"Munitions didn't fill our long-range missiles," Skitson said.

"You rarely use them," Highwood said.

"That doesn't matter. I only have two barrages worth."

"Make it work. Not much we can do about it now. When we get back, I'll talk to the munitions officer."

Skitson said something under his breath.

Highwood clicked a few buttons, opening the comms channel.

"Control. This is Mr. Cuddles," Highwood said. "We are five by five."

"Roger that, Cuddles," the communications officer replied. "All kreigers are good to go. Passing you to the captain while the ground crew clears the hangar."

Highwood clicked on his external sensors, and his vision changed. His vision changed as they morphed. His eyes saw from the top of the machine. He was the kreiger.

"Attention all pilots," Duffey said into the comm unit. "We lost contact with the *Aurora* five minutes ago. Gun corvette and four kreigers have a parallel course. Highwood. Call it."

Highwood pressed a button and activated lance comms.

"We are going with Alpha defense," Highwood said. "First team will take the outer perimeter with a second team on the *Shenanigans*. Keep your eyes peeled for targets."

"Hurrah," the response came.

Red lights appeared across the hanger roof. Control let the harness, which attached to Cuddles' shoulders, loose. Highwood moved his controls, marching the machine forward. He stepped across the hanger to the start line.

Mr. Cuddles stood as the machine pulled him to the launch tube. The doors closed behind him as he settled into the airlock. The launching chamber readied itself. With the atmosphere cleared, a red light changed to green, and the doors opened.

The darkness of space appeared in front of him. Highwood pressed the comm unit button.

"Mr. Cuddles. Ready," Highwood said.

"Roger, Mr. Cuddles. Launching," the communications officer replied.

THE FORCE OF MR. CUDDLES' launch from the suit frigate pressed Highwood into his seat as he blasted into space toward his designated point. Two kreigers moved behind him in a line formation.

It was the kreigers, Smokey and Clownboy. They weren't Phantom-class like Mr. Cuddles. They were of the Giant class. The suits were taller than Highwood's, though without the rail gun. Short-range missiles and a rattling cannon on each arm filled their armament. The cannons fired a massive 25mm rounds a second.

"Alpha leader," Smokey said. "This is alpha two. Do we attack?"

"Negative, alpha two," Highwood said. "We're buying time."

"Affirmative."

Highwood glanced at the scanners. The two other teams took up their positions. The concept was to have a defense in depth. When the enemy were to attack, he could call the others in for support with longer range weapons. They would move back into the range of the kreigers on the *Shenanigans* only if they had to. They were the last line of defense.

The Purpz corvette and kreigers moved closer. They moved in a slow arc in front, not directly to them. Skitson pressed a button, and a range countdown appeared in their vision.

"I've got long range loaded first," Skitson said. "Give the order and I can let a volley off."

Highwood pondered the situation. If he attacked now, then they would counterattack sooner. If he waited, then it delayed the combat.

"Sir?" Skitson asked.

He pressed a button, moving his rail gun out of the way.

"Target the frigate. Fire when in range," Highwood said, pressing another button on his comm unit. "First team. Let them come into range then engage."

Acknowledgment came over the comm unit as he waited. The counter ticked down. Right before it neared zero, the Purpz changed course. They burned straight for them and would be on them in a moment.

"Skitson?" Highwood said.

A volley of missiles left the tube. As soon as the last one was safely away, he jerked on the controls. He moved to the side, expecting a counterattack of missiles and rail guns. Except no munitions came.

The enemy force burned toward them as fast as they could.

Highwood smashed the lance comm button down. "Third team. Attempted breakthrough. Converge on the enemy. Second team, this may be a diversion. Keep eyes peeled."

He didn't wait for a response. Highwood trusted his pilots would follow his orders.

"Fuck it," Highwood said, jerking on the controls, moving for the Purpz.

Highwood swung his rail gun into position, drawing a bead on the lead craft.

"What are you doing?" Skitson asked.

"Getting close and personal," Highwood replied, listening to the targeting computer beep at him.

He aimed his weapon at the lead kreiger. The targeting computer clicked tone and Highwood squeezed the trigger.

"Shot out," Highwood said, as Mr. Cuddles vibrated.

His target swerved at the last moment and the shot went wide. Highwood shot forward at the lead kreiger. The machine tried to move away, except it wasn't fast enough.

Highwood activated his smasher knuckles and smashed the Purpz kreiger in the leg. The force ripped the limb apart. The blow spun it out of control.

Before the three other kreigers could respond, he was through them. Highwood burned for the enemy gun corvette. It was a long, phallus-shaped object with a cannon in its center. The ship had to move its bow to aim.

Alarms blared out as five missiles from the Purpz kreigers blasted toward them. Skitson went to work with the point defense cannons. He used every ounce of skill to blast at the incoming warheads.

Four detonated by Skitson's defensive fire. The last one neared him. The speed of Mr. Cuddles kept them ahead of the deadly warhead. Highwood corrected his course, heading for the enemy warship. As they neared, the gun corvette aimed its charged cannon at them.

"Sir," Skitson yelled. "This is a bad idea."

The gun corvette went off, shooting its main cannon. Highwood jerked away, tumbling to the side. The green blast rocked by them. If it hit them, it would melt half of Cuddles. The cannon struck the missile before dispersing into the dead of space.

Behind him, Smokey and Clownboy moved to back him up. They fired salvos of missiles at the remaining enemy kreigers before following up with their mini-guns. They targeted the one closest to them with their guns while letting the missiles harass the last two.

Highwood didn't see if they were successful in their attack. He flared his engines, racing for the star craft. Banks of point defense cannons lined the side of the gun corvette. Highwood ignored them as they ripped chunks of his armor from his hull. They wouldn't be able to penetrate his armor. He neared the craft as he raced toward it.

He aimed his rail gun at the craft's engineering bay. Being a corvette, it was the smallest capital ship the Purpz could send at him. Anything smaller would be a gunboat. A corvette had paper-thin armor compared to others in the Purpz fleet.

Mr. Cuddles' targeting computer buzzed and reached tone. At a short range, he squeezed the trigger.

"Shot out," Highwood said, as the rail gun fired.

The weapon blasted through the thinly armored hull of the ship. Atmosphere burst from its side, sending it into an out-of-control spin.

Highwood let his momentum take him farther along as he lined up his weapon. He waited for his targeting computer to find a target. Except the spin confused the machine, making a shot impossible.

He took a chance by firing blind and squeezing his trigger.

"Shot out," Highwood said, as Mr. Cuddles vibrated once more.

The shot pierced its opposite side. Atmosphere burst from the craft as it violently decompressed. Pieces and chunks of the craft blew apart into the void.

Smokey and Clownboy destroyed the two kreigers they faced. The last fell back from the fight, now missing a leg. Smokey had taken damage to its side with its left arm being ripped apart. It hung together by a dozen exposed wires.

Highwood glided his craft toward them, boosting his scanners. He didn't want to be surprised by the fleeing Purpz kreiger.

"Attention control, this is Mr. Cuddles," Highwood said. "Last enemy is falling back. Other targets are destroyed or disabled."

"Roger, Mr. Cuddles," the communication officer replied. "I have two more groups of targets on the scope. There is a dozen each."

"Acknowledged," Highwood said. "We can't take that. Recommend pulling back."

"Orders from the fleet. Destination selected, jump imminent. We need to get to the jump point. The captain has ordered a recall."

"On the way," Highwood said, turning the comm unit back to his pilots.

The nine kreigers of Highwood's lance folded in toward the *Shenanigans*. They would move in pairs onto the ramp. It was a slow process, but it allowed them to still have kreigers active and protecting them from an attack. They completed this maneuver while the suit frigate was burning at high speeds toward the rendezvous point.

The team stationed on the ship would be among the last in on the ramp, while Highwood and the first team would be the first. Despite protocol, he made sure he was the last kreiger on board.

Smokey and Clownboy were the first down the ramp as Highwood took up a position on the back of the ship. He let every one of them down and in.

As the last two kreigers moved down, a blip appeared on the scope. They were at long range, nothing more than colors on a screen.

"Sir. We've two contacts inbound," Skitson said.

"What are they?"

"Two more gun corvettes."

"Shit," Highwood said, clicking a button. "Control. Do you see those?"

"We do, Cuddles," control said.

"Does the fleet have anything to intercept them?"

"We're the end of the line."

"Roger, control. Moving to intercept," Highwood said.

"Will launch—"

"Negative control," Highwood said. "Burn hard and fast. Make that rendezvous. We will catch up."

Highwood lifted off the end of the *Shenanigans*, burning for the enemy. They would have minutes before they were in range and there were no Purpz kreigers in range to alter their firing patterns.

"J.R.," Skitson said. "Is this a good idea?"

"No," Highwood replied. "But if someone doesn't, they'll take the *Shenanigans* out."

"Understood. We'll be in their range in thirty seconds. I'll have missile range in sixty."

Highwood jerked on the controls. "I am speed."

"Fuck me," Skitson replied.

Highwood maneuvered the kreiger into an unusual pattern. He kept it random, moving vertical and horizontal. His intention was to keep the Purpz targeting computer guessing. A green blast missed them as he gunned toward it.

"Missiles away," Skitson yelled, as five munitions left the tube. "Reloading."

They blasted toward the two enemy gun corvettes. Highwood moved his arm back into position, letting the targeting computer take aim. Except they were moving in too fast. He didn't have time to let the system calculate.

Highwood aimed his rail gun at the nose of the closest corvette. He squeezed the trigger.

"Shot out," Highwood said, as Mr. Cuddles vibrated.

The shot slammed into the ship's upper glacis. It bounced harmlessly into space. Highwood maneuvered the kreiger to the side of the ship, aiming at its side. Firing blind, he pulled the trigger.

"Shot out," Highwood said as the five-shot magazine ran empty.

The 50mm tungsten carbine shot slammed through the port side of the corvette, denting the inside of the starboard hull. The ship listed as atmosphere vented, tumbling the ship to the side.

It missed impacting the second corvette as the live ship maneuvered to the side. It burst vertically, aiming its massive cannon at Highwood.

"Fuck," Highwood said, jerking on the controls.

He burst horizontally, attempting to get away.

"Missiles," Skitson said.

Highwood moved the rail gun arm out of the way as a horde of missiles left the tubes. They were close-range models. The young man chose the correct load.

The five warheads slammed into the front section of the corvette. They didn't have the strength to destroy the ship, but a green spark raced along the capital ship's hull.

The cannon glowed green, signaling it was going to fire. Except the weapon exploded first, and then the rest of the corvette followed. A million pieces blew apart into the void of space.

"Yes," Skitson said. "I got one."

"Good job, kid," Highwood said, switching comms. "Control. Both targets destroyed. I'll meet you at the rendezvous point."

"Acknowledged, Cuddles," Duffy said. "I owe you two a case of beer. Get here safe."

HIGHWOOD BURNED MR. CUDDLES, moving as fast as the machine would let him. Fighting the two corvettes put him dangerously close to running out of time. He had no choice but to make it to the jump location. If he missed the jump, the fleet would leave without him. His kreiger didn't have the ability to make jumps on its own.

Ahead of him, his scope flashed with life. It was the entirety of the Seventh Fleet. The jump ship filled the center of the fleet. The vessel moved entire fleets from one solar system to the other through known jump points. This was the heart of the fleet. Its destruction would be the last nail in the fleet's coffin. To the side of the tight formation was the *Shenanigans*.

"SF *Shenanigans*. This is Cuddles. Do you read?"

"Loud and clear," Duffy said. "Glad you can make it. You almost missed the jump."

"Roger that. Will be in momentarily."

He landed the kreiger on the lift and lowered it into the hanger. The process took longer than he'd like. With Mr. Cuddles clamped into place, both left the cockpit.

As Highwood stepped onto the catwalk, a cheer erupted from the crew. They chanted "Cuddles" repeatedly.

A whistle erupted across the ship. "This is the captain. All hands to jump stations. All hands to jump stations. Two minutes to jump."

Highwood and Skitson climbed back on-board Mr. Cuddles, as did all the pilots. They didn't have any fight capacity left, but the standard procedure allowed for a quick deployment on the other side. Highwood knew that if the suit frigate broke apart on the other side, they would survive in their kreigers.

Two minutes later, the *Shenanigans* jumped. Highwood checked his scope.

"Fucking transit tunnel," Highwood said.

Depending on how far the jump was and the state of the jump, it could be a short, bumpy trip through hell, or a smooth, month-long journey to the other side. This jump was the latter. Unless it was a regular route, he had no way of knowing till he got into the tunnel.

Highwood and Skitson disembarked. After exchanging his helmet for his service cap, he left the ready room for the bridge.

The crew moved to settle the ship for the long transit. No one knew how long it would take, but the order was to remove flight and combat gear. They were to dress in proper uniforms. Highwood stepped onto the bridge and spotted Duffey at his chair.

"Good. Come to my office," Duffey said. "I have an inter-ship comm meeting with the admiral. I'd like you to sit in."

"Of course," Highwood said.

Duffey glanced over at his watch officer. "You have the con."

"Aye, sir," the officer said.

Duffey followed the captain into the office as the man shut the door behind them. There were six officers from the different departments of the ship in the room. Duffey clicked another button, and the room disappeared.

The holographic image of the meeting room in the battlecruiser *Iron Sides* took its place. Images of the fleet's captains stood around the admiral, who sat in the large chair in the center of the room.

"We are in trouble, captains," Admiral Heinze said. "In seven days, we'll jump into the system, JD-1538A. This is a bare system with nothing but a few asteroids and dust to aid us. We're outmaneuvered and have no place to go. This is it. The enemy will be right behind us. This is where we make our last stand, gentlemen."

A murmur erupted from the commanders as everyone talked at once.

"Let me remind you. There is no surrender. Remember the Thirteenth Fleet and their fate. They slaughtered them all and didn't accept a single survivor," Heinze said. "We are out of time and supplies. It's fight or die."

Duffey raised his hand.

"Go ahead, Captain McLuckie," Heinze said.

"What are your orders?" Duffey asked.

"I will transmit ship formation before we get to the system," Heinze said. "We will form up and catch them before they arrive. We need to bottleneck them. Put them down in ones and twos. Not the entire fleet at once. Those with scout drones, get them out using the standard fleet pattern. Find me their jump location."

The admiral glared at the commanding officers. No one said anything else.

"If that was all the questions, give 'em hell," Heinze said as the hologram ended.

The small office appeared back in its place, with the metal desk taking up most of the space. The captain turned to face Highwood.

"Are your Devil Dogs ready?" McLuckie asked.

"We will be ready to do what's needed. We'll fight," Highwood replied.

"Get going," McLuckie said. "I'd like them ready and loaded with weapons, ready to fight."

Highwood saluted and left the room. He marched from the office to the ready room. He needed to organize his teams and ready them for the coming fight. There was repair work to do, simulations to run, and a night of drinking to be had. It would be the only time for it.

Over seven days, the kreiger's crews repaired and rearmed machines. Pilots rested and trained, going over enemy craft classes and ship types. Then the order came down the chain of command that they were coming out of the jump. Highwood and the kreiger pilots rode the exit out in their machines. The ship jerked as it slipped into the new system.

The system sported a single star with a scattering of asteroids. There was no sign of sentient occupation. No research stations, mining stations, or even a rebel base.

The Seventh Fleet spread out across the region of the sector. Thousands of sensors spread out around them, hunting for the faint reactor signatures. After two days of hunting, one sensor recorded readings, which were followed by a dozen more. The fleet's computer systems hacked the numbers, giving the brass a gate location.

The fleet gathered, forming a wall of ships with weapons aimed and ready to go. The ships burned their engines, keeping from drifting away from the location.

Highwood and his pilots spent their time in the ready room. The crews had their preparations complete, and everyone welcomed the collective boredom. Highwood preferred the boredom. He had experienced too many dark days where he lost friends and comrades.

Time ticked on. His comrades fidgeted, anxiety written in their expressions and interactions. Highwood had to stop a few altercations between crew members.

Highwood sat in Mr. Cuddles, examining the systems. He went over the various weapons. The door to the cockpit opened, and Skitson floated inside.

"I thought I would find you here," his copilot said. "What are you doing?"

"Going over the systems. It's going to be a hard fight."

"Nervous?" Skitson asked.

"No. Being careful."

Skitson glided into his seat and flipped on his terminal. "Then let's go over the weapon systems."

"Start close range and move out," Highwood replied.

"We have the smasher knuckles. The plasma pulse is in prime shape. It'll emit three thousand Celsius upon impact, burning up everything."

"The point defense weapons?"

"Both of the 15mm missile defense weapons are good to go. Those should stop any missiles. We have thousands of rounds of ammunition."

"Which you will go through faster than the quartermaster would like," Highwood replied. "How about the missiles?"

"They fixed the auto-loader, but we still don't have the capability of unloading any of the six tubes," Skitson said. "Though the shoulder-mounted rail gun is on the fritz. You'll have to count the shots. But we have eight mags of five rounds. Too bad those ten rounders don't fit."

An alarm echoed across the hanger into the cockpit. "Reactor signatures inbound. All kreigers prepare to launch."

HIGHWOOD SAT in the cockpit of Mr. Cuddles. All his kreigers formed up in a wedge formation around him. Clustered around him were the machines from half the fleet. They numbered in the hundreds. Highwood hoped it would be enough.

The *Shenanigans* was farther behind them, protected by battle frigates, just in case some of the enemy got through.

Their job was to shoot down any enemy kreigers circling up and around them. The fleet would do the fighting. The kreigers guarded the flanks.

The advantage and disadvantage of FTL technology was that they could spot reactor signatures from far away. It allowed them, the admiral, and his staff to find the jump location. Now all the fleet had to do was to wait for them to jump in and kill them one by one.

Spread out in a semi-circle, the fleet was close to a single point. Their weapons were ready to fire. Above and below the fleet were two kreiger wings. Highwood and his kreigers waited with the upper wing.

Admiral Heinze appeared on his screen. The old man stood before them.

"This is it. This is the moment of our lives. We were all born for this moment. Either we will win the day, or we will be dead. There is no retreat, and there is no surrender. Remember the Thirteenth Fleet. The enemy will murder us all. It's time to show them what we are made of."

Blue light flashed in the space before them. First it was one, then a second. A dozen lights appeared before him. The first of the enemy appeared before them. Two battlecruisers with a light cruiser and destroyer escorts. Scattered around the vessels were dozens of kreigers.

"All vessels. Open fire. Kreigers wait for further orders. Don't waste your lives. Now fight," Admiral Heinze yelled.

The fleet opened up hell, firing broadsides into the incoming fleet. Escort ships exploded on impact as the shots landed in the vessel's superstructure. Highwood watched as they ripped apart the enemy ships. The last ships to be destroyed were the battlecruisers.

"That was it?" Skitson asked as the debris moved past the vessels.

"That was the first wave," Highwood replied. "With luck, the enemy will arrive in a thousand waves over the course of a month."

"But we won't be that lucky."

"No, we won't. We haven't yet."

Another wave appeared as blue lights appeared. The fleet fired a barrage of missiles and rail guns at the vessels. Results were the same as the one before. The vessels blew up one by one. The main battlecruiser launched a single round of torpedoes at them. A few of the crafts landed blows on vessels, but Highwood couldn't see any damage to any ship.

Over the course of the day, seven squadrons of the enemy burst into the system. Each fight was short and swift, with a total loss of the enemy before they could get a second volley off.

"What is the purpose of this?" Skitson asked.

As if on cue, dozens of bright lights appeared above and below him. When each light disappeared, it revealed dozens of enemy capital ships. Highwood counted dozens of dreadnoughts, battleships, and battlecruisers. The escort ships were innumerable. The enemies outnumbered them three to one.

"Shit," Highwood said as hundreds of kreigers soared down toward them.

An order flashed across his screen. "All kreigers attack."

Highwood clicked a few buttons, switching the screens. He set his comm-link to his squad.

"You heard them. Let's do this. Stay close. Stay together. Fight hard," Highwood yelled.

He jerked the controls, aiming into the mass of incoming troops. Highwood gripped the handles as the mass of kreigers gathered around them. The enemy outnumbered them. The fight was going to be tough.

Highwood clicked a button, pulling up his shoulder-mounted rail gun. He targeted a shot on the closest kreiger, waiting for tone. After what seemed like forever, the tone beeped.

"Shot out," Highwood said, squeezing the trigger.

The weapon rocked, sending the shot out. It struck the Purpz craft, sending it spinning before it exploded.

The salvo of shots left the kreigers as the enemy responded in kind. Highwood spun and moved as machines exploded around him. The screams of his dying comrades rose as he counted his soldiers dying. He watched as both Smokey and Clownboy exploded into a scattering of debris.

Highwood didn't give up. He jerked the controls, pulling left then right. He gunned the engines and swerved. Skitson fired missiles as fast as he could load them. His point defense turrets fired, detonating incoming missiles.

He lost track of his lance as the swirling ball of fighting and dying kreigers went on. Highwood concentrated on firing at the Purpz and not letting up. He smashed the torso of one Purpz with his smasher knuckles, sending it into another.

It all seemed like a blur to him. He closed in on an enemy kreiger, a Warfighter class. He grabbed ahold of its hand with his left hand and shoved his right into its torso.

"Shot out," Highwood yelled, blasting the round through its body, ripping apart its cockpit.

Highwood roared away before it exploded. He twisted and turned in the air, aiming for another target. Highwood slammed his smasher knuckles into its shoulder, melting armor plating. He kicked the malfunctioning machine with his feet before blasting a rail gun through its body.

He glanced around him and at his sensors. Half of his lance was downed. He had a hard time spotting his own side.

"Target rich environment," Highwood said.

"What?" Skitson replied.

"Take control of the shoulder mount. I need to move faster."

"Roger that."

Skitson flicked a button, and the rail gun was his to control. Highwood pulled and jerked on the controls, moving in a random pattern. The computer lit up targets and incoming projectiles.

He couldn't miss them all, but it wasn't for the lack of trying. Highwood dodged and ducked, moving close to and far away from the enemy. He edged near an enemy and smashed it with his smasher knuckles.

Skitson aimed and placed a short-range missile up its backside. The machine exploded, sending shrapnel into a wide arc.

Then they were alone in a swarm of enemies. Each one tried to fire upon him, to destroy him. Highwood moved and swerved around as a cluster of missiles followed him.

Then they were through the swarm of kreigers. The enemy had shifted their focus from him to the fleet. This left the enemy fleet wide open.

The friendly fleet shifted formation, inverting the semicircle to face out. The enemy surrounded them and soared toward close range at flank speed. Ships that had targets were firing shots at enemies, whether they were kreigers, escorts, or capital ships.

Highwood glanced at the enemy and gunned the engine. He aimed for the closest of the enemy capital ships. Point defense weapons fired out at him, bullets hitting and bouncing off the armor plating. He soared toward the ship.

"Give me my gun back," Highwood said.

"I don't like this," Skitson replied.

Highwood blasted forward, aiming at the dreadnought. He aimed his rail gun, placing three rounds into its front heavy turret. The shots pierced its armor, blasting into the ship. The turret set off like a candle, sending debris out behind him.

The ship shuddered as its main magazine exploded. It wouldn't be enough to destroy the ship, but it would get their attention.

The enemy fleet fired a salvo. It zipped by him, heading for his fleet. One by one, the ships exploded. First Admiral Heinze's flagship core exploded, and the craft disintegrated into small chunks. Then the rest of the capital ships.

The escorts turned and fled the battle.

"Mr. Cuddles. Mr. Cuddles. Come in," Duffy said.

"I read you," Highwood replied.

"You're the last one, get out of there. We're pulling back to the rendezvous point Alpha Zeta Delta."

"Roger," Highwood replied, ending the link.

Then a rail gun bullet struck Mr. Cuddles. The shot bounced off his armor, though not before it scattered shrapnel throughout the cabin. One struck him below the armpit. Skitson took two in the face and fell limp in his chair.

Highwood grunted in pain as he corrected his craft. He gunned the engine away from the enemy fleet. They weren't interested in him. The enemy rocketed toward the disintegrating fleet. They had smelled blood and were moving in for the kill.

He concentrated on remaining conscious and moving forward. Highwood set the autopilot to get him there, but it wasn't long before he was losing consciousness.

Highwood slipped in and out of consciousness before he finally gave up the ghost. The Armainian Empire would become no more with the Purpz Alliance destroying its armies and salting its planets.

ABOUT THE AUTHOR

Nathan Pedde is a sci-fi author from the dark reaches of Vancouver Island. He has been writing for over a decade with multiple titles published. He has a wife and two kids who encourage his crazy storytelling. You can find him on his website, *www.NathanPedde.com*.

ASCENDANCY

By Theodore Hodges

Captain Frank Davidson of the Dionysian Navy is at the height of his career. With the newly dubbed "313th Naval Reconnaissance Squadron" under his command, he has met wild success fighting pirates, terrorists, and criminal interest groups. However, that is about to change.

From the bowels of the Dionysia's oldest enemy comes a fourteen-kilometer-long space leviathan called the HMS Ascendancy. Thousands drift in the cold void as corpses from its first assault, and Davidson is ordered to do the impossible. He must kill the monster, no matter the cost. Even if that means sacrificing everything...

|

DRS *VICTORY*
313th NAVAL RECONNAISSANCE SQUADRON
CAPTAIN FRANK DAVIDSON, COMMANDING
UNCHARTED SYSTEM
CLOSEST DIONYSIAN REPUBLIC COLONY: NEW PITTSBURG (5 LY)

I never enjoyed translating in and out of FTL. Humanity has been doing it for centuries now, but I've never escaped the feeling of unease every time a ship bends reality to propel itself from point A to B. Something always seemed unnatural, and in my defense, it was. Whenever I ordered my ship, the DRS *Victory,* into that place between space and time, I couldn't help but remind myself that it wasn't something we should be able to do. The knowledge that FTL was used across thousands of worlds millions of times a day did nothing to reassure me either.

Physicists from every corner of the galaxy have debated on the nature of FTL. Even after seven hundred years, they are no closer to an answer than when they started. All anyone agrees on is that we can launch warships, bulk transports, yachts, and a million other variants through its extradimensional embrace. Countless of them drift as abandoned derelicts within FTL, some dating back to the origins of space travel. Others are more recent additions. Regardless of the risks, we needed an answer when Earth and our native solar system were no longer viable. Our options then were narrow and continue to be so: survive, or fade into obscurity.

Commander Gabriel Reed, my executive officer and friend of at least a decade, walked over to me after the *Victory*'s automated system reported over the 1MC that our translation was successful. Unlike most naval officers, Reed was short, squat, and covered with cords of hard muscle housed within his tan skin. I was a far cry from his almost obsessive adherence to physical standards. That was to be expected when a man crossed the threshold into his fifties, but I still resented my subordinate for making the most of his youth. Decisions like that only become clear after you pass the point where you can change them. I had a lot of those in my career.

"Captain," Reed said, eschewing a salute because he knew I hated wasting time on pointless ceremony. "*Victory* is in system. Comms has a signal from the drop buoy and is deciphering the data package now. Scanners report no other vessels in the area."

"Very well," I said. "Let me know as soon as we have everything decoded."

"Aye, sir," Reed said, then returned to his post ahead of my own on the *Victory*'s bridge.

DRS *Victory* was a Shadow pattern light cruiser. Most of the fleet's cruisers are the Liberty or Defiance pattern and eschew the Shadow's reliance on stealth for better armor, armaments, and crew capacity. Their goal remained as simple as the earliest aquatic navies of old Earth, that being killing as many of the enemy as possible. If it wasn't for the Dionysian Republic's steadily growing issues of low enlistment in the armed forces, that approach would work. However, the last few decades have proven time and time again that a republic is as beneficial to the citizens as it is detrimental to the military. So, the navy finally agreed to develop the Shadow pattern vessels.

Turn out for the Shadows was low, despite my best efforts in proving their advantages over the past few months. In fact, I only know of the *Victory* and her sister ship, the *Victoria*, that are cruisers under that design philosophy. Considering the fact that I was a major advocate for their construction in the first place, I am reasonably confident the War Department didn't pull the proverbial wool over my eyes. Then again, Dionysia is no stranger to off-book projects, so it is possible that hundreds of Shadow patterns exist in operation or drydock on some galactic underbelly.

What makes the Shadow pattern unique compared to its contemporaries is a prototypal armor system that reduces its scan signature to something comparable to a small asteroid or a debris cloud. Shadows are hideously expensive, and therefore the process of getting them approved took a decade of my life away. Trying to get it approved by the Department of the Navy, the War Department, the Dionysian Senate, and finally, the president was an arduous task, but I met a lot of important people over those tedious years. Honestly, I would have rather spent that time in the void or with my family. That's because I'm a sailor at heart, unlike many men and women who wear the navy's uniforms. A true sailor's home is and always will be the untamed spaces between civilization. When we aren't with our loved ones, that is.

A few minutes passed, which I wasted thinking about my ship. Junior officers walked, or jogged when something was important, from station to station across the bridge. The Marine Corps guard detail, which all Dionysian Navy vessels have, shifted uncomfortably in their assigned positions. Doubtless, they were thinking about their own natural habitat: hostile territory. None of my crew activated the emergency general quarters alarm, though, and that was as good a sign as any we were alone in this abandoned section of space. All that remained was to figure out what Admiral Michaelson, the commander of the 5th Fleet, had to say. If the routine we'd established over the past six months held up, it wouldn't be much.

Michaelson was one of the major detractors on the Naval Reconnaissance program, and I was prone to the belief that is why the War Department chose him to command my squadron on its maiden voyage. His opinion, which I heard repeated hundreds of times since I started lobbying for the Shadow patterns, was that the fleet was best served by building three times as many traditional ships. I couldn't fault him for exaggeration either. The 313th was literally the price of that many ships of similar tonnage. However, Michaelson never placed much stock in intelligence gathering like I did. He was a staunch traditionalist in that way, which was consistent with his austere bearing and dislike of men like me who sought to challenge established doctrinal practices.

"Sir, priority message from the War Department," Reed said, interrupting my musings. "They are ordering us to disengage stealth systems and activate the quantum communication array."

"Shit," I said below my breath. "Alright, Commander, spin up comms."

"What about the *Whirlwind* and the *Justice*?" Reed asked. "They're reporting successful translation alongside their escorts."

"Tell them to maintain current status. I'll take the call in the Black Room."

Reed nodded, then said, "Aye, captain."

Besides *Victory*, the destroyers *Whirlwind* and *Justice* were the only ships in the 313th with Black Rooms. We called them that because the entire chamber was paneled with opaque screens when not in use. When they are operational, thousands of projectors set in the ceiling form a three-dimensional environment that matches the other side of the call. This was one of the few systems I opposed when the Shadow pattern went through the appropriations committee. The War Department, however, felt that if they were going to build ships that swallowed up most of the annual budget, they might as well squeeze every fancy toy they could out of R and D.

"Authenticate, Davidson, Frank, Captain, DRN," I said after the door to the Black Room slid shut.

"Identity confirmed," the chamber's automated system droned.

An uncomfortable amount of time passed while I waited. A side effect of the Black Room was complete sensory deprivation when you were inside and without power. Concealed air filtration systems even suppressed smells. If it wasn't for the tug of artificial gravity on my boots, I would have felt like I was floating in a vacuum, which wasn't something any sailor enjoys. After all, we spent our careers trying to stay out of the void, not in it. Even if our ships did exactly that.

Suddenly, a woman's voice came over the speaker. "Captain David-son, this is the War Department. Stand by for the secretary."

"Standing by," I said, happy to have her voice as something to focus reality on in the surreal room.

The projectors started whirring when I finished. At first, they flashed bits and pieces of an artificial surrounding, but they eventually settled on a cohesive display. What appeared was an office smaller than my wardroom. An elderly man in navy dress blues sat behind the office's lone desk. Varnished cabinets, various ornaments, and wall decorations nearly encapsulated him there were so many, one of which was a certificate from the DRS *Majestic* in appreciation for its former commander, Admiral Silas North. Besides that modest note of the man who worked here, all I saw were furnishings that looked like they might pay off another Shadow pattern vessel if the government auctioned them off.

"Sir," I said, rendering a salute for the War Secretary.

North returned the salute and said, "Frank, how's it going?"

He didn't really want to know how I was doing, but I told him anyway. "All things considered, sir, I would say quite well. Have you looked over the 313th's mission reports? We've gathered more intel in six months than the fleet has in the last six years."

That earned me a small smile before North said, "I have. If it wasn't for recent developments, I was going to give you a personal commendation for your work on the frontier. Hell, there was even some movement on giving you admiral stars."

"'Recent developments,' sir?"

"Yeah," the admiral-turned-secretary said. "When was the last time you reported in?"

"Two weeks ago, sir. That's been our standard operating procedure for this tour," I said.

"Well, then I have some bad news for you."

Instead of prodding him with speculation, I waited in silence. North and I had known each other since I served under him as an ensign. We were well beyond juvenile games like twenty questions. If he was wait-ing, and his look of consternation made me believe so, it seemed likely that he was working up to dropping a bombshell on me. One that neither of us would enjoy.

During the few seconds that North hesitated, my mind wandered to the persistent threat of the administration shutting down Naval Reconnaissance. My pitch hardly convinced the president when I gave it two years back. If he hadn't just taken up office, I doubt he would have said yes at all. Several active programs had gotten the axe since then, and I could easily see my life's work as his next target. Politicians are merciless in their efforts to spend money or slash budgets, depending on their prejudice. Our current Commander in Chief was the latter kind.

Eventually, North let out a long sigh and said, "As of yesterday at nineteen hundred hours standard, we are at war with the Europan Hegemony."

My jaw dropped, "Wait, what? I thought Intel said…"

"They were wrong," he interrupted. "As usual. There's a lot of heads rolling right now. Let's just say that the president is… upset."

Before I could reply, North continued. "Don't worry about your ass, Frank. Analysts are getting it, not the operational side. Like you said, your reports have made some waves around here. I just wish we deployed you to Hegemony space instead of the frontier."

"How bad is it?" I asked.

North's face darkened, and I saw every line that comes from over thirty years in the service. "Bad."

"So, I need to rally with the 5th? Or am I going behind the lines? The 313th could stir up some trouble if we play our cards right."

He shook his head. "Neither, I'm afraid."

In the lifetime I had spent as Silas North's friend, I had never seen him so cautious. Though far from a bellowing leatherneck, he was one of the more direct officers in the fleet. In fact, that was why we got on so well. Both of us agreed the navy had become absorbed by politics, infighting, and territorial disputes. Our fear of a war we weren't prepared to fight had become a reality, despite all assurances by the intelligence apparatus we were wrong, but I didn't see any pleasure in North at his vindication. All I saw was something like fear in his studious features.

What could make him so hesitant? I didn't know, and I was

growing more certain by the second that I didn't want to. If the situation was bad enough that he admitted it, I knew Dionysia was caught over a barrel. North wasn't the type for melodrama, after all. The only real question then was how many colonies and ships we'd lost since I last checked in with Admiral Michaelson.

"The 5th is gone," he said like a man admitting infidelity to his wife. "One hundred percent fatalities over New Pittsburg."

"What? How?" I stammered.

North pressed a button on the underside of his desk, and a holographic projector on the topside activated. The Black Room struggled to manifest the image because holographics were difficult for the system to recognize and model. When it finally snapped into place, an unfamiliar warship floated above his desk in ghostly green light. There wasn't anything to scale it off of, but by the weapon mounts on its broadsides, I was confident in guessing the vessel had to be over ten kilometers long.

"This," North said with a gesture at the ship, "is the HMS *Ascendancy*. It is the first of the Lion pattern dreadnought, and if our intel people are correct for once, it is the largest warship in human history."

"Shit," I said while studying the image. "What am I looking at exactly?"

"From bow to stern, she measures at thirteen kilometers. Crew capacity is somewhere near two hundred thousand, with an additional forty thousand ground troops onboard. Tonnage is unknown, but we know it has something like twenty-seven hundred weapons batteries and nine hundred missile launch tubes."

"There are fleets with fewer weapons than that!" I exclaimed.

With a scowl twisting his features, North said, "Exactly. That's what the 5th found out the hard way when she jumped into New Pittsburg. We lost four carriers, four battleships, and a shitload of escorts in less than six hours. Worse still, they barely damaged the goddamn thing."

All I could do after that news was stare at the green image floating between us. Where the ship was once a curious development, it was now a source of genuine fear. Europan vessels, unlike Dionysian craft, were long and narrow like a blade, and I could almost feel the sensation of that murderous machine ripping through a fleet of a hundred thousand people. As I studied the beast, a question came to mind.

"Shouldn't they have done more damage? I mean, sure, it looks formidable, but the 5th should have at least given it a bloody nose."

"Michaelson is getting the Dionysian Cross for his defense," North said. "I just signed the recommendation personally when we figured out what else the *Ascendancy* has on board."

"It gets worse?"

"I'm afraid so," North said, then exhaled loudly before going on. "You remember those rumors about energy shields that started turning up a few months back?"

I hadn't, but I also wasn't the War Secretary. When I told North as much, his expression somehow got darker. If I wasn't receiving notice of a potential end of our civilization, I would have made fun of him for it. Not even our firm friendship could shelter me from the hammer blows reigning down with every additional piece of information, though.

"Well, the Hegemony figured out a way to rig a kinetic energy shield on the *Ascendancy*. It's a major power leech, and I was just informed by intel before this conversation that they had to put two backup fusion generators onboard to support the damn thing. However, Prince Henry's efforts have paid off. He's got one tough son of a bitch to crack," North said.

"But not impregnable?"

"Thankfully, no. Michaelson had to broadside it with all four of his battleships to overload the system. That was his... last pass. Poor bastard died to prove that monster could bleed from conventional weapons," North said.

"And the prince is using it as his flagship? I thought he and the king weren't on good terms."

"Tensions in the Hegemony appear to have been... exaggerated. There was no falling out between the king and his son. Henry wasn't at court because he was overseeing the last steps of the *Ascendancy*'s construction. Now, he's leading their fleets into our space."

"'Fleets'" I said in disgust. "Of course we weren't lucky enough to have *one* insurmountable task."

"That's where you come in," North said.

"I'm linking up with the 9th?"

"No," North said, then forced me to suffer through another long pause. "Before I go on, I need you to understand that I did not recommend this operation. The president himself signed the order this morning. It's over my head, Frank."

I knew where this was going now. "You're shitting me, right? I've got one cruiser, two destroyers, and four frigates. What the hell can I do against that?"

North cleared his throat and said in an official tone, "At zero nine this morning, I received orders from the Office of the President of the Dionysian Republic to promote captain Frank Davidson to the rank of rear admiral. Billet position is 5th Fleet, commanding."

"Fantastic, Silas," I said sardonically. "Now tell me how the hell I am supposed to kill that thing."

North paused while a brief flash of anger crossed his features, "Sarcasm? Really?"

Chastened, I said, "Apologies, sir. Just a lot to take in."

"Right, I understand, Frank. Like I said, this isn't how I would have used your squadron, but this is over my head."

"I know, sir."

North nodded, which was as close as he ever got to saying a hatchet was buried. "Do you still have the area denial weapon onboard *Victory*?"

By "area denial weapon," North meant a fifty-megaton hydrogen bomb. Because of the Naval Reconnaissance mission, they gave the *Victory* one in case we discovered a priority threat on the frontier. After all, the frontier was home to people who didn't want to live under galactic law. Terrorists, cultists, genetic abominations, the frontier had it all. Occasionally, someone stumbled upon something so dangerous that it needed to be eradicated by nuclear Armageddon. It wasn't a common occurrence, but it happened.

"Unless I misplaced my only one between now and the last inspection ten hours ago, we've got it," I said.

"Standby for authentication code," the War Secretary said almost atop of my words.

I pulled a small notepad and pen out of my blue fatigues and said, "On your go."

"Delta, gulf, gulf, three, four, niner."

I repeated the sequence, and North said, "Read back is correct."

"Does the president understand what will happen if we break that seal? There's no way the Hegemony will hold back if we aren't, and they have easily twice as many nukes as we do. Half the goddamn Republic will be a parking lot by the time this is over."

North nodded. "He does. Frank, the situation is dire. The 9th and 12th are decisively engaged over New Richmond and Prosperity as we speak. Their situation is still developing, and we're moving the 20th and 3rd to support them. However, if Henry brings the *Ascendancy* back on the field, it's game over. King Edward's diplomats said they aren't stopping with a minor territorial gain. This war is for all the marbles. If we don't disable or destroy the *Ascendancy*, intel believes we have a few weeks before total collapse."

I was about as far from happy as a man could be, but I understood why I was getting this mission. It wasn't because I was the best equipped, prepared, or most capable officer in the fleet. The reason they ordered me to take a stab at the *Ascendancy* was that I was the *only officer they had*. In a war for survival, which this apparently was, Dionysia would need to use everything at its disposal to eke out a victory. Maybe the Hegemony or the Rykarion Empire wouldn't if they were in our shoes, but we never had a military as big as them. Constitutional republics had their downsides, and that was decidedly one of them.

"Alright then," I said. "Do you have any good news besides announcing my last promotion?"

"Some," North said. "We had the 315th jump into New Pittsburg this morning. *Victoria* reports that, apparently, Michaelson did enough to force the *Ascendancy* to use the orbital yards for repairs. Safe bet is they won't be in that state for long, but if you can get in and deploy the area denial weapon, you just might take it out."

"What is Intel's probability estimate on that?" I said.

"Thirty percent, with a five percent margin of error. It all depends on if you can hit them before they get their shield up."

"And if they do?"

"Less."

I broke the silence that followed with a pointless question. "Any chance I can get support from the 315th?"

"Sorry, Frank, but I cannot give you any additional support. If we... well, you know, if you can't complete the mission, we will need them more than ever."

My frown did the impossible by deepening. "Of course. I just wanted to make sure this suicidal attack was as difficult as possible. It's high time I get the Dionysian Cross myself. Apparently, they hand them out like candy when it's posthumous."

North gave me an irritated look, then it eased when he said, "At least you were right. Shadow pattern might be our only chance at winning the war. Not the one you expected, sure, but you still were right."

"For God's sake, Silas!" I said, barely containing a scream. "There is no reason to sweeten this shit sandwich. Even if we somehow deploy the weapon, I'm about to lose a lot of people in the process. We both know there is no other way this is going down."

"You're right," he said. "I'm sorry, Frank."

I could sense that this meeting was almost over, so I quickly asked, "Does the *Ascendancy* have any support craft? A picket?"

"We don't know."

"Right," I said, then saluted the War Secretary for the last time. "If that's all, sir, good day."

North stood from his desk to return my salute. "Get this done, Frank. You already know what the stakes are. This is what we all signed up for when we took the oath of service. Don't be afraid to remind your crew of that."

"Yes, sir," I said and dropped my salute.

Regardless of the War Secretary's suggestion, I wouldn't stoop to that level. My crew was as good as any captain could ask for. They would do this, and they didn't need any rousing speeches from their fearless leader to fulfill their duty to Dionysia. That was always something North and I disagreed on, but then again, he was the War Secretary. I, in comparison, was pinning admiral half a decade after I was supposed to.

The last sight I had of Silas North was him dropping his salute and nodding to someone offscreen. I assumed was probably one of his army of junior officer aides and adjutants that swarmed him like flies did to carrion. Whoever it was, they had access to the quantum communication controls so they could cut the transmission. Before he fully faded away, I saw North sit back down and stare at his personal computer. If this war was as bad as I guessed, he probably had a lot more meetings like this to handle.

II

DRS VICTORY
5TH FLEET
ADMIRAL FRANK DAVIDSON, COMMANDING
UNCHARTED SYSTEM
CLOSEST DIONYSIAN REPUBLIC COLONY: RICHMOND (15 LY)

Within the hour, I had the newly dubbed command staff of the 5th
Fleet in the *Victory*'s operations center. Ops was one of the largest
rooms on my ship. This was because of the occasional necessity of
briefing hundreds of junior-grade officers for missions that had a
longer window than we currently did. However, it wasn't much more
than a standard auditorium that would have been equally welcome in a
university on Dionysia. Well, besides the fact that they didn't plan wars
in classrooms. That was the responsibility of those who waged it.
Figuring out why rested on the shoulders of academics in the
aftermath.

Only four officers sat in the room on cheap folding chairs
surrounding the holographic projector table. What we decided today
would determine the fate of thirty-five hundred marines and over six
thousand sailors. That bothered me more than I cared to admit. After

all, even if we pulled this off, a lot of Dionysia's best would be dead in the next few hours.

North was right though, damn him. If we didn't kill the *Ascendancy*, there wouldn't be a home for us to sail back to. The Hegemony had a long record of bloody military tribunals whenever they added new worlds to their kingdom, and they would label most of my people as seditionists or rebels instead of honorable combatants. Such was the way of the Hegemony and a lot of the galactic community. I would be lying if I said I hadn't seen Dionysia do it in the past as well.

Sitting on my right was Colonel Fredricks, commander of the 313th's marine contingent. He was in his early forties, like Reed. Also like my XO, Fredricks looked like slabs of hard muscle tacked on to a skeletal frame. Graying hair was shorn close to his head, which brought all attention to his dazzling blue eyes. They looked like a caged chemical fire as he stared at me, and I knew a cold-blooded killer lived behind those sapphire gems. Caution was best when dealing with men like Fredricks; though he was loyal to Dionysia, I always wondered if that was just a front for his more homicidal ambitions.

Commander Jacob Davidson of the *Whirlwind*, my only son, sat to Fredricks's right and across from me. He looked so much like Rebecca, from his jet-black hair to his sharp, angular features. Even though she had been dead for over a decade, I couldn't help but see her charm, wit, and fiery spirit with every gesture my son took or word he said. That wasn't his fault. I knew it, but it was still challenging to see the last evidence of my late wife in the world of flesh and blood.

Finally, there was Captain Jessica Dufresne of the *Justice*, sitting to my left. She was the closest to me in age, at somewhere near her early fifties. Like me, she had also fallen out of favor with the War Department. Accusing a four-star admiral of sexual harassment had that effect on even the best of officers, and she was. I was happy to have her around, though. Dufresne's folly proved to be a major benefit for me, and I had promised her in the past that I would get her promoted as soon as I put on admiral stars. It was a promise that both of us hoped for but knew wasn't a likely outcome of our tumultuous careers.

This assembly was far from the glamour of briefings on a carrier or battleship, but Naval Reconnaissance had already developed a more relaxed atmosphere than the fleet abroad. What came with looser regs was lesser accommodations. All said, I was satisfied with the tradeoff. If you could balance order and breathing space, I found it made efficient crews.

Jacob was first to speak. "Admiral, congratulations on the promotion."

I nodded, then said, "Thank you, Commander."

Fredricks ignored this formality, which was his way. "My marines are getting restless, sir. There's a lot of rumors running through the squadron. What's going on?"

I pressed a series of keys into the holoprojector to bring up the diagram of the *Ascendancy* and said, "Well, the situation is not favorable. Feast your eyes on the HMS *Ascendancy*. Our mission is to kill it."

After I laid out the details, which took about fifteen minutes, Jacob erupted in protest. "Sir, with all due respect, are you serious?"

I pursed my lips, then said, "As a heart attack, I'm afraid."

"You said the 5th hit it with four broadsides?" Dufresne asked, proving that she was the voice of calculated reason, as always.

"Simultaneous saturation," I said. "According to the War Department, they dropped its shields and did enough damage to force them to refit in New Pittsburg. It's safe to assume that they are far from dead, but the 5th did hurt it. The War Secretary and Intel believe that may be enough for us to finish the job with our nuke."

"Shit," Jacob hissed.

Fredricks gave Jacob a stern look, doubtless because of his consistent outbursts. Dionysian marines were a group of ironclad discipline, all the way to the top. I suspected Fredricks saw my accommodation of Jacob's behavior as nepotism. However, I knew the truth better than he did. Our chances of success were slim, everyone knew it, and normal men like my son struggled to cope with that. Considering the fact that he couldn't air his grievances to his crew, I would rather have him do it here.

"Thirty-five percent is sure?" Fredricks said, voicing his opinion on Intel with a question rather than a rebuke.

"A systemic collapse of the Republic is 'sure' enough that they're willing to take the risk," I answered.

"What is the plan then, sir?" Dufresne asked.

"Thank you, Captain," I said with a forced smile and wink. "If Intel is correct, which I admit is an *if*, then we should have easy passage to the New Pittsburg shipyard. *Whirlwind* and *Justice* will lead us in with their escorts. Everything depends on when they are detected. Assuming that happens, lead elements will engage the pickets while the *Victory* comes in from behind and deploys the nuke. Afterward, we scurry away, FTL back here, then prepare for link up with the 9th or 12th at the War Department's direction."

"But we don't know if there are any pickets," Jacob said.

"No, we don't know *how many* pickets there are. No way the Hegemony is leaving that brute to fend for itself while it's weakened," Dufresne corrected.

"Right," Jacob said with a nod at the *Justice*'s captain.

"Contingencies?" Fredricks asked.

"You have something in mind, Colonel?" I asked.

"*Victory* has fifteen launch tubes, right?"

"Yes."

"How many boarding torpedoes do we have?"

Jacob scoffed. "Oh, here we go."

Fredricks shot my son another sinister look, then continued. "I want my people on that ship if the first attempt doesn't pan out."

"We have enough to deploy all your marines stationed on *Victory*, *Justice*, and *Whirlwind*," I said. "Problem will be timing. Each torpedo takes a thirty-man platoon?"

"Correct," Fredricks said.

"*Victory* has fifteen tubes, *Justice* and *Whirlwind* each have ten. If we account for one during the first wave for the area denial weapon, and there's thirty-five hundred marines across all the three ships, that means we'll need… three and a half launches before everyone is out," I said after crunching the numbers.

"That's well and good, but how are we going to stay in torpedo range? *Ascendancy* will not let us get that close without something to say about it," Jacob said.

"EM disruptors might buy us the time," Dufresne said.

"I'm not convinced," Jacob said with a deep frown marring his handsome features. "There's no way they won't be packing some serious sensory equipment."

"It's a good thing you don't have to be convinced," I said. "That's my job. In case you forgot in the last thirty seconds, *Commander*."

"Apologies, sir," he grumbled.

I thought it over for a moment while the room descended into silence. The estimated ground component on board the *Ascendancy* was somewhere near forty thousand. Could Fredricks's leathernecks put a dent in that? My instinct was no, but the DRMC had a long history of defying the odds. After all, they didn't need to take the entire ship. They just needed to disable the three fusion reactors to cripple the beast.

Then again, if the reactors overloaded, that would put everyone in a pickle. Three fusion reactors running at four megawatts each would produce a titanic explosion. The 5th, the shipyards, the *Ascendancy*, and a large portion of New Pittsburg's surface would get evaporated if that happened. That easily added up to millions of civilian and military casualties, but what other option did we have if the nuke didn't work? How many Dionysian civilians would get the harsh end of Hegemony justice if we lost?

I knew that the War Department calculated this before they ordered the mission, so I said, "You're green on my end, Colonel. Have your marines loaded up when we enter the system. Captain Dufresne, Commander Davidson, help the colonel in any way he needs. This is do or die, people. FTL in two hours. Dismissed."

My staff snapped to attention and rendered salutes. Dufresne and Fredricks left after I returned the gesture without another word. Jacob had more to say, though. He always did, and for once, I was tolerant of his attitude. Knowing that this was probably the last time I would see my son softened my typically hard edges with officers who spoke out of turn.

Regulations were clear about not having family members serving in the same squadron, let alone a fleet. However, my rivals in the navy broke every rule in the book to get Jacob off his assignment to a destroyer in the 9th and in command of the *Whirlwind*. They said it was a favor to me, but I knew they had done it to chain my entire family to the same cause. If the Shadow pattern failed, then we would both have a major black spot on our record. I couldn't help but feel sick when I considered the fact that my boy was going to die because of my ambition and the navy's politics.

We stared at each other for a moment before I blurted, "I'm sorry, son. I wish there was another way, but this is where we are. The *Ascendancy* is too valuable of a target. Even if we don't make it, we have to try."

Jacob waved away my statement. "Dad, I knew that I may be called to give my life when I signed on. Can't say that I wanted it to be like this, but I knew. Now is the time for us both to answer that call, and I plan on doing that like a sailor in the Dionysian Navy."

On a whim, I decided to hug my son. It was a massive breach of protocol. However, I also didn't care. The navy had stolen enough years from me already. It was time to steal a few moments back. Especially when these fleeting seconds were probably the last we would ever have together.

"I love you, son," I said quietly into Jacob's ear as we embraced.

"You too, Dad," he said. "Now let's go kill this goddamn thing."

I laughed at his bravado, knowing it was all a man could do in moments like this. "Let's."

We pulled away from each other then and parted ways as two naval officers instead of a family. If we hadn't, I would have abused my power to send the *Whirlwind* away to join the 9th. I needed every gun I could muster, though, even if I hated myself for not trying to save him. Without *Whirlwind* under my command, our chances went from impossible to slightly more impossible. All I could hope for as I left the ops room and headed toward the bridge was that this last mission would be worth it. Maybe another father somewhere could keep his son at the cost of mine.

III

DRS VICTORY
5TH FLEET
ADMIRAL FRANK DAVIDSON, COMMANDING
NEW PITTSBURG SYSTEM
CLOSEST DIONYSIAN REPUBLIC COLONY: RICHMOND (20 LY)

A consequence of my promotion was Commander Reed moving up to the captain's chair of the *Victory*. I couldn't promote him to the rank, but I could give him the position. It would have taken too much time to push the paperwork. And what did that matter in the face of a real command? After all, every one of us who took the oath and put on the uniform wanted to captain a warship before we got out. My only regret was that it had taken so long for one of my oldest friends and best officers I'd ever served with to get his shot.

From his position on the bridge, Reed turned to me and said, "FTL cycle down begins in five minutes, Admiral."

"Very well," I said. "Everything within nominal parameters?"

"Yes, sir."

"Excellent," I said, then after a few quiet seconds I asked, "how does it feel being in the big seat?"

He grinned. "Not as comfy as you made it look. You've got all that extra padding, though, so I suppose anything is comfortable."

Despite myself, I smiled back. "You old son of a bitch. You're damned lucky I won't be able to write a disciplinary report after this."

Reed wasn't deep into middle age like me, but he was far too old for the rank of commander. That was another unfortunate aspect of the battles surrounding the Shadow pattern. He had been an ardent supporter of it as well as my personal aide while we waged our political war on Dionysia. Just like when they assigned my son to the 313th, my rivals systematically denied every opportunity Reed had for promotion. I hated them for it, but now I realized it might be for the best.

When you know it was now or never, the truth comes easy. Reed was, without question, the only sailor I would trust to command the *Victory* in my absence. I wanted, no, *needed* him to hear that. Two decades of honorable service to the Dionysian Navy, and Reed deserved to know that he was one of the best.

With a meaningful look to Reed, I said, "Commander, I want you to know that you are one of the finest officers I have ever served beside. You are a credit to the naval profession, and this promotion is long overdue."

"Thank you, sir," he mumbled.

"I wish it was under better circumstances."

"'Better circumstances?'"

I frowned. "Gabe, you know this is a one-way trip. For all of us."

"We might get lucky. Crazier things have happened."

A sigh exited my lips before I said, "They have, but I don't think today will be one of them."

"Remarkably poor morale for an admiral," Reed whispered in a conspiratorial tone.

"That's why I'm not making a stink. How well-briefed is the crew?"

"They understand what we need to do. I failed to mention you think they're all going to die. Do you want me to correct that error?"

"I'll let it pass, just this once."

Reed gave me a meaningful stare. "Sir?"

"Yes, Commander?"

"In case there's not a better time, it was an honor serving with you."

I nodded, then said, "It was, Gabe. It really was."

"Captain," the helmsman said, "thirty seconds to FTL translation."

"Weapons primed, sir!" the gunnery officer called out.

"Standing by, Skipper!" the sensor officer reported.

"Comms are up!" the signal officer said.

"Admiral," Reed said in a professional tone while staring at the countdown on the bridge screen, "*Victory* is... twenty-five seconds from translation."

"You know what to do," I said, eschewing protocol for simplicity.

"Aye, sir."

I stepped away from the captain's chair and pulled out my personal communicator. "Piledriver Six, this is the admiral. Report status."

"Personnel are loaded with void seals on." Fredricks's voice crackled over the communicator a second later. "We're ready to hit it on your go, sir."

"Roger that, Piledriver. Stand by for deployment."

"Roger, standing by."

"Semper Fidelis," I said on a whim, quoting that ancient axiom the DRMC said with pride to this day.

"Ooh-rah," Fredricks said, offering another piece of history back to me.

"Fifteen seconds!" the helmsman shouted.

We waited as the automated countdown droned on in silence. I briefly wondered if this was the time FTL space would finally consume me, but the *Victory* broke back into reality without issue. Of course, my stomach still flipped for a second with the translation like it always did. Even after two decades on void ships, I couldn't avoid that unpleasant bout of nausea. Thankfully, the feeling passed as soon as data started coming in from the sensor officer.

"Captain," she said, "detecting one massive contact on long-range scans. There's one, no, three... wait, ten additional contacts. Tonnage is consistent with Hegemony frigates."

"The larger contact?" Reed said, leaning forward in his chair.

"I… I don't know, sir, but there's no way that isn't the *Ascendancy*. I've never seen a ship that big before."

"Stealth systems?" Reed said.

"Active, sir," the helmsman said.

"What about the rest of the 5th?" I interrupted.

"*Whirlwind* and *Justice* look like they're translating now, Admiral," the sensor officer said.

Reed didn't look at me for confirmation before giving out orders. "Comms, send a tight beam to them when they're clear. Sensors, keep a firm eye on that monster. If it so much as dumps garbage, I want to know about it."

"Aye, sir," they said in unison.

Five agonizing minutes passed with us waiting for the *Justice* and *Whirlwind* to signal back. Once we were in position to start phase one, the remnants of the 5th Fleet waited at the system's edge in case we needed to perform an emergency jump. After all, this entire plan relied upon stealth. If we lost it before we were ready, the *Ascendancy* and its pickets would tear us apart. We were ready for that, too, but only when we were close enough to make a difference. I wouldn't sacrifice my fleet before then.

"Fleet is mustered, and we are undetected, sir," Reed said at five minutes and one second.

"Begin the mission," I said with more confidence than I really felt.

"Helm, plot a course to the *Ascendancy*. Tell engineering to run us at fifteen percent power. Comms, tell the *Justice*, *Whirlwind*, and our escorts to do the same," Reed said.

"Aye, Captain. Fifteen percent," the helmsman said.

A lifetime ago, I had served as an ensign in the 12th Fleet. North was only a lieutenant back then, and Reed wasn't even in high school. That was the last major war the navy had taken part in against the Hegemony. What immediately stuck out to me as we crept closer to New Pittsburg was how much easier battle was in those days. All we had to do was jump in and batter the Royal Navy into submission.

This new war presented new opportunities, though. Shadow patterns can, and would, provide the Dionysian Navy with opportunities we wouldn't have dreamed of in more clear-cut engagements of the past. Even though I was the man who spearheaded the initiative, I found the operational realities of stealth difficult for me to handle. Every second that passed made me want to order the 5th to go weapons hot and bracket our enemies with enfilading fire. However, the only reason we weren't burned-out hulks was that I hadn't. So, it forced me to wait with growing impatience while we eased our way into the demarcation point for phase two.

"How close are we?" I said after an hour.

Reed was an avatar of calm when he said, "Helm?"

"Just about there, sir. Tough to get a read on the *Justice* and *Whirlwind*."

"Damn stealth systems," Reed said with a chuckle.

"Whoever thought of that should be retired," I said.

Reed smirked, then said, "No kidding."

Tight beam communication was notoriously unreliable and only useful at close range, so we had agreed that the *Justice*, *Whirlwind*, and our escorts could go weapons hot at the captain's discretion. It was a surprise for all of us when our twin destroyers opened up with their batteries. That didn't last for long, though. *Victory*'s crew was too competent to freeze in a fight.

"Captain!" the sensor officer shouted. "5th Fleet is officially engaged with the enemy pickets!"

"Very well," Reed said. "Helm, accelerate to eighty percent power. Gunnery, plot solutions on any incoming hostiles. You may fire at discretion."

"Aye, Captain!"

Almost instantly, the gunnery officer started calling out targets to his ratings. Dionysian naval doctrine requires all vessels to take part in annual gunnery drills, so I had felt the *Victory* fire before. However, I hadn't been on a ship at war in a long time. The sensation of all sixty twin-linked sixteen-inch batteries discharging simultaneously was incredible. Though it wasn't audible in the void outside, the *Victory* roared a titanic battle cry which shook across the hull. It felt like the wrath of an iron god made manifest. That was the last time I ever openly smiled. Despite everything, it felt good to hear my baby let fly.

The bridge was a model of controlled chaos as we drove the

5thFleet like a wedge into the Hegemony picket. They outnumbered us, sure, but without the *Ascendancy*, our vessels were larger and better equipped than theirs. *Whirlwind* scored the first kill on a Hegemony frigate about ten minutes into the engagement, and I couldn't be prouder of my son at that moment. Of course, there was no time to tell him, but I hoped he knew, anyway.

"*Justice* has three frigates on her! Captain Dufresne is reporting moderate damage!"

"*Whirlwind* is moving to engage the final Hegemony vessels!"

"Captain, I have a solution on one ship engaging the *Justice*!"

"Fire!"

A roar, followed by a tectonic shake, rattled the *Victory*, then the helmsman said, "Missile strike on the fore section, Captain!"

"Damage report!" Reed shouted over the din.

"Minimal," the helmsman said after spending a second to look over the ship's systems display. "Damn lucky that was from a frigate. The *Ascendancy* would have ripped us apart."

"Accelerate to attack speed! Sensors, give me a status on the *Ascendancy*!"

"She's powering up, Captain! Far as I can tell, no energy shields!"

"Far as you can tell?" I snapped.

"Sir, I have no fucking idea what I'm looking for. All I can tell you is the biggest ship I've ever seen in my life is showing power fluctuations strong enough to supply half of Dionysia."

That was a fair point, so I said, "Very well."

Inertial dampeners kicked into overdrive as the *Victory* tore through the battle space toward the *Ascendancy*. Artificial gravity struggled to compensate as a result and tugged at everyone on the bridge with immense pressure. Most of the younger sailors were forced to grab on to something to remain standing. Some fell over from the force of the *Victory*'s charge. I only stayed upright by leaning far enough forward that I would have toppled over in better circumstances. Seeing your admiral flip over was bad for morale, so I knew I had to put on the airs of a man completely under control. Even if I felt more like vomiting all over the floor in front of me.

"Distance to target?" Reed asked when things settled down to a point where communication was possible.

"Sir, *Ascendancy* is firing her engines!" the sensor officer interrupted.

"What? Isn't she still docked at the station?"

"Sir, look," she said and brought up the sensor feed on the bridge display.

Sure as hell, the *Ascendancy* was breaking from New Pittsburg Station. It wasn't a graceful exit, either. Docking arms ripped off the station, and the *Ascendancy* literally rammed its way through everything in its path. The complete process took less than thirty seconds. Once it was over, New Pittsburg Station wasn't much more than orbital debris descending downward to the surface of the planet that fed it. I wondered how many people would die from the impending ecological disaster of skyscraper-sized chunks slamming into the ground. That was quickly overshadowed by the grim realization of how many Dionysians would die if we failed.

"Gunnery, plot that solution, now!" Reed barked.

"Captain, *Ascendancy* is training her guns on us!" the sensor officer shouted.

"Gunnery!"

"We're still outside of optimal range, captain! We need thirty seconds!"

"Sensors, how long do we have?"

"Less!" she cried.

"Fuck," Reed growled loud enough that only I could hear him. "Orders, sir?"

"Gunnery," I said, "margin of error on the shot?"

"Twenty percent, Admiral!"

I nodded to Reed, and he said, "Gunnery, you are clear to launch."

"Aye, sir. Standby!"

Unlike the guns, which were continuously hammering the Hegemony pickets with devastating volley fire, we heard nothing when the area denial weapon launched out of the torpedo tubes. The only reason we knew it happened was that the gunnery officer told us. The young lieutenant called out the distance from munition to target, sensors tried to shout over him with data from the *Ascendancy*, and Reed was screaming at the helmsman to redirect our course away from the blast radius of the weapon. In short, it was absolute madness, and only the detonation stopped the quagmire.

What I can only explain as the largest explosion I have ever seen in twenty years of service flashed across the bridge displays. Some navies foolishly had reinforced glass observation windows on their bridge so they could view the majesty of space. Dionysia didn't indulge in the practice, and it relieved me that such was the case. All we saw was a wide yellow ball of light before the displays shorted out. Admittedly, it was unnerving standing in a room with a blank wall ahead of us where there had been a heated battle seconds earlier. Unease turned to horror when they reactivated, though.

"My god," Reed said in the silence that had overtaken the bridge.

"Wha– how?" the gunnery officer said louder.

"I'm… I'm trying to scrub radiation, sir. There's a lot of it bleeding off of her, but I think the shields are down. No way to tell, though," the sensor officer said.

Now was the time to be an admiral, it appeared, so I walked over to Reed and put a hand on his shoulder. "Gabe, order your helm to bring us around. Marines are ready to deploy. Now is the time."

"But we didn't even scratch it!" he said.

"You are the captain of this ship, Commander Reed," I said with a bit more steel in my voice. "Do as I say. We will kill this thing."

"Right, of course, sir," he said mechanically. "Helm, bring us around. Comms, inform Colonel Fredricks his marines are going in."

"Aye, sir," they said.

"Keep it together, Gabe," I said with my best attempt at reassurance. "We aren't out of this yet."

He nodded. "Yes, sir."

IV

DRS VICTORY
5TH FLEET
ADMIRAL FRANK DAVIDSON, COMMANDING
NEW PITTSBURG SYSTEM
CLOSEST DIONYSIAN REPUBLIC COLONY: RICHMOND (20 LY)

Five minutes after detonation, we realized our initial damage estimates were off. Not by enough to end the battle, but enough that the *Ascendancy* was struggling to get her weapons back online. Based on speed projections, we were confident that we had one pass without it being able to fire. Everyone knew that each successive pass after this one was going to be a much more difficult proposition, so this had to be done as effectively as possible.

"Get us in tight," Reed said to the helmsman. "There is no way we are doing this stationary. Maintain speed and prepare for rapid course correction after the first salvo."

"Sir," the gunnery officer said, "are we certain about these deployment points?"

"Have we been sure about anything since this started, Lieutenant?"

"Right, sir."

"Message from the *Whirlwind*, Captain. Captain Davidson is reporting all picket vessels are destroyed. *Justice* has suffered extensive damage, but they are asking if they can deploy marines," the comms officer said.

Reed looked over his shoulder at me, and I said, "Yes, Lieutenant, *Whirlwind* and *Justice* are clear for launch. Tell them that in the chance that we go down before this is over, they are to deploy all marines and hammer that goddamn thing with broadsides until it says uncle."

"Aye, sir."

"How do you rate our chances now?" Reed said while the *Ascendancy* grew on the bridge displays.

"Don't ask," I said.

Truthfully, I did not know our odds. Intel had been so goddamn certain that the nuke would work. They hadn't given me anything else to go off of. We couldn't even tell how hurt the *Ascendancy* really was. There was no data to make an informed decision. That in mind, I decided not to make one. All we could do now was what we planned to from the start: destroy that ship.

"You're clear, gunnery!" the helmsman called out a minute later.

"Firing boarding torpedoes!"

A pause, then the comms officer said, "That's a good launch, sir. Piledriver Six is onboard."

The comms officer laughed after that, and Reed wheeled around on her. "Something to say, Lieutenant?"

"Uh, sir, Piledriver is reporting that Hegemony forces are... surprised to see him. Resistance inside has been minimal."

There wasn't any cheering or hurrahs, but that lightened the mood a bit. Perhaps Fredricks's ground pounders could pull this off. I wasn't willing to take a risk on that alone, though. Prince Henry seemed to agree with me too.

"Incoming!" the sensor officer screamed.

Where the first hit the *Victory* took was minimal, I was certain this one was telling. Kinetic fury slammed into our ship, tossing everyone around like rag dolls. I hit the ground and felt my nose crack off the hard metal deck plates. Hot liquid and a smell like copper immediately overwhelmed my senses, and it took me longer than I'd like to admit getting back up.

Alarms howled across the bridge when I rose. The helmsman was frantically dividing his attention between damage reports and course calculations. Reed somehow bashed his head against the back of the captain's chair, and blood ran free from a deep gash in his scalp. He was a tough bastard, though, and didn't let pain distract him from his duties.

"Damage report!"

"Extensive!" the helmsman said, still parsing through the data.

"Don't give me that shit, ensign. I need details."

"Aye, Captain."

Three seconds later, he said, "Portside batteries are gone, sir. Engineering reports a reactor leak that is flooding the local area. The marines are... well, the torpedo array took a direct hit."

"What is the status of our outside decks?" Reed asked with more patience than I expected of him.

"Decks ten through fifteen are holed through to varying degrees. Fires on deck nine. One hundred percent casualties on exposed decks. Deck nine looks like somewhere near fifty percent."

Reed turned to me. "Sir, there is no way we are putting a scratch in the *Ascendancy* as we are. Current status is combat ineffective."

I said nothing, so Reed prompted me with, "Orders, Admiral?"

Another explosion flashed on the left side of the bridge display, and the sensor officer said, "That was the *Justice*, sir. She's gone."

"What's the situation on the *Whirlwind*?" I asked.

"Captain Davidson is saying *Whirlwind* is about as bad as we are, and escort frigates are destroyed," the comms officer said. "He's, uh, advising a ram, Admiral."

"Twenty seconds until projected enemy reloads are complete," the gunnery officer said. "Captain, Admiral, I feel confident in saying we can't take another hit like we just did."

I turned to Reed and said, "Ask engineering if they can spike our reactor."

"Yes, sir," he said.

After Reed asked, the helmsman said, "They're saying they can't without starting a catastrophic failure."

Here it was, the final decision. If we were lucky, I could order the 5th to retreat. However, the *Ascendancy* would still be there. Fredricks had about a thousand marines on board, but there was no way they were going to take the ship with so few of them. So, either I finished the mission, or Dionysia would die like the eleven hundred marines and God knows how many sailors on the *Victory*.

"Shit," I whispered, then raised my voice. "Captain, I am ordering you to spike your reactor and perform a ram alongside the *Whirlwind*. Tell captain Davidson to do the same to his reactor. Make sure he understands I want him to generate a catastrophic failure, not just to overpower his engines."

"Aye, sir," Reed said, then turned to his crew to hand out the *Victory*'s last order.

Bringing the *Victory* around for its last pass proved difficult. The only way we pulled it off was by driving the reactor to one-hundred-fifty percent power. Since it was already leaking, the increased radiation exposure killed the engineering crew in seconds in one of the most painful ways imaginable. However, they followed my orders without hesitation. Though I expected nothing less from sailors of the Dionysian Navy, I was proud to see they did what had to be done at the end.

"Bring us in, helm," Reed said.

"Aye, sir. It was an honor."

"It was, ensign," he said.

"I feel like I should read off some sappy poetry," I said to Reed as we sped up toward the *Ascendancy*.

"I'd rather you tell me this was worth it," he said glumly.

"Comms," I said.

"Admiral?"

"Message to the *Whirlwind*. Tell my son that I love him."

"Done, sir," she said in a low tone when the *Ascendancy* dominated our viewscreen like I had only seen planets do before now.

"Reactor meltdown imminent," the helmsman said.

"Gabe," I said.

"Frank," he replied.

"Thank you. For everything."

"I wouldn't have done it any other way."

Maybe that was the best any of us could ask for. A life lived without regret. Telling those we love we loved them. Doing what's right, no matter the cost. Making the sacrifices we all fear, but all respected in equal measure. I hoped my son, Colonel Jeremiah Fredricks, Jessica Dufresne, and the thousands of Dionysian heroes I had just killed understood that I did the best I could for them at the end. If there was any other way, I would have chosen it.

Those were the final thoughts that ran through my mind as the *Victory* rammed the *Ascendancy* amidships. The prow, which was moving at hundreds of miles per second, sunk deep into the dreadnought. I didn't see the *Whirlwind* hit, but that was okay. Life owed me that, at least. No father should have to bury his son, let alone see him die.

V

DIONYSIAN REPUBLIC WAR DEPARTMENT
ADMIRAL SILAS NORTH, SECRETARY OF WAR
DIONYSIA SYSTEM

"Word from New Pittsburg, sir," the aide said to North, handing him a tablet.

The War Secretary studied the tablet for a moment, then said, "This is confirmed?"

"Straight from the *Victoria*, sir."

"Survivors?"

"Check page two, sir."

North did, and he saw nothing short of devastation. A thirteen-kilo-meter hulk of irradiated steel drifted above New Pittsburg, heavily charred from nuclear annihilation. Davidson had done it, and he sacrificed his life and his own goddamn son to make it happen. If he had the time to grieve or feel anything besides the need to save his people from extinction, North may have wept in that moment. There was no time for that, though, even with the 9th and 12th's recent victories.

"Put him and his son in for the Dionysian Cross," North said, handing the tablet back.

"What about the crew, sir?"

"Can't give everyone a medal, son. It's not like it's going to bring them back. The Davidsons' sacrifice is a sign for the living. In my experience, the dead care little about honor."

ABOUT THE AUTHOR

Theodore "Ted" Hodges is a US Army Veteran, Father of Three, and a lifelong fan of various Science Fiction, Fantasy, and Classical Titles. When not writing, he spends most of his time questioning the nature of reality, immersing himself in speculative universes, and studying human history.

A MOTHER'S LOVE

By J. R. Handley & Liska McCabe

What would you sacrifice for family?

A MOTHER'S LOVE

Tick-tock, tick-tock.

The ambient noises grew louder as she met her opponent's deep-blue eyes, questioning every decision that led her to this moment. When she'd taken a commission in the United States Space Force, Major Lainey "Sauce" Parvin thought it'd be a lark. Just another fun distraction in her never-ending quest to find meaning. A search for answers she'd thought she'd find in the inky voids of space.

Now what? Lainey asked herself, looking for solutions to the puzzle before her. She mentally stepped back, observing the entire battlefield, just as she'd learned at the Academy all those years ago. There were three possible moves, each more desperate than the last. Only one would allow her to survive. The others meant certain elimination, though the end would be spectacular.

Watching the steps, her face frozen in anticipation, Lainey waited.

One.

Two.

Three.

The second the fourth and final step finished, her nemesis met Lainey's eyes. The foe smiled brightly and snickered sarcastically, "Sorry, Mom!"

Lainey smiled and laughed along with her family over the board game. "Oh, you got me again!"

"I'm good at this game," the little girl said confidently, eminently pleased with her temporary victory.

"Yes, you are," Lainey said. "Do you know what I'm good at?"

Her daughter looked up at her expectantly.

"Tickle Monster!" Lainey yelled as she grabbed her squealing five-year-old. She tickled her daughter's sides, grinning at the sound of raucous laughter.

"Wow, she really got you good!" Lainey's husband, Michael, said over the viewscreen.

"I know," she said, equally as surprised at her youngest daughter's legitimate win. She was sure that shock was still evident in her voice but was too proud of her little girl to hide the raw emotion. "Ariella is becoming quite the little Trouble shark!"

"Your turn, Dad," said Lainey's eldest daughter, fifteen-year-old Zahra.

It's nice to see her enjoying herself, even if she did try to hide her giggle behind a coughing fit. Lainey was happy to finally see the moody teenager smile again. She didn't let her gaze linger too long, though, knowing never to bring attention to an angsty teen's happiness.

"Chase!" Lainey called to her twelve-year-old son. "Hurry up and get in here! You're missing the whole game; it doesn't take that long to get a snack. What are you doing?"

"Coming, Mom!" came the disembodied reply.

While Michael took his turn through the virtual interface, Lainey surveyed the room again. She couldn't help herself; she just couldn't turn off the military. It had seeped into her bones, as much a part of her as the children she had carried inside of her. *Ok, maybe not as much a part*, she thought, chiding herself. *But you need to stay in the moment, Lainey, like the head-shrinkers suggested. Be in the moment for your kids.*

Despite her broken focus and imperfect concentration, she was glad to have this quality time together. She volunteered for the director of operations position at the 4001st Expeditionary Space Defense Squadron "Tigers" because the job was an accompanied tour, despite

its remote location. The squadron was oversized in the usual complement of manned SF-44 Valkyrie space superiority fighters and even
had its own attached armed reconnaissance drones, QSF-32 Reavers.
They were the main defense for the newly established and mostly
civilian Athena Outpost in the barely charted Musk system. The location was quiet, predictable, and boring for a fighter pilot. It was ideal
for a family. For her family.

The kids hadn't relished the idea of moving again, especially after
they found out that they'd be separated from their father for several
months. He still had to complete his own assignment at the Space
Force's Ganymede Station. It was close to where they'd be living; only
one bumpy trip through the Archangel Gate separated Michael and
their new home.

Everything was different on this new world, on Athena. The
atmosphere was just slightly more metallic, the planet revolved around
a thirty-hour day, and even the planetary rotation was off. The adjust-
ment had been rough, but after six months, the family was finally
settling in.

"So..." Michael said, drawling out the word to break through
Lainey's thoughts. "I've got some good news!"

"Oh yeah?" Zahra asked, cautiously optimistic.

"Yeah, I think you're really going to like it."

"Don't leave us hanging!" Zahra said, all pretense at indifference
gone.

"So you don't want to be surprised?" he asked.

"Daaaad," the kids groaned in a unison born of practice.

"Fine, I guess you might like hearing that the transfer orders just
came down. I've got three more weeks here, and then I get to join you
guys for good!"

Lainey smiled as her children celebrated the happy news with
exuberant shouts and clapping hands. The volume continued to esca-
late until Chase's shout of "Finally!" resonated throughout the living
quarters.

"How did you manage that? I thought it was going to be at least a
year," Lainey said.

"Seems Colonel Wood decided she needs another engineer on site.

I put in the request and said a quick prayer. Whatever happened after that was above my pay grade."

"Regardless of how it happened, I'm glad to hear."

"Me too." He sighed. "I miss you guys so much."

"I miss you too, Daddy!" Ariella said much louder than necessary in the small room and blew him a kiss.

She's such a ham, Lainey thought as she smiled indulgently. *She must've gotten that from his side of the family.*

The family continued enjoying their game night, thankful for the virtual interface. The outpost commander's decision to loosen the security lockdown was a godsend. It'd given them the time for Michael to play along, instead of simply watching them after the fact.

Or worse, she thought, of playing with them via message with the frustrating delays. Now, the game became a time for shared memories and bonding.

Several rounds later, after repeatedly sending each other's pieces back to home and moving their own pieces along, the game was back in full swing. The laughter almost drowned out Lainey's communicator.

She shared a glance with her husband. "You guys keep playing. I'll be right back."

Her smile faded quickly as she gently closed her office door. Everyone in the squadron knew it was her day off; they wouldn't have contacted her for anything shy of a full-scale invasion. *And even then, they'd wait until aliens had been sighted and a mothership was in orbit*, she smirked.

Frowning, she looked at the ID to see who was calling her. Lainey shifted from mom to major in a heartbeat. *All business, all the time*, just like her instructors at Patrick Space Force Base on the far away Florida coast had drilled into her. *Was the Academy really that long ago? It feels like just yesterday that I threw my cap into the air when it was finally over.*

Opening the comm channel, she answered, "Major Parvin speaking."

Immediately, she saw the nervous face of Technical Sergeant Flores on her screen. "Ma'am, I'm sorry to bother you on leave, but the commander wants to see all senior leaders ASAP."

"Why didn't Lieutenant Colonel McCullough just call me?" Lainey asked, confused by the overly proper adherence to protocol.

"No, ma'am, you misunderstand. Not the squadron commander. Colonel Wood wants everyone in the briefing room in the next thirty minutes."

Lainey's wide eyes were the only indication of her surprise. "Oh," she started slowly. "Right. Yes, thank you, Tech Sergeant. I'll be right there."

She took a deep breath, calming herself for the headache she knew was coming. After she was able to recenter her inner zen, Lainey quickly threw her flight suit on over her extremely comfortable pajamas and grabbed her boots. Being recalled while on leave was bad enough, but if the outpost commander was calling everyone in, something had gone seriously wrong.

"Hey, guys," she called as she reentered the living area, "bad news."

The three saw her flight suit, and their faces immediately fell. Tears sprang to Ariella's eyes as she scooted closer to her brother while Zahra spoke, "But you said you had today off. You promised!"

"I know I did, and I'm sorry," Lainey said, donning her boots and trying to sound as soothing as she could manage in a rush. "But when the boss calls you in, you go in. That's all there is to it. Hopefully, this won't take too long, and then we can get back to our day, alright?"

"Is everything okay?" Michael asked, seeing the worried expression she was trying to hide.

"Don't know yet. I'm sure it's nothing major, but I'll find out in a few minutes. Why don't you guys keep playing, and I'll jump back in later, okay?"

Ariella jumped to her feet, rushing over to hug her mother. "No fair!"

Lainey picked the small girl up easily and tried to placate her. "I know it isn't, but I promise I'll be back as soon as I can, okay? I love you, bug."

"I love you too, Mommy."

She squeezed her youngest and handed her the beloved stuffed shark she carried everywhere. "I'll be home soon. Zahra, you're in charge until I get back."

SHE WAS out of breath when she entered the briefing room. Scanning the room as she moved, Lainey took her designated seat. Her uncomfortable office chair was next to her immediate supervisor, Lieutenant Colonel Jacob "AERO" McCullough.

He looks as confused as me, she thought in surprise. *Heck, everyone looks confused.*

She observed the others in attendance, taking it in. The bloodshot eyes and mugs of coffee clued her in that this was serious. They'd kept people from going home at shift change and even brought in a junior officer who reeked of booze. *That was always a safe hedge against a recall on leave*, she thought. *Drunks can't be recalled from leave unless shit hit the fan.*

Even the civilians looked like they'd just rolled out of bed, as one of the staff bureaucrats was still wearing his pajamas under a lab coat. Most of the senior personnel at the outpost were civilians, purportedly experts in their respective fields. All the civilian department heads were present and thoroughly vexed: the clinic, the research station, and the civil engineering directorate.

The nervous tension is palpable. This is not a crowd that thrives on uncertainty.

McCullough leaned over to Lainey. "Hell of a way to spend your day off, isn't it, Sauce?"

"Do you have any idea what this is about?"

He opened his mouth to respond as the door opened and Colonel Michelle "Pecker" Wood took her spot at the table unceremoniously. Stern and brusque, she was a woman of few words whenever she could manage it. She would never win a "Miss Congeniality" contest, but she was an effective leader and very likely on the fast track to a star.

"Ladies and gentlemen, I'm sorry to bring you all here so cryptically. As you know, I detest the telephone game and I want all of us on the same page regarding the information I just received." She gestured to a scared lieutenant. "LT, if you would?"

That kid doesn't look old enough to shave, Lainey thought. *He wouldn't look out of place in Zahra's high school class.*

The young officer stood and clicked something on his pad, sharing it to the large screen behind him. He cleared his throat several times before beginning. "Ladies and gentlemen, I'm Lieutenant Gwaltney from the Intel shop. One hour ago, at 1347, long-range radar picked up a contact bearing two-seven-five, approximately two light-hours from here and closing, well inside our Space Defense Identification Zone. For those unaware, that is the general direction of the closest known stronghold of the People's Republic of Proxima Centauri. At this time, contact is still too far out to positively identify; however, we know of no other life-forms capable of interstellar travel. Rules of engagement still require positive ID prior to engaging; therefore, we will attempt communication when they come into range"—he looked at the chronometer on the wall—"three hours from now."

Aren't we too far away for those godless Commies from the PRPC? This can't be right!

"What about a defector?" McCullough asked. "Wouldn't be the first time."

"That's a remote possibility, sir; however, that is another reason we will attempt communication with it once it's within range to confirm or deny that. Currently, the ship is far enough away that the signal is degraded, but the best estimate of the engine signature indicates a Uragan-class ship. That's an extremely short-range vessel. Even with modifications, it's highly unlikely that it could make the trip here from the PRPC's closest installation and maintain its current track. The most-likely scenario given available information is that this is a scout, launched from a ship still outside our range."

"What would they want with such a small, remote moon?" asked the medical director.

The director of research answered her. "Doctor, this moon has a remarkably high concentration of a volatile compound not found on Earth. It's extremely dangerous and expensive to mine, and we can't synthesize it yet. Theoretically, we can make some interesting alloys with it, the kind that increase tensile strength and tolerance of materials a hundredfold. Better yet, potentially, we can make ship parts a lot lighter and using a lot less material."

The crowd's murmuring highlighted how uncomfortable some people were with sharing this information. "How dangerous is this stuff? They thought it was smart to move families here? Why weren't we fully briefed?"

The director continued, speaking louder above the din. "If the Commies took control of this place and figured out how to mine it—and they would, one way or another—things could get bad for us. They could develop ships, armor, and weapons that we couldn't penetrate with our current weapons and make lots of them."

"Not to mention," McCullough chimed in, "that the Archangel Gate would give them direct access to the Sol system."

"The Gate's the more-likely target," Lainey said.

"But how would they even know about it?" asked the doctor.

"We told them," the signal and communications officer answered plainly. Seeing his colleagues' surprised, angry faces, he continued, "Not intentionally, of course, but we did. The problem, you see, is that we don't know how these things—the Gates—were originally powered. We've learned how to apply our own power sources to them, but we have to do it slowly, at a continuous trickle, just to keep them from blowing out. But while it's charging up, and right up to the instant when it generates the warp bubble for a ship, you get constant emissions of Cherenkov radiation. Glow-in-the-dark kinda stuff. Nothing inherently unusual about that, but it puts out a lot of it, so it just screams 'artificial source.' And it gives off huge bursts of electromagnetic pulses, jets of highly charged particles, at routine intervals like a pulsar. We can manipulate smaller warp fields to cause a lensing effect, to send effective FTL comms signals through the Gate, and we can even tweak that effect to behave like a pseudo-synthetic aperture radar. That's how we found this Commie ship.

"The larger the bubble we generate, the bigger the bursts get. It's not the warp bubble itself causing that; it's powering the damn thing up and down. Generating larger fields, like for ships, will naturally cause larger bursts, but even standard communications through it will cause some level of pulse. So we can see something coming our way, but it can also see us. I suspect the PRPC intercepted that signal and are coming to investigate."

"So what you're saying," Colonel Wood started slowly and deliberately, "is that we've been flashing a giant Eat at Joe's sign above our outpost this entire time?"

The signal officer shifted nervously in his seat, fidgeting with his hands. "I'd say it's closer to running a radar when the other guy has homing missiles, but yes, ma'am."

"Can't you just shut it off or something?" the doctor asked, her voice rising in pitch.

"With all due respect, Doctor, it's too late for that. They know *something* is here, and they're on their way," McCullough answered. "Even if we could just shut it down, that would hurt us more than them."

"How long before it gets here?" Lainey asked, already considering several courses of action.

"Approximately eight hours at current course and speed. It doesn't seem to be accelerating or decelerating; it's probably just coasting right now. We have about three hours until it's within comms range, like the LT said."

The assembled directors murmured and argued the situation amongst themselves. *About time these civilians see what chaos actually looks like*, Lainey thought. *These paper pushers want to talk shit about us one second then demand that we be their human shield the next. Guess they've decided that we're useful after all.*

The conversation continued to flow around her until something caught her attention. She perked up, listening to the bureaucrats calling for a total evacuation of all civilians.

"Knock it off!" Colonel Wood said, loudly slapping the table. "Thank you, Lieutenant, great job."

After the young officer sat down, Wood stood to keep the attention of the raucous crowd. "I'm not one for rash judgements. If we were all service members, this would be an easy decision. Gate Defense Command has ordered us to protect this station by any means necessary. Despite our task, the safety of everyone here is my utmost priority. I won't bet our civilians' lives on the chance that this might be a defector or even another life-form on a first contact. Since this is a Space Force base outside the Solar System, authority to order a Noncombatant Evacuation Operation is delegated to me. Prepare to evacuate all civilian personnel back to Ganymede Station. Take ore samples and hard copies of all your research. Zeroize the memory drives, leave the Commies with nothing."

"Ma'am," the logistics officer said, "that's going to get really expensive—"

"Then we bill it as a large-scale exercise and continue mission. Space Force Public Affairs will handle any fallout. Directors, you're dismissed. Commanders, we'll reconvene here in five minutes."

Lainey smiled to herself. *Only someone with a star just waiting for her can afford to be that confident.* Pecker was on the fast track, and even if she made an overly cautious call here, it wouldn't slow her down.

Those still assembled dashed for coffee or mumbled their ideas to each other, immediately ruling out the terrible ones before suggesting them to Colonel Wood. Without the civilians present to distract them, they were able to slip more easily into warfighter mode. Lainey preferred that while working instead of constantly having to mind her manners and explain terminology that was a second language to her.

Lainey stood by the interactive, 3D holographic projector dubbed the "whiteboard" after the ubiquitous tool of generations past. She conferred briefly with her Weapons and Tactics officer, Captain Tyrone "Crunch" Hodges, before the meeting came to order. Crunch was the tactical heart of the squadron, a fresh graduate of the Weapons School, young and hungry. He had the bare-bones outline of a plan already scribbled out on the whiteboard's display to show her.

Lainey, now in pure "Sauce mode," studied his work. "Yeah, that looks good; just remember to stay flexible."

"Semper Gumby, ma'am," Crunch said as Colonel Wood reentered the room and gestured for all present to find a spot where they could see.

"Alright, everyone, I couldn't say this with the civilians around, but with the information at hand, preliminary as it may be, hoping for anything other than a PRPC scout ship is a pipe dream at best, so we'll be planning for that and for every contingency we can think of." She turned and gestured to Captain Hodges. "Crunch, you have the floor."

"Yes, ma'am. In three hours, this ship will reach the point at which we can maintain voice communication with minimal delay. Before that time, we will stage a four ship of drones in orbit for a combat patrol. I will honcho the battle space from SCAT's ops center here on the ground. Once we make voice contact with the ship, we will intercept, detain, and escort them to a secure area for debriefing."

Lainey loved that code word in particular. "Debriefing" always sounded great in the media reports, leaving civilians to assume it meant "to have a nice, civil chat." Whereas she, and every other servicemember, knew it really meant "to throw in a dark hole and interrogate the shit out of someone."

"What if they resist?" asked a young flight commander.

Colonel Wood gave the final word on the matter. "Bring them in if you can; bring them down if you can't."

The silence hung heavily, with no one wanting to address the elephant in the room. "We can defend the station," Major Vitter insisted, looking around the room for support. "My Security and Police personnel are trained for more than just guarding Gates. We can support the fight."

Lainey's eyes narrowed, wondering if Vitter missed the implication of the inbound ship. "Do you think that ship is really wandering out here on its own? If this is PRPC, it was launched from a carrier. Has a lone carrier ever operated this deep within our space at any time during this decades-long war, either in its hot or cold phases? No, if that ship pinged our sensors, there is a fleet behind it. One we're not equipped to engage."

"Crunch," Captain "Fletch" Singer, the squadron's newest flight commander, spoke up, "when should we know if there's anything trailing that ship?"

"No way to tell at this time, Fletch, but we can extrapolate a few likely approach vectors based on the scout's flight path," Crunch answered honestly. "However, we'd be idiots not to plan for the worst-case scenario."

"Ma'am." Lainey spoke. "What about reinforcements from Ganymede?"

"That request is already at Garrison, Sauce."

"We shouldn't count on that," Crunch said grimly. "There are maintenance requirements for every ship that passes through the Gate. Garrison isn't known for waiving those requirements regardless of the circumstances. We should plan for what we have and fold any rein-forcements we may get into our plan. I recommend we form a blockade to deny the enemy access to our space."

"Are you insane?" AERO interjected. "We only have thirty-six fighters here. We can get thirty spaceborne, maybe thirty-two or thirty-three, if we bend some rules. We'll be slaughtered!"

"Sir, you'll have thirty-six. Period," the grizzled maintenance chief promised with a nod.

"If you have a better suggestion, AERO, now is the time," Colonel Wood said. She stared at him expectantly until he sighed and shook his head. "All flight personnel will remain to form a blockade. Crunch, retain any support staff you need in order to manage the battle from orbit. We'll do what we can to protect our assets here and reassess when we know what we're facing. Sauce, Intel, see what you can do to extend the long-range sensors. We'll probably get a ton of false positives and background noise, but we need as much warning as we can get."

"If we're assuming a fleet, though, how can we possibly hold them off long enough to even ensure the civilians get away?" Lainey asked.

"I have some ideas about that," Crunch smiled. "Buckle up, every-one. It's about to get wild."

The planning meeting lasted another two hours. Led by Crunch, they finally laid out a game plan that Pecker, AERO, and Sauce could sign off on and a few contingency plans. Lainey was mentally exhausted but felt they'd prepared as well as could be expected.

As they wrapped up, the installation's logistics officer timidly raised his hand. "Colonel Wood, these plans involve a lot of war reserve materiel. If all this turns out to be nothing..." he trailed off.

"Like I said earlier. 'No-notice snap-alert exercise.' We'll all get awards for being 'innovative' and 'readiness focused.' HQ will love it, really. In the meantime, let's make it happen."

The assembled room jumped to attention and waited as Colonel Wood left the room. The time for discussion was over.

———

WITH MARCHING orders disseminated and preparations begun, the situation was under control for the moment. Lainey walked back into her quarters in a daze.

"What am I going to tell the family?" Lainey wondered, talking to herself. "How am I going to pull this off without panicking the kids?"

She desperately hoped that the lone ship was just a defector, but she knew in her heart that it was something more. Life was about to get far more interesting than she'd ever wanted. *"May you live in interesting times,"* she thought. It was the quote her dad often told her when she was a kid. *I never really understood that proverb until today... son of a bitch.*

She was glad to see Michael still on the viewscreen when she walked into the house. He was watching a movie with the kids, cheerfully talking over parts to analyze. Lainey paused in the doorway and watched them cuddled on the couch, Zahra's arm gently wrapped around her sleeping little sister. She silently entered the living area and sat with them, gesturing for them not to wake the small child. Ariella shifted in her sleep to lean against her mother, squishing her ever-present shark between them, and sighed contentedly.

Lainey had to prepare the kids, and quickly, but the ship wouldn't even be within comms range for nearly an hour yet. She didn't know if she could afford the time to simply enjoy this, but she was going to take it anyway.

Zahra saw Lainey's eyes shining and lightly tapped her arm. "Mom," she whispered, "what happened?"

Lainey smiled tightly and blinked the tears away. "It's okay. I'll tell you after the movie."

For twenty blissful minutes, she sat with her children, stroking Ariella's back as she napped, stealing glance after glance at Zahra and Chase, memorizing them as they were in that moment, heartbroken that she'd have to ruin their peace. *They're worth it. Whatever happens, they're worth it.*

As the movie ended, the older kids stood to stretch, and Lainey shifted enough to wake Ariella. She rubbed her eyes and focused on Lainey. "Mommy!" she said happily and lunged forward to wrap her tiny arms around Lainey's neck. "I missed you!"

Lainey squeezed her harder than she intended. "I missed you too!"

She shifted to face the kids, Ariella still perched in her lap. "Okay, let's talk for a minute. Michael, I'm glad you're still on, because this is important. Turns out there's someone headed here, to the outpost."

Ariella perked up. "Is it Daddy?"

She had to chuckle a bit. "No, baby, it's not Daddy. We're not one hundred percent sure who it is just yet or what they want, so we're going to play this one extra safe. The good news is that you guys are going to go stay with Daddy for a bit until we get everything sorted out here."

"When?" asked Chase nervously.

"Tomorrow. Now, can you guys go and pack so I can talk to Daddy, please?"

Michael waited for the room to clear before speaking. "What's going on, Lainey?"

"It's the PRPC. There's a ship inbound—we think it's a scout. No telling what might be following it."

"Shit. So, what's the plan?"

"Attempt communication and try to bring it in. Prepare to evacuate all civilians."

"What about military?"

"The top priority is defending the outpost and the Gate. It's called Operation Red Rover and includes the noncombatant evacuation order.

We establish a perimeter around the moon and blockade as best we can, hopefully take out a few of the bastards in the process."

"I don't like it. What happens if you can't hold them?"

"Then we blow the Gate."

"You're light-years away. You'd be trapped out there!"

"I know," Lainey whispered. "But that's a last resort and only if things go tits up. We push as many people through the Gate as possible before that and hope they don't rip apart in transit. But Sol would be safe. I need to know that you and the kids are safe. That's enough for me."

"I don't like this," Michael said, frowning.

"The decision's already been made. Besides, this might be nothing. There's still a lot we don't know yet. Best case, the kids get to spend a few days with you before coming back out here and we get to count it as a major exercise. What I need you to do is make sure you're there to get them when they arrive. Promise me that."

"Of course."

They sat in silence for a full minute, sharing with a simple look all the hopes and fears coursing through them in that moment, each afraid to speak the words aloud.

"I wish I could hold you right now," he said, resigned.

"Me too," she sighed. Taking a breath to steel herself, forcing the confidence into her voice, she insisted, "But everything is going to be okay. We have a good group here, and with any luck, reinforcements will be arriving in a few hours. We've got this."

They smiled tightly at each other and nodded, both wanting to believe her.

"I love you," he said simply.

"I love you too. I'm going to go help the kids and check in with work. You go get some sleep while you can."

"Yeah right!"

"I'll call you when I know more," she promised.

He nodded and disconnected the call.

She briefly checked on the kids, spending a few minutes with each of them, and ducked into her office. Based on previous course and speed, the ship would be entering communication range within minutes, and she wanted to see what they were dealing with firsthand.

"Are we up?" she asked as a view of the operations floor came into view.

"Yes, ma'am," came the disembodied voice of Chief Master Sergeant Rayburn, the senior enlisted leader on the outpost.

Good, she thought, *he obviously wants to handle this personally. We need hands-on leadership right now, maybe more than we ever did.*

She muted her end and listened intently. All unnecessary noise on the floor died down as all eyes fixated on the inbound ship. The red star with hammer-and-sickle emblem of the PRPC contrasted brightly with the pristine hull of the spacecraft. Even the distortions she received from her piggybacked signal weren't enough to hide that hideous insignia.

"We have visual, Chief. Interrogating now," said a radar operator hitting the IFF switch. "No response."

"Damn. Alright, let's do this the old-fashioned way." Chief Rayburn nodded to the comm tech to his right. "If he won't squawk, let's see if he'll talk."

"Frequency is open."

"Inbound vessel" came the chief's booming voice, in his most authoritative tone. "Decelerate to one G and identify yourself."

All activity ceased as they awaited reply. She held her breath as she watched the screen impatiently. Seconds rolled by. Thirty seconds passed. Then a minute. The ship continued its passage, with no sign of retro burn or maneuvers.

"Inbound vessel, this is Athena Station. Decelerate to one G and identify yourself," Chief Master Sergeant Rayburn tried again.

No response.

"Are we sure they're hearing us?"

From the vantage point of the camera she was viewing, she saw a twitchy young specialist double-check his screens. "Yes, Chief, they should be receiving."

"Proxima Centauri vessel, this is Athena Station Control. You have violated sovereign US space. Respond or you will be intercepted."

Another tense minute with no response.

Toggling the camera to the left, Lainey watched as Chief Master Sergeant Rayburn looked towards Colonel Wood.

"How long until we can intercept, Specialist?" she asked, never taking her eyes from the screen.

"Approximately ninety minutes, ma'am," the young enlisted man replied.

"Crunch," she addressed the weapons officer, "as briefed, push the intercept. Update every fifteen minutes."

"Roger, ma'am. Push SCAT flight."

While the pilots prepared to assume control of the Carter-class picket drones, Lainey turned on her own drone station. The stations were included in the secure offices of every qualified pilot, though she'd only used it for training simulations. She much preferred flying with a real stick between her legs, and she chuckled at the thought. *Someday, I'll be mature enough to not laugh at that, but today is not that day.*

Lainey strapped into the boxy cockpit, a functional mockup of the one in the SF-44 Valkyrie she normally flew. Lainey waited for the link that would give her command of one the drones. Normally, she'd seal the home secure vault door and use her real flight helmet. This would give her a more immersive experience, but she couldn't leave her children unsupervised. Instead, even though it violated every security regulation she knew, she kept the door cracked just a little, and she turned up all of the other sensor outputs to compensate. She hoped no one called her on it and hoped it didn't negatively impact the mission.

"SCAT Lead, this is Two. Rejoining on your left. Let's make this bandit talk or squawk," Lainey said.

"Lead" came Captain Lance "Guppy" Macrae's acknowledgement.

"Three."

"Four."

Crunch, running the whole mission from the base operations center, issued the order. "Line abreast by elements. Monitor contact group, copy two mikes out. We'll do a dry pass to get their attention. They either bug out, or we make the return flyby a gun run. Arm safety off."

They were one minute out when their single radar contact split into three, five, and then seven enemy craft. The PRPC scout ship was escorted by six long-range fighter support vessels, a little bigger than standard fighters, although it wasn't a class Lainey was familiar with.

Crap, they must have been trailing just a few feet behind, and they exploited our sensor resolution limits. That's sporty. They've learned.

Crunch wasted no time issuing tactical orders. "SCAT flight, Dark Star, bandit group hostile engaged, seven targets. Sort: Lead and Two, take bandits one through four. SCAT Three and Four, take bandits five through seven. Weapons-free." Crunch said to the flight.

"Lead copies," Macrae acknowledged. "Sauce, target third and fourth. I've got one and two. Pick up any spitters."

"Two," Lainey responded as she pulled a hard right to engage her target. "Fucking Commies."

For the first time in her career, she forgot proper radio protocol. She was distracted by a sound behind her—one of her kids had entered the room and gasped as they watched her. "Mom!"

Muting her comms, she spoke over her shoulder, "Zahra, go back to packing! I have to handle this, okay? I need you to help take care of your siblings for me. Everything's going to be okay, but make sure they've got all of their important things in an overnight bag."

Turning her comms back on, Lainey resumed her focus on the screen in front of her. Her distraction cost her the chance to fire on the fighters during her first pass, but she doubted she could have gotten a high probability of kill shot anyway. By twos, SCAT flight arced a vector roll and, flipping end over end, hit their retros hard and shot toward the enemy group. She saw that one of the enemy fighters was gone, and the drone's debris warnings filled her speakers. She saw glints of light here and there, flashing into and out of view for mere seconds. Likely tracers. The drone's automated flight systems would help avoid streams of bullets and debris from destroyed targets. A human pilot could override the drone's own control inputs if he or she needed to.

Lainey ignored the whooping from Three and looked for her target. "Sauce tally bandit three," she said, arming a missile.

She waited for the high-pitched whine to tell her the radar was locked to her target. "Sauce locked bearing two-seven-five, Fox three!"

The missile fled its cage straight to the engine compartment on the enemy fighter, blowing the craft apart like a popped balloon.

That's when the remaining three enemy fighters abandoned the scout ship and broke off to engage SCAT flight.

Lead pinged her: "Two, target the scout. I've got the lead fighter." Lainey quickly saw her opportunity to engage the scout ship and took it before Crunch had the chance to assign her the task. "Dark Star, judy judy," she said to Crunch, telling him she had the matter well in hand. To Guppy, she said, "Lead, I'm going to the merge."

As she spoke, she kept the same vector but crab-angled her drone's facing toward the enemy scout ship, struggling to bring all of her weapons into play. The scout barreled on like a train. She struggled to match its speed as the ship accelerated. When she was within maximum engagement range, she brought her reticle onto the target and fired. Her missile separated, engine igniting dangerously close to her drone, and sped toward the enemy vessel. It appeared to track. While it flew, she armed her second missile and waited for the chance at another, more optimal shot, should her first miss.

"Splash one!" she heard Four shout over the comms.

"He's on my six. I can't shake him!" said Three.

She ignored the chatter, focusing on pursuing the enemy scout ship. He was only lightly armed for self-defense, with a gas-powered machine-gun turret on both its dorsal and ventral side for anti-missile coverage. While small caliber, they were still dangerous to her drone if she was dumb enough to fly through his lanes of fire. The bullets would go on forever until they hit something, so they were a hazard to SCAT flight and the surviving enemy fighters as well. So far, her first missile was avoiding the streams of bullets.

Growling, she fought the urge to curse when her first missile collided with a piece of the debris left from a destroyed enemy fighter. Adjusting her aim, she pushed the engines to their maximum capacity and used the extra delta-v to close some of the distance. The scout continued, speed its only real defense. When she was within the optimal zone for her weapons, she fired.

The missile shot outward, but the enemy scout pilot put in a full roaring white-hot burn from a maneuvering jet cluster. Instead of

getting a high probability of kill hit center mass, she sheared off the
bulbous right wing loaded down with pods. The combination of kinetic
impact from the missile and high-power maneuvering caused the bird
to tumble off axis, ass over end, before attempting to stabilize itself on
its new vector. It was still spinning. *At least I took out his weapons
pods*, she thought. *And it won't be landing in an atmosphere.* Checking
her weapons pods, she cursed under her breath.

"Chain gun is malfunctioning, need an assist. Does anyone have
missiles left?"

"Negative," said the flight lead.

Crunch came over the channel: "Keep them busy. We're scram-
bling some backup for you."

"Roger, Dark Star," Guppy acknowledged.

"Ramming authorized," Colonel Wood said, cutting into the
comms channel.

"Mom," Zahra said from behind her, sounding panicked.

"Mommy's busy right now," Lainey said, her focus on her drone.

Got you!

Lainey's missile had damaged the Uragan's internal gyroscope, and
the vessel slowed while the pilot struggled to determine which way
was now up. She used that time to close the distance with her drone
and turned off her collision overrides. The scout ship hadn't fully
stopped its tumble when her ship collided with it. Her feed cut to static
as both the target and her Carter-class picket drone ceased to exist.

Swapping over to monitor her subordinates, she saw her pilots ram
their drones into the remaining two enemy fighters. Her heart pounded,
amped by the excitement of the battle, despite the lack of real-time
consequences to her own immediate safety.

"Was that a drone too, Mom?" Zahra asked, her voice sounding
off-kilter.

*Oh God, they didn't cover this in the mom manual. What do I even
say to that? Do I lie? Do I tell her she just watched Mommy kill
people?*

"You're not answering. Someone was in there, weren't they?"

"We protected the colony. Those were bad guys with bad inten-
tions," Lainey said quietly. "I know you've learned about the war in

school. Unfortunately, sometimes taking out the enemy is a part of that."

"Are you scared?"

"Yeah, sometimes. Right now, though, I'm way more concerned about you guys. Go help your siblings; make sure they have everything important."

"But…"

"No 'buts.' I need your help. Please, get Chase and Ari ready to leave tomorrow without scaring them," she said quietly.

In the time she was talking to her daughter, the rest of SCAT flight had rammed the remaining enemy fighters. Although Crunch called them both kills, as she scanned the data, she saw that one had somehow survived was slowly heading on a reverse course.

"We've got a leaker," she said. "Can we cycle through to another picket drone to pursue it?"

"Negative," Colonel Wood said. "Distance is too great to intercept."

As they watched the debris scatter into the void, the senior radar operator called out over the shared video feed. "Ma'am, I've 'gonku-lated' all the new sensor data with Intel's help, plus data from the drone sensors collected during the fight. We got something big."

"What is it, Master Sergeant?" Colonel Wood asked. Lainey watched the woman as she approached the workstation, the camera following just over her shoulder.

"We were able to extend the sensor field a few thousand kilome-ters. Not much, but it gives us an extra half hour or so to react. This just entered that new range." She pointed to the new contacts on her screen. "Multiple signatures, ma'am. Coming from the exact course as the bandit."

"Fuck me—that's a carrier group. It's confirmed," Colonel Wood said grimly as she looked over toward Chief Master Sergeant Rayburn. She continued speaking as she looked at him, but it was obvious that she was addressing everyone present and online. "We have our answer. Red Rover is a go. Execute."

FROM HER APARTMENT, Lainey nodded involuntarily and opened a separate comm line to Lieutenant Colonel McCullough. "AERO, Red Rover is a go. I'm sending you all the estimates I have. Littoral ships from Ganymede are expected to arrive within the hour."

"Good. The cargo ships are already being loaded. The moon's rotation puts the station closest to the Gate in eight hours. That's when the civilians will depart. They need to report to the hangar in seven."

Only seven hours left with my babies, she thought as she worried about the safety of her kids.

Lainey barely squeaked out an answer as Zahra squeezed her in a deep hug. "Yes, sir."

McCullough's tone softened. "Look, I know this is hard for you. There's not a lot of time, but the wheels are already in motion. If I need you, I'll call you. Spend the time with your kids. Then when you get here in the morning, be ready."

"I will. Thank you."

As she disconnected, she turned to see Ariella standing in the doorway. She beckoned her in with a sad smile and wrapped her arms around the two girls.

"Mom," Zahra mumbled into Lainey's flight suit, "I'm scared. Please tell me what's going on. If things are bad, then you should come with us. We need you. Why can't you come with us?"

She pulled back and looked into her firstborn's terrified eyes. "Okay, here's the truth. You already saw some of it, but the PRPC are coming here. I know that you're aware of them. We don't know if they're after the Gate or the moon or what. Really, it doesn't even matter. What we do know is that you kids, all the scientists, everyone living here, are too important to take chances. So we all felt it was safer to evacuate you all. I have to help protect everything here, including you as you go through the Gate."

"When are you coming through it?" Zahra asked.

"As soon as it's safe to do so. In the meantime, I need your help to take care of Chase and Ari. You have grown into such a wonderful, beautiful young woman. You are so strong, such a great big sister, and they're going to need you until I can get back. Can you do that for me?"

Zahra couldn't speak, just nodded her head.

"I'm a big girl. I can take care of myself," Ariella said, though the other women ignored her.

"Good girl," Lainey said as she gently placed her hands on Zahra's face. She saw those determined eyes, a perfect foil to her younger sister's uncertain ones. "I am so proud of you. You are going to do amazing things one day. I love you so much."

"I love you too, Mom."

They squeezed each other tightly for all too brief a moment.

"Go ahead and get ready for bed. We have to be at the hangar early. I'll be there in a few minutes."

Nodding, Zahra left with Ariella's hand in hers. Lainey watched them go, feeling her heart swell with pride as she ran through a checklist for her own preparations.

Lainey called Michael to update him on the ever-changing situation and then checked on her sleeping son. *That boy could sleep through anything, even the end of the world.* She watched him for a moment, trying to swallow the crushing ache in her chest. He lay there on his bed, his gentle snores reverberating through the room, so much like his father. She wasn't sure how long she stared at him, but she knew she needed to check on his sisters, so she moved on.

When she got to Ariella's room, she found it empty and continued down the hall to her eldest daughter's room. The light was on, and Zahra was reading a bedtime story to her younger sister, hugging her as she gently rubbed her back with her free hand. When she opened the door, her eldest glanced at her and smiled.

Lainey entered the room and joined them on the bed, cuddling them both. She took the book from Zahra and continued the story. *I may never get to do this again,* she thought sadly.

The girls tried to fight it, but both nodded off quickly, contentment on their faces as they listened to their mother's voice. Lainey stayed until she finished the chapter, happy to give and receive as much affection as she could for a few precious moments. She carefully extricated herself, kissed their foreheads, and packed the book into Ariella's bag.

She moved to the kitchen and sat in one of the uncomfortable prefab chairs that came with every residence. As she sat there, Lainey stared at the locked liquor cabinet. There was a good bottle of scotch inside, one that she'd been saving for the right occasion. Checking the clock, she saw she had six hours until the kids had to depart. *Seven hours bottle to throttle*, she thought.

"Screw it, I'm having one."

She pressed her thumb to the biometric scanner and unlocked the cabinet, removing a Glencairn whiskey glass and the twenty-five-year-old Speyside single malt she and Michael had picked up at their first duty station. She had intended to open it when he joined them at Athena. That plan, like all of the most well-meaning ones, hadn't survived contact with the realities of a nation at war. She poured three fingers, resealed the bottle, and sat alone with her digital pad and her thoughts.

Eyes closed, Lainey let the smooth, brown liquid burn her throat and warm her belly. The subtle sweetness danced on her tongue, reminding her of the day she'd bought the bottle with her husband. *We should be sharing this drink together, like we planned. I promised him when I took this assignment that it would be a safe one.* Surprisingly, her thoughts were free of bitterness. She merely regretted that she'd been asked to leave her kids alone when they would need her the most.

Picking up the pad, she alternated between studying the operation and looking at family pictures. Goofy, smiling faces contrasted with missile placements and fighter formations. She needed to be absolutely sure where the no-fly zone was going to be.

An hour later, her glass empty and mind exhausted, Lainey walked to her bedroom and shuffled out of her flight suit. As she approached her bed, she saw a small, still figure occupying her pillow and smiled.

She quietly climbed into the bed, drawing little Ariella to her. The little one instinctively wrapped an arm around Lainey's waist. She fought back tears, not wanting to wake her, and pressed kisses into the girl's soft hair. She watched the little girl well into the evening as she fought to stay awake.

She knew she needed sleep—they all did—but tomorrow would be dangerous for everyone, and she didn't want to lose a second of time with her precious babies.

As she nodded off, she heard the door creak open, and a soft voice called from the darkness, "Mom?"

She craned her head to see Chase, looking much smaller and more vulnerable than his usual aloof preteen attitude would allow. She smiled and beckoned him over. He climbed into the bed as she shifted to wrap an arm around him too.

She never said a word, just smiled in the night and soaked in their affection, gently kissing each crown as the whim took her, and drifted off more contentedly than she had since their arrival.

MORNING CAME TOO SOON. Lainey awoke to find that Zahra had also joined the family cuddle huddle at some point, bringing a smile to her exhausted face. She'd only been asleep for three hours, but it was time to get the kids ready for departure. They had two hours left before they had to board the cargo ship that would take them through the Gate.

She wanted nothing more than to hit Pause on the universe and stay in that spot a while longer. Lainey knew it would never be enough, but she wanted a few more moments cocooned in the loving embrace of her kids. She squeezed them all lightly. "Guys, it's time to get up. Your flight leaves soon."

Some things never change, she thought as the moaning and whimpering met her ears. Their little arms tightened their grip on her, and she hugged them tighter. She couldn't help but snicker softly, but she continued pushing them to get moving.

Her kids reluctantly disentangled themselves, her younger kids griping throughout the process. Zahra stepped up, her maturity making Lainey smile proudly as she urged Ariella and Chase to prepare themselves and their bags. *She's growing up so fast, almost a woman in her own right. I just hope she doesn't rush to get there.*

While the kids finished packing, Lainey prepared breakfast for her family and checked in with AERO. When he told her that the radar picture had updated overnight, it caused her stomach to drop to her feet. An overstrength carrier strike group was rapidly descending upon the small moon colony, one they were ill-equipped to defend against. Their station was only defended by one manned fighter squadron, the drone jockeys, and three littoral combat ships.

Fighting off waves of panic, Lainey took a deep calming breath. She stared at the fleet bound for her family and whispered, "Oh, fuck me."

"Did you say something, Mommy?" Ariella asked.

"No, honey, go put your bags by the door so I can cook breakfast."

Time dwindled down as they finished their meal. She didn't bother cleaning up after them; they had to begin their trek to the hangar housing the cargo ships. As they walked, Ariella became increasingly restless and combative. Lainey could tell she was scared—they all were. She tried to calm her, but her reassurances and redirections fell on the deaf ears of a bright child.

"Let me hold you," she said as she bent down to pick Ariella up.

Chase and Zahra each took one extra bag as Lainey carried the young child, her tiny arms clinging tightly to Lainey's neck. When she tried to set her down at the boarding site, Ariella refused to let her go, screaming loudly.

"No, Mommy!" Ariella screamed, thrashing around in her arms. "Please don't make me go! I want to stay with you! I promise I'll be good! I promise! Please!"

Lainey whimpered but tried to keep her pain from her kids. Tears threatened to spill from her eyes. "Oh, baby, I know. I know. You're such a good girl." She squeezed the inconsolable girl as tightly as she could, thankful she'd allotted time for this.

She managed to get Zahra to hold her sister while she addressed Chase. "Do you have any idea how great you are? How proud I am of you? You have blessed my life in more ways than I can count."

Chase's eyes brimmed with barely held tears; he no longer cared if his sisters saw him cry. He launched himself at his mother and briefly sobbed into her chest. "Please be safe, Mom. I'm sorry I was so mean to you."

"Hey, it's okay, buddy," she cooed to him as she stroked his hair. He was on the verge of becoming a young man, but in so many ways, he was still the little boy who hid behind her legs when he met a stranger. "Don't worry about that. Just make sure you look out for your sisters, okay? And listen to your dad."

Chase sniffled and nodded his head before he reluctantly pulled away from her. She hugged him again and kissed his cheek, wiping away the tears with her thumbs. He took Ariella and held her close to him while Lainey turned to Zahra.

She could tell Zahra was trying with all her might to hold back the tears. They both wanted to be strong for the younger ones. "Mom..." She trailed off, not knowing what to say.

Lainey shushed her. "It's okay. Remember what I told you. And never doubt how amazing you really are. Here." she pulled a small sack from inside her own workbag. "Make sure you give this to Daddy when you get there."

Zahra nodded and hugged her. They stayed that way for a moment before gesturing to Chase and Ariella to join them in a family hug.

She somehow heard the boarding call for their flight through the fog of her emotions. It sounded distant, coming through viscous fluids, muting, and deadening the sound. Lainey forced herself to release her hold on her kids and picked up little Ariella once more. Tears still streaming down her tiny, cherubic face, Ariella tried to give Lainey her beloved shark.

"For you, Mommy. He'll keep you safe," Ariella said, her voice more subdued.

Her breath caught in her throat at the selfless gesture. "Thank you so much, honey bunny. Why don't you hang on to him? He's going to need you to get him back to Daddy's house. Can you do that? Be my big, brave girl?"

Ariella nodded. "When are you coming back?"

"As soon as I can, baby. As soon as I can." She hugged her once again. "I love you so much. I love all of you."

They all hugged her once more before she gave them each a kiss and pushed them on their way. "It's time. You guys have to go."

She walked them as far as she could, not wanting to let go, and let Zahra lead them the rest of the way onto the waiting spacecraft. She backed away, still watching them, as she heard Ariella become more and more frantic, struggling against her siblings.

"I'll keep you safe," Lainey whispered, her voice fierce. Her decla-
ration was drowned out by the ambient noises, but it stamped itself on
the depths of her soul.

"No! Mommy! Mommy, please don't leave! Please come with us!
Please, Mommy!" She wailed into the crowd of people, each word
louder than the last. "Mommy!"

Oh, baby, Lainey thought, anguished at the display.

Ariella broke her grip and sprinted back to Lainey, who scooped
her up in a final desperate embrace. "I'm so sorry, little bug. I know it's
scary, but you're going to be okay. Everything is going to be okay. I
promise. I love you so, so much. Don't ever forget that."

"I love you, Mommy," she cried into Lainey's neck as the other
kids came back to collect her, picking up the shark she'd dropped
along the way.

She managed to get Ariella into Zahra's arms, and with one last
kiss, they were off through the security checkpoint. Lainey stared after
them, yelling "I love you" into the din until she could no longer hear
Ariella's cries. When she couldn't see her kids anymore, she fell to her
knees and openly wept.

After a few minutes, she pulled herself together, turning the gut-
wrenching devastation she felt into a coldly burning anger. Getting
back to her feet, Lainey swiped at her tears and breathed deeply
through the nose as she threw her shoulders back. *Those assholes are
going to pay for this,* she swore to herself as she turned sharply and
made a beeline for the briefing room.

LOOKING AROUND THE ROOM, she saw a mix of emotions. It was
easy to tell who'd just sent their families away and who were simply
itching to get into the fight. The room was thick and uncomfortable
with tension. Those without families tried to distract their distraught
colleagues with banter and jokes as they waited for the final briefing
from Colonel Wood.

I love these beautiful bastards, she thought as she watched the
pilots of her squadron. *My second family.*

Lainey was quietly observing the room, blowing on a hot cup of coffee, ignoring how terrible it was. While she mused, a new lieutenant came to stand next to her. He'd only been assigned to Athena for a few weeks, barely long enough to get current on the airframe they'd be flying. She could practically smell the fear on him. The more he tried to hide it, the more obvious it was.

"How are you holding up, LT?"

"Oh, you know, ma'am, living the dream. Ready to kill a Commie for Mommy, right?"

"Yeah, something like that." They snorted derisively at the tag line they'd been spoon-fed since they signed up. "Sauce," she said as she informally introduced herself, offering a handshake.

"Kelvin."

"How'd you get that?" she asked, always curious about callsigns.

"Instructor pilot at flight school said I was an absolute zero. How did you get 'Sauce?'"

Lainey smiled at the memory. "Running late for work at my first duty station after I reclassed and embraced the fighter life. My daughter spilled a bunch of applesauce by the door. I didn't see it, slipped, and went down hard enough to break my arm in three places. Showed up at the squadron later that day in a regen cast with applesauce smeared down my entire leg."

The lieutenant chuckled politely, beginning to visibly relax when Lieutenant Colonel McCullough joined them. Kelvin snapped to attention. "Relax, LT." He placed a hand on Lainey's shoulder, genuine concern in his eyes. "You okay, Sauce?"

She met his gaze and answered honestly, "AERO, I'm pretty fucking far from okay, but I'm ready."

"Atta girl." He squeezed her shoulder and went to take his seat.

Kelvin looked at her quizzically. "AERO?"

"He had a faulty bird in flight school. Had to bail out on his first solo flight. AERO stands for Already Ejected in Round One." She smiled at the young man as Colonel Wood approached to get a coffee for herself.

They chatted a moment while Lainey introduced her to Kelvin and spun her up on the callsign story exchange.

"Ma'am, I'm sorry to ask, and I know it's none of my business, but I may never get another chance. How did you get the name 'Pecker?'" Kelvin asked.

If he's that bold in the cockpit, the kid just might survive, Lainey thought, impressed with his moxie.

Colonel Wood answered straight-faced, "I like to go bird-watching to relax."

Realization dawned on the young officer. "Oh, woodpecker. That makes much more sense."

"Why, what did you think it was?"

Kelvin's eyes widened. "Uh, nothing, ma'am. Excuse me," he said and hurried away to find a seat.

The commander winked at Lainey before making her way over to Crunch.

One by one, the aviators took seats facing the podium where Colonel Wood would give them their final update before takeoff.

"Okay, Task Force Viking, I suppose tradition dictates that I give a rousing speech on the eve of battle. Well, I'm not exactly Henry the Fifth here, so I'll keep this short. There's a lot on the line today, for some more than others, but I am standing in front of the best group of warriors I could ever hope for. I know we'll all get up there and give them hell together. No one knows how today is going to end, but I want you all to know that you have done your country, the Space Force, and your families a great service. It has truly been an honor and a privilege to serve with you. Godspeed."

The squadron jumped to their feet with a roar of the 4001st squadron rally cry, "TIGERS!" Lainey was moved by just how tight-knit the unit had grown in such a short time.

Crunch assumed his position for the final mission brief. "Our strategy is simple, layered defenses. Overnight, we marshalled a package of modified missiles as our first layer. They are armed and set to detonate on impact; however, we've bypassed the seeker so they will not emit any radar signal or boost engines until the warhead's prox-imity sensor gets a passive return. This means they won't track like missiles. Instead, they will act as a minefield that turns into a wasp's nest of live active missiles at the very last second to disorient and hopefully destroy as many enemy ships as possible.

"Next layer, SCAT flight in a picket line. As all combat mission–ready pilots will be in the Valkyries, we'll throw our technicians into the mix to help pilot the drones. We'll send them into their formations and take out as many of those bastards as we can. Your target is the carrier. I will manage the battle from the *Tallahassee* in orbit. Then our fighters and littorals will be waiting for them.

"We'll push a twelve-ship gorilla package and retrograde. We'll lull them into thinking we're making a run for it, and when they charge in, the other two flights will slam into their flanks. It'll be chaotic, but we have a chance at winning. Either way, it buys time for our families to get away. I know there are no questions, so let's get to work."

As the assembled squadron stood to head to the flight line, AERO pulled Lainey aside. "This is the real deal, Sauce. With a full mobilization, we can't control the drones ourselves. We're so remote that Gate Defense Command never planned for a full invasion fleet hitting us here. I need someone I trust to supervise the pickets. None of these techs have done more than ferry the drones around for maintenance."

"Roger, sir. I'll take them. Can you have my bird hot and ready to go? When the enemy gets close or the drones are eliminated, I'll go wings up."

"I'll make it happen. We'll leave the bus to shuttle the dirtside techs to the Gate. It's doubtful they'll make it, but it beats a PRPC labor camp."

"Happy hunting, AERO."

"Give 'em hell."

He didn't wait for her to respond, leaving Lainey to organize the drone pilots while he rushed off to get the manned fighters into the void. Following this, she rushed into the drone's squadron bay to find the newly minted pilots gathered around the dais in the front of the room.

"Listen up," Lainey shouted to be heard over the crowd. "I know your piloting skills are rudimentary, and you've never fought a live enemy before. However, this is just like every sim you played as a kid. The stakes are real, but the mechanics are the same. Unlike in the games, we can't afford to get cocky. There's no respawn point, and the enemy gets a vote. Our picket line needs to slow down the enemy without prematurely sacrificing the drones."

"What happens when our craft is destroyed?" someone shouted from the crowed hangar bay.

"Once your bird is gone, make an orderly exit from the bay. A bus is waiting on the flight line to take you out of here. Once there, you'll wait for the rest of the drone pilots to join you. Nobody leaves until the last drone is gone, so fight smart and we'll win the day. We just have to buy enough time for our families to escape. They're counting on us."

"You heard her," shouted Senior Sergeant Terry Mixon, a crusty-looking former maintainer. He was a lifer, and to stay in he had to reclass when the Valkyrie replaced his airframe. As he bellowed at the technicians, he ushered them into their cockpits. "Strap in and fire it up. You've already been assigned to your sections, so this shouldn't be too different or difficult for you. We've worked with each other for over a year, and now we get to do it in space."

She watched the station's ground crew with pride. The technicians were highly motivated, if poorly trained. Their families were also on the shuttles heading to the Gate. Everybody had a reason to fight hard so they ensured that their drones hurt the PRPC.

"When you strap on your birds, you'll see your sections and flights. Link into the appropriate comms. We've lucked out—we're already in the path of their assault—so we don't need to execute any crazy maneuvers to get ready. Alpha Flight, we're going hunting. Form up on me. Bravo Flight, you'll pull back and come at them when they're in among us or past this. Do *not* activate until we give you the signal."

Lainey divided the twenty-four remaining drones into two flights of twelve. She'd take the first flight herself, dubbed SCAT 01 through 12. Mixon's would be 13 through 24. That callsign came down from one of her ancient heroes, and she had made it the standard one for the Tigers' drones. She counted on Senior Mixon to manage his flight and trusted the other Senior NCOs to help them both manage their woefully underprepared pilots. While Mixon worked, she took charge of her flight and started issuing orders. "We'll boost out to the hold point and then spread out in a vertically stacked U-formation. Once established, keep your engines in idle until I say otherwise. All of your weapons will be slaved to mine for the first salvo. Once I fire, you're to spread out in pairs and try to get more shots off against their capital ships. When you're out of missiles and chain-gun rounds, crash into something expensive. It's too easy, can't be any questions, so now we wait."

The wait seemed to drag on. What felt like hours staring into the void was only roughly thirty minutes before they noticed the first flashes of the enemy attempting to traverse the ersatz minefield. Lainey's sensors pinged with the signal of incoming enemy ships. Checking the reading, she saw that the entire fleet they'd discovered earlier was there. The PRPC super carrier was escorted by a destroyer and a frigate squadron, two cruisers, and a handful of support tenders and supply ships.

If our intelligence is right, their carriers carry a one-hundred-twenty-fighter spacecraft wing, she thought glumly. *All of that and two dozen warships against thirty-six Valkyries and twenty-four picket drones. We'll be lucky to hold out against them for ten minutes, let alone long enough for the great escape.*

Reading the incoming reports, she noticed some irregularities. The entire enemy fleet appeared to be state-of-the-art for the Commies, vessels new enough that she couldn't determine which class they were.

The missiles were having the intended effect, though weaker than they had hoped. The carrier launched a flight of their fighters to investigate, slowing their approach but not stopping. Many of the enemy pilots flew directly into the mines, being unable to see them until it was too late.

The maneuver certainly did not defeat the enemy but succeeded in putting a small dent in their numbers. Taking out ten fighters and disabling a frigate wasn't much, but it was eleven fewer ships they would have to deal with later.

The fleet continued its passage, entering SCAT flight's engagement zone, the larger ships taking some damage on the way. Even a slight weakening of the hull was a welcome advantage.

"Here they come," Lainey said to the techs, fighting the urge to use proper radio procedures that she knew they wouldn't understand.

She could hear them shifting in their seats and smell the nervous sweat in the air.

"Wait for it," she whispered to herself off comms.

She let them get in close, desperate to ensure the optimum range for all twelve of her drones. She needed all of them to get a successful shot against the enemy before they knew she was there. Only the low observable ability of their drones bought them the time they needed to launch their salvo.

"Got you!" she said as she locked onto the carrier. "Firing again," Lainey said into the comms. "We've got the carrier!"

The second salvo launched before the first were halfway to their objective. After the second missile salvo had launched, she turned over control of the drones to their individual pilots.

"Use your chain guns," she said. "Make a gun pass on the ships; let's try to take them out. I want each section to focus on one ship at a time. We swarm it like angry gnats until they swat us out of the sky."

She received a flurry of affirmative responses from her drone flight and focused on flying as she brought her picket through the enemy. She frantically looked for another chance to hit the PRPC carrier. As she searched for a window to maneuver through the enemy fleet, she saw the results of their missiles. They'd achieved total surprise, the drone's passive stealth getting through the enemy's ring of defensive support vessels to strike from the shadows.

The missiles slammed into the carrier just as she dropped her bay doors to launch their own fighters. The timing couldn't have been better if she'd planned it. Lainey almost forgot to fly her own craft as she watched the destruction roll across the hull. The flashes of explosions grew as leaking oxygen from within fueled the fires along the hull. Three missiles made it through the opened door to slam into the fighters prepped for launch, igniting their own warheads. Her sensors showed the extent of the cascading failure as the carrier died in real time.

"All Vikings, SCAT Zero-One," she said into the battle network. "Splash one carrier."

Without waiting for a response, Lainey turned her drone into a barrel roll. Her corkscrew maneuver barely gave her time to avoid escape pods jettisoning from the dying enemy carrier. She had no interest in killing an enemy who was already off the chessboard of combat. When two cruisers moved alongside the carrier to provide relief, she tagged them as the new priority targets.

Crunch came over the coms channel, echoing what Lainey already knew. "All SCATs, mark the cruisers as priority targets."

"Roger, Dark Star."

Swapping channels, she continued, passing that priority to the second flight of stealthed drones.

Lainey continued dodging the escape pods as well as the unfortunate bastards who were sucked into space without them as she lined up a gun pass across the hull of the massive cruiser in front of her.

"I'm Skosh on missiles!"

"Guns totally Winchester!"

She heard the shouts over the comms, but she didn't have to remind them to slam their drones into the enemy vessels.

"Got the engine!" she heard someone shout with joy.

Scanning the sensors, she saw the ineffectual nature of their crash course in intergalactic warfare. Their kamikaze run hadn't done more than dent the hulls of the enemy carrier strike group.

"SCAT One-Three, launch now. We've lost the element of surprise... don't wait," she said as her picket drone was shot out of the sky.

The swarm of missiles aimed at one of the enemy cruisers trying to rescue the dying carrier brought it down in another glorious fireball. She watched their efforts to make successful strafing runs with their chain guns achieve the same lackluster success. Without the element of surprise, their pickets were woefully understrength in a stand-up fight against an enemy carrier strike group. Taking out a cruiser and the carrier itself was more than she'd ever expected to achieve.

"Senior Sergeant Mixon, surprise these heroic pilots. Get them out to the shuttle and through the Gate. Your flight did awesome," Lainey said.

"It's been a privilege, ma'am. Go get 'em!" Mixon said quietly as Lainey unstrapped her helmet from the drone cockpit.

Opening the door to the hangar, Lainey was momentarily blinded.

She'd been in the dim hangar, and her eyes hadn't adjusted to the early-morning sunshine. Despite the sunspots dancing across her vision, she took off at a jog across the flight line to where her Valkyrie awaited her. It was an eerie experience, as the flight line was devoid of life except for Lainey and her dedicated crew chief, Sergeant Sandlin. Her fighter sat next to the remaining two without pilots. Like any squadron, the Tigers had more jets than ready pilots, with the "extra" planes only expected to be maintenance spares or hangar queens.

Seeing her bird, painted with six stars for her verified kills at the fight in the Jackson system, brought her a sense of grim pride. The inspiration added a renewed pep to her step, and she kicked her sprint up a notch. She was breathing heavily when she reached her fighter to begin the preflight inspection.

"Sergeant Sandlin, you need to leave now!"

"No, ma'am, I'm launching you. I won't budge until you taxi. You can court-martial me later."

Lainey realized the pointlessness of arguing with him. When she finished checking over her impeccably prepared ship, she checked the other two and found them functional as well. She was surprised to hear the clamping of boots coming up behind her, the sound startlingly loud on the deserted line. Turning, she saw Senior Sergeant Mixon and a young specialist sprinting toward her with their helmets in tow.

"I can handle my own preflight," Lainey said. "Catch that shuttle before it's too late."

"We earned our flight wings," Mixon said, barely out of breath as the young kid panted beside him.

"There's a galaxy of difference between a simulation and the real thing," she said firmly.

"If I turn on the training mode, you can slave our controls to yours. We can fire when we've got locks and add some more missiles and bullets in the mix," Mixon said.

"My wife is pregnant," the kid said. "I need to make sure she gets out. Let us help protect them."

She didn't know what to say, so Lainey grasped both of their shoulders and gave a teary smile, her chest aching with pride and gratitude. She nodded at them before she stepped back and resumed her checks of the three fighters. Once she was done, she helped them strap into their cockpits and showed them how to use the ejection handles and every other piece of emergency equipment. Twenty minutes after she'd left the void battle with the pickets, she was taking her fighter back into the skies.

"AERO, this is Sauce. We've taken out a cruiser and the carrier and are en route to join you in the defense of the Gate."

"Welcome to the party, Sauce. They're already here, so be quick. We've got to hold them off until the last ship escapes. Escort the bus and then rejoin the squadron. AERO, out."

Time wasn't on her side. Lainey pulled her SF-44 Valkyrie and the two slaved to her up in a launch arc steeper than regulations allowed. When they caught up to the shuttle escorting the drone pilots, it had successfully cleared orbit and was hauling it toward the Gate with a frigate on its tail, sending a wave of missiles.

It'll never make it. That flying kettlebell can't evade all of them; it can't jam, and they don't carry countermeasures.

"We're going in," she quietly told her little three-ship. "We've got to take out that ship, or those techs won't make it home."

"Roger," the two men said in unison.

She engaged their thrusters, pushing their fighters to their limits as she chased after the frigate chasing her friends. While frigates weren't huge ships, they were massive compared to a Valkyrie. It was a daunting task, but her people were worth the effort. Worth the risk.

"They won't notice us right away; they're hunting glory and high body counts. We'll sneak up behind them and send three missiles right up their ass."

"Up the poop shoot, aye," Mixon said grimly.

Flying one Valkyrie fighter was relatively easy, despite the chaotic nature of the space around the Gate, but maneuvering three was slightly more difficult. They had to navigate through a lot of traffic clustered around one chokepoint. The jump Gate back to the Sol System served as a bottleneck that the entire enemy fleet concentrated on.

She watched in horror as the Commies focused their attacks on the fleeing civilians.

"We can't let them pursue our people through the ring. We have to stop them," she grimly told her pilots.

"Lead the way," said the kid whose name she'd never learned.

"Let's do this," echoed Mixon.

The giant cluster of destructive power from the enemy fleet complicated her attempts to get behind the frigate. It was a target-rich environment, but she was singularly focused on chasing down the frigate trying to kill the drone technicians who'd recently savaged the Commie carrier.

Pulling up hard, she adjusted her trajectory on a ninety-degree angle to avoid a destroyer pursuing one of their trash haulers carrying classified material. *Destroying that beats the bastards capturing it.* She banked hard and to the left to get above and behind the vessel chasing her men. Adjusting her angle, she lined up her shot and pinged the exact spot in their shared targeting reticle.

"If we hit them here, it should cause a cascading explosion or two along the rear of their hull. Even though I haven't encountered this type before, Commie ships are laid out pretty similarly. There's a waste-heat exchanger under that armor plate. Won't destroy the ship, but it should be big enough to knock them off course and take a lot of their weapons out of the fight. Once it isn't a threat to our people, we can ignore it. Best we can do is buy those technicians time."

"Aye, ma'am," Mixon said. "Tell us when to fire, and we'll send a little surprise buttsex."

That brought a scared chuckle out of the kid, making Lainey smile slightly. "That's the spirit," she said.

"Set a three-second timer in the HUD, and we'll fire on your mark, ma'am," the kid said, his voice shriller than it had been earlier.

When the target timer hit zero, Lainey and her two wing mates each fired a missile at the enemy frigate. While the rounds were en route, she fired a second salvo. She adjusted their course to stay on its tail as she waited to see what would happen. They couldn't afford to waste a missile, as each of their fighters only carried eighteen of various types. They needed to make each one count.

The impact against the heat exhaust for the frigate's engine was underwhelming. Her wing mates' two rounds exploded on the metal shield around the port.

When it went off, it briefly flared before winking into nothing. Her round struck, soundlessly, before it skidded across the port guard and tumbled ass over end into the port. There was a momentary pause before it exploded outward, obliterating the protective covering for the engine's heat sink.

Their second set of missiles slammed deeper into the heat exhaust, exploding brilliantly. It caused the desired result, the enemy warship was pushed sideways by the force, hitting the nose cone of one of its own squadron mates. The impact would've been loud had there been sound in space. Lainey watched the second hull crumple inward under the weight of its sister warship.

"We got a twofer!" Mixon shouted, joyfully whooping.

The crusty sergeant spoke too soon. Once the shuttle had a clear flight path toward the massive Gate home, the young kid with them chose that moment to act. He assumed command of his own fighter, ignoring the last transport vessel on their side of the transport ring. She watched in horror as he pulled off to chase after the second doomed frigate instead.

"Come back!" Lainey shouted the comms. "It's dead already; fall in on us! We've got to protect that last transport. Our families could be on board!"

The kid didn't answer, but he'd heard her. She could tell by the way he pulled back and corkscrewed his Valkyrie so that he was facing the enemy. Three destroyers were chasing down the troop transport vessel carrying some of the civilians and families escaping the station.

As she flew closer to the destroyer, chasing the errant kid from her section, the warship fired a salvo of four missiles at the transport vessel. Their rounds were larger than her Valkyrie, designed to take out capital ships. Their missiles were slower than her nimble fighter.

"Hold on kids, Mommy's coming," she whispered as she prepared to make a gun run against the missiles.

The kid chose that moment to play hero. He juked his Valkyrie and aimed his fighter right into the path of the oncoming missiles. Pushing the throttle, he got in their path, his craft blocking their firing lock and messing with their onboard targeting software. The first of four missiles struck his cockpit, exploding outward. Shrapnel spewed outward in all directions, confusing the last three missiles. They exploded, harmlessly pulverizing his already atomized fighter.

"Godspeed," Mixon whispered.

Those poor buggers, she thought. *They're riding along helplessly in the fighter I control—can't be easy.*

Just when she thought the transport was in the clear, the debris from the exploding fighter slammed into its engine. The damage was minor, but she watched in horror as the flare from its exhaust port flickered and died. It wasn't going to make it.

"If you cover me, I can nudge it a little, give it enough juice for the transit," Mixon said, his voice neutral.

"Your fighter can't stand up to that," Lainey said, mentally dismissing the idea.

"Let me go, ma'am. I can nudge it. Won't take much," Mixon said quietly, his voice resolved and earnest.

"That's suicide," Lainey said quietly.

"If I have to go, let me go out like a lion."

"I'll make it count," she said, giving him her solemn word.

Checking her sensors, she looked for any targets that might be in their way. She fired a missile at an enemy escape pod in between them, silently begging for forgiveness for her actions. She had to protect Mixon on his run; there was no other option. She saw him line up for his pass while she vectored underneath him and to his right so she could destroy another large piece of debris blocking his path to the Gate.

There's nothing I can do to save Mixon, but I can ensure that his death matters. She vowed fiercely to ensure that it wasn't in vain. *We'll make 'em bleed today.*

She maneuvered, deftly combining her main engines and her maneuvering jets in a well-choreographed survival ballet. Her HUD updated her on the rest of the battle. Her squadron was running on empty, weapons dry and half of their number dead or dying. They were swatting above their paygrade, always a deadly proposition.

Skimming through the update, she saw that her boys had taken down several frigates, but the battle had been costly and not stopped the destroyers hot on the heels of the civilians. *So many names, and so young*, she thought as watched names she knew scroll across her feed as KIA.

"Snap out of it!" she told herself. "Your kids need you."

When she had a path cleared for the troop transport, Lainey tried to prevent the Commie pricks from getting off another salvo. Checking the countdown clock, she noticed that the last remaining ship would be through the salvation ring in a few minutes.

"Three more minutes. I just need three more minutes."

Her Valkyrie screamed, twirling on its axis to point her weapons in just the right angle to nail one of the destroyers hot on the heels of her kids inside the transport vessel. She hammered down on the pickle button as she tracked parallel to the ship, pointing her nose at the target and unleashing every remaining gun round she had. The destruction was spectacular, her rounds striking through poorly repaired patches from previous combat damage. It wasn't enough to completely kill the ship, but it did give their troop transport time to make it through the ring.

"AERO, we need to destroy the ring! The civilians are through; it's just us!"

"We won't get to you in time, Sauce. You're gonna have to work miracles one more time.

No kill like an overkill, she thought as she weighed her options. Time seemed to slow down, and her focus narrowed to the Gate in front of her. Her entire mission, her reason for being, was to destroy that link to her home. To her babies. To her husband. *I'll protect you*, she vowed.

She had two missiles left, not enough to take out the ring. She couldn't do enough damage to knock one of the enemy warships into it either. She was out of options. *Out of options, save one*, she corrected herself.

"I've got the situation in hand. AERO, get the survivors to the emergency escape facility in the outer system. Sauce, out."

As she flew right into position for her final run, two enemy destroyers made it through the Gates leading back into the Sol System.

By God, please be ready to receive those Commie bastards, she prayed. *My kids deserve a chance to grow up, to have a life.*

She flipped her fighter and did a rapid deceleration burn, trading speed and momentum for precise maneuverability. Lainey inched her way close to the gate. Her world existed in the microseconds between time, propelled by her single-minded quest. *I love you, Michael*, she thought as she toggled the switch to arm the weapons. She fired her last two missiles at the opposite side of the Gate, where she intended to give the PRPC her final salute. The timing and angles would be paramount to her success.

The range was short, and her missiles impacted where she'd intended in a matter of seconds. There was no room for error; the two explosions had to happen in close chronological proximity to each other. A localized explosion could be compensated for, so Lainey needed to spread the pain.

A third destroyer made it through the Gate before her missiles struck the ring directly above her. When she was almost upon it, the Gate so big it dwarfed her entire canopy viewport of her cockpit, she made her last play. Lainey hit the one button that instructors always told her to never hit.

Ironically, the Valkyries' self-destruct button wasn't red; it was a brilliant neon shade of yellow. It was meant to give a pilot a means to deny a crashed or stricken Valkyrie to an adversary for exploitation. She set the internal timer to zero and broke the hard plastic cover free. She pushed it to its first detent. Armed. With one last prayer, she conjured a memory of the family that she so regretted leaving, her dearest loves. Closing her eyes and smiling at the image of their happy faces, Lainey hammered down on the button. Her world exploded into nothingness as she set off a cascading explosion that collapsed the warp field and destroyed the Gate and the last destroyer still in transit. One minute, the ring was there; the next, it was space dust.

IT'D TAKEN six months before the US Space Force closed its investigation into what had occurred. The events leading up to the attack on Athena Station and the subsequent destruction of the Archangel Gate were the subject of every news reporter looking to make a break into the big time. Ultimately, they concluded that the events were unavoidable and that collapsing the Gate had indeed cut off a PRPC invasion fleet. It was a cold comfort to the families of those who'd died in the fighting.

Sure, we saved the Sol system, but at what cost? Michael wondered, trying not to be bitter. His wife had been posthumously awarded the Medal of Honor and given a hero's funeral. *Not that it'll keep me warm at night... or tuck my kids into their beds.*

On the family-room wall in Michael's quarters on Ganymede, between wedding and family pictures, hung Lainey's medal. The award rested on her official plaque, just above the shadow box containing her flag. The final tribute from her country, given to him at her funeral, sat prominently displayed on shelf below just below the medal.

As he stared at the picture of Lainey and the kids, he reflected back on their last call. There'd been so much he wished he could've said, but he'd been forced to make peace with the way his marriage had ended. Therapy had helped, but it had taken his kids much longer to begin recovery.

Michael immediately enrolled the kids in mental health services, but it took several months before he saw even a semblance of the way things were before. He lived his life that way; there was now, and there was before, when things were bright and his soul was complete.

I can't be you, Lainey. I can't be their mom. Heck, I can barely braid Ariella's hair. How will I teach them to be women you'd be proud of? I wish you were with me, now, in this home.

Persistence was paying off, though. His kids were just beginning to adjust to their new normal. They still grieved and missed their mother intensely. Chase started getting into fights with other children, and Michael spent many sleepless nights cuddling an inconsolable Ariella. His baby screamed and begged for her mommy, but together, they were all getting through it.

One day, as the kids were finally ready to unpack the last of their things, Zahra found the bag that Lainey had given her in the hangar before they left. She'd promised she would give it to her father but had completely forgotten about it. The chaos that had followed their collective loss had swallowed his baby. By the time the dust settled, she'd forgotten that last maternal request.

Michael looked up when Zahra walked into the living area, where he was reading a book to Ariella. "Dad, look what I found. Mom asked me to give this to you."

Confused, he opened the sack and pulled out the bottle of scotch she'd wanted to share with him. The packaging was damaged, but it was just like he'd remembered. He could recall the day they'd bought the bottle. It had been one of his precious memories of them together. He held it gingerly in his hand, relishing the talisman to his past.

Turning to put it away, he dropped the bag and heard a light thump on the table. He set the bottle down to investigate. Digging inside, he found a few small keepsakes for the kids, some jewelry and other mementos, and a data stick bearing the logo of the US Space Force. They were as common as the Bic pens and stolen just as often by the servicemen and women.

Michael plugged the drive into the family workstation, finding copies of vital records and some video files for each child. The largest file was labeled *Trouble*. Curious, he opened it and found a basic AI programmed to play the game.

"Hey, guys, check this out!" he called to the kids as he opened the file on the large viewscreen.

When Lainey's smiling face popped up, he felt his world constrict. The image of what he'd lost stared at him. She'd been his life, his joy, for so long. Now she was staring at him from the past, as if to remind him that he was still alive. That he still had three reasons to continue fighting. Smiling through the tears, he waited for his kids to arrive.

"Mommy!" cried Ariella.

Michael looked at their surprised faces and made an executive decision. "What do you guys say? Do you want to play a game?"

They smiled and nodded, setting up the game pieces like they always did. This time, however, nobody complained when Ariella took the first move. The memory of their last game was too close to the surface for such petty sibling rivalries.

Thank you, he thought as he stared at the smiling face. *Thank you for reminding us to live.*

Michael knew that nothing would bring Lainey back to them—he'd been over that too many times in therapy. But seeing her on the screen and feeling her love once again brought comfort to his bereft family. For just a moment, life felt somewhat normal. In that moment, his kids understood the depth of their mother's love.

The End

ABOUT THE AUTHOR

J.R. Handley is a pseudonym for a husband and wife writing team. He is a veteran infantry sergeant with the 101st Airborne Division and the 28th Infantry Division. She is the kind of crazy that interprets his insanity into cogent English. He writes the sci-fi while she proofreads it. The sergeant is a two-time combat veteran of the late unpleasantness in Mesopotamia where he was wounded, likely doing something stupid. He started writing military science fiction as part of a therapy program suggested by his doctor, and hopes to entertain you while he attempts to excise his demons through these creative endeavors. In addition to being just another dysfunctional veteran, he is a stay at home wife, avid reader and all around nerd. Luckily for him, his Queen joins him in his fandom nerdalitry.

My web page is *www.jrhandley.com.*

 facebook.com/sgt.jr.handley

ABOUT THE AUTHOR

Liska McCabe was born in St. Louis, MO, the youngest daughter of an Army Reserve nurse and a USAF veteran-turned-engineer. She graduated from Seattle University with a Bachelor of Criminal Justice and a US Army commission. She is a veteran of the Florida Army National Guard and US Army Reserve, having mobilized for Operation Noble Eagle in Washington DC. Currently, she is a USAF spouse to her husband, Chris, a stay-at-home-mom to their daughter, and fledgling author of military sci-fi, space opera, and crime thrillers. They reside in the Florida panhandle.

www.ingramcontent.com/pod-product-compliance
Lightning Source LLC
Chambersburg PA
CBHW011804010726
47498CB00009B/2866

* 9 781734 025767 *